THE PERFECT

Royal Mistress

ALSO BY DIANE HAEGER

THE PERFECT

Royal Mistress

~ A NOVEL ~

DIANE HAEGER

THREE RIVERS PRESS · NEW YORK

Copyright © 2007 by Diane Haeger

Reader's Group Guide copyright © 2007 by Three Rivers Press, an imprint of the Crown Publishing Group, a division of Random House, Inc.

Published in the United States by Three Rivers Press, an imprint of the Crown Publishing Group, a division of Random House, Inc., New York.
www.crownpublishing.com

THREE RIVERS PRESS and the Tugboat design are registered trademarks of Random House, Inc.

Crown Reads colophon is a trademark of Random House, Inc.

Library of Congress Cataloging-in-Publication Data

Haeger, Diane.
    The perfect royal mistress : a novel / Diane Haeger.—1st ed.
    1. Gwynne, Nell, 1650–1687—Fiction.   2. Charles II, King of England,
1630–1685—Fiction.   3. London (England)—History—17th century—Fiction.
4. Great Britain—History—Charles II, 1660–1685—Fiction.   5. Great Britain—
Kings and rulers—Paramours—Fiction.   6. Mistresses—Great Britain—Fiction.
7. Actresses—Great Britain—Fiction.   I. Title.
    PS3558.A32125P47   2007
    813'.54—dc22   2006025803

ISBN 978-0-307-23751-4

Printed in the United States of America

Design by Nora Rosansky

10   9   8   7   6   5   4   3

First Edition

FOR ELIZABETH, MY DAUGHTER AND MY FRIEND

I SING THE STORY OF A SCOUNDREL LASS,
RAISED FROM A DUNGHILL TO A KING'S EMBRACE . . .

—*Sir George Etherege*

Chapter 1

FOUR days after the blaze began, consuming half of London and cutting a wide swath from Tower Hill to Fetter Lane, Nell stepped cautiously through the doorway of the tavern into the harsh light of day. For a moment, she lingered on the stone landing that jutted into Lewkenor Lane before stepping down into the tangle of lost souls, prostitutes, piles of garbage, and animal dung, so overpowering that her eyes watered. The canopy of sky remained gray with smoke and obscured the sun. A rash of smaller fires still blazed as the odor of charred wood and burned pitch mixed with the putrid stench of decay. It blew across the city, and would not let go.

The flames had spread as far as Fish Street, and the Thames. The wide, serpentine river, normally dotted with thousands of decorated barges and boats with billowing sails, was still thick with debris and a heavy layer of soot. The ravages of the fire had spared the Cock & Pye, where she rented a garret beneath the eaves, as well as the other timbered and gabled houses around that end of Drury Lane. But the ashes, smuts, and little burned bits of paper still rained down upon the city. They were like feathers, she thought, until they landed, marking everything a desolate gray.

Beneath her feet was a carpet of the same ash, dung, and soot that the wind had carried. Many Londoners, in one devastating evening, and the four days that followed, had lost every worldly good. It seemed unfair that a city should suffer such devastation after the ravaging plague of only a year before. But that was not her problem, then or now. Survival was. She tried not to look at the still smoldering ruins, like a tangle of skeletons against the skyline, as she quickly walked. Still, it was odd to see untouched buildings in the foreground—timber all neatly painted, window boxes still full of geraniums, sitting before a skyline of mangled and charred debris. She lowered her head and kept walking. Life was like that, really, she thought. One simply had to put one's head down and keep going along.

Nell's thick copper hair was stuffed into a drab mobcap, and her gamine body was sheathed in a mud-brown dress with beige mock-sleeves. The tie at her bosom was ages-old leather. As she made her way from the area of close-packed timbered houses and dark, narrow, straw-covered alleys, the frayed hem of her dress licked the muck-drenched cobbles that led her through crooked Wych Street.

She moved on toward Drury Lane until the great King's Theater, a stone-and-brick building, revealed itself like a great giant before her. The theater, with its long sets of windows, columns, and portico, was still pure magnificence. Not even something already called "the Great Fire" had changed that. Under the direction of a woman named Orange Moll, Nell had found a way to avoid the bawdy house and earn a few shillings as an orange girl. Orange Moll stationed her girls outside the theater doors, and in the pit beneath the stage, where the fops and dandies collected. Newest among Moll's girls, Nell was to tempt those with a few extra pence and an eye for a pretty face. Nell thought of the new work and those garishly dressed fops, who lived expensively and behaved outrageously. Allowing pinches on her bottom, and a bit of banter, amid all the pushing, shoving, and shouting, generally garnered her more tips. "I fancy clever girls," Orange Moll liked to say. "The clever ones earn more, so *I* earn more." Stopping outside the theater, closed now like most everything else, Nell glanced down into the small wicker basket covered with vine leaves on the crook of her arm. Two softening oranges remained, each now sporting a tiny spot of mold. She should have returned them to Moll.

"Orange? Two pence! Orange! Who will buy an orange?" she called out in her sweetest work voice.

She saw her then, a woman huddled inside the dirty alcove between the doors where the tickets were sold. The canopy, protection from the elements, hid her face in shadows. In her arms she held a tiny, dirty-faced child. But she was not a beggar. Nell could see that by the fabric of her soiled gown. Once there had been a world of difference between the two of them. The fire had opened up a doorway between the two worlds and, for this moment, made them very much the same.

"Would you fancy an orange, ma'am? I've got one 'ere I'll not be needin'."

The woman lifted her head. Her face was smudged with soot, as was that of the sleeping child in her lap. "They're gone," she said so flatly and quietly that Nell almost did not hear. "All of them but the wee one. Even my man. All burned to death."

Nell felt her stomach recoil. "God save you, ma'am."

"There's no use to it. 'Tis all gone now."

Nell reached out with an orange. "'Tis a point with the wee one though, ain't there? You've got to think of 'er."

The woman, at last, took the piece of fruit but seemed not to realize, even as she did, what she was meant to do with it. Nell stood lingering for a moment, then heard a man's voice. Startled, she spun around to see four men, two in the crisp periwigs of noblemen, and the other two with their hair closely shorn. Their wigs and waistcoats gave them all away. They were gentlemen of the first order.

"You see? Perfectly unharmed," one of them was saying to another, as they stood gazing up at the theater. "A bit of soot only, but that can be easily enough washed away."

One of the men turned to look at her critically. His periwig was the color of corn, matching a neat mustache and trim beard. His eyes were brilliant blue and clear, but colder than any eyes she had ever seen. "Do run along, girl," he said in a pompous tone. "You've no business here."

"I'll go nowhere, sir."

He tipped his head, surprised. The others turned then to regard her as well.

"I work 'ere."

"*You?* As what?"

She held up the orange. A flock of blackbirds flew across the sky. "I sell these, sir."

"Is that *all* you sell?"

"It is, sir."

"Nonsense! You're all for sale, girls like you."

"You are vile."

"*You* are predictable."

Another of the men intervened. "Enough, George. Back to the business at hand, shall we?"

This man was taller than the other three, and he was one who wore no wig. His close-shorn hair was very dark. He had strong, masculine features, an ebony mustache, and a swarthy complexion that was stained with soot and sweat. His eyes, as they surveyed her, were dark as coal, and oddly intriguing.

"Still have a taste for the low ones, Charles ol' friend?" asked the other man.

"And *you* have a foul mouth, sir," Nell snapped, interjecting herself again.

The blue-eyed man shot her a glare. "Saucy!"

"Coxcomb!" she called back without thinking.

"Jade!" His voice went deeper, more menacing.

Her body tensed, preparing for a fight. The brothel in which she had grown up fetching wine and linen was a breeding ground for raw violence. But the other men only chuckled. "Well! She got the better of *you*, it's plain to see!" said a stout, dough-faced man, wearing a black velvet cape and beaver hat.

As they laughed, Nell risked a second glance at the tall man with the mustache. He was handsome, she thought. He smiled for only an instant at the surprising exchange, his cheeks dimpling as he did, yet still she could see that he was different. He wore a rust-colored leather waistcoat and, over it, a long surcoat the color of chocolate. His buff-colored trousers and nut-brown buskins, like his hands, were mud caked and stained with soot. He was a wealthy man, she saw, but one who had somehow tried to help.

"Those oranges are worth sixpence each, Charles. She has clearly pinched them from Orange Moll's supply, and I certainly think the old bird needs to know that she—"

"I ain't pinched a thing!"

"Oh, leave her be," the tall man said, his voice as deep and rich as French wine. "Let's return to our purpose, George. It appears that performances can continue as soon as the players are ready."

"T'would be right insensitive of the king!"

"Girl!" The man called "George" glared at her. His tone was full of condescension. "Merriment helps one to forget the tragedies of our world."

"Aye, for those with money enough."

"And those with a certain gentility. Which certainly does *not* include the likes of you."

"I may well be low, sir." She crossed her arms. "But what, I wonder, is *your* excuse?"

"Excuse?"

"For the rough way you speak to perfect strangers, sir."

Again the group of men chuckled, although this time with a hint of embarrassment. Nell had bested the same man twice.

"What is your name, girl?" asked the tall man, with what seemed to her like appreciation.

When she looked at him, she saw a hint of amusement in his eyes.

"Who are you that wants to know?"

"Listen, girl! Do you have any idea who this—?"

"Be silent!" The tall man cut him off. "That is quite enough, George."

"But, Your M—"

"Enough!" The tall man raised his hand, and his companion was instantly silenced by it. He turned his attention to Nell. There was a hint of a smile playing at the corners of his mouth. "You are quite an extraordinary girl."

"In that case, Eleanor Gwynne's the name. But most call me Nell."

"Well, Nell. I believe I rather fancy an orange just now. George, pay Mrs. Gwynne for the orange, *and* for having to spar with the likes of you."

"'Tis not necessary, sir. And I ain't no one's missus."

"Forgive me, but where I come from a lady is called missus, out of respect. And believe me, Nell," he smiled kindly. "It *is* quite necessary. There are few around who could go more than a round or two with old George Villiers here. Much less a—"

"Much less a low girl?"

Bested as well, the tall man smiled. "There's nothing in the world low about you."

Nell felt herself smile, too, and her guard fell by a degree. He had a kindness about him.

"Here." The man called George Villiers handed out a coin to her, pomposity and pity in his gesture. Nell took it and, for a moment, held it tightly in her hand. There was cold, hard reassurance in it for her. Enough to buy food, perhaps even a pair of shoes not already worn at the soles. But she simply could not take it.

"I do thank you, sir, all the same, but the lady over there, the one with the babe, she'll be needin' it more."

As the collection of men stood incredulous, Nell walked the few paces back to the woman and her child, and then knelt beside them.

"Here," she softly said, holding out the coin for a moment, then tucking it into the woman's shirt. "I know a place, the Cock & Pye, 'tis very near, where you and your wee one'll find a proper bed, and a bit of peace, to think through what you're meant to do next."

When Nell stood and turned around, she saw that the men were still watching her.

"Extraordinary."

The tall man had murmured the word, though more to himself than to his companions.

"Nothing extraordinary about it. 'Twas only what's right, sir."

He was studying her now. For a moment, neither broke their gaze. Her knees were suddenly weak. She could only imagine the number of well-bred ladies whose heads he had turned with that same stare.

"You are an intriguing girl, Nell Gwynne."

"I'll be takin' that as a compliment, sir."

"It was intended as one. And this coin I wish you to take for yourself. Think of it as any other tip a customer might offer you. I would say you've more than earned it."

The man held out a single shining silver crown to her. Nell thought of declining, but there was no expression of pity or condescension in his offer, as there had been from the other man. She accepted the coin.

"We really must be on our way," said George.

"So we must."

"I'll remember what you said, sir," Nell called out.

"You do that," said the tall man, glancing back as he disappeared into the gathering crowd. Nell moved quickly down the narrow, sunless alley, through soot ground into black mud that came up through the holes in her shoes, until she was back at the Cock & Pye. People seemed always to have money for ale, and a crowd had grown down in the tavern. Four days after a fire that nearly wiped out the city of London, life went on.

Inside the dark tavern, there were low, rough-hewn beams, chipped plaster walls, and mice scurrying across the cold stone floor. Tankards full of foaming ale were lifted by meaty hands as she pulled back the roundtop door, letting a rush of street light inside. Amid laughter and the clink of pewter, the barman called out to her as she moved toward the rickety staircase.

"Your money's owed me long since, Nelly Gwynne! Ye'd best find a way to pay me or I'll toss your arse straight out of 'ere, I will!"

The crowd, most of them drunk, red-faced men in soiled shirts, from the harsh, neighboring streets of Cradle Alley and Paternoster Row, laughed, coughed, and tipped their heads back at the great jest. This was not a neighborhood that housed compassion.

Nell met the barman's gaze squarely. Patrick Gound was simply a businessman. More nights than she could recall he had helped her press her gluttonous, drunken mother up the staircase, toss her into bed, then bring Nell a clean pan as her mother wretched up gin. But it was about survival in these alleyways of London. In that, they understood one another. Amid chuckles, she went to the bar and slapped down her glistening silver coin. "This is all I 'ave in the world, Mr. Gound. I 'ope 'twill be enough 'til the theater opens again and there is work for the lot of us."

"'Twill do 'til Michaelmas, but not a night longer." He leaned forward, lowering his voice. In it, there was a hint of compassion, hidden like a thief behind the warning, "You've got to pay me what ye owe, Nelly girl, or you're out!"

"I'll pay your rent, Nelly," a man called out from the back of the room. "If ye pay me a bit of time."

"I'd rather be paid by the devil 'imself!" she shot back in a deadpan drawl.

The crowd erupted in shouts of rough laughter at the girl with the wild copper hair and the dagger-sharp tongue. Nell knew that no matter how hungry she got, she would never do what her mother did for money. Giving herself to old, vile men like this one. *One must be resourceful,* she thought, walking toward the staircase, *but never a fool.* She was not ever giving herself like that to a man. There could be nothing for her in it.

"Oh, Nell!" called another. "I'd pay your rent just to 'ave you insult me personally!"

"Now *that* might just be arranged!" she laughed broadly, holding on to the wobbly banister and batting her eyes in the bawdy way a barmaid might, for she had learned the skills of a good whore, even if she had no intention of using them to their full extent.

"Ye'd find yourself in line behind *me!*" The tavern owner chuckled and poured another ale that foamed over onto the bar top. "A day isn't proper unless our Nelly has personally taken ye to task!"

"'Tis a thought to fancy! That my mouth could see me out of debt!"

"Knowin' you, it could also see ye into a fair amount of trouble!"

She flicked her hand in the air at them. "You do know how to flatter a girl!" she laughed charmingly, heading up the stairs before the conversation could descend into something she had no intention of pursuing. Better to keep them guessing. Guessing and wanting. Knowing that was the single useful gift she had received from her mother.

Nell trudged heavily up the steps, each one creaking beneath her weight. Then she fumbled at the garret room door, the warped floorboard making the door stick. A memory tumbled back at her. It was a time, a year earlier just before the plague struck. She had struggled with this same door on that day, then opened it to see Helena Gwynne, wild and unwashed, her corpulent body spilling out of a soiled dress. Her eyes, then as always, projected criticism. And Rose . . . Poor Rose, always defending them both against her . . .

"Where is it? Where's the money you owe me, Nelly girl?" Their mother stood before them in the mellowing lamplight that could not

warm the damp room, hand extended. "Ma, there isn't any!" There was sweat on her brow as she lunged at Nell, fingers seizing her daughter's neck. "I've got to 'ave it, d'ye 'ear me?" "Let 'er alone, Ma, and I'll get it for you!" Rose cried. "Just let 'er alone!" Her sister was at the door as she paused and glanced back. "Don't worry, Nelly. I'll be back in a thrice! You'll see . . ."

The memory of that day tumbled over and over now in her mind.

Rose, the sister who cared for her, stole for her, who had become a prostitute to survive. Rose was the one who shared her fleeting memories of a father long away. Only a few memories of him lingered—the scent of ale and sweat, the sound of boot heels clicking across floor tiles when she was meant to be asleep. Mainly, she saw his eyes, happy, smiling eyes, sweet and creamy brown, offering a protection she had not found since. Like their father, Rose had not returned. Her bones aching, Nell sank onto the little bed. She lay down and curled her legs up to her chest surrounded by damp, cold walls and a low, sagging ceiling. As slumber began to take over, she was no longer thinking of Helena Gwynne, or even of Rose, but rather of the tall stranger standing in front of the King's Theater, and wondering if he had actually eaten her orange.

"He really should not be allowed to go out among the masses like that," said George Villiers, the Duke of Buckingham, behind a raised, jeweled hand that glinted in the light from the leaded windows, with their diamond-colored glass. "It does depress him so."

The fires in every room were lit against the pervasive dampness. The men—courtiers, ambassadors, and servants—stood collected in the king's private audience chamber at Whitehall Palace, surrounded by those well-enough placed in society to enter this private chamber to plead for the king's help. Men in velvet coats, with laces and ribbons, hats plumed with great ostrich feathers, their shoes ornamented with jeweled buckles, waited patiently to be heard.

"It is his past, of course, that did it to him," the king's brother, the Duke of York, quietly observed. "All of those miserable years of poverty in exile. There is some part of him, heaven help us, that feels like one of those low wretches himself, and is ever drawn to them."

Every day since the fire had begun, the king had ridden his horse headlong into the thick and dangerous warren of burned-out streets. He had given out coins, and passed buckets of water along a human chain, until his hands were chapped, and his clothes were as soot stained and sweat drenched as those of who had no idea who he was.

"My Lord of Buckingham," the king called out deeply across the perfumed and mirrored chasm. "You may approach."

The duke made a sweeping bow before a very different king than his companion of earlier that morning. Charles II sat on a gilded throne beneath a richly textured canopy of red satin. He wore official Garter robes, billowing ivory satin, crimson velvet sewn with gold thread, and tall lace cravat, and his long, muscled legs were crossed at the ankles. His hands played restlessly at the lion's head fixtures on the arms of his throne. The man he had been that morning was all but hidden now by luxury and obligation. A long, jet-black wig, perfectly matched to his mustache, now adorned his head and trailed down meeting the shoulders of a rich cape. And across his chest lay a heavy bronze medal once belonging to his father, which he often liked to wear when he did the business of his people here in Charles I's favorite public room.

"Your Majesty," flattered the king's oldest and closest friend, rising from the exaggerated bow.

"So, George, have you spoken to Charles Hart? Will the players be ready?"

"He tells me the theater can open again when you decree."

"And that young girl today in front of the theater?"

"The orange girl?"

"The very one. What was her name?"

"I'm afraid a frivolous recollection such as that has slipped my mind."

Another man took two small steps forward. "You will pardon me, I pray, but *I* remember it, as it was a thing of consequence to Your Majesty."

Everyone facing their sovereign, including Buckingham, pivoted around, heavy satin rustling, plumes bobbing, to see the Earl of Arlington, one of the king's other companions earlier that day. Arlington, the secretary of state, a tight-faced little man, was unscrupulously ambitious, with an uncanny ability to know when to pounce. "It was Gwynne, Your Majesty. Her name was Nell Gwynne."

"So it was indeed." Charles's grin was broad. He enjoyed seeing George bested for the sheer pleasure of what his old friend would do or say next, as it happened so rarely. He knew the two men loathed each other. "A selfless soul in one so poor."

"A calculating soul is more like it," George snarled, beneath his breath.

"Coming from you, George, there is a certain element of irony when one speaks of calculation," said the king.

"Your Majesty, I am calculating enough to know a conniving wench when I see one. With those doleful green eyes of hers, she ought to be selling her wares *on* the stage of the King's House instead of in front of it."

"Arlington?" Charles glanced at the other man. "I trust you can find out about her. Some need she might have, or rather, should I say, the most pressing need among the many. I find that I should like to do something for her."

"It is done, Your Majesty,"

The king stood then as Arlington bent into an overaffected, sweeping bow.

The gilded doors were pulled back by two liveried Yeomen of the Guard. A tall, elegant woman swept past in a rustle and sway of blue satin skirts, hoops, and petticoats. Lady Castlemaine had a large entourage behind her, and the fabric of their gowns was a sudden, rich kaleidoscope of color and rustling fabric. All of the king's courtiers bowed to her, and to the finely dressed ladies. Her absolute power over Charles demanded it. Or at least the power she had held for eight years had begot a pattern between them that had held. But now her histrionics and bold manipulation had begun to weary the king. He watched her glide forward, honey-colored hair, smooth skin, and he thought how surprisingly little he felt, looking at her now. The conversation ceased as she approached the throne. Facing her lover, Barbara Palmer made a slight, perfunctory curtsy. It was only just enough.

"Your Majesty."

"My Lady Castlemaine knows this is the hour of my audience—"

"Indeed, I do," she cut him off breezily. "But *my* need to speak with you dictates my actions."

Charles's anger flared. He thought of banishing her from his presence chamber altogether, to remind her of her place. But she could be dangerous. She had proven that too many times. And there were the children to consider. She was not above using them as weapons, just as she had once used his heart when she had still mattered to him.

The courtiers fell into an immediate and collectively reverent bow as Charles took her arm and they began to walk away from the dais, and toward the tall, gilded and heavily carved double doors at the opposite end of the room.

"Lady Castlemaine and I shall walk," he announced.

Amid the low grumbling of subjects who had waited hours for one moment to petition their sovereign, Charles and Barbara left the vaulted, echoing chamber. The shoes he wore clicked across the rich inlaid floor; they were brocade and ornamented by costly buckles of Spanish silver, nothing at all like the simple soot-caked buskins in which he had trod through debris only hours ago. But this was another part of his life entirely, as was she.

"Very well," he said coldly, once they were alone. "What is it this time?"

"I require additional funds, Charles."

"Additional? God's blood, woman, I have already given you half of my own purse!"

"Three-fourths would please me better."

In spite of how ridiculous she sounded, he knew she was deadly serious. They continued down a long corridor, with a high vaulted ceiling painted by Rubens to represent Peace and Plenty. It had been commissioned by his grandfather James I. Their shoe heels echoing was the only sound for what felt to Charles like an eternity, amid the ghosts of all the kings who had gone before him in these rooms, men who had not dallied quite so much with foolish women.

"What you ask is impossible."

Her expression now held a spark of pleading. "Tell me, then, how can I be expected to clothe and feed all of our children in proper elegance, if you insist on being such a spendthrift?"

Of course, she had never paid for any of that herself. The care of His Majesty's children had always been costs of the Crown. But this was Barbara's way of tightening the noose. She was aware of his interest in Lady Stuart. In his zealousness to make her his new mistress, Charles had been indiscreet. Barbara was about to make him pay for that, as she just had warned by embarrassing him in front of his court.

"And pray tell me, my Lady Castlemaine, why this could not have waited until after my audience?"

"Now, darling," she said condescendingly, linking her arm with his as they continued walking. "You know you have been too preoccupied lately for me to approach you any other way but boldly. That whole fire business. Then Lady Stuart. Not to mention the nasty distraction of that twopenny actress, Moll Davies."

"Yet I always have time for you."

"And you will have even more time once you have won the fair Lady Stuart to your bed. After all, Your Majesty is not known for your attention span."

He looked over at her, biting back a smile. God, how he adored the unexpected. Even if it must be with Barbara Palmer. One day it would likely be his total undoing.

"And yet *you* have captivated me for all of these years."

"Indeed I have. As I have done with others. Following Your Majesty's model."

He laughed out loud at that, the absurdity of a competition between them. He was the king of England. He was expected to have other lovers. They were both referring to the Duke of Monmouth, his eldest illegitimate son, who she had been bedding for several months for the mere sport of it. "Let us not delve into *that* arena," he said, still chuckling.

As a chastened expression highlighted her own smile, they moved down a wide limestone staircase and into the privy garden. Splashing fountains, neat hedgerows, and fat, blooming rosebushes sheltered them from the ugliness of London by the high walls of the many buildings forming his palace. "I shall see what I can do," he finally recanted.

He had far too many legitimate concerns at the moment, with the rebuilding of almost an entire city. He certainly did not need another of her tirades. Nor did he fancy the damage she might do with Lady Stuart, who he felt so close to winning. A happy Barbara, he had discovered the hard way, was a quiet Barbara, and that suited his purposes quite nicely. At least until he had won the lovely Lady Stuart to his bed.

"Conniving bastard!" Buckingham charged. "Villainous opportunist!"

As a punctuation mark, he hurled a heavy silver candleholder and candle across the paneled sitting room of his private apartments. He had come away from the king's chamber, in a fit of fury, followed closely by Thomas Clifford, a young, quick-witted man, who was at court by the grace of his uncle, and who was intent on making his own connections.

As the candle and holder clattered to the floor, the guard posted at the door flinched then signaled for a maid. A moment later, a young girl entered the room, curtsied, and went to clear away the mess.

"That bastard, Arlington, seeks to undermine me with the king at every turn!"

"And yet, is there a soul alive who can achieve such aims?" Clifford flattered him. "You are, after all, His Majesty's dearest childhood friend, and his closest confidant."

"I shall not remain so if Henry Bennet has his way! And all over some low wench who caught the king's eye!"

Clifford burst out laughing. "It always *is*! Yet, might this not work to your advantage since our king seems to be getting nowhere with the virginal Lady Stuart?"

"And how can you fathom that?"

"I thought Your Grace was hoping to unseat Castlemaine with someone new?"

"Not with this wench! This was a pathetic orange girl! Nevertheless, our great ruler actually gave her a moment, a compliment, *and* a silver crown for her pluck, if you can imagine anything so vulgar!"

"Well, he has shown a penchant for low girls, actresses, and the like."

"Penchant or no, *I* am the power behind the king of England, and that power I mean to remain!"

"I fancy Lady Castlemaine would disagree. Unless we find her weakness."

"Other women are her greatest weakness. We need only wait for the right time, and the right woman to remind her."

"We, my lord?"

Buckingham turned to him. "You need an entrée into the higher echelon at court, dear Thomas, and I . . . well, I could do with a *protégé*."

Thomas tipped his head in agreement. "I am honored, sir."

"I shall squash Arlington like the insect that he is. Castlemaine, too."

"There was a time, not so long ago, when you and Lady Castlemaine were . . . close."

"That was a lifetime ago. Yes, one has to learn that timing is everything."

"Indeed. I had heard that."

"Good," said Buckingham. "Now prove to me that you know what it means."

"How might I do that, Your Grace?"

"By helping me vanquish the king's great secretary, Arlington, my enemy. And yours now as well. Castlemaine will come next."

As barge lights lit the Thames, masking the horror of charred wood and debris, Charles entered the candlelit banqueting hall with Lady Castlemaine a half pace behind him. The queen was already seated. Courtiers dressed in lengths and swirls of brightly colored silks and satins bowed as the royal musicians played the tune for a branle from the carved Tudor gallery above. As Charles was seated with great ceremony, a kneeling page, in royal livery, held out a silver ewer of scented water for his hands. Another held the cloth. From a linen-draped table, arrayed with silver platters and crystal flagons, a gentleman of the banqueting hall tasted first the food His Majesty had selected before a plate could be put before him. The same process was repeated before the queen. Then it was repeated for the king's mistress.

Queen Catherine, a small-boned Portuguese woman with a plain face, sallow skin, and watery dark eyes, had watched the entrance with a well-honed combination of disgust and resignation. She had married a man who was never, and could never, be faithful to her. Or to anyone. It was one thing to know that. It was quite another to be forced to see it played out before her eyes with humiliating frequency. The only compensation, if there was one, was that Charles was equally as unfaithful to his trollop, Castlemaine, as he was to her. And Catherine was quite certain it bothered Castlemaine more. She felt a smile turn up the tight corners of her mouth, then forced it away. Gloating had no place in the life of a pious queen. She would force herself to pay for the unholy sentiment with another hour on her knees on cold stone in her private chapel.

Lifting the wide, outdated farthingale of her buff-colored gown, she stood, having taken only a single bite from her plate. Then she backed away from the table. If only Castlemaine had an ounce of civility, or a modicum of culture, to compete with her ambition . . . The queen looked across the table at them. It was not that Charles wished to hurt her. She knew that. Rather, it was that he could not bear to hurt anyone at all, least of all a woman with whom she still slept on a revoltingly frequent basis. What was it, she wondered as she watched the court fall to a hush at her abrupt departure, about a calculating woman, aging rapidly, that held Charles? She wondered with voyeuristic curiosity precisely *how* she achieved it. In her mind, heart, and in her soul, intercourse was for the creation of children only, an heir for the king. Something that, in four years of marriage, she could not do, while Castlemaine had given him four children who, to her horror, he had quickly acknowledged as his own. That, she reminded herself, was the reason Castlemaine reigned supreme. But a vengeful heart made a poisoned soul, and she would have to do penance for those thoughts, as well.

At first, naively, she had loved him. But that seemed a lifetime ago. Now there was only the longing for home, for Portugal, for the soft lavender-scented breezes near the seashore, and for her family. Catherine glanced back one final time at Charles. He and Castlemaine were laughing and chatting happily. At least, with the years, the raw part of the wound of his infidelities had healed. That was God's blessing. With a sigh, Catherine, followed by her entourage of Portuguese ladies, left the banqueting hall.

After dinner, the king walked with friends through the outer gallery and past the old tiltyard of Henry VIII. On the path that led to the privy gardens, the Earl of Arlington approached. Charles waited as he bowed.

"I have found what Your Majesty desires to know."

"Then tell me."

"It seems that Eleanor Gwynne, the orange seller who calls herself Nell, is from quite a—shall we call it—*colorful* family. Her mother is a whore plying her trade on Pudding Lane. Her father is dead, and her only sister is in the Newgate gaol. Nell refuses to ply the family trade, which brought her to Orange Moll."

"Bring me a petition to release her sister."

"Your Majesty must know that Rose Gwynne is there for theft."

"It is my wish that she be released, and so she shall be. Once you have organized that, you are to give Rose Gwynne one hundred pounds, which she is to be instructed keenly by you, personally, to share with her sister, Nell, that the two of them might get their lives in order. Is that clear?"

Once again, Arlington bowed deeply. "Crystal clear, Your Majesty."

Near midnight, Barbara Palmer rolled onto her back, her bare, fleshy body glistening with a sheen of perspiration, and began to laugh. The canopy above them was blue silk. The tapestry curtains were closed.

"Was I that dreadful?" the young man asked, his dark brown eyes as wide and discerning as his father's, but without the jaded depth of difficult experiences, and years.

James Scott, Duke of Monmouth, was perfectly sculpted, taut, and deliciously olive skinned, Charles's Medici blood dominating in his eldest son's veins, as it did his own. But Monmouth, unlike his father, was an abysmal lover, still as quick and unskilled as a colt.

"Not dreadful," Barbara sighed. Apparently, in this past month, she had taught him nothing. It all seemed pathetically comical. "Just a dreadful bore, I'm afraid."

"Well, thank you very much indeed for that!" he said as he bolted from the bed and bent to retrieve his silk pants.

"Oh, now, my dear Jamie," she began, trying hard to stifle what she knew was a cruel-sounding laugh. "To succeed in this world, one must be as realistic about one's strengths as one's weaknesses. Did the king never teach you that?"

"My father has taught me nothing about how to be a king because he does not believe his bastard son will ever be one."

She went to him then, her hands moved tautly down along his hips as she pressed her moist lips to his ear. "But do *you* believe it? You are his only heir!"

"His bastard son. Only Catherine's children can be heirs."

"Well, the little Portuguese does not have any children, does she?"

"You know my father wishes his brother to be king if Catherine remains barren."

"James is a Catholic. Protestant England will never stand for that."

Monmouth turned around and embraced his father's principal mistress, their bare bodies still warm and wet. "I appreciate your wanting to help me, my Lady Castlemaine, but—"

"Oh, for the love of God! Since we have rutted like this more than a few times, can you not see your way clear to address me informally? Or am I too old and motherly for such consideration?"

"You are a goddess! There is nothing old about you!" he reassured her enthusiastically, enough to make her smile.

"Then heed my advice. As the Duke of Buckingham dares to scheme against me, so do I scheme against the king's brother with you for your place. It is what we at this court do."

In the prison between Newgate and Ludgate, just beside the river, a cell door opened with a low squeal. It was past two in the morning and the tormented sounds, the cries and pleadings, were quieted. The lone sound echoed down the long, stone corridor as a guardsman in a soiled uniform, holding a flickering lantern, along with a tall man in an expensive black cloak, entered the cell.

"Rose Gwynne?"

"Who wants to know?" came a weak but defiant voice from a straw mat on the stained and refuse-strewn floor.

"Are ye she or no'?" the guard gruffly pressed, holding the lantern higher.

Rose looked from one face to the next, dream soaked and defensive. She feared a trick. It was not uncommon for guards to steal into a woman's cell in the wee hours, to do with her things she would have no power against which to defend herself. But the presence of the other man, well dressed, recoiling from the odors, as he placed a silver pomander to his nose, told her clearly he was not of this foul, hopeless plate.

"I am," she finally replied.

Rose saw the well-dressed man nod. "You're to come with me," the guard announced.

"I'll not, 'til I know why!"

The two men exchanged a glance.

"You're being released," the guard declared.

"Released? I'm 'ere for the rest of my life, and you well know it!"

"I haven't the inclination to tarry with you, girl. I say you're free to go. Unless, of course, ye're inclined to remain as you fancy the accommodations," he cackled, and then began to bark out a rheumy cough.

As Rose staggered to standing, he spat, then wiped his mouth with the back of his hand. "Come on, then! Be quick about it. I fancy a bit of a lie-down meself before dawn sometime."

Rose lingered near the door with the small opening covered by a rusty iron grate. "But I don't understand . . . why?"

It was then that the well-dressed man spoke. "Consider it a gift, young woman, and make the most of what you do from here on out."

Ten minutes later, Nell Gwynne's older sister, in a soiled shift and cloth shoes, was shown the street. As the great iron door closed mysteriously behind her, her hand was heavy with a shockingly large number of coins. She looked down a long, cobbled street that was silent and full of shadows. It was the middle of the night and a thick fog rolled around her ankles and made her shiver. She coughed, then drew in a trembling breath, the first fresh air she had breathed in over a year.

Chapter 2

THEN ENTER NELLY ONTO THE PUBLIC STAGE.
—*James Shirley*, The Lady of Pleasure

FIVE weeks after London's fire, the King's Theater reopened amid a sudden autumn cold so frigid that it froze the Thames. Notices were posted, and handbills were given out announcing that the king's players would be performing Thomas Killigrew's own play *Siege of Urban*. Admittance to the pit would be free of charge by His Majesty's command. It was said the sovereign hoped to bring a bit of joy to his beleaguered subjects with a rousing comedy.

Nell stood outside the theater in the cool gray air, a basket of plump oranges at her elbow. She was wearing an olive-green dress. It was almost new, even a bit stylish, with an attached, ruched, pannier skirt made of pink floral cotton to the middle of her calves, and puffed half sleeves. It had been offered to her by one of the other orange girls for ten pence. It had been almost a month, yet Nell still could not quite believe her sudden and mysterious good fortune.

The dress was only the smallest part of that.

The memory of waking with a great start, hearing the door handle click. Casting off her blanket, she had fumbled for the long wooden stick she kept beneath the mattress for the nights when Helena Gwynne brought home more than a hangover. But it was not Helena. It was Rose. Rose! Standing in the pale light cast from the corridor, looking like a ghost and an angel at the same time. Rose, who was meant to die in the Newgate gaol. It had been a miracle. But her sister had come back changed, weakened by the ordeal. She had a stubborn cough now, and her face was no longer that of a girl, but of a hardened young woman. Nell was committed to caring for Rose forever now that she was back, and helping her recover her health, no matter what it took.

"Well, don't *you* look fine today," Orange Moll proclaimed.

The declaration brought Nell back to the front of the theater, where a throng of people was pushing past her to get in. Orange Moll stood before her in the cold, gray noonday, a blue shawl closed over her swelling bosom, and a large basket brimming with fruit slung over her own arm and resting against her ample hip.

"I've a new dress," Nell smiled.

"So I see. And 'tis a stroke of good fortune, too. I've lost one of my best inside girls. Just this mornin', in fact. Ran off to marry a linkboy, a pox on 'em both!" She shook her head. Her hair was dark and frizzled, hanging onto her shoulders. Her eyes were shrewd, her face wrinkled and painted. "She needs replacin', and in your new dress you 'appen to fit the part. If you'd fancy a turn at it, that is."

An inside girl. Their baskets were full, not just with oranges, but a bounty of delectable lemons, apples, and sweetmeats. They were the clever ones who bantered with the theatergoers, the girls who made the real tips, the girls who glimpsed the other side of London life. Money. Dresses. Jewelry.

"Oh, yes! Yes, if you please!"

Nell's open smile made Moll flinch. Her expression was suddenly full of warning. "Now, ye'll 'ave to learn quick if you mean to make a proper livin' at it. Banter with the patrons, and a little flirtation comes to no 'arm. The more they fancy you, the more they buy, and the better they tip. Just never let me see ye cross the line. Not at least in a public way. What ye do on your own time's your own business, but 'ere at the king's house I've a reputation to maintain."

Nell caught her breath. "I understand."

Since Rose had found her way out of the Newgate gaol, they had been achingly careful with their precious windfall. Now, perhaps they could think of a larger room, something with a bed big enough for both of them.

Orange Moll, whose real name was Mary Meggs, took Nell's basket of oranges and replaced it with her own full, lush basket. "Ye'll be workin' the pit. 'Tis no fine walk in the park, I'll warn ye. The lot of 'em can be loud and boorish, and the fops won't want to give ye the time o' day for the attention it takes from *them*. Those pretty little boys, with their noses in the air, can be a mean lot. But I've heard ye, Nell, and I believe ye'll hold your own."

"Thank you, Mrs. Meggs!" Nell was beaming.

"Eh, don't be too quick to thank me. 'Tis a chance only, Nell. If ye don't sell the fruit, I'll toss ye out as quick as ye were ushered in, understand?"

"I'll not let you down. I might not even 'ave enough fruit for all I mean to sell!"

The doors to the King's Theater were drawn back at noon, as they were every day, and the crowd that had gathered scrambled for a place on the backless pit benches. Orange peels from the day before were scattered over the seats, covered in green felt, and strewn into the aisles. Foul-smelling men and women surged forward like a great tidal wave and, for a moment, Nell could not quite catch her breath. For the first time, she was in the very midst of all the glorious pushing and struggling for place. The theater was more magnificent inside than her mind had ever conjured, with its three-tiered interior, a middle gallery, and, above it, private boxes gilded and draped with velvet. Crowning it all, to let in light, was a glass cupola above the great apron stage protruding into the audience framed with heavy draperies and painted pictorial scenery behind.

I am 'ere among them all! I am actually inside the King's Theater! It was a heartbeat after the thought, a moment only, when two men wearing lace sleeves and long silk coats, one of eggshell blue, the other an opalescent ivory, clearly the fops about whom she had heard so much, bumped into her. "Watch yourself, girl!" one of them said tautly. He was gaunt faced, his lips were red and wet, and Nell could see pale powder and a small black patch on his cheek. Just as she moved to apologize, she felt the power of another man's hand on her back.

"Two oranges, love, and be quick about it!"

She quickly plucked two of the prettiest pieces of fruit, then looked down into the face of a stout little man with protruding teeth and deep pox scars. In spite of how repugnant he was, Nell gave him her sweetest smile. "Best I 'ave, sir!"

He leaned nearer, his breath smelling of gin, as he handed her the coins to pay for it. "I'll wager those are nowhere near the best that a pretty thing like you has on offer!" His voice was lecherous, and she felt her stomach constrict as his hand, tight on her back, plummeted to the rise of her buttocks.

"True enough! But they *are* the best I'll be sellin' to anyone 'ere!" she declared. Her charmingly wicked laugh made him smile and the little man was disarmed.

He reached into his pocket for extra coins to tip her. "I see that is indeed my loss."

"Now, if all of my customers are as generous as you, sir, I fancy I'll be a duchess before I'm a right proper lady!"

A woman called out then, breaking the moment. "Here girl! Your sweetmeats. Let me see what you have. The offerings from the girl over there were paltry."

Nell fished inside the basket and pulled out one of the small pastries filled with honey and nuts. She handed it to the woman as the din of laughter and yelling around her reached a crescendo. And the play, she knew, would not begin for another hour.

"This looks quite dreadful!" the woman sniffed. "How long ago was this made, girl?"

"I ain't certain, ma'am. I'll warrant you, it tastes delicious, though!"

"And I am going to trust an opinion from the likes of *you*?"

"Pomegranate then, perhaps?" Nell held it up. "Ripe and lovely as they come, these are."

"Better," the woman declared, handing sixpence to Nell. There was no tip included.

"*I* shall take the sweetmeats."

The declaration had come from a young man standing behind the woman in the still-growing crush of bodies. He was handsome, Nell saw, with wavy auburn hair and kind, blue eyes. He moved forward, coins in hand. "And I *would* absolutely trust the opinion of this lovely girl, Lady Russell."

"Bah! That is *only* because you are a lecherous young jackdaw!"

"Lady Russell," he smiled, showing mock indignation, and with it, surprisingly boyish charm. "I really would have expected better from you."

"And *I* would have expected precisely the same as what I saw from *you*, Lord Buckhurst!" she declared, turning on her heel as others clambered forward.

As Lord Buckhurst handed her the money for the sweetmeats, along with an astoundingly generous tip, Nell felt herself being pushed and prodded, but she managed to keep her smile, and her attention, on him. "I thank you indeed, sir."

"Ah, if only they were pearls instead of coins, I would cast them willingly before you," he sighed with enough overaffected drama that Nell could not quell a loud burst of laughter that erupted in a very unladylike fashion. "And when you say that sort of thing to proper ladies, does it actually work?"

"Nearly always," he laughed charmingly.

"'Ow fortunate for me that I'm not the least bit proper!"

A more sincere smile crossed his face. She saw that he was surprised by her clever tongue. "If you are here tomorrow, I shall be delighted to buy your sweetmeats once again."

"'Twill be my pleasure to serve your pleasure, sir," she flirted openly.

Her attention was quickly drawn to another customer, but her thoughts eddied a moment longer on Lord Buckhurst. The power she had felt in that brief interlude was a heady sensation.

Nell began to work the pit with ease after that, smiling and laughing as openly as she did at the Cock & Pye. Drawn by her infectious laugh and her raw beauty, men flocked to her, and Nell reveled in the attention. "Give us an orange, love!" called a stout man with black button eyes. "And there shall be ten pence more in it if you will add a kiss!"

"For six pence more I'd kiss the orange but not you!" she chuckled. To her surprise, with a wide happy smile, he added the ten pence, pinched her cheek, and was gone.

It would be easier than she thought to charm her way to a good meal for Rose and herself, she realized even before the next man pushed his way forward. Proper food, at last!

"Two oranges! I shall take two!"

"'Old your 'orses!" she called back through the din, reaching into her basket as she leveled her eyes, and her smile, directly upon him.

"I would hold anything belonging to you!"

"You'd best settle for the oranges, sir!"

"Today, perhaps! But I will be back for whatever you have on offer tomorrow!"

Even at sixpence an orange, half the cost of a seat in the pit, it was not long before Nell sold almost every one. As the performance drew nearer, she held an orange back, hiding it within the folds of her skirt, so that she might have reason to stay inside and glimpse a bit of the play. She wanted to ensure an explanation should she be asked why she had not left along with the other orange girls.

Selling outside the theater, she had only been able to hear the laughter of the audience and the faint strains of the musicians. Now she greedily drank in all of the atmosphere, the sense of anticipation that was growing in the crowd, until candles were snuffed by young men who worked for the theater company and a young actress came from the wings and onto the stage. In the role of a maidservant dressed as a man, she stood in the center of the boards that jutted out into the musicians, and began the opening monologue.

"Now good people, listen well, I know in your hearts you hate serious plays, as I hate serious parts, but if you sit now calmly you shall see before you not drama but a world of fops and tarts!"

The audience responded by erupting in laughter. Standing back near the entrance doors, Nell listened intensely to the dialogue. The audience responded with great fits of laughter as the girl was joined by two men in guard's costumes. Nell studied each of the actors and made note of the voices they used, how they projected their lines, and used them for what they desired from the audience. As each actor spoke, Nell found herself standing in the anonymous darkness and shadows, mimicking their upper-class accents. Men's lines, women's. It did not matter. She quietly repeated them all. As the actors moved across the stage, her lips mirrored what they said. She studied each sound and inflection. On the way home, her body tingled with fatigue and her mind hummed with all that had happened. She had sold the contents of two baskets, and earned five shillings in tips for herself. It had taken an extra hour, and half the tips, but she was returning home with a new dress for Rose. Like her own, the dress was used, bought through a woman whom Mary Meggs knew, the wife of a prosperous tailor whose wealth exceeded her good sense, shown by discarding perfectly suitable dresses after a few wearings. Nell could not imagine the luxury of discarding anything. The dress was the color of dried rose petals, and Nell knew it was meant for her sister.

Nell was so full of excitement she was not prepared for the sight of her sister huddled against the bed, a bruise swelling on her cheek, and her top lip cut. But she knew what had happened.

"She took it," Rose said, weeping. "All of it."

Nell sank onto the sagging mattress that dominated the tiny room.

"Forgive me, Nelly."

Music and laughter from the tavern below came through the floor and swelled up around them. "I should never've left it 'ere with you, Rose. Ma can smell money, I swear it." Nell put an arm around her sister, feeling suddenly like the older of the two. She drew out her tip money. Watching the open shock on her sister's face made her smile. "I suppose we shall simply be forced to use this instead."

"Oh, Nelly, you didn't sell yourself for me—"

"Not a chance in the world! I'm far too smart for that!"

Rose touched the coins. "You ain't stealin' it then, are you?"

"I'm now a proper orange girl *inside* the King's Theater." She was preening, sitting up a little straighter. "In a month's time, I'll be the best bloody orange seller Moll has ever employed, I'll warrant ye! Most of this is tips. As long as we give 'er the profit, the tips are ours to keep, whatever we're clever enough to earn."

"Knowin' you, Nelly Gwynne, that could end up bein' a small fortune indeed!"

Nell stroked the side of her sister's face, and Rose grimaced a little when she touched the bruise there. "You've always believed in me, Rose, always loved me, and *always* taken care of me. Now its my turn. Oh, and I nearly forgot!" she said, lunging for the dress lying in a fabric pool near the door. Rose gasped when she realized what it was, then her eyes filled with tears.

"'Tis the color of roses," Nell said proudly. "Just like your name."

"You shouldn't 'ave spent your money on me."

"*Our money.* And I cannot think of anythin', or anyone, better to spend it on."

Women swirled past her, cloaked in dark velvet to conceal their identities, and vizards to hide their well-known faces so that they could do as they pleased. Dandies were in their lace and jewelry in a select area of the pit called Fops Corner. They preened and strutted up and down the narrow, overpacked isles, crushing orange peels under their elegant shoe heels, holding snuffboxes and pomanders stuffed with fragrant cloves. The aroma of cooked food mingled with perfume, with the rank stench of body odor, and from those who had relieved themselves in the corners. Nell gripped the basket of fruit with determination, and smiled broadly. She loved it all. Just then, an excited call came from beyond the doors.

"The king comes! The king! The king is coming to see the play!"

All around her, patrons began making way for the great royal party that approached. Nell's heart rocked in her chest. She might actually catch a glimpse of the king!

The swell of the crowd pushed her back as His Majesty's party drew nearer, but Nell resisted, remaining close enough to the front of the crowd to see fine quilted silk coats, jewels, heeled shoes, and plumed hats approach her. Women in bright scarlet, emerald, and sapphire, all of them laughing and glittering like jewels in the sunlight; most prominent among them was a striking golden-haired woman. She breezed past Nell in a swirl of champagne-colored velvet, bell sleeves edged with fur and studded with tiny pearls. Her rosewater perfume held the air for an instant and then, as she did, faded into a rumble of excited chatter and gossip.

The woman was his mistress, without a doubt.

She was grand and breathtaking.

And then, finally, Nell caught a glimpse of him in a coat of lavish emerald brocade and wearing a shining onyx-colored periwig. He was surrounded by others, but he was taller and more magnificent. Yet there was something more; he looked, in that brief instant as he passed her, *familiar. Impossible*, she thought as the royal party rounded the corner and began their ascent of the staircase that led to the king's box. She had never been closer to Whitehall Palace than Charing Cross.

After they had gone, the crowd dispersed, returning to their places in the pit. The spectacular moment vanished. But throughout the play, Nell could not stop herself from gazing up at the royal box from the dark of the alcove shadows, hiding her beneath the gallery. How could the king of England seem familiar?

He watched her with interest from behind the side curtain, the length of velvet tightly in his hand as she stood in the shadows, gazing up at the king. *New blood*, he thought with a smile. But he would need to tread cautiously. His reputation would likely precede him.

"Mr. Hart!" a voice called. "Five minutes until you're onstage, sir!"

"Thank you, Bell," he replied, using his best verbal flourish, the one that had made him a star.

By the end of November, Nell had developed a regular following of customers. They bought her fruit, tipped her handsomely, and engaged her in the witty banter at which she excelled well above the other girls. They found her funny without being boorish, flirtatious without being crude, and the men loved it. One of her most ardent customers, one who always bought the quince pies, was Charles Sackville, Lord Buckhurst.

Buckhurst was kind, handsome and, since her very first day, an exceedingly generous tipper, often giving her more on the side than what he paid for her fare. "If it isn't lovely Nell!" he called out to her early one Saturday afternoon as people were clambering around her for seats.

As always, it was a pushing, shoving maelstrom for places on the pit benches.

Nell spun around, knowing the voice now. He seemed, she thought, a friend. "Your Lordship's usual?"

"Am I really so predictable?" he sighed dramatically.

"Afraid so."

"Have I nothing then at all of the mystery to challenge you?"

Her robust laugh was as distinctive as it was endearing. "Certainly a fine, high manner, Lord Buckhurst. But mystery, with you, I'm afraid, is in short supply."

"Oh, you wound me!" He pressed his hands to his chest in a gesture befitting one of the actors they were about to see onstage.

"An orange girl could do no such thing to a man of consequence."

"She could if her name was Nell Gwynne!" he parried as she simultaneously sold one orange each to two plain-faced women standing before her, hands extended. "And trust me, Nell, I am worth far less consequence than it may seem."

"Lord Buckhurst!" one of the women sniffed. "Pray, do not tell me a man of your stature would tarry with an orange wench!"

Buckhurst glanced at Nell. He was wearing his endearing grin. "I'd not dream of it, Lady Penelope. But then there is little I would *dream* of telling you. Our conversations have always been something more of a *nightmare.*"

Nell put a hand before her mouth, but not before a laugh burst past it. She felt a hand press firmly onto her shoulder. The face that met hers, when she turned around, was long and thin with a square jaw and patrician nose. "If old Moll's most popular orange seller has an orange left, I should like to buy it," he said to her in a deeply cultured voice.

"Indeed I do, sir."

After he took the orange, he handed her coins, which amounted to an excessively large tip. "I thank you, sir. 'Tis right generous of you."

"Worry not. I always get what I pay for, Nell."

When he had gone, Lord Buckhurst asked her, "Have you any idea who that was?"

"Not a clue. Should I?"

"Charles Hart is the star of this theater, and one of its principal managers. And, if I may say, he has clearly taken a fancy to *you*."

"Oh, everyone fancies me, Lord Buckhurst. The same way they do a pup in the street. I get a moment's notice for a clever tongue and a smile, then no more."

"Well, in all my time at this theater, I have never seen the great Charles Hart come out from behind the vaunted curtain, and certainly never as directly for an orange from one of you."

"Maybe he was hungry," she smiled slyly. "I wouldn't make too much of it."

"And I would not discount it, lovely Nell." He drew up her hand and, for the first time since she had met him, his expression became serious. "Take care with Mr. Hart, Nell. He can be a dangerous man."

"He seemed perfectly charmin' to me."

"He's an actor, the finest one in London. Boasts to everyone that he is a grandnephew of William Shakespeare. Mark me, he sought you out for something more than a piece of fruit."

"If you're right," she laughed, "we have only to wait and see what that is."

Before she left the theater that afternoon, Nell received a message, brought by the girl, still in rouge and lip paint, who had delivered the epilogue. It was from Charles Hart. Nell read the brief words with difficulty; she could barely read, and could not write at all. Still, the message was clear. Mr. Hart wished her to join him in his private tiring-room.

There was something he wished to ask her.

The king sat at the head of a long, polished table, with the Duke of Buckingham. The Earl of Arlington, who Buckingham openly despised, sat across from him, fingering a silver snuffbox. Thomas Clifford, Buckingham's new protégé, slouched, while John Maitland, the barrel-chested Scottish Duke of Lauderdale, whispered to the Duke of York at the table's other end.

As England's Lord High Admiral, it was the King's brother, James, Duke of York, who was spearheading a new effort to locate revenue for England. All of the councillors, with the exception of the gout-ridden, cantankerous lord chancellor, the Earl of Clarendon, were young and enthusiastic for the continuation of the yearlong war with the Dutch. In spite of the enormous cost of sea battles, the potential in victory was too seductive to be denied. "We simply haven't enough money to continue on! It takes money to make war! We have barely enough to man our harbors as it is!" Clarendon declared, slamming a liver-spotted hand onto the polished oak table. The earl was alone against the younger council members. Their sighs and rolled eyes were a reminder to the king of that.

"The Dutch have wealth beyond the needs of three countries," argued Buckingham.

"That has never meant it is ours for the taking!"

Clarendon was a stubborn old man, with a shock of snowy hair and a rugged, somber face. He was tolerated, not only because his daughter was married to the king's brother, but because he had been a great supporter of Charles's father. But the times were slowly shifting.

"It will be ours if we are victorious," Clifford observed in support of Buckingham.

The Duke of York leaned back in his chair and put a hand on his chin. "There *is* another way."

Arlington rolled his eyes. He, like the others, knew what would come next. The views of the king's secretly Catholic brother were well known to this intimate council. An alliance with Catholic France was his standard proposal. Accepting money from the French would mean an end to the Dutch hostilities, and a respectable sum for England in the bargain.

"Your Majesty could still accept Louis XIV's generous terms. Then the Dutch would become inconsequential. After all, why have you sold our sister to his brother, if not ultimately for a treaty with France?"

"Keep Minette out of it," Charles interjected, stiffening. "We are talking about war."

"The terms with France are still too high," Buckingham put in. "If there were even a hint that His Majesty meant to convert England to a Catholic country, there would be anarchy the likes we have not known since—" He bit off his words, but the reference lay raw still between men who had survived the dark days of Oliver Cromwell, watched a king's murder, and had worked for the Restoration of his son, who now reigned.

"Since my father was brutally butchered right outside these walls, you meant to say? His death will not be in vain, by God! I will rule as he ruled, bravely and boldly!"

"The country is glad to have Your Majesty," Arlington amended, purposely seconding Buckingham. "We rejoiced openly in your Restoration. But England is a staunchly Protestant country."

"I have it on sound authority that not everyone is so staunch," James said quietly.

"This is taking us too far afield from the point," Buckingham interjected. "England requires money, and ahead lies two distinct paths toward realizing that. One will require continued sacrifice at sea, but earn great wealth in our certain victory. The other, while asking less sacrifice, calls for an intolerable spiritual compromise."

"And a dangerous deception to my subjects," the king added. "We need a sound victory if we are ever to rebuild London."

"Mark me," said Clarendon. "You shall *all* rue the day that you continued on with this."

The king looked at Clarendon, his father's trusted adviser, trying to recall what he had seen as worthy in the advice of a fearful old man. His gaze then slid to Buckingham and Clifford.

"We need money. The Dutch have more than enough," decreed the king. "Any treaty with France contains the provision that I declare myself a converted Catholic king. And, at the moment, that is a price even I am not willing to pay."

"Why not make Louis a counterproposal?" offered James. "Protect our harbors from attack, then wait and see."

Clarendon stood, then hunched over, his knuckles meeting the oak table. "You know perfectly well we cannot afford the cost of manning docked ships! The city cries for rebuilding, and there are still the effects of the last plague with which to be reckoned. It would be a foolish waste of money, Your Majesty, one which your father, the king, would never have allowed!"

The king settled his eyes first on the broad-shouldered Clarendon, then on his brother. "At least we must man our unused ships that are still in the harbor. Keep them at the ready. As they are, we are vulnerable should the Dutch decide to retaliate."

"Keeping them at the ready will cost more than we have," Clarendon grumbled. "You must propose a truce with the Dutch and put an end to all of this, no matter our circumstance, if you have a prayer of rebuilding London!"

"James, are you prepared to continue on as Lord High Admiral, leading us at sea in spite of our difference of opinion on this?"

"My duty is to serve my king."

Charles arched a brow. "And your duty to your God?"

"I shall pray that the will of one shall follow the path of the other."

"And George, what of England if the prayer goes unanswered?" asked the king.

"Then we are all doomed, a devastation throughout the world the likes we have never seen before." Buckingham's glance slid from one privy councillor to the next. "But, of course, that will not happen."

The king's gaze followed Buckingham's. The silence stretched out for what felt an eternity. "My father trusted you implicitly, and I am prepared to trust you, Clarendon," he finally said. "For the time being, until the French respond to our counterproposal, we take no further aggression toward the Dutch, and we will patrol our harbors but keep the ships unmanned so that we can begin to help the people build shelter."

"Rob Peter to pay Paul?" said Lauderdale beneath his breath.

"Mark me, it will be a grievous mistake," said Buckingham, who turned his head and gave a little grunt of disapproval which no one but the king heard.

He was propped by a spray of tasseled velvet pillows, in his tall poster bed, with a massive tester behind it. At his feet, and near the fire, was a collection of his beloved spaniels, dozing. The girl would be quietly brought to him, like all of the others, by William Chiffinch, the keeper of His Majesty's privy closet. Afterward, she would be led away. Like the same tune played too many times, the melody now was gratingly predictable. There was no love in the act, nor any longer even the wild excitement of anticipation. Other than what he felt for his children, and he loved them all deeply, there was no love in his life, no passionate love, any longer. Though he had all of the richness and grandeur that had eluded him in his poverty-ridden exile, his heart was a more difficult void to fill. The harder he searched for someone he could love, the more he found women seduced by the trappings of royalty. Hortense Mancini was first to make an impression on his heart, Lucy Walter was first to make an impression in his life; she was Monmouth's mother. Then Barbara. Moll Davies. It had become a game to him, to see how long it might take to uncover an honest heart. Catherine loved him. Why, the Portuguese ambassador queried, did a lonely king not pay greater heed to that? Charles did care for her. He enjoyed her company. He even trusted her judgment. But to Catherine, duty *was* love—he was her duty, not a great passion. They had married, sight unseen. Yet still, even after four years, she was rigid with him. Beyond the necessary encounters to, God willing, produce an heir, there was no playfulness, scant show of affection, and unrelenting prayers every time immediately afterward.

The decision about war with the Dutch plagued him almost as much as his private life. Continuing on with aggression could prove a dangerous mistake. Like infidelity. Charles remembered well what had happened the last time. Common sense gave way to English avarice. Hundreds slaughtered at sea. A devastating cost. A humiliating defeat. There was a soft rap at the door, and thoughts of war vanished into a light swirl of juniper perfume.

An hour after she had gone, Charles could remember nothing about the girl.

Unable to sleep, he rose, and drew on a brocade dressing gown. He went toward a ring of moonlight cast through the grand Elizabethan oriel window, which looked onto his own formal gardens. Here, protected on all sides by Whitehall Palace, he could almost make believe he lived a quiet life in the country where everything beyond the palace walls was clean and safe. Yet, in spite of the danger, Charles was often drawn beyond his protective cocoon. He loved to be anonymous, to slip in and out of the world of which he could never truly be a part. The ordinary world. It was why he went into London so often without his wig and his finery. While there had been hunger and fear in his impoverished exile years, Charles had found a kinship with common people that had changed him forever. He opened the window and a cool rush of night air washed over him, reviving him. Ghosts . . . so many ghosts at night . . .

"Stop! No, I'll not listen!"

"You will listen, Charles! They've cut off his head, and you are king of England now! You will survive, and one day you will return to England to rule!"

Charles squeezed his eyes and let the cool night air dry the sheen of perspiration on his face and chest. The ghosts faded. He shivered. Though she had remained exiled in France for nine years, the sound of his mother's determined voice was as clear in his mind now as it had been that day. That moment would forever haunt him, knowing the savagery of Cromwell's men. God, the images that came when he lay his head on the pillow! He squeezed his eyes against the image of a river of blood. He could almost hear the thump of his father's severed head landing in the wicker basket beside the stump. The place it happened was here, outside these very castle walls. Now, as he often did, when he could not drink enough to find a bit of peace, he drew on a long leather coat, trousers, soft boots, and a wide-brimmed hat, and went alone down the same back stairs on which the girl had been brought to him. Alone, he walked into the freedom of morning's earliest hour, when the fog rolled and swirled at his ankles, obscuring him. He lowered his hat and passed a guard sleeping on duty, slumped in a chair, lightly snoring. Charles knew the soldier should be punished, but, in this case, the boy had done him a favor. He moved quietly through a narrow corridor, lit by candles in wall sconces, then down a flight of stairs to the outer courtyard that faced the Thames. There, by Charles's order, the block remained, still starkly stained with his father's blood. "So I might never forget," he once told his brother.

Charles knelt beside the block and lowered his cheek onto the flat surface. Barbara had found him here once and berated him for his foolishness. But no one understood. Not even his own brother. James called it God's will, and refused to speak of it again.

Help me be a better king, Father . . . and help me be a better man than I have been . . .

Footsteps were crunching the gravel behind him. The moment, the image, snapped. Charles pivoted around. William Chiffinch, in dressing gown and crimson velvet robe, his salt-gray hair wild, approached flanked by two royal guards. "It is the queen, Your Majesty, you must come quickly!" said Chiffinch, the only royal servant who knew precisely where the sovereign would be.

"Is it the child?"

"I'm afraid it is, sire."

Chapter 3

As England's Monarch in his closet lay
Chiffinch stepped to fetch the female prey.
—*Poems on Affairs of State*

Spring, 1667

"THE selection for last evening met with Your Majesty's approval, I trust?" Chiffinch asked casually as he held out two large plumed hats for the king's consideration.

Charles stood before a full-length French mirror, framed in gold, a gift from Louis XIV. "It would have, if I could remember a thing about her."

"She was quite comely, sire."

Charles glanced over at the man he knew was as faithful as he was discreet. "Love would be better, Chiffinch."

"So the poets do claim. I am told that the queen is still very hopeful. Perhaps—"

"I am dearly fond of the queen. But fondness is a far-off thing from passion."

Chiffinch did not propose Lady Castlemaine because he found her deceitful and vain. "Perhaps Mrs. Davies then?"

Charles chuckled as the chosen hat was placed on his head, then tilted properly. "She is only a dalliance, Thomas. Nowhere near to touching my heart, or anything higher up than my prick, I'm afraid."

Chiffinch nodded but did not respond.

"Fun and games to press away the darker images that would haunt me. Until the unlikely moment when I discover a real passion, I must settle for as much of the former two commodities as you are able to procure for me."

He and Chiffinch were followed silently then down the long corridor by a collection of his aides as he approached the queen's apartments. It had been two days since her miscarriage, and Catherine was still confined to her bed by the doctors. But her ladies played a game of basset beside her, and beneath the window a young boy played his harp to entertain her. When Charles entered the private bedchamber, all motion ceased. Catherine's ladies all stood and dropped into deep curtsies. Rustling skirts was the only sound.

"You're looking much better today," he said kindly. "The color is back in your cheeks."

The waiting women slowly rose and moved away from the royal couple, affording them privacy. Charles motioned to the boy to begin playing his harp again as he sank into one of the chairs beside her bed. Charles held out his hand to his wife. She took it to her cheek and closed her eyes. She was still horribly pale, he thought, nowhere near the picture of health he had married. In his own way, Charles loved his wife, much as a brother cares for a sister.

"I am so very sorry, Charles," Catherine whispered, tears filling her eyes. "I truly believed this time—"

"There is still time," he soothed her, even though they both knew it was unlikely. They had been married for five years, and in that time he had fathered four of Barbara's children, and two others by ladies of the court.

Buckingham whispered to him about divorce. But she did not deserve that injustice, certainly not yet.

Charles Hart's private tiring-room behind the stage was lit by three small lamps with shining pewter bases. Delicate etched glass covered the dancing flames. An elegant tapestry chair was positioned at a dressing table littered with bottles and jars, and in the corner was a daybed of blue velvet fringed in gold. It was the dominant feature of the small, private room. Nell glanced at the boy who showed her inside, then she watched as the door was closed, leaving her alone. She felt an odd mix of anticipation and dread. She waited, listening to the sounds of laughter and foot-steps of people going past, beyond the closed door. Finally, from behind a folding screen, Charles Hart emerged and stood before her. His eyes were devilishly wide and green, and there was something unmistakably dangerous about them.

"So you are the new orange girl."

"And *you* are the famous actor I've been warned about."

He was smiling, charmingly. "As principal actor and part manager, I like to have my hand on all things concerning this theater."

"And are you satisfied with what you see?" she asked.

"Satisfaction has many layers. I reserve judgment until I know a bit more of you."

He was saying suggestive things intentionally. He was, after all, a famous actor who certainly did not need to entertain com-mon orange girls. With beautiful actresses everywhere, and wealthy women waiting for him by the theater curtain, she could not imagine what he wanted with her. He poured a glass of wine, then two. He handed one to her. Nell had never seen glassware so fine, beautifully beveled and cut. She took a grateful swallow.

"So tell me," he said, and his cultivated voice was a rich, catlike purr. "Have you seen any of my plays?"

"I watched you play Mr. Wellbred in *The English Monsieur* yesterday."

He straightened his back. "And how did you find it?"

"What an orange girl thinks can 'ardly interest the likes of you, Mister 'Art."

"You'd be surprised."

"All right, then. I thought you were too serious in the first scene. There was a grand opportunity for a laugh you missed."

His confident smile fell swiftly. "You thought so, did you?"

"Well, sir, you did ask."

"You sound as if you believe you might have done better than a grandnephew of the vaunted William Shakespeare."

"I'd 'ave got a laugh."

"And just how would *you* say the line?"

"All right then. The line Lady Wealthy 'as is 'Go 'ang yourself.' And Mr. Wellbred *should* say, 'Thank you for the advice.'"

He scratched his chin. "You say I'll get a laugh like that?"

"I've no doubt."

His charming smile returned. "Allow me to take you to dinner, Nell. I would like to hear more of your views on my untapped comedic potential. I know a lovely little place very near here where we can dine quietly, and talk."

"You want to take the likes of *me* out in public?"

"I asked you, did I not?"

"True enough, Mr. 'Art."

"You're a cautious girl. And quick for your age."

"Do you not mean quick for a girl from modest means?"

"Nell Gwynne," he laughed out loud. "You *are* a charmer."

She let him lead her down the street to Long's, in the Haymarket. It was a delightful establishment, all brightly candlelit, with draperies around the back tables, and linen on some of them. Charles Hart was ushered in with great ceremony, and Nell followed him, unnoticed in her secondhand olive-colored dress. They went to a small alcove, paneled in rich oak, and hung with long swags of vermilion velvet. He sat down at a table, and two women came over to speak with him. Charles Hart did not notice that they blocked the only other chair at the table so that Nell was forced to continue standing.

"If you please!" Nell finally said. She might not be a lady, but she knew well enough she was a guest. Her comment required the women to turn and regard her. The first one was petite, with dark hair and huge breasts peeking over her lace trim. She bit back an unkind smile as she moved just enough for Nell to reach the chair and sit. "Poor Charles, dredgin' the depths again?"

"My dear Moll, it is the variety in life that sustains me. Nell Gwynne, may I present Moll Davies, the finest actress the Duke's Theater has ever had the fortune to possess. And I say so even if they did steal you away from our far superior King's Theater, and from me."

"Superiority, Charles, is a matter of opinion." She laughed in a way Nell thought more suited to Maypole Alley whores than a prosperous, well-dressed actress.

"Not according to our receipts! You know we outsell you every month!"

"'Tis only because you've Mr. Dryden. A distinctly unfair advantage."

She *was* from Maypole Alley. Her earthy accent and bawdy manner told Nell as much.

"Word is, you're doing well enough for yourself," Charles said, as the second woman was distracted, then called away, by another group of patrons across the crowded dining room.

"As long as I stay in His Majesty's good graces, I am indeed."

"So then it *is* true."

"Everyone knows the king's passion for the theater. I simply made it my business to know that . . . and anythin' else 'e was passionate about!"

Intimidated by the grand surroundings, and the celebrity of Charles Hart and a royal mistress, Nell tried to think of something even half as clever to say.

"So those devilish poems about our king are true?" Hart asked.

"Every bit. 'Is Majesty is a great bear of a man with the most massive—" She abruptly dropped the final word hanging on her tongue and, with jarring condescension, lowered her gaze on Nell. "Perhaps I've said too much."

"Oh, this is just Nell, an orange girl in need of a meal. Your secrets are safe in this room."

Moll looked directly at Nell. A spark of competition flared between them. "Of course. But a girl simply can't be too careful if she fancies keepin' 'erself in the style to which the king of England 'as made 'er accustomed. And, believe me, I *will* remain accustomed! Mark me, girl, if you've a mind to actually captivate this fabulous man 'ere, for more than the indiscretion 'e expects, you'd do well to find yourself a mentor like me. Not to be overly boastful, but—" She touched the large stone at the end of a chain that stopped at her ample breasts. "My success *is* one to learn from!" She embraced Charles Hart, and then was gone.

Nell wanted to learn nothing from a woman like Moll Davies, no matter where she had come from. But as they dined on courses of oysters and roast leg of pork served on gleaming pewter dishes, Charles Hart was charming. He overwhelmed her with his attentions, and his clever tongue, and she found she rather liked it and him. After dinner, they walked in silence back toward Drury Lane and the theater, linkboys running back and forth around them lighting the path of others for a small fee.

"You're awfully quiet," he said as they passed through a shadowy little cobblestone courtyard.

"I speak when I've somethin' to say."

"Did you not enjoy your dinner?"

"The meal was fine. 'Twas the performance before it that set my teeth on edge."

"Mrs. Davies, was it? Now, you mustn't take a woman like that too seriously, Nell. She's a cock-if-you-please sort of girl, just bedded the king of England, and is enjoying her status as royal tart of the moment."

Nell stopped abruptly beside the dirty windows of a closed tailor's shop and looked at him. "I may be *just* an orange girl, Mr. 'Art, but I've a sight more pride than to go boastin' about like a tart on Sunday."

"People do a lot of things to get ahead in this world, Nell."

"Maybe so. But there's a limit to what *I* would do."

"Is that a fact? Until you've been offered the brass ring like Moll has, or something close to it, you may want to reserve judgment. There are men who can make a working girl's life far more comfortable, so long as she is open to the possibilities."

"I may be common, as well, but I've my priorities."

"Priorities rarely keep one warm at night, Nell. And there truly is not a common thing about you."

They went up the pathway to Drury Lane and into the main door of the theater with his last words still echoing in her head. Standing inside, with the vacant pit and the rows of benches stretched before them, there was a great hollow grandness to the space. As they paused, Charles Hart turned and softly kissed her.

The only other man Nell had been kissed by had been one of her mother's drunken lovers. The taste of his hot, wet mouth, dirty teeth, and breath stinking of ale had been with her since. Hart's kiss was not repulsive; his breath smelled like the fine wine they had drunk at dinner. With his hand on the small of her back, he led her to his tiring-room. He began to kiss her again, more deeply this time, then roughly. Nell's knees went weak. Her response turned to fear. She tried to protest, but he was stronger than she could have imagined, and when she struggled it only encouraged him.

Charles Hart pressed her forcefully against the closed door and was struggling with her dress. There was a tearing, then the sound of buttons clinking onto the floorboards. She tried to turn her head so that her mouth could break free from his, but he lifted his hand to her face and held her chin. Another childhood memory surfaced then. She could have been no more than seven or eight. She had hidden behind a divan on the first floor of the brothel. There had been a man doing this very thing, pressing one of the women up against the wall. His trousers were shoved around his thighs, the pink flesh of his buttocks pushing against her with a frenzied rhythm. Nell had felt curiosity then. She felt shame now. She had kept herself all those years. She had avoided them all. And now, with no more ceremony or care than the woman in the brothel that day, she was to become one of them.

"Pray, let's not dally longer!" Hart said as he pushed her toward the velvet-covered daybed. "I do fancy a challenge," he panted into her ear as he tossed her skirts and petticoat up onto her bosom, and into her face. "But too much of the coquette can surely sour any moment!"

She beat at his chest, hitting him with her fists. In an odd dance of pull and push, he had fumbled with his codpiece, lifted himself back onto her, then lunged forward. From then on, it was all tearing and thrusting, pushing into her, until suddenly he collapsed, an unbearable weight, and it was over. "God's blood, but you had me wild for you," he said to her then, kissing her forehead. "But I promise you, 'twill be better between us next time." Arranging his shirt, waistcoat, and trousers, Charles looked back down at her, and saw something that stopped him. There were streaks of blood on her thighs. "Great God above! Tell me you were not still a maiden!"

"I tell you nothin' now when you wouldn't listen to anythin' a moment ago."

"A pox on it!" He gripped his head with both hands. "You should have told me! I'm not in the habit—" Charles Hart's words fell away. He looked at Nell for another moment, his expression pained. It twisted his handsome face. He was shaking his head as he walked out of the room. "Damn orange sellers! Damn the lot of you!"

After he had gone, Nell slid from the daybed and onto the floor. She reached up to cover her breasts, where he had torn away the bodice, and only then realized how violently she was trembling. She smoothed out her dress and tried vainly to catch her breath. She tried to tell herself she was all right, that her mother and sister did *that* as a matter of course. She was not certain she could ever learn to actually enjoy it. For all of his reputation as a smooth and confident actor, Charles Hart had been a moaning, sweating pig. She wished she had at least been paid a few shillings if she was going to be forced to live the indignity of her mother and sister's world after all. But that was her defenses talking, certainly not her heart. She felt a complete fool that her usual judgment had been so impaired by an outwardly charming and famous man. She really should have known better, she thought.

"Are you all right, mistress?"

A tentative voice shocked her and she turned, grasping the torn fabric tighter to her chest in response. "Who the devil are you?"

"Richard Bell, mistress."

"Why are you 'ere?"

"I'm one of Charles Hart's actors," he replied. Then, in the awkward silence, he shrugged. "Actually, I'm more of a cleaning boy, one who gets onstage from time to time when Mr. Hart needs a larger crowd scene. But I have hope, anyway. It's my foot in the door." He waited a moment. "But you, you're different from the others. I've seen you. You've a way with words."

"'Tis only what I'm supposed to do to sell oranges."

"But if you'll pardon me for being bold, Mrs. Gwynne, you've got a spark."

"And didn't *that* just start a flame I didn't want."

They both knew what she meant. He ran a hand behind his neck. She looked away, aching to be somewhere else, even to be someone else.

"I have an idea how you can best him *and* better your own situation in the bargain."

She truly looked at him then and saw a thin young man with limp hair and a wide, flat nose covered with a smattering of freckles. He had remarkably gentle brown eyes. He was everything Charles Hart was not. That registered with her, especially now. "No one goes up against a powerful man without his own reasons. What's in it for you, Mr. Bell?"

"I don't like Charles Hart. And I *do* like you."

"You don't even know me."

"I know I'd fancy getting the better of that rapscallion. And, I don't know it for certain, but I believe you are the one to help me do it. If I'm right, we both win."

"And if you're wrong, we'll both be out of the King's Theater on our very common arses."

"That you can be so witty after . . ." He took a breath. "Well. It tells me all I need to know."

Richard Bell pushed past a collection of stage props and painted pictorial scenery after Nell had gone, pausing at the empty stage upon which Charles Hart was sitting, hunched over, head in his hands. "Something wrong, sir?"

"Foolish, foolish!" He was murmuring the word. He did not look up.

"The girl, sir?"

"She was still a maid. Blast! How was I to know?"

The obvious response was that a woman's virtue should not be made an easy target of conjecture. But a confrontation with someone so much more powerful did not now suit his plan. His was a grander game of resourcefulness and opportunity. "She *is* but an orange seller, Mr. Hart."

"And Mary Meggs'll have my hide for knowing it! She's lost three girls this past fortnight, and you will never convince her they weren't all my fault!"

Richard Bell stepped closer. "Why not give Mrs. Gwynne a small part, as an apology. Nothing grand, mind you, just something in the background. A crowd scene along with me, perhaps."

Charles Hart looked up. "The girl is no actress!"

"She has agreed to work on my lines with me for the performance tomorrow morning herself, playing Morgana. Mrs. Knepp once again wants my head on a platter for, she says, trying to upstage her in the second act, and she won't rehearse with me. Why not watch from the side, and make up your mind about Nell then?"

"A more colossal waste of both our mornings could not likely be had."

"And yet you might appease your conscience."

"I've little conscience left about me, Bell. In this life, my concern has become self-preservation only."

And a good dose of self-aggrandizement, thought Richard Bell. But he wisely chose not to say it. Something told him from the beginning that Nell Gwynne was worth holding his tongue.

Rose Gwynne's hand went to her mouth. "What in blue blazes happened to you?"

Nell slumped against the warped door. It was not supposed to have been like that. Her life was meant to be different. Somehow, suddenly now, she felt herself on the same path as her sister. "'Tis all right."

"The devil it is!" Rose moved across the room and put the back of her hand gently to Nell's cheek.

"You and Ma manage it. Why should I not learn as well?"

"Because you're different, Nelly. You are the 'ope of the Gwynne's!"

"I'm no one's 'ope."

"You've 'eld out for so long."

"'Tis what 'appens sooner or later, right?"

"I expect so."

"And you make somethin' of it, if you're pretty enough. Ma used to say that to us. I can't remember much else she ever said, much I'd want to remember."

"If you're pretty *or* very clever. That's what she used to say," Rose answered. "Ma used to say men always fancy the clever ones, and 'tis no tellin' what a pretty, clever girl can achieve."

Chapter 4

A PRINCE OF MANY VIRTUES, AND
MANY GREAT IMPERFECTIONS.
—*John Evelyn on King Charles II*

H E swam with powerful strokes through the calm waters
of his private canal at Whitehall Palace. Behind him,
fighting one another to keep up, was a length of aides
and courtiers who fancied not the swimming so much as the
bragging rights. Keeping pace with the energetic and athletic
king of England was a necessity to retaining one's place. Aware
of it, and amused by it, Charles plunged beneath the surface
again. Some days it was just good to be king.

After tormenting them sufficiently with his superior skill, he
moved toward the mossy bank, beneath a branching oak, and
stepped out of the water. His Medici skin was naturally tanned
and glimmering in the midday sunlight. The others shook, shivered, and grumbled as Charles stepped toward a waiting blanket
and a fresh pair of velvet slippers lined with down. Then, without
turning to acknowledge them, Charles moved up the embankment and began to walk with long-legged strides as each man
scrambled for his own place nearest him. None of them, not even

Buckingham, would ever fully know his painful, twisted course to the Crown. To flee his father's murderers, Charles had been forced to seek safety in France, until troops could be amassed to help him win back England. There was no other way. To accomplish his escape, Charles was forced to send all of his faithful courtiers away. All but one made their way toward Scotland, and were captured and killed. Alone, vulnerable, and entirely impoverished, Charles had been forced to depend upon the loyalty of a simple country family, one that disguised him and helped to spirit him out of England. He had been aided by Richard Penderel, a brave Royalist, and his small party of supporters. Charles was exhausted by hunger and pain when the group headed down the steep edge of an embankment to the sandy shore where there was only hope of swimming to safety. "I cannot swim, Your Majesty!" came the voice of one of the Royalist followers, the simple man who had risked his family's safety, and his own, to help the king escape. Charles had led his guide through the water that day, and toward the safety of the other shore. The opulent life of excess and entitlement he now lived remained startling to him in contrast to that dark memory, and a dozen others like it. They were never gone, nor buried beneath comfort, privilege, and debauchery.

Charles never forgot the loyalty of the Penderel family. When his throne was restored, he saw to it that they were made comfortable for the rest of their lives.

"Come on, the lot of you stragglers," he called out now, the dark memories put away. "I'll not keep Mr. Wren waiting! I am told this great young architect has a plan for rebuilding London!"

Ahead of them, sitting beneath a bristling evergreen, dressed in volumes of pale blue and gold brocade, was the most recent object of his attentions, Frances Stuart. He had hoped to find her here. Beside her, on a tufted stool, built just noticeably higher, Lady Castlemaine sat. She was now the object of his greatest regret. He paused for a moment between two huge urns, the gateway to a small flight of stone steps. Then he approached the two women with utmost caution. Barbara never did anything without a purpose. By her presence, she meant to say that she knew precisely what was transpiring. Buckingham came ahead of the others, meeting the king's stride, then, seeing the women, he leaned over to whisper, with a clever smile, "Did Your Majesty ever consider monogamy?"

"I did once, actually. But I've since recovered from it quite nicely."

Both women rose, then fell to deep curtsies.

"Pray, Lady Castlemaine, tell us in what sort of conversation might you be engaging so young and impressionable a girl as Lady Stuart here?"

"Anything Lady Stuart could glean from my many years at court would be time well spent on her part, Your Majesty. The details are unimportant."

"Did someone not once say that the devil is in the details?"

"Your Majesty knows I have always been devoted to you."

"In deed, if not always in your words."

"One would never be wise to say any but the most glowing things of Your Majesty."

"Since when was wisdom one of my Lady Castlemaine's great assets?"

"Since spending eight long years at Your Majesty's side and, if I may say so, surviving."

A soft murmur of amusement ruffled the air behind him, and irritated Charles. He did not like to be outshone in front of his court, and certainly not by such a fading star as Barbara Palmer.

Charles turned to the girl who had become his obsession. "Lady Stuart, you would be wise to take with a very fine grain of salt every utterance of the lady before you."

"Yes, Your Majesty." Frances Stuart blushed and then curtsied again. Charles saw that she had decided wisely not to enter a fray of such long and tangled standing.

Looking from one woman to the next, Charles suddenly began to laugh. Having Barbara so well entrenched at court was murder on his love life, and she knew it. As he nodded to each woman and then proceeded away, Buckingham leaned over once again. "Perhaps some things are worth trying *twice* in a lifetime, Your Majesty."

"For the right woman, George, I think I actually might."

"Something *must* to be done about that old fool! We are at a crucial juncture, and Clarendon could ruin it all," Buckingham spat as he sat with Lady Castlemaine, well concealed in a grotto draped and curtained off by wisteria and thick ivy. It was far out beyond the privy garden, and past the grove of lemon trees where the former king used to stroll and the present king rarely dared to tread for the ghosts hidden there. "If he has his way, the king will be surrendering to the Dutch before a fortnight and England will be the laughingstock of the world! He will ruin everything we have worked so hard for!"

Lady Castlemaine agreed.

As Charles met with Christopher Wren, Buckingham plied the king's mistress with brandy from a silver flask in their hidden refuge. "Nostalgia does have such a damnable way with our sovereign." He began brushing her neck with kisses as his fingers snaked down beneath the fabric of her bodice.

"But I suspect, between the two of us, we can do battle with his nostalgia. Either through the king's loyalty, or his prick."

George laughed, running his other hand up her bare thigh, happy to find no pantaloons. "You *are* a wicked she-devil, and it is the thing I adore most about you."

"The very most thing?"

"Well, perhaps the second thing."

As he moved on top of her, as he had done a dozen times before, Barbara pressed him aside. She lowered her skirts and petticoats, and moved to the edge of the bench. Then she took a long swallow of the brandy, draining his flask before giving it back to him. "We're better accomplices now than lovers, George."

"I believe we are up to the task of both."

"Alas, it should not be a task, yet it is."

"Lady Castlemaine," he said indignantly. "You have no plans of using me to your own ends somehow, do you?"

She leaned forward then. "I have plans to help you be rid of Clarendon, and seeing *you* made chancellor of England in his stead. Shall I not use you in that particular way?"

Buckingham groaned and fell back against the iron bench and the lattice above it. He had come to her side when called, and he had expected his usual reward. Barbara could be vicious, he thought, self-centered, lethal, but always effective. He struggled now to put his ardor away; finding the means to vanquish the chancellor would be worth the sacrifice. She was right, after all. Clarendon *did* have the element of nostalgia with which to play his hand. But Buckingham would trump him in that, as he always did. There was no one at court more ambitious, or more clever. Buckingham leaned back, crossed his hands behind his head, and exhaled deeply. "What exactly do you suggest we do?"

"We are bound to have a small setback or two against the Dutch. They are, after all, an undeniably powerful force." She smiled with the devilment of a fully ripening plan. "And when we *do* suffer that defeat for our unpreparedness, which is all too likely, I am sad to say, the king shall be made to see the need to be rid of the old goat for his poor advice."

"Made to see it by you and I, do I presume?"

"You know as well as I that Charles never has liked taking responsibility for things in life. Enduring his father's murder, escaping assassins of his own, and living all those years in exiled poverty have wrought a man who is driven to make up for that by avoiding any and all critical thought for pleasure's sake. He needs the two of us."

Now Buckingham grinned. How perfectly her ambition met his own! As long as she was on his side, he would not show her who possessed the ultimate power. "Clarendon really is all that stands in the way of my having total influence over the king."

"Clarendon . . . and me." Lady Castlemaine laughed.

Chapter 5

FATE NOW FOR HER DID ITS WHOLE FORCE ENGAGE
AND FROM THE PIT SHE MOUNTED TO THE STAGE;
THERE IN FULL LUSTRE DID HER GLORIES SHINE,
AND LONG ECLIPS'D SPREAD FOR THEIR LIGHT DIVINE.
—*The Earl of Rochester*

S HE knew he was standing there, watching. Nell could feel his eyes upon her from behind the heavy stage curtain, lecherous, imposing. Richard had told her Hart would come to observe them rehearsing, and so he had. For the first time since considering Richard Bell's plan for her, Nell smiled. It had never occurred to her, watching her mother with men, that there might be another element to be harvested from sex. *Power.* And seeking power was certainly better than tolerating the shame. Guilt was a powerful weapon she could use; it would empower her and wound him. With great determination, Nell smiled more broadly, and prepared to manipulate Charles Hart into offering up something to her—though this time it would be a thing of her own choosing. Looking to Richard, she spoke the next line for a laugh. "Well, then, shall I see you again?"

"When I have a mind to it. Come, I'll lead you to your coach for once," Richard responded with flair.

"And I shall let you for once."

"Oh, Mr. Hart! Nell here was just helping me with my lines," Richard said, pretending only just to have seen him standing there. "But, I confess, she outacts the lot of us. Did you get to hear her?"

Hart was scowling. "I heard her."

"And? We could use a girl like her in the troupe. She's got a natural instinct for comedy."

There was a long pause. "Very well. See the wardrobe mistress. You can try a place in the crowd scenes."

Nell glanced at Richard. Another awkward moment slipped by. "You wish to give me a part in the production?"

"Let's say I've been made to see the value in giving you a try."

"Well, what I *want* is a proper apology."

"What have I to regret to you?"

"You were wrong to behave like a stag in season."

"A rather vulgar way to put it."

"I've no patience for dressin' things up, Mr. 'Art. With Nell Gwynne, what you see is what you get."

"Exactly what I'm afraid of."

"Well, I accept your apology, such as it is, but I'll not take a place in the crowd. I'll be playin' Lady Wealthy to your Mr. Wellbred, thank you very much indeed."

"Lady Wealthy? You?" He barked out a laugh. "That is a lead role!"

"And I made her the comedian she should be! I saw you laugh in spite of yourself!"

Hart glanced back at Richard Bell, who merely shrugged his shoulders, as if to say he had indeed enjoyed Nell's interpretation of a character who, played each afternoon by Rebecca Marshall, called Beck, never garnered more than a few tepid chuckles.

"There's simply too much at stake to risk making an *orange girl* into a leading player."

"What will you gain if she is a success? She does have that spark, sir. And if another of Mr. Dryden's plays should fail—"

"I'd wager what you'd lose is a playwright to the duke's house," Nell interjected.

"Is this blackmail?"

"Not if it's workin'."

He was getting angry. "What would you call it then?"

"Compensation for a girl's stolen virtue," Richard put in.

"Rather easy virtue, if you ask me." Hart's face was tense. He looked like a man backed into a very uncomfortable corner. And he was. "Oh, very well. You may have a more substantial role. But *not* Lady Wealthy. This afternoon, you will go on as the niece. Then, if you don't mangle the part too horribly, we shall see."

"But sir, she doesn't even know that role!"

"Then that'll be a challenge for her, won't it?"

"How much does it pay?"

"Now that really is too much!"

"Well, Mr. Hart, you cannot expect her to do something else for you for nothing. You won't want it to get around that she is being given some other means of compensation, or the rest of the actresses that you've—"

"I take your meaning, Bell. Twenty shillings and not a penny more."

"Thirty," Nell said, smiling broadly up at him.

"You haven't even been onstage!"

"I performed well enough for you, didn't I?"

"Vulgar as any other doxy!"

"But 'alf again as clever!"

Richard laughed, and Charles Hart even did battle with his own bitten smile. "Thirty shillings, and if you foul this up, you shall be pleading with Mary Meggs for your old job back before sunrise tomorrow."

The next afternoon, she stood behind the heavy red velvet side curtain, filled with fear. Beyond the rhythm of her heart pounding, there was ribald laughter and jeers from the capacity audience who sat stuffed into the pit.

Nell had been fitted into a costume of layered, emerald-green velvet and flouncing ivory lace. She was to play the daughter of a countess. That, of course, was to be the joke, with her thick accent and streetwise manner. Having stood outside the theater with her basket, then worked the tumultuous pit, Nell understood the remarkable chance before her. Waiting for her cue, she saw the faces of the men at the Cock & Pye in her mind, how she made them laugh with her bold humor, a wink, or a curtsy. She felt her knees stop knocking. *Just be yourself,* she thought. *You ain't a well-brought-up lady, and that you'll never be. The best you can 'ope is to make 'em laugh.*

She glanced out at the players already onstage and getting a tepid response. The worst of the audience out in that sea beyond the lamplights waited for just the right moment to toss overripe fruit at the characters they disliked the most. There was no going back. The candles at the foot of the stage flared so brightly that she could see no one, not a single face beyond them. She could only sense them there, judging her, waiting. Whispers. A muffled cough. Then frightening silence. Smiling her brightest smile, she skipped onto the stage.

"This life of mine can last no longer than my beauty; and though 'tis pleasant now, I want nothin' while I am Mr. Wellbred's mistress, yet if 'is mind should change, I might even sell oranges for my livin'!" she exclaimed, hands on her hips and a broad, confident smile lighting her face.

The first rumblings of laughter rose from the pit, stunning her. For an instant, Nell was almost rising out of herself. Everyone in London knew the players—knew who were lovers, and which ladies were connected to which men. The reference had been lost to no one. Scene after scene unfolded after that, with Nell weaving herself into each of them with nothing more than a nod, a wink, or a sigh.

Afterward, Charles Hart was there to see her first, though a dozen others clambered at the tiring-room door. "You surprised me," he said, a tone lower than usual.

"I surprised myself."

"The audience loved you." He moved nearer to touch her cheek. "Ten shillings a week raise, and tomorrow afternoon you play Lady Wealthy."

"You're replacin' Mrs. Knepp?"

"*You* are replacing Knepp. I admit it, the role is perfect for you."

She bit back a victorious smile. She would be clever enough to make what happened work to her advantage. "You'll not be sorry Mr. 'Art. I'll make you proud! I'll make the theater proud, I promise!"

"I have no doubt," he replied. "Nell, you are a delightful breath of air, one I am proud to have in the company. And who I would be even more proud to take into my heart."

Her mind raced to think of something to say that would not offend him. "Mr. 'Art, I—"

"You must call me Charles." He framed a canvas with his hand. "People will come from all over London to see us perform together."

"Mr. 'Art—"

"I shall see that you have the best costumes *and* the wittiest lines."

"But I—"

"The other girls will all envy you, and you will have to be cautious about the men and the gifts. Richard and Beck Marshall here can certainly warn you about all of that. And I will be your teacher. I shall teach you everything I know."

Charles pressed a sensual kiss onto her earlobe, and the muscles in her throat constricted. But the choice was clear. It was a pivotal moment in her life, and there would not likely be many others like this. For a life of security, for herself and Rose, there was a price to be paid. Women always paid a price it seemed. *This price.* She drew in a deep breath, knowing all that lay before her, and all that her response implied. Nell was fully prepared to make Charles Hart think she found him attractive and that, since he had apologized, there was no real harm done from their "encounter." The cost of security was high, but she would gladly pay it. "Mr. 'Art, I accept."

After he had gone back to his own private tiring-room, and Nell felt herself breathe again, an actress with frizzled, tawny hair came forward, grinning. "I'm Beck Marshall," she said. "Happy to have you on board our topsy-turvy little ship, tormented by high seas though it can be." Nell felt an instant kinship with her. "And don't worry about Mr. Hart. He's far more interested in the business aspects of our little theater company than the women in it. Once he's had you, most of the time he'll let you alone."

"You and Mr. 'Art—"

"Mr. Hart and every new actress in the company," Beck Marshall said.

Chapter 6

To the King's House, and there did see a good part of
'The English Monsieur' which is a mighty pretty play,
very witty and pleasant. And the women did well,
but above all little Nelly.
— *The Diary of Samuel Pepys*

THE next afternoon, as Lady Wealthy, Nell garnered three standing ovations and a brimming bouquet of lilacs, and not a single piece of fruit was tossed at her. It was proof positive, Richard Bell assured her, that she was a success. As she walked down the long, low-ceilinged corridor that led from the stage to the tiring-rooms, all of it lined with racks of costumes, hats, and props, she heard the whispers. Who was she? And from where had such a comic talent come? She smiled to herself and saw one thing clearly. She had gotten a thing of value after all from her mother—her stubborn nature.

"They're calling for you, Nell!" Richard charged excitedly into the tiring-rooms after her third performance that week. "They're absolutely mad for you!"

Exhilarated, and feeling triumphant, Nell sank back into the chair at her dressing table. She liked the stage, the command, the attention. As she gained some ease before the crowds, she watched what it was she did: the inflection on a line, the tilt of her head, whatever brought a laugh, and what did not. Each performance was an education. "Thanks, Richard." She stretched her arms over her head.

"You know," he said in a lowered tone, "the other ladies are none too happy. They say you are sleeping your way into the best roles."

"Well, they're right, I am. Just as all of them did before me," she replied. She had accepted Hart as her lover, and was determined to enjoy the rewards, rather than regret what she had done. "But I'm also a better actress, and that's what really bothers them."

"That you are."

Charles Hart was at the door, his smile broad and proud. "Come, Nell. They're calling for you! The crowd is a hungry beast you've got to feed if you want it to keep a taste for you!"

Nell, with calculated seduction, pressed a kiss onto his cheek. "You're the boss, Charlie."

Around her, actresses whirled in their costumes of tired velvets and frayed silks, gleaned from some countess or duchess who had donated her castoffs. As she brushed past him to return to the stage, Nell pressed a finger to his crotch, giving him the promise for later she knew she must in order to keep her place. Lying with him was no longer the horror it had been at first, nor was it pleasant. Fortunately, he had not made her his only mistress. There were other actresses, and Nell would not lose the security she had gained from Charles Hart, no matter what it took.

She went back out onto the stage with the other actors, bobbed a curtsy with a quirky smile. The catcalls and applause rose up. She felt the sly grin on her face begin to grow, but she held it back. Wild laughter was the result, deep, rich laughter, far bigger than before. As her hands went onto her hips, and she leaned into it, a man from the pit called out, "Toss us a kiss, Nelly!"

"Yeah!" chimed another. "Somethin' to hold us till we see ya tomorrow!"

She thought of what she had done in the tavern to get a laugh, and to have Patrick Gound go easy with her on the month's rent when she did not have it to give. Then she lifted the hem of her skirt, just enough to show her calves, did a little shuffle step, and blew a large, exaggerated kiss. Just as the prop manager began to close the heavy velvet draperies, the still nearly packed house erupted in more laughter and more applause. At that same moment, Nell felt a broad hand clamp onto her arm and pull her from the stage.

"Always leave 'em wanting more," said Richard Bell. "Besides, Mr. Hart is calling for you again."

"Thanks for the warnin'! I'll get out while I still can. Meet me at the Cock & Pye in ten minutes time?" she whispered. "I owe you an ale or two in thanks."

"I'll be there."

The tavern beneath where Nell lived was crowded to capacity with drinkers and a few, in the back behind the frayed curtain, eating meat pies and lamb stew.

"If it isn't our own prettiest little success story, Nelly Gwynne come home to us!" called out Patrick Gound from behind the bottle-strewn bar.

Nell made him a theatrical little curtsy, and was immediately surrounded.

"Did ye give 'em what they asked for, Nelly?"

"And then some, I did!"

"I'd fancy seein' such a fine lady grace the stage," swooned an older woman, missing a front tooth, her hair graying and frazzled.

Nell slapped the bar. "Then you'd best not be comin' to see *me*! Fancy isn't what they pay for with Nell Gwynne before them!"

Patrick Gound raised his own tankard, ale sloshing over the side." Well, ye're finer than this lot by half."

"Which ain't sayin' much," volleyed Nell.

Richard Bell came through the door, entering in a shaft of silvery light that was swallowed up quickly as the hinges squealed and the door closed with a deep thud. Everyone looked up. The laughter fell away. Nell looked as well. "It's all right. 'E's my guest," she said.

"A fine-lookin' gent!" a man called out.

"Bell's no gentleman," Nell corrected with a burst of deep, bawdy laughter. "He's an actor, like me!"

After they had both had a tankard of ale, then two, Nell felt herself begin to breathe more deeply. "Does it ever grow tiresome, hearing that applause?" she asked Richard as they sat together. She leaned forward, elbows balanced on the tabletop. Her eyes were glittering in the lamplight, and her long, coppery hair lay in ribbons across her shoulders.

"Only if you grow weary of being adored."

Nell took another long swallow of the comforting ale at the very moment that a woman approached them from the crowd near the bar. Her dark hair was done up into a fussy black hat with a little red plume that did not suit her face. Her dress was sewn of red silk, and she wore a little black jacket that reached her waist, and a huge ruby glittered at her throat. The voice was unmistakable, but Nell would have known her anyway.

"Evenin' to you, Mrs. Davies," she said.

"Smart you are, if not so terribly pretty," Moll Davies replied.

"*I* happen to think Mrs. Gwynne is divine," Richard defended. "And so does London. She's already a sensation!"

"I 'ear she's makin' quite a name for 'erself on the stage, and I'll warrant she 'as you to thank for it, Richard. You always was the quiet, resourceful type." She took his hand, forcing him to stand and face her. Her smile, gap-toothed and yellow, revealed her commonness, as her voice did. "So, Richard Bell. Whatever brings you to a place like this?"

"I was going to ask the same of you."

"And so you 'ave. As it were, I'm stayin' nearby while my new 'ouse is being readied. The 'ouse the king has bought for me."

Richard glanced over at Nell. "The king of England has bought *you* a house?"

"And don't you believe I 'aven't earned every floorboard! 'Tis a grand place, too! Right in St. James's Square, where only the finest people reside!"

"I thought His Majesty had just fathered another child by Lady Castlemaine?"

"Times change. A king's head turns." She leaned forward, balancing her hands on the table so that her ample breasts plunged over her tight bodice. "Lady Castlemaine'll not be the only one to benefit this year from royal progeny."

"You?"

"As pregnant as a Cornwall sow, I am!" She sank into the empty chair behind them, her tone going low and gossipy. "Apparently 'e can make anyone pregnant 'e likes, except the queen!"

"Does he acknowledge your child as his own?"

"Why else would 'Is Majesty buy me a proper 'ouse? If you don't mind my boastin', the king is absolutely besotted by me. Apparently, the charms of elegant court ladies 'ave their limit."

"Are you still onstage at the Duke's Theater, then?" asked Richard, his eyes sliding to Nell, and then back to Moll Davies.

"For the moment, I am," she replied with a shrug. Then she patted her still flat belly. "But that won't be for long. I know we're meant to be rivals, actresses at opposin' theaters, Mrs. Gwynne—"

"Call me Nell, if you please."

"Very well then, Nell." Moll smiled condescendingly. "You make it easier to offer a friendly word of advice."

"I don't know she should be taking advice from an old jade like you," Richard warned.

Moll slapped his arm playfully and smiled at him in a way Nell had seen her mother do too many times with new men. "'ow better is there to do in this life than be mistress to a king? Trust me, Nell, an actress's life onstage is like 'er beauty: fleetin' at best. The crowds are a fickle lot. They'll always demand the newest thing. The prettiest fare. You've got to make plans for yourself. You've got to find yourself a well-placed man, then make 'im fall in love with you."

"Child's play for Nell," said Richard. "I mean, it would be, if she wanted it, that is."

"You'll pardon me for tellin' you what to do, but take it from me: You've got to learn to look like you want it, Nelly. And if you could convince a man you fancy the experience, in the same way you draw 'em in onstage, so much'll be the better for those rapidly declinin' years."

Moll Davies was bawdy, crude, and obnoxious, but what she said did make sense. The thought of being at the beck and call of a self-centered man like Charles Hart for the rest of her life was a chilling prospect. And how different from her own mother's life would hers truly be? That could not be her future. Not when she had come so far. "Well, there is only one king of England," said Nell on a laugh, "and I don't suppose I'd fight you for 'im."

"Can you imagine that?" cackled Moll, slamming her fist on the table, a movement completely unbefitting the dress, the hat, and the sparkling jewels. "'Is Majesty is well beyond the likes of you, naturally. But the theater's filled with lords and dukes aplenty, lookin' to add a bit of glitter to their dull lives. Ain't no better route."

"You'd be better off listening to your heart," offered Richard Bell.

"And where 'as *that* ever gotten any woman without a dowry, I ask you?" Moll challenged. "Broken'earted, or locked up in the Newgate gaol. No. Mark me. You might not know it to look at me now, but I come from a place like you did, not far from 'ere, as it 'appens. I tell you, security's the route. Look out for yourself, Nelly. In the end, that's all girls like us really 'ave anyway."

It made sense. Every day now brought something, and someone, new into the King's Theater and into her life. The question was merely who she would see sitting out over those glittering lamplights next and how she might use them to her own advantage.

Chapter 7

GLORY IS LIKE A CIRCLE IN THE WATER, WHICH NEVER
CEASETH TO ENLARGE ITSELF, 'TIL BY BROAD SPREADING IT
DISPERSES TO NAUGHT.

—*William Shakespeare*

OVER the winter of 1667, and into the spring of the
following year, as Nell's star rose at the King's Theater,
hostilities with the Dutch continued. The English fleet
had taken heavy losses during a surprise attack it had launched
on the Dutch. Money to press on toward victory remained in
short supply as rumors of a retaliatory attack swirled throughout
London, setting nerves on end. The Earl of Clarendon, the sage
and seniormost privy councillor, had gained the ire of the others
by continuing to push not only for a truce, but also to force the
English fleet to remain at anchor, and therefore in a vulnerable
position. By summer, the worst fear of the English, and the
younger members of the king's Privy Council, came true as King
Charles sat presiding over a summer ball at his grand palace of
Hampton Court.

He was being entertained by music and costumed dancers, with
Buckingham beside him, when the Duke of Buckingham received

word in his ear from a liveried courtier. They spoke rapidly back and forth, but their conversation was masked to the others by the sound of music and raucous laughter. A moment later, he leaned over to the king and drew a hand before his mouth.

"It has happened, Your Majesty. The rumors were true. The Dutch have attacked us at Gravesend Harbor."

Charles glanced at him, his face going white. "How bad is it, George?"

"Our men are not defending the ships, just as Clarendon advised. Now, they say they haven't been paid enough to risk life and limb. Our own are mutinying rather than fighting."

"But Clarendon assured me, since there was talk of peace, that the Dutch—"

"I've told you all along he has gotten too long in the tooth for real and delicate negotiation. This is a certifiable disaster, sire!"

Charles bolted from his throne, which caused the music, and the merriment, to come to an abrupt halt. All eyes turned upon their king. A crescendo of worried whispers rose up. But Charles disregarded everything, dashing in long-legged strides from the Great Hall and out into the corridor beyond, the Duke of Buckingham following closely. "Perhaps now you will believe me that I am better suited as chancellor than that dithering old fool!"

A collection of courtiers followed at a discreet pace. Charles groaned. "You did try to warn me. I know you did."

"And Clarendon now has cost this country greatly."

They strode more quickly together, nearly at a run now, up a wide flight of stone steps, past a stone balustrade overlooking the gardens, and into an arched corridor with dark, paneled walls. The barrel-chested Duke of Lauderdale huffed while trying to meet their pace, in order to tell the king more. "They've taken the *Royal Charles* with absolutely no resistance at all and destroyed the *Royal James*, the *Royal Oak*, and the *Loyal London* in a single attack! The ships were, if you'll pardon me, sitting ducks. At Clarendon's obstinate insistence, we refused to man them!"

They were heading for the Privy Council chamber now, Charles's velvet cloak flying out behind him like a billowing blue sail. "How many souls have been lost?"

"There's no total yet, sire, but—"

"I should have thought after the fire the Dutch would have shown some modicum of restraint in attacking us here at home!"

"I am told they consider the fire God's revenge, sire, for our burning their fleet last year," said Clifford, Buckingham's protégé.

Only once they were all seated around the long, polished oak table was it apparent that the chancellor himself, Clarendon, architect of the move toward peace, and James's father-in-law, was not among them.

"Where is he?" the king bellowed, without saying his name.

"Lord Clarendon has been sent for, Your Majesty," said Clifford.

Charles slammed the table. "Well, you are my Privy Council! Advise me!"

"As you know, sire, I believe we should have found what money we needed and attacked again last summer. We needed to show our strength, especially with our losses, and this waiting on the French to help broker a peace for us has shown our weakness. We played right into the very center of it!"

"The Dutch did smell our vulnerability, it seems, and seized upon it," the king's brother, the Lord Admiral, carefully concurred, newly returned from surveying the damage.

"Might I remind Your Majesty," Buckingham slyly added, "that Clarendon was the only one among us to look to the French, and then wage stubbornly for inactivity."

Charles washed a hand over his face. "The people will be furious with this, after the fire, and the plague, not to mention our previous losses."

"I am afraid Your Majesty has taken an old friend's age for wisdom, when it might have better been taken for the senility it clearly is."

"That will be quite enough, George." The king shot him a warning stare. Charles had a long history with Clarendon, as he did with Buckingham. Clarendon's father had faithfully served Charles's father, and had endeared himself into Charles's memories, and his life. He had been, in many ways, like the father Charles had lost. Growing into manhood, he had depended upon Clarendon greatly. Yes, he had married his own brother, the Duke of York, to Clarendon's daughter Anne as a show of support. Charles had loved and trusted the old man, even with his Privy Council set against him.

"I'm only saying, you cannot let him go on when it has cost us so much!"

"Enough! When I wish your further opinion on the matter, I shall ask for it!"

"But Your Majesty must hear the younger voices above the aging chorus! Even if I risk my own standing, it shall be worth England's safety!"

Charles shot to his feet, his face blazing with sudden fury. "George, I warn you!"

"Someone has got to reason with Your Majesty, and if it takes your oldest and dearest friend to highlight the utter incompetence of an old man who—"

"To the Tower!" Charles cried, his face mottled red with rage.

"You cannot be serious! This is me, your truest friend!"

"Guards! Escort the Duke of Buckingham to the Tower, and keep him there until he has learned to honor his king, and hold his tongue!"

George Villiers did not plead his case further. He only continued to meet the gaze of the man he had helped to escape from London long ago, and to whom he had devoted his life—even if he had done it through politics and manipulation. "You can put me away if it pleases you, but not the truth!" he seethed. "Clarendon's weakness will bleed through no matter what you do! And at the end of the day, you will realize that not only did I have our best interest at heart, but I had the courage to see it through!" He looked toward the guardsmen, then, with a flourish, turned from the king. "Now, take me where you will, and be done with it. I have shown honor to our sovereign the best way I know how. I've nothing further to say."

Chapter 8

ALL THE PLEASURE OF THE PLAY, THE KING AND
MY LADY CASTLEMAINE WERE THERE, AND PRETTY
WITTY NELL, AT THE KING'S HOUSE.
—*The Diary of Samuel Pepys*

AFTER MAY DAY, 1668

J UST after the great May Day celebration, a new play opened
at the King's Theater. John Dryden, the most celebrated
playwright in London, had written a comedy, *The Maiden
Queen,* and the role of Florimel was created particularly for Nell.
She, not Charles Hart, was to be the star. The role was her
largest and most demanding yet, and Nell was plagued with a
sudden case of nerves. It was rumored that the Duke of York, and
perhaps even the king himself, might well be in the audience for
the first performance.

His Majesty, it was said, was trying to recover from the devastating attack by the Dutch at Gravesend Harbor, and from having consigned his dearest friend, the Duke of Buckingham, to the
Tower for having tried to use the incident against the elderly
Clarendon. Theater was a passion of his, but he rarely indulged
in past months, and when he did, he went to the rival Duke's

Theater, where his current paramour, Moll Davies, performed. Or at least she would continue to perform until she bore the king's child, which was rumored to be soon.

It was Moll who had caused Nell to look beyond Charles Hart and to begin considering wealthy candidates that might look her way. She thought of Hart, at this very moment in the next room "rehearsing" alone with Mary Knepp, the actress who was playing her friend. Hart had grown as bored with Nell as she was disgusted by him. Still, business and survival, these were what mattered. And she must think of Rose, and what their lives could return to if she failed. She stood, layered in heavy velvet skirts, made wide by a volume of petticoats. Light from the tiring-room window glinted against the amber fabric, the folds and shadows enriching them the more. The dress had been donated from Lady Argyll's personal wardrobe. It was the most luxurious thing Nell had ever pressed against her skin. In spite of protests by the more senior actresses, Dryden had seen the valuable dress given to his star. Nothing was to hamper her performance, the playwright insisted. He wished Nell to *become* Florimel.

Charles Hart came into the ladies' tiring-room a quarter of an hour later, flushed and distracted. He bent and kissed Nell absently on the back of the neck as she sat applying her own lip paint. "You look lovely, my dear."

"And *you* look spent."

She watched his expression in the mirror's reflection. He smiled in an overly sweet manner that instantly put her on edge. "Nothing to trouble yourself over. I shall be right beside you as you triumph this afternoon. The whole lot of us are counting on it. The theater is already packed to capacity."

"But we don't go on for an hour."

"Such is their thirst for Mrs. Nelly. That's what they are

calling you now, you know. How far you have managed to come when you started your career in a brothel."

"I'd no choice, bein' there, you know that. I was a child made to fetch wine for the patrons. But that was all that place ever got from me."

"Of course it was," he said condescendingly. "Now. Do you know your lines?"

"Better'n you know yours, I'll warrant."

"We shall see."

"Just don't try to make me look bad to make yourself look better. Mr. Dryden won't like it," Nell said. Then she turned from him and went out of the tiring-room alone.

"I don't know why we must come to *this* theater when we have a perfectly clever little play staged over at the Duke's," Moll Davies carped.

"This is His Majesty's theater, my dear," Arlington responded dryly.

The king added nothing as the royal party paraded between the swiftly parted, deeply bowing throngs of theatergoers stopping to gape and wave. Moll bored him to tears already, and she was far too shrill to keep his mind from comparing her to Barbara. Since the novelty had worn off, there was little reason to keep her around, but for the child she carried. He tried not to notice how garish Moll looked, heavily pregnant, dressed in rusty-orange brocade and mock sleeves, her hair long and loose beneath a little velvet hat. His libido certainly could lead him astray, he thought ruefully. He sank into his chair in the center of his private box and gazed down into the pit at all of the craning necks, faces turned up to see him, flirtatious smiles, bows from dandies and fops, nods from ladies hidden by their vizards, and orange girls plying their trade up and down the narrow isles. A woman in one of the other boxes lowered her vizard and smiled at him. She looked familiar, but he could not place her. She was too old to have been a dalliance . . . perhaps it was one of her daughters he had known? It could have been anyone at all.

"That new actress, Nell Gwynne, is starring today, Your Majesty," Arlington leaned over to remark behind a raised hand. "They say Dryden finds her absolutely fascinating." He was clearly glorying in his place beside the king, with Buckingham now locked away in the Tower.

Nell Gwynne . . . why was the sound of it familiar? The old woman was still smiling at him and now clearly trying to suggest something with her eyes. Great God, was she trying to suggest *that*? She looked old enough to be his own mother!

"I saw her last month in *The English Monsieur*. She was hilarious. Had half the balcony throwing flowers to her, instead of oranges."

"Now there's a switch to note," Charles chuckled.

Moll, who had been listening from the king's other side, shot him an irritated glance. He chose to ignore it. Finally, the candle lamps rimming the stage were lit and the crowds in the pit, and around him in the various other boxes, broke into thunderous applause.

First onstage was a stout, white-haired man in velvet robes, who acted as the narrator for the prologue. By his presence, the cheers turned to thunderous disapproval and great shouted choruses of "Bring on Nelly!"

Charles bit back a smile and settled against the high-backed gilded chair. This afternoon might shape up to be a bit of fun, after all. As he glanced down again, even the woman with the vizard was shouting for Nell. This girl must be something unique indeed. A moment later, wearing a remarkably elegant dress, her full copper hair cascading down her back, Nell Gwynne took the stage. Before she spoke a single line, the entire crowd erupted in applause, whistles, and catcalls. Brazenly and with a charming smile, she looked directly out at the men before her in the pit. She smiled broadly, blew a kiss, and then turned to her costar, Charles Hart, who was making his own entrance from the other side. They met onstage, joining hands, as a couple intending to marry. The rumor of their real liaison was so rampant that the audience began to chuckle at once.

"As for the first year, according to the laudable custom of new married people, we shall follow one another up into chambers, and down into gardens, and think we shall never have enough of one another. So far 'tis pleasant enough, I hope," he said loudly.

"But after that, when we begin to live like 'usband and wife, and never come near one another, what then?" she said with a bold wink.

The crowd rewarded Nell by laughing so boisterously that Hart's next line was completely lost. The king bit back a smile and remembered Nell Gwynne. Of course. How delightfully surprising! The orange seller with the big heart, standing outside after the fire, had become a star. Absolutely marvelous!

"She has only been on the stage for six months and already she has captured London," said the Earl of Arlington, who leaned forward from his chair behind the king.

"And a number of hearts, I would imagine."

"It is well known in the theater that she is Charles Hart's mistress," said Moll gratingly.

"Fortunate Mr. Hart," said the king, as the crowd erupted for her once again.

The next hour rushed by in a whirl of laughter, surprise, and delight, and the king was charmed as he had not been for a very long time. As he watched Nell, he could feel her sensuality even with the theater's length between them. That, combined with her wit, made her positively irresistible to every man present. She was gamine, saucy, and wildly exciting; knowing she was from the darkest streets, he recognized her as a consummate survivor. The King was disarmed.

When Nell took her bows, he leaned casually toward Arlington and lifted a hand across his face to mask his words. "Keep Moll occupied as we leave, and I shall owe you a favor."

"It would be easier to keep the plague out of London in September."

"It was not a request, Arlington, no matter how kindly delivered."

The two men exchanged a glance as Moll Davies clamped onto the king's forearm and gazed up adoringly at him from his other side.

"I need a moment, lovely. Arlington here shall see you safely to my coach." He stood, and she stood as well, still holding on fast to his arm.

"I'll come with you."

"Nature calling, my lovely girl, is a largely private matter."

Nell was just coming off the stage, her face glowing with triumph, her skin bathed in perspiration, when she heard a voice break through the shouts of applause. "Nelly! Where are you, love? Un'and me, sir! Nelly Gwynne's me own daughter, she is! *Nelly!*"

"Oh, good lord," said Mrs. Knepp beneath her breath. "I've one of those creatures myself to taunt me when I least expect it."

"As do I," said Beck Marshall, shaking her head in camaraderie as each unlaced the stays of the other's tight, high corset. "But I wasn't ever likely to tell her about the life I'd made here or I'd never have seen a shilling of my own."

"I didn't tell her," said Nell on a sigh. "She smells money like a huntin' hound."

"There you are, Nelly! Be a love, then; tell these gents your poor Ma'd only like a word?"

Helena Gwynne, as usual, was drunk. Her dress was stained with mud, food, and perspiration, as if she had fallen into the street on her way to the theater. Quite likely she had. Stout and ungainly, Helena grabbed onto the doorjamb to steady herself. Her eyes were bloodshot. Nell felt her heart seize. She had not seen her mother in nearly three months. The urge to say she had never seen the woman before in her life was overwhelming. She was embarrassed by her, afraid of her, and felt far more shame in her company than anything close to affection. "'Tis all right, William," she nodded. The men who stood guard after the shows, in order to protect the girls, lifted their brows in surprise.

Helena smiled a gap-toothed smile, and ran the back of her hand across her face as the two men turned to leave. "My, don't *you* look ever the lady! Such is the stage life, I suppose; magic at turnin' a sow's ear like you into a right proper silk purse for an 'our or two."

The other actresses went to one of the dressing tables to give Nell a moment of privacy. Nell lowered her voice. "What do you want, Ma?"

"Actually, I'd 'ave thought to see you in one of these plays by now, properlike. I'd 'ave thought you'd 'ave bought me a seat."

"You don't care about the theater, or me. So what do you want?"

She shrugged. "Only a penny or two, then, hmm? 'Tis all."

Nell went to her handbag and pulled out two coins. Before she could say anything, they were interrupted by the shouts of Richard Bell. "The king comes! The king is coming here!"

Nell did not believe it—for how unlikely such a thing seemed!—but she could take no chances with her mother. Pressing the coins into Helena's hand, she led her to the back door personally to be rid of her swiftly. As those around her stood, only to fall into deep curtsies, Nell turned and saw him in the doorway. This close, she saw that he was handsome, and so amazingly tall. *Tall . . . great God in His heaven, it is . . .*

She quickly dropped into a low curtsy herself.

"Mrs. Gwynne, your performance was most entertaining."

Oh, ballocks, smile, you fool! a silent voice urged. *Smile like you couldn't care a whit!* She looked up and managed a disarming smile. "So long as Your Majesty 'as found it so," she said, as though she had been speaking to him all of her life, "I shall do my best to disregard the critics, should they not find the same favor in my performance."

Charles indicated that all present should rise. Then he replied, "I am told they are as fond of you as the audience is."

"'Tis not a fact I know of, and one should never indulge in speculation, Your Majesty. The opportunity for disappointment is too vast." Charles smiled at that, straight white teeth shimmering in the lamplight, and she was flooded with memories of that day, well over a year ago now, in front of the theater. *So that is how Rose made it out of the gaol! Of course it was him! Who else?* In her mind, Nell saw him as he had been that day, the simple costume, his unadorned head, the lack of jewelry or ornamentation. There had been nothing of the pampered royal about that man, with the two-day growth of beard, the bloodshot eyes, and look of shock on his face, she thought now. That day, they had both been someone else. It was a dark time in London's history that oddly linked them.

"It is a great pleasure to meet you, Mrs. Gwynne."

"But of course we've met, you know, Your Majesty," she said.

"So we have," returned the king. "But in circumstances somewhat divergent from these. May I say, you have changed, and charmingly so."

"And you are exactly 'ow I remember you, but now with the wig."

"And how is your sister?"

"She is well, sire, very well, thanks to a mysterious intervention of kindness."

In the doorway suddenly stood a man with auburn hair and youthful blue eyes. Nell remembered him at once. Seeing the king before he saw Nell, the man lowered himself into a courtly and proper bow, sweeping his plumed hat before himself.

"Your Majesty."

"It has been a while, Buckhurst," said the King. "How is your mother?"

"She is well, Your Majesty, thank you. Completely recovered from her ague."

Both men, named for the previous King Charles, looked at Nell then.

"Lord Buckhurst," said the king with a slight and bemused smile. "May I present London's newest sensation, the lovely and talented Mrs. Gwynne."

He was ever the gentleman about meeting her as an orange girl, silent and discreet. "A pleasure to meet you, Mrs. Gwynne."

Nell nodded. "The pleasure's mine, Lord Buckhurst."

"You were magnificent just now. I find I never laughed so hard at anything."

"Lucky for me the play was a comedy."

Hearing the swell of chuckles around her, Nell felt herself draw a breath, standing between two such impressive and noble men, one of them, quite amazingly, the king of England. She lifted her face and looked into his dark eyes. His gaze upon her was direct and intense, as if they were the only two in the room.

"There you are! I should have known!"

Moll Davies's harsh accent was like a brittle twig snapping.

"Oh, do let's depart, Your Majesty," said Moll. "The force of a royal child grows weighty on such shapely little legs as my own." The soft cackle that escaped her lips then was a taunting, ugly sound. Nell watched the king's expression change. He looked back at her more formally, the connection between them extinguished.

"Mrs. Gwynne," he said with a courtly nod. "Best of luck to you with the new play and the ones to follow. Though I doubt you shall need it."

"I 'ope Your Majesty will be watchin'."

Moll Davies glowered as the king nodded to Nell once again. Then they turned together and left the tiring-room to a rising crescendo of whispers from the crush of costumed actresses who, once he had gone, broke apart and went back to changing. No one cared that Lord Buckhurst had remained. Soon two other gentlemen entered, each bearing flowers for someone. Nell turned then to face Buckhurst, suddenly alone in a sea of other activity around them.

"You must be quite impressed to have caught the eye of the king."

"If I wanted to end up like Mrs. Davies, I might be."

A smile played at the corners of his mouth. "Have supper with me."

You've got to find yourself a well-placed man, then make 'im fall in love with you . . . Moll Davies's words came at her almost like a response. Even for his open flirtation, the king was not an option. But this man before her most definitely could be. "I'll not be wantin' a meal," she replied, remembering how things had begun between herself and Charles Hart. "But I might well fancy a ride through St. James's Park in a proper coach."

"Would you now?"

Buckhurst smiled boyishly, and Nell saw, for the first time, truly how handsome he was. He was a proper gentleman, a noble one at that.

"Aye." She smiled back. "I fancy I would."

"Well, then. In that case, I shall be honored to be the one to take you."

Chapter 9

OLD FRIENDS BECOME BITTER ENEMIES ON A SUDDEN.
FOR TOYS AND SMALL OFFENSES.

—*Robert Burton*

WHEN the king returned from the theater that afternoon, he had intended a brisk swim in his private lake, before a quiet supper he had carefully arranged with Lady Stuart. He found not Lady Stuart in his private apartments, but rather his brother, the Duke of York, and Lady Castlemaine. Clearly, they had found a way to amuse themselves while they waited.

James was standing before the freshly stoked fire, his back to the wood-paneled fireplace hearth. His hands were linked, and Barbara was leaning against him, playing with the folds of his white cravat.

"Pray God, Barbara, is there not a man at court you will not seduce?" The king's voice boomed with irritation.

"Apparently not you any longer, so I take what I can get," she said.

"So what the devil *are* you doing here?"

"Pity, to hear that tone," Barbara purred. "You used to be so welcoming of this delicious sort of thing—you, me, another willing creature—for the variety of it."

"And you used to be delicious. But times do change. Now, I shall thank you to say what you have to say, and be done with it, so that I may dine with Lady Stuart."

"Ah, yes, about her." James brought his hands forward and pressed them together as his expression changed. "It seems I have the unenviable task, since no one else fancies time in the Tower, of telling you about that."

He rubbed his temples. "Well, out with it. I've suddenly developed a dreadful headache."

"I'm afraid she has eloped with the Duke of Richmond," James confessed.

As if he had been struck, Charles sank into a chair, edged with gold fringe, his expression going very blank. For months he had wooed her, courted her, and taken her rebuffs, all in the hope of an eventual victory. Now she had betrayed him.

"It cannot come as too grand a surprise," Barbara said cautiously, pressing back her obvious delight. "They've been stealing away together for months. Everyone at court has known about it."

Charles shook his head. "Everyone, it seems, but the king."

"Oh, really, Charles. You cannot mean you truly cared for that empty-headed chit? She'd have been no challenge at all once you'd had her." She twisted her hand in the air with a flourish. "Pretty enough, I'll grant you, but dull as dirt, really."

They were silent with each other for a time after that. Charles was too stunned to say anything clever. "If you mean to gloat," he finally said, slouching in his chair, legs wide, "you can take your leave now."

"Actually, I came to give you a piece of advice."

He arched a brow. "Oh, I can hardly wait to hear it."

"You should have poor Buckingham released from the Tower. That is my blunt advice, and apparently you are in need of it."

Charles looked at his brother, who stood saying nothing. "George is where he belongs for opposing his king."

"And where is Lord Clarendon for costing England so dearly? It is the question all of England is asking."

"She's right, you know," said James, finally. "The country has turned against him. He is too old, too out of touch, they are saying. We have had to surrender to the Dutch, for God's sake. After what happened to Father, I ask you: Can you truly risk that attitude on all of us?"

Charles was silent. The tug of memories came at the mention of their father. *Tell Cromwell I shall gladly die in the king's place! Only let my father live!* . . . Charles looked at his brother. At this moment, he did not feel very much like anyone's king. "Well, you've said what you wished to say," he said at last.

Glancing at the two brothers, Barbara kissed the king's cheeks, then left the room.

"What did I do with my own life?" Charles asked rhetorically of his brother, as he raked a hand through his dark hair. "I've rather made a mess of things without meaning to. And I feel I've let Father down in it. I've no heir; I certainly haven't anyone who I dare delude myself by saying she loves me. And no one I particularly love in return. Unlike you, I do not wish to divorce my wife, and yet, God forgive me, I do not love my own in any other way than I love our sister, Minette." He curled his fists over the chair arms. "Do you think of him, ever?" Charles asked in a quiet voice. "Do you see his face, as I do; hear his words, as I do?"

"That is madness. I do not hear the dead."

"He died for England, on a stump outside these very walls. He died for the Protestant faith, and you would smite him at every turn."

"I don't know what you are going on about," James hedged.

"The devil you don't! I may not hear everything that is whispered in my court. But I hear well enough the gossip about the friend you are to the Catholics. That's why you're *really* here, I'll warrant you. You are hoping I shall change my mind and grant you a divorce, because your faithful wife has gotten fat and unappealing."

"Don't be absurd."

"Do not lie to your king, or your brother!"

"Charles, I do remember our father! And what I remember the most is that he was a man passionate about his family! He would not have forced me to stay in this marriage!"

"Then with any luck, perhaps your wife will die early and free you of your burden of fidelity!"

"You're a fine one to talk to me about fidelity, with your own share of mistresses!"

"If the queen gives me an heir, you can have your divorce."

"The queen is barren, Charles. A barren, Portuguese embarrassment!"

"Then start your Catholic prayers that she experiences a miracle. You will not have your divorce without it!"

The Duke of Buckingham was accorded his own servants, his cook, a grand poster bed, his books, and all of his papers. Yet still, he was a captive in the Tower of London at the king's pleasure. Marking the long days, he sat in an upholstered chair facing out into the courtyard, where guards paced beneath a dreary spring sky. It was the thrill of court life he missed most. The chase. The bawdy jokes. The endless card games, the dancing, the drinking . . . the sex. Charles knew that well enough, which was precisely why he was here. Taking all of that from him would make a king's point in spades. When the heavy door opened, he did not hear it at first, in spite of the long, low squeal and the clank of the iron handle. But he recognized the king's unmistakable ambergris scent.

Charles lingered in the doorway for a moment, two guards bearing halberds behind him. He was elegantly dressed in blue velvet with silver ribbons, but his face was drawn, his eyes tired.

"So, how do you find the accommodations?" Charles asked as a second chair was set for him beside Buckingham's own. Buckingham waited for the king to sit, then he slouched again as he had been before. "How one might find a case of the grippe. Eager for it to be at an end."

"At least you have not lost your sense of humor."

"Only my self-respect."

"Then come away with me, George."

"Need I remind you that it was Your Majesty who wished me here in the first place?"

"I was angry."

"So I gathered."

"You have but to apologize, and all will be forgiven."

"Apologize for telling you the truth? Is the very foundation of our friendship, and your trust in me, not based on that very crucial thing?"

Charles closed his eyes. For a moment, he said nothing else. "My father's friendship with Edward was long based on trust, as well. Honoring my father's memory to me is—"

"Honoring his memory, to the exclusion of other things, is dangerous, not only to you, but to all of England."

Charles shot him an angry stare. "You are an insolent hound!"

"I am an insolent hound who would rather spend eternity in this hole than see you continue on with so grave an error that will have you despised by your own people."

"You are right about Clarendon, of course. He has made a grand mess of things."

"And I am right that it is *I* who should be your chancellor."

"Humility never was your strong suit."

"Fortunately for both of us, loyalty is."

"Apparently, you will need to get in line on that claim. Arlington and Lauderdale both desire the distinction."

"No one has known you longer, or better, Charles."

"There was a time when I thought Clarendon did."

"You are loyal to your father's memory. Clarendon was a part of that. But you are a new king, with your own challenges, and England cannot afford the humiliation we are now facing, having to submit to Dutch peace terms, as if it were outright surrender. Not after the fire *and* the devastation of the last plague!"

They both heard the guards pacing outside.

"Just apologize, George. In the name of friendship, it is all that I ask."

Buckingham propped himself on an elbow, chin on his hand. They were facing each other. "Say you need me and I will do just that."

Charles rolled his eyes. He lowered his voice. "You know perfectly well that I need you, George."

"More than Arlington?"

"More than any of the others."

"It was all I wanted to hear. And I *am* sorry I forced you in front of them to see how much you need a true friend."

"Not exactly the tone of apology for which I had hoped. But it will have to do," said the king, knowing he had just been manipulated, but letting an affectionate smile light his face anyway.

Arms linked, Nell and Rose moved quickly along the cobblestone, grins wide, hands gripping string that held a collection of shopping boxes. Inside were hats, lace gloves, a new silk fan for Nell's upcoming carriage ride, and two new pairs of shoes made of white kid with silk embroidery. All around them was the clap and echo of hammers and the smell of fresh wood. There were still the scars everywhere, reminders of what had happened— charred ruins, piles of rubble and debris—but London had begun to recover from the devastation.

Their lives, too, had changed greatly. New furniture, richer coverlets, and silk pillows made their evenings more comfortable, but the Cock & Pye remained a touchstone, and they had continued to live together above the tavern. Helena Gwynne, however, had been mysteriously absent. She would come around again when she needed money, they both knew, but for now her absence added to their new contentment. Happy and breathless, they ducked inside and were greeted rousingly by the patrons who welcomed Nell as their local celebrity. Patrick, the proprietor, held up the most recent copy of the *London Gazette*. "Our Nelly 'as made 'istory!" he proclaimed. "It says 'ere she is the queen of the King's Theater!"

"Long as I'm still queen of your old jaded 'earts in this place, I'm quite the real success," she joked. She could read little, but Nell wanted to see the words for herself. As the laughter faded, Patrick pointed to her name, and Nell touched the black letters gently with her fingertips. Thinking of herself in print made everything that had happened to her more real. She was celebrated. Loved. She felt tears prick her eyes. How very far life had brought her! She and Rose exchanged a glance. Only Rose would ever really know.

"You've done well, Nelly," she said softly.

"I've done it for us," Nell smiled. "So let's go up then. I fancy seein' you try your new shoes on again!"

"I told you Clarendon would lose. I *always* win. It really was only a matter of time."

"Stupid old fool," Barbara said as George Villiers, Duke of Buckingham, newly released from the Tower, stroked her feet. He was rubbing the little area behind her toes as she lay naked on a daybed at a bank of open windows that faced onto the barge-filled Thames. The king had gone into London to see Moll Davies's newborn daughter and so, for a time, they were free to behave as wantonly as Barbara directed them.

"We are close to being rid of Clarendon altogether. I can smell his vanquishment."

"*If* we work together." Her hand was snaking down her own body, softly stroking.

"We have always been a splendid team. I owe you my life for interceding with the king to get me out of the Tower and back in favor."

"I have my ways with him, even after all these years. He is still such a sentimental man. He didn't really want you in there. He just wanted you to apologize."

"And so I did. Rather theatrically, too, I must say. I learned everything I know from the best partner a court could ever provide." He moved to kiss her mouth, but she opened her eyes. There was enough censure in them to press him back.

"In the biblical sense, I am no longer your partner. I believe I have made that perfectly clear."

"Young blood is still trumping experience?" he moaned, collapsing on the pillows. He meant the king's eldest son, the Duke of Monmouth. "What on God's earth is there still beyond that in it for you?"

"Besides stamina, youthful determination, *and* the chance of seeing such a moldable vassal made heir?"

"Charles will never legitimize Monmouth. He's a king's bastard, nothing more."

"Perhaps. And then again, perhaps the stories that in his own youthful zeal and loneliness abroad he secretly married Lucy Walter are true. They certainly do persist, as does the evidence."

"Just because you are losing one king does not mean you can fabricate another out of whole cloth!"

"Now, George," she said. "You, of all people, know perfectly well that I can do virtually anything to which I set my mind. Is that not why you came to me about Clarendon in the first place? My relationship with the king may have changed, but you can clearly see, by your current taste of freedom, that it has not ended."

"The king still fancies you a confidante, I'll grant you that."

"There's more power in that than being his lover. Now, you leave my ambitions for Monmouth to me, and let us concentrate on driving that last nail into Clarendon's coffin, shall we? You do still want to be lord chancellor, I presume?"

"I only wish to claim the post that should have been mine all along."

"As *I* should wish to claim my place as rightful queen."

"Ah, you *are* evil!"

"In that I am in proper company," she laughed.

Unfulfilled, George Villiers left Lady Castlemaine and strolled out along the private pathway that fronted the Thames within the compound of Whitehall Palace. The worst of his resentment toward her was gone now. And he was tasting every aspect of his freedom. The wind was in his hair, the sun warmed his upturned face, and a new ruby on his finger pinched his flesh, just ever so slightly. If they were no longer lovers, he knew he could no longer trust her. Finally, Lady Castlemaine had truly outlived her usefulness to him, just as she was doing with the king. It was time for both of them to be rid of her. She knew too much. She needed to be replaced. Charles's full attention on another mistress was the only way to achieve that. Moll Davies was irritating and low, not a viable candidate. Lady Stuart was now married and away from court.

It would take some cunning, and bold manipulation. But he would find Lady Castlemaine's replacement himself. Then he alone would control the king.

In two days' time, the court left for Newmarket. Dozens of eligible and willing young lovelies could be found there. And, after all, Barbara had brought this all upon herself. One of the most important things about court life was knowing how to keep your friends close, and your enemies closer. Lady Castlemaine had forgotten that, and it was just about to cost her, dearly.

Chapter 10

. . . THEY CALLED US ALL IN AND BROUGHT US TO NELLY,
A MOST PRETTY WOMAN, WHO ACTED THE GREAT PART OF
CELIA TODAY, AND DID IT PRETTY WELL; I KISSED HER AND
SO DID MY WIFE, A MIGHTY PRETTY SOUL SHE IS.
—*The Diary of Samuel Pepys*

THE oversized coach, with its black lacquered paint, gilding, rich velvet cushions, and six sleek black horses pulling it, swayed along the paving on the Strand. They passed the coffeehouses, the taverns, the hat maker, and the glove shop there, and then clattered onto the cobblestones of Drury Lane. Nell could not stop herself from looking out the window, taking it all in: the press of the other coaches nearly up against one another, the painted sedan chairs, couples strolling in extravagant ornamentation. Gold and silver passementerie. Lace and ribbons adorned silk. Buckles shone on heeled shoes. Men were in their plumed hats and carrying walking sticks, ladies in velvet capes and shawls, their hair dressed in fashionable ringlets, some in silk hoods.

It had been a fabulous day already. She had played Celia to capacity crowds, and they had kept her onstage for ten minutes longer than the others to cheer her afterward. Lord Buckhurst stole her from the throng then and drove her past the elegant houses on the fashionable square called Lincoln's Inn Fields, down the most fashionable strip of St. James's Park, and out to Mulberry Garden. His driver was careful to avoid the areas of London she normally saw, those ravaged by the fire, because he wanted the experience to be grand. He said he wished for nothing that might make her sad.

The coach slowed in traffic at Charing Cross, where there were mansions, shops, and stables, and they were buffeted by the strong, pungent odor of horse dung. But that did not matter. Buckhurst sat on the opposing coach seat, holding the silver tip of his walking stick with gloved hands, and he looked to Nell like the most elegant man in the world. When he turned to her with his dimpled smile, she felt a little giddy. In spite of his standing, he did not put on airs, and he made her laugh. He was very clever, too, which was a good match for her own quick wit.

"Have you enjoyed this afternoon?" he asked when the ride was over, his voice rich and sweet, like honey.

"Very much. You've given me a lot to consider."

"As I meant to do," he replied, enormously pleased with himself.

The coach came to a stop and a footman opened the door. Nell thought they could not possibly be back at the theater so soon. Lord Buckhurst got out first and waited for the footman to help her down. Standing before the wide stone steps of the theater, he made a sweeping bow to her. "May I call on you tomorrow?"

"I've got another performance."

"Then I should be no other place in the world than right there on the very front bench to cheer you on, my face full of encouragement for you, and for all the world to see."

"What a way you 'ave with words."

"I leave all of that to poets like Lord Rochester. I only say what is in my heart."

A hint of a crooked smile turned her lips. "Then I'll look forward to what else you'll 'ave to say."

She let him press a very light kiss onto her cheek, then dashed up the wide steps, holding the hem of her skirt, and went back inside the theater. Richard Bell was there when she returned to the tiring-room. He sat at her dressing table waiting for her. His expression was more grave than she had ever seen it.

"Are you certain you know what you're doing with him, Nell?"

"I can only 'ope."

"You must at least promise to be careful."

"You've misunderstood 'im. 'E's a right perfect gentleman."

"Buckhurst is a libertine and a reprobate. His name is constantly linked with Lord Rochester, who is the worst of them all! At least don't say I didn't warn you."

"Do stop worryin', will you? For once in my life, I'm 'appy and I know what I'm doin'."

"It's not *you* I'm worried about," Richard Bell said, shaking his head.

"Well? Tell me everything!" Rose bid her sister amid the thunderous noise and music that filtered up from the tavern below, through the very walls and the warped floorboards, rocking their little room.

Nell's sister was sitting on top of their bed, arms wrapped around her legs, her eyes wide, as Nell moved forward, floorboards creaking.

"'E wants me to go to Newmarket with him for the summer!

'Tis where the wealthy go to watch the races and drink French champagne! Where they visit with the king!"

"And what else?"

Nell giggled and flopped onto her back on the bed. "I suppose that'll be a part of it, but 'e's a nobleman, by my 'eaven! And 'e fancies *me*, if you can imagine."

"So does 'alf of London, but there're not many among 'em who watch you on the stage who'll make you an 'onest woman. Don't do this, Nelly! Don't give up what you 'ave—somethin' of your own makin', your own talent—for a man's black 'eart and empty words!"

"I know 'ow it's been for you, I do, and I am sorry. But this is different." Nell shook her head; Rose's life could not have been more different. Rose wanted to have work of her own, too, but Patrick downstairs could show her none, because of the cough Rose could not seem to quiet, and the look of illness etched deeply into her face that he said would remind customers too much of the plague. So Rose could only content herself in the shadow of Nell's bright star. "I don't fancy 'er, but Moll Davies was right, Rose. The theater 'as given me a chance, but only just that. Girls like me can't grace the stage forever. Soon, I'll be gone like all of the other pretty faces, replaced by someone new. So I've got to use it while I can, find some sort of proper life where we'll never 'ave to worry about a roof above our 'eads again, you and me. I mean to see to that!"

"So you're goin' then?"

"I've no reason not to."

"What about Mr. 'Art?"

She turned onto her side and propped her head with an elbow. "'E doesn't love me, Rose. The only thing 'e loves is the stage. There's no future for me with 'im, and the theater'll never pay me as much as I plan to 'ave for the two of us. You know the money is not anywhere near what people think."

"God above, Nell, what I wouldn't give for the life you 'ave! And you're sayin' you'll give up everythin'? The stage and the public who wait in line for a chance just to see you?"

Nell drew in a deep breath, then sighed. "For a chance at a proper life for us both. 'Tis precisely what I'm sayin'."

"Oh, Nelly, I *'ope* you know what you're doin'."

The words of caution were nearly Richard Bell's. "So do I," she said, trying not to think what would happen to her life at this very crucial crossroads if she was wrong.

Chapter 11

AND VIRGINS SMILED AT WHAT THEY BLUSHED BEFORE.
—*Alexander Pope*

JUNE 1667

NELL tipped up her head, feeling the sun and the wind together as the coach turned off High Street and moved down a twisted little lane shaded by evergreen boughs. She leaned back against Buckhurst's elegant leather coach seat, aware of the string of other coaches ahead of them, and one behind, feeling as if she were a part of something, and as if she were leaving Lewkenor Lane and the Cock & Pye very far behind.

An image of Charles Hart flared like a candle flame before her. *Whore*, he had called her, and bid her never to come back to the King's Theater if she meant to abandon him now. It was only his pride that was wounded, she knew. Still, he had cursed at Nell so furiously that it had drawn a crowd of actors who collected near the door of his private tiring-room as he warned her it would never last with Lord Buckhurst, that she would return to London a laughingstock.

"Penny for your thoughts. You do look awfully pleased with

yourself," Charles Sackville, Lord Buckhurst, noted as the coach clattered and swayed. He took a small silver flask from his pocket.

"Just pleased, in general. No particular thoughts worth sharin'."

"It's the company, I hope."

"Oh, undoubtedly." Nell smiled at him.

Buckhurst took her hand then and brought it to his lips. "I'm not Charles Hart, you know. It won't be like it was with him."

"I'm certainly glad to hear that!"

He opened the flask and took a long swallow of the contents. He then offered some to her, but Nell declined. She did not need spirits to make her any more giddy. This trip was a girl's fantasy, and Lord Buckhurst was Nell's grand knight, she felt absolutely certain of it.

They arrived in Newmarket, a charming village of thatched cottages and clean streets, nestled amid the lush heath land of Suffolkshire, at half past seven that evening. Outside, it was still as light as day. Buckhurst stepped from the coach amid a porte cochere ringed by neatly trimmed emerald hedgerows, and held out his perfumed hand. Before them was a vast brick estate nestled into greening woods.

"*This* is yours?"

"My family's, actually. But they do take pity on their dissolute son in springtime and allow me the use of it."

He held her hand as Nell was presented to the staff that stood in a starched straight line on the outside stone stairway.

"'Tis very grand," Nell said as she looked up at the entrance hall, with its gleaming black marble floors, soaring ceiling, and portraits lining the walls in heavy gilded frames.

"Designed to impress, like everything about the Sackville family."

"Well, *I* am rightly impressed."

"Good," he smiled, still holding her hand. "Now. Do you wish the staff to show you to our rooms, or would you be more comfortable in having me show you privately?" He ran a seductive finger along the line of her jaw. "I hope that I made the nature of my proposal clear."

"You did."

Buckhurst smiled as though he were indulging a favored child. "I've no intention of making a wayward woman of you, Nell."

"Some would likely say I already am one."

"A wayward angel, perhaps, but only just that. I do care deeply for you."

He kissed her at the top of the landing, and she realized only then how powerful was the taste of liquor on his lips. "Might I lie down alone, just for a little while?"

He fingered a coil of her coppery hair, then he smiled his charming smile. "I'm a bit spoiled, so do not take too long."

"Oh, it'll be worth the wait, I can promise you that," she smiled.

The lovely collection of rooms to which she was shown in Lord Buckhurst's grand country house looked down into the little town. From the windows, she could see people strolling before the open shops. She could see the horses in the street, the coaches and carts, hurrying past it all. Inside, there was a large, pale oak bed with thick turned posts, a bedcover of intricate ivory crewelwork, a dressing table with a mirror framed in silver, and velvet draperies ornamented with fringe. She unhooked the latch and drew back the windows, letting in the cool country air, mixed with honeysuckle and roses. This was nothing at all like the air in soot-choked London. Here, she could almost breathe in the possibilities. Nell felt herself smile again.

Buckhurst had agreed to let her rest before dinner, but rest was the last thing she wanted just now. What she had needed was a moment to calm herself, to drink it all in, and convince herself that something this grand was actually happening to her.

After a while, she crept down the stairs, holding on to the polished mahogany banister, and followed the sound of his voice, and the laughter of others, coming from a room tucked behind the entrance hall. The oil-painted faces in the row of portraits along the wall drew her eye. They were dour, serious faces, nothing like Buckhurst himself. Nell paused for a moment, then went on until she was surprised by a small, black face gazing out at her from beneath the staircase. It was a little girl wearing a pretty dove-gray dress, lace at the sleeves. Her ebony hair was shaved close to her small head so that all Nell saw was the sweet face and the most enormously expressive coal-black eyes. She had never seen anyone like her in all the world. "And who might you be?" she asked, but the child disappeared almost before the words left her lips. Nell was so struck by the almost-encounter that she nearly forgot where she had meant to go. She moved through an arch and went to the open doorway, where she could still hear Buckhurst. Lingering there unseen for a moment, she watched. The room was a paneled library, stuffed with leather-bound books. There were two other men with him, and they were all standing against a wall of windows, with a view of the rolling green lawns behind, all of them holding full glasses of wine.

"Certainly you cannot mean that," one said. "It'll be so frightfully dull."

"I mean it, entirely. You are both to be on your absolute best behavior," Buckhurst warned. "Give me at least a chance to appear redeeming."

"Appear, if not quite become, I hope?" the other man quipped.

Buckhurst looked up, seeing her then. He smiled and held out a hand to her. "Ah, Nell. Do join us. Gentleman, this beautiful lady is the famous Nell Gwynne, about whom you have heard so much in London. I don't suppose my father shall ever quite believe that I have won so fair a prize, but at least you two will be forced now to declare how clever I am when next we are with him."

Nell moved forward and took his hand. The other two men were slim and elegantly dressed, like Buckhurst, but not nearly so attractive. The tallest had thinning sandy blond hair, which gave him a high forehead not hidden, at the moment, beneath a periwig. His eyes were a bland shade of blue, and his front teeth were noticeably crooked.

"Nell, may I present my dearest friend in all the world, Sir Charles Sedley. And this other old rake here is Sir Thomas Ogle."

Ogle was clearly younger, with straight dark hair that fell into his eyes, and could not hide large protruding ears. Both of the men smiled at her and then nodded deferentially. "Right charmed I am, gents," she said smiling in return.

"Do join us for a glass of wine, Mrs. Gwynne," Sedley said affably.

She moved forward and took a large, etched crystal goblet, then Sedley refilled each of their own. "I do believe it is going to be a grand springtime here in Newmarket," he said, drinking his newly filled glass in one long swallow, as Ogle and Buckhurst did the same.

"To grand adventures!" Buckhurst toasted.

As a warm breeze ruffled his elegant slashed sleeves and blew back his hair, King Charles stood at the front of his royal barge.

It was lacquered in crimson red, gilded, and proudly flying the Royal Standard as it floated down the Thames toward Newmarket. He was anxious to arrive. The wonderful little town his father had so enjoyed for the peace it had brought him was his grounding place. He could breathe the air there.

To that thought, he drew in a sweet breath and gazed out ahead at the lush, green landscape, the trees and shrubbery softening the banks. *Freedom* . . . This was the first trip to Newmarket in three years unaccompanied by a lover. Even with Buckingham, his courtiers, privy councillors, pages, cooks, and dressers, and a large group of friends for companionship, he felt the faint chill of disquiet. Both Barbara and the queen had remained in London. Moll, who was too newly delivered of her child, was mercifully not yet fit to travel. He watched the charming little town known for horse racing and revelry come slowly into view as the barge was prepared for docking along the mossy banks.

"Shall we proceed with the banquet tonight, Your Majesty?" asked Buckingham.

Charles turned. "It *is* what we do here, is it not?"

"That and a few other interesting things."

"Is Clarendon entirely out of London, then?" he asked uncomfortably, forced to think of the old man's downfall.

"Lord Clarendon is on his way to his country home as we speak. And, may I say, Charles, good riddance to him for what he has cost England."

He looked at his old friend, a man he did not believe he would like if he met him now. But for the rich and long history they shared, Buckingham would seem a persistent fly in need of swatting. "We all made our decision with regard to the Dutch. I daresay there's none of us without blood on our hands," he said.

"Goodness. You really are in need of a bit of revelry."

Charles turned and watched the ramp being fitted for his disembarking. "Perhaps you're right. The queen is despondent, and it is a relief to be away from her when she is like that. She had led me to believe once again this month that she was—"

"Not again." Buckingham groaned, rolling his eyes dramatically. "Your wife is lovely, but as barren as a Devon hag, and after this long that is not likely to change."

"For the good of England, I have got to keep hoping though, do I not?" He gripped the polished ebony handrail. "My brother is again pressing hard to divorce Anne, using her father's banishment now as impetus. And my spies have told me that he wishes to replace her with a staunchly Catholic bride."

"There *is* always Monmouth to be named your heir if the Duke of York proves unfit."

"My brother is my only heir. The rightful succession of this monarchy is in large part what my father died trying to preserve."

They began to walk down the little carpeted gangway followed by Thomas Clifford, John Maitland, and Henry Bennet, and their wives, the warm breeze ruffling the edges of their elegant capes, skirts, and the plumes of their hats, and then an unending line of servants.

"Some ghosts speak too loudly for their own good," Buckingham carefully offered as they climbed together into the same coach, and the door was closed.

Charles settled against the seat across from him, his mouth a firm line. "I will *always* do what he would have done."

"Even if your brother succeeds you and turns England Catholic?"

"I cannot consider that. And I will thank you, my old friend, not to darken those prayers with your own dissonant cloud."

Buckingham shrugged. "In the meantime, I would say the return of our jolly old blade is well in order, here in Newmarket at least."

"I don't know how jolly I am, considering the events of the past month. But I find I *am* in the mood for a bit of revelry."

"Ha! Splendid!" Buckingham smiled as the coach lurched forward, the sound of horses' hooves heavy around them. "Now let us find Your Majesty a girl in town with whom you can quite properly revel!"

"I am not in the market for another mistress, George."

"Who said anything about a mistress? Let us just both settle for a rousing good whore!"

Chapter 12

'TIS NOT THE DRINKING THAT IS TO BE
BLAMED, BUT THE EXCESS.
—*John Selden*

THEY walked, hand in hand, through a field of bluebells behind Buckhurst's country house. Charles Sackville also held a full silver goblet of French wine. They had been in Newmarket nearly a month, and to her surprise Nell found that intimacy with Lord Buckhurst was a fleeting thing built on vain attempts and then endless apologies. She had concluded that Buckhurst's attachment to drink was stronger than anything he felt for her. Still, he wished her to remain, and so still she hoped for the security a miracle match like this one could give her.

"Here now." He reached across to touch her chin. "Why look so sad? Do tell me you are enjoying Newmarket as much as I am."

"The countryside is lovely."

"And my friends adore you."

Sir Thomas Ogle and Sir Charles Sedley, the two wealthy libertines, were Buckhurst's shadows. They stayed at Lord Buckhurst's house, and spent most of their time drinking, playing cards, or going out with him. Where they went, or what they did when they were gone, she never knew.

Beneath a sky pillowed with white clouds, Buckhurst looked at Nell. Studying her for a moment first, he pressed an absent, feathery kiss onto the tip of her nose.

"How would you like to attend a banquet with me this evening Nell?"

"What sort of banquet?"

"It is an evening's entertainment given by the king himself. Lots of dressing expensively, dancing, and drinking, of course."

Nell felt a shiver at the unexpected thought of the king. She sank into a patch of flowers so thick that it swallowed her up. "'Is Majesty is here?"

"He is. And it is his custom to host them as often as twice a fortnight when he is in town," Buckhurst said, as he drained his goblet in a single, long swallow, then sat down beside her. "I am rather well connected, you could say. My father was a great favorite at court when His Majesty was a boy, and, fortunately for me, this king is given to strong bouts of nostalgia."

"Is that so?" She leaned back on her elbows. "'E seemed different when I met 'im."

"Royal persona. Important for things like war and asking Parliament for more money. Both full-time occupations, the way I hear it," Buckhurst said blithely. "Once you come to know him here at Newmarket though, he is a different sort altogether. You will see he is really quite tolerably human, full of all the same warts as the rest of us."

"Speakin' of warts, is 'e likely to bring Mrs. Davies?"

Buckhurst laughed. "I rather doubt it. The king is not known for his consistency with the fair sex. Especially not here in Newmarket, where there is an abundance of beauty and options. And speaking of being human, Nell, I know I haven't been the best host, or the best paramour, so far, but I promise you, I've turned over a new leaf." He brushed a hair back from her face and then kissed her passionately.

"I'll keep you to that," she said, but all she could think was what a girl like her should wear when being entertained by the king of England, and what clever thing she would say to charm His Majesty if she were given the chance.

The rolling green Newmarket Heath had been transformed into an exotic sheik's harem. Lights twinkled over a canopy of red silk like stars in a summer night sky. Servants, dressed as slaves, strolled up and down bearing silver trays filled with figs and nuts and jeweled goblets of wine. As the royal musicians played just beyond the tent so that he could hear them from the house, Charles sat in his small presence chamber with his head in his hand.

"Forgive me, Your Majesty."

Charles shook his head. "Is the queen all right then?"

"She is, sire. She knows now it never was a true pregnancy."

He washed a hand over his face. "God, Catherine."

"There shall be others, of course," said William Chiffinch encouragingly.

"Of course," Charles blandly agreed. "Is she resting then?"

"Yes, sire. Resting comfortably at Hampton Court with her ladies."

At last he stood and allowed his dresser to drape him in the flowing purple robes of a sheik. He turned, and a flash of gold braid at his broad shoulders caught the light. "Very well, then. Enough of this melancholia. The Dutch . . . Moll . . . *my wife* . . .

We are at Newmarket!" He lifted a hand jeweled now with two large rubies. "Let us away to some revelry at last!" *And to forgetting*, he thought. But he did not say that.

He walked outside, encircled by a coterie of self-important men in costumed robes of their own. As they laughed and talked, he thought suddenly again of Lord Clarendon, the old man he had been made to turn against to save England's place in the world. Clarendon had been with them last time here, in autumn, coming out of this same door with all of them, laughing about something trivial. Now his laughter was forever silent at court. Chancellor of England once. Exiled forevermore.

Charles had not allowed himself to miss him, until now.

The politics against him had been too great, the force for change too insistent. Chiffinch walked beside the king now, down into the gardens, but they did not speak. Charles knew Clarendon had been a potent political liability. But surrounded by men who fed continually at the trough of his generosity, the king missed his deeper friendship. Buckingham was a friend, but he was also dangerously motivated by self-preservation. Charles loved him, and the camaraderie between them, but he was not a fool. He saw his friend's strengths and weaknesses for what they were. He sank into a throne set up for him at the back of the tent, garlanded in vines and grape leaves. The music was exotic, the costumes of his servants creative enough to set a mood. Yet still there was a mounting sense of boredom. Chiffinch's efficiency led him to the same result, night after endless night. As it would again this night. It was a compulsion he had almost begun to dread. Then, she was there. *Nell* . . .

The thoughts in his mind stilled, and he was caught entirely off-guard.

She did not see him, so he was free to watch her. She came forward into the tent through an arched opening, dressed in layers of violet silk, edged in gold thread. Her extraordinary hair, the long copper curls, were loose and full on her shoulders. The many candles and lamps created a golden halo of light around her as she paused. It did not surprise him that her smile was wide, and she was softly laughing. What he did not anticipate was that she would be on the arm of Lord Buckhurst, and that she was laughing with *him*.

How could she have thought to give up the theater for a reprobate like that? Lord, but she was a deliciously complex creature, always saying and doing the precise opposite of what was expected. His pulse sped, and though noise swirled around him, he heard no other sound. "Is that not Nell Gwynne?" he asked Chiffinch, knowing exactly who she was.

"The very same, sire."

"Tell her I would speak with her."

"Yes, Your Majesty."

The king watched Chiffinch walk over to her as he had wished to do himself. But he would not battle with Buckhurst like a commoner. He watched Chiffinch speak.

Nell turned to the king then with an unexpected little frown. He sat absolutely still, music and guests swirling around him. He was glad suddenly that she did not know what Chiffinch's customary role was in his life. The moment of her indecision lingered for what felt like a lifetime. Finally, she tipped up her face, never breaking her gaze from his, and came away from Buckhurst with Chiffinch.

"I had no idea you would be here, Mrs. Gwynne," he said, feeling instantly foolish for how ordinary that had sounded.

"And I 'ad no idea Your Majesty'd remember me."

"Ah, there is no way that I could ever forget you."

She frowned slightly again, then, very suddenly, her happy smile returned. "'Tis true what they say, that you can charm any girl you please."

"Being king does have its privileges," he smiled back at her, feeling as if he had known her forever. "And what of my theater, which they tell me you have recently abandoned?"

"I've left it for greener pastures." Nell glanced back at Buckhurst, who was clearly beating both Ogle and Sedley at a drinking contest. She grimaced at the way they laughed and swayed, and how they were cheered on by the others who had gathered around them.

The king's eyes followed hers. She was embarrassed by the display that was all too common at court. *Good*, he thought. His gaze intensified. "It's Buckhurst, the biggest libertine in England, you're with?"

"If Your Highness will pardon me, I thought that was *you*."

"It is just that I rather expected more from one of London's great new actresses."

She gave him a wide-eyed look. "Speakin' of that, where, might I ask, is Mrs. Davies?"

Charles could not have imagined allowing someone to speak that way with him even an hour ago. But for a moment, she had bested him, and he had actually enjoyed it. He stood then, took both of her hands, and drew her against him in a way that surprised them both. "As it happens, Mrs. Davies is in London, along with the queen and Lady Castlemaine. Now then. Have you any *more* clever questions for me?"

"Not at the moment. But, if you'd like, I'll let you know when I do."

He threw his head back and laughed. He was feeling enormously invigorated, and desirous of doing far more with this absolutely wild, delectable creature than merely spar. But all in good time. The chase, the thrill of the chase, that was the thing. They were so close now that he could smell the fragrance of her skin. It was cool and lightly floral. "So. You are here with Buckhurst as his what?"

"As whatever it takes to change my life, and 'elp me to care for my sister."

"Ah. The notion that every actress should find herself a nobleman and settle down."

"Indeed, Your Majesty, not every actress can find 'erself a king now, can she?"

"Fortunately, I'm certain you have heard that the king has a dreadfully wandering eye."

"And just who might that be dreadful for?"

"Any girl not clever enough to tame it, I suppose."

"And is there such a girl in all the world?"

"Not so far. But the king before you is an optimistic man with a benevolent heart."

"Your Majesty shall keep tryin' to find that girl?"

"I might well have done it."

"And yet, there is a problem?"

"Sadly, it appears *she* may well be preoccupied at the moment by another man."

"That would be dreadfully sad," she teased.

"Indeed, it would."

They were still so close that in spite of the flurry of guests and music around them, he kissed her as if they were entirely alone. Her lips were warm, and he felt her knees give just slightly as he wrapped an arm around her shoulder. It had not ever felt like this to kiss anyone. It was a moment more before they came apart. He took her hand then and ran the tip of his tongue across the inside of her wrist. "Tragic not to know what might have been," he said on an exaggerated sigh.

He could see her struggle to swallow. The tide had turned. Now he had entirely bested her, and they both knew it. How utterly delicious.

"'Tis 'ow Your Majesty greets all your lady guests, is it then?"

He was smiling. "Only the truly special ones."

"My ma always said to beware of strangers with honeyed tongues."

"Did she not also tell you the value in a bit of risk?"

"She never really took many risks at all. Which likely explains why she's been 'appier all of these years stayin' drunk."

"I'm sorry, Nell," he said, speaking her name aloud for the first time, and feeling an odd little shiver at the sound of it on his tongue. "My own mother's rather fond of drink as well."

"Oh, you couldn't compare the two. Yours is a queen, and all mine has ever been is a royal pain in the arse!"

He laughed outright. "Tell me, do you always have such a quick reply to *everything*?"

"Thinkin' things through is dangerous work, Your Majesty."

"And we couldn't have *that*, now, could we?"

"Not if a girl from Coal Yard Alley expects to get 'erself to a proper square like Lincoln's Inn Fields one day."

He was not listening now. He was thinking only of what he longed to do with her, and how he meant to make that happen with Buckhurst only a few feet away. How difficult could it be? The fool drunkard had not even noticed that the king of England had taken his mistress and kissed her, in front of his entire court.

Feeling his insistance, she tried to turn from him, but he held her hand, tightening his grip.

"Lord Buckhurst needs me."

"Oh, my dear. Do take care with *that* illusion. Lord Buckhurst may be many things, but—"

"He's kind and generous . . . and he is goin' to change my life."

"I hope you're right about that. The good Lord above knows you'd be the best thing ever to happen to him."

"Well, now, that's right diplomatic of Your Majesty to say."

"It's only the truth, Nell. I cannot seem to speak to you any other way. Most women make me want to run as far from *that* as I can get."

When she began to turn from him again, he gently pulled her back. A heartbeat later, he pressed a last kiss onto her neck, just beneath her earlobe. The heat between them pulsed, then flared as their eyes met.

"Will you be at the races tomorrow? My horse, Old Rowley, is competing."

"Old Rowley, is it? 'Tis not a name I would've chosen for a king's 'orse."

"And he's not actually a horse a king might have chosen. But I had one just like him when I was a boy. Those were good, carefree days I like reliving whenever I can."

"I'll tell him I would like to go. But I can't promise. You know Lord Buckhurst."

"I don't suppose it would help if I commanded him to attend?"

"No." She paused a moment. "But you might invite 'im. 'E's ever so impressed to be known by the king of England."

"And you, Nell, are *you* impressed?"

"Flattered, surely." Her gaze held his fully. "But if I were too impressed, I couldn't be myself."

"And I certainly would not want *that,*" the king said in reply.

Another *actress?* thought the Duke of Buckingham condescendingly. *That jade from in front of the theater? When had* that *occurred?* He knew well enough when the king was besotted. He had stood through the entire conversation with his back to the king and Nell, in disbelief at her spirit and wit. Nell Gwynne was voluptuous, clever, and deliciously unique. It was not at all likely that she could find the powerful place Barbara had held at court—or in the king's heart—but she might do quite nicely as a temporary replacement. The only impediment, he thought, watching them together, was that wastrel, Buckhurst. The king was led away by Arlington's wife, Isabella, to dance a spirited courante, and now Nell was struggling to help Buckhurst to his feet, his having just collapsed with Sedley into a fit of drunken laughter. *A damsel in distress. How perfectly priceless.* Buckingham calmly strode the few paces to her, and gave her his most charming smile. "Do pardon me, Mrs. Gwynne, but might I be of some assistance?" He watched her expression: At first, she was grateful for the intervention, then she recognized him as the man who had been with the king that day in front of the theater, and only too willing to insult her.

"I don't suppose a girl like me needs Your Grace's sort of 'elp."

He nodded. "The problem is, if you do not forgive our unfortunate misunderstanding, you will likely be on your own in getting a very dissolute man back to his house."

She stared at him. "I'm all right on my own, Your Grace. Gettin' by on my own's the way it's always been. Rather good at it, I am."

"I'm certain life has made you the resourceful woman you are. But learning to accept assistance when it is offered shows your wisdom."

Buckhurst was vomiting on the ground now between them, and Sedley had passed out in an equally unattractive heap.

Nell did not want to trust him, he could see, but he pressed on. "I shall send two of my stewards and my coach. You cannot handle him as he is now, and you should not be made to. You need not trust me in order to accept. I shall remain here at the banquet in order to prove I have no ulterior motive."

Nell tipped her head, looking at him cautiously. The night air between them was bright with fireflies. "Very well, then. Thank you."

"Don't think another thing of it. You were right to be wary of me, and I was wrong to have underestimated you. It has been quite a long while since I have done that. Hopefully, we can start again on a better footing."

"I don't suppose a duke 'n me would find ourselves very often in the same company for any sort of foot at all."

"One never knows, Mrs. Gwynne. Look at you, present at an affair given by the king of England. Would you have expected that a year ago, you with your oranges in front of the King's Theater?"

"That seemed about as likely then as you offering your friendship." *Lord, but she was quick. Yes, indeed. In need of a bit of training, a bit of style, but she would definitely fill the bill for now.* "Well said, madam." The Duke of Buckingham smiled and led her away to find his coach.

Nell wanted to return to London. But one thought alone had stopped her. To what would she return? She had not allowed herself to see truth for fantasy; she had come to Newmarket with a nobleman who had never actually offered to marry her. But the reality she could no longer ignore was that Charles Sackville was a drunkard. Life with him, no matter how richly decorated, would not be far from the one she had escaped in childhood with her sodden mother. Nell was sitting beside his bed when he finally opened his eyes the next afternoon.

"Pray, tell me what time is it?"

"Past one," she replied flatly.

He squinted and tried to sit up. The stale odor of wine lingered. "Oh, dear. There you are, lovely as a picture, and I am quite dissolute."

"You retched all the way home from the king's banquet."

He lay against the spray of pillows behind his head as Nell stood up and pressed back the heavy velvet draperies on their thick iron rod, revealing the great bare window.

"Oh! Show a bit of mercy! The light is blinding, and my gut feels like the site of the Battle of Hastings!"

"You really shouldn't drink like that."

"It was no grand drama, Nell, just a bit of frivolity with friends."

"Frivolity for you, perhaps. But if I'd wanted to go on cleanin' vomit off my dress, I'd 'ave stayed above the Cock & Pye and faced my own ma!"

He squinted at her again and put a hand at his brow to shield the blaze of silvery white daylight streaming in through the large picture window beside his bed. "At least move away from there if you mean to go on chastising me. I cannot see a bloody thing with you as you are!"

"'Twould serve you right to feel a bit more pain. It might 'elp you to knock your good judgment back into place."

"Speaking of mothers," he groaned, trying to sit up. "If I'd have wanted to hear harping, I would have invited my own." For a moment, they were at an impasse. Then he turned his lip out in a charming little pout. "Tell me you had *some* fun on your own last night."

"The king tarried with me. And aye, 'twas good fun indeed. In fact, 'e wishes me to come and see 'is 'orse in the race today."

Charles's smile was sudden and broad. "Oh, splendid!"

She lifted a brow suspiciously, uncertain of how to gauge his response. She had hoped to make him jealous with the revelation. "You're not angry, then?"

"Hitching myself to that star, if it's going somewhere, would be a good bit of work for the Sackville family."

"Hitched, as in you want a position in the king's court?"

"A position, as in *work*?" he gasped, then chuckled. "Oh, good Lord, no! But being in the king's company a bit more often would be a splendid accomplishment for my family, and achieving that would bring me great reward! Nell, you *are* an amazing creature. With all of the women there, how did you manage it?"

She was still wary of his response. "'E found *me*, actually."

"Extraordinary."

"So, shall we go to the races today then?"

"I wouldn't miss it."

"Will you be drinkin' less?"

"Not at all likely."

"Then we're not likely to remain as we are," she warned him, "if every evening ends as the last one did."

Buckhurst shrugged, then smiled sheepishly at her. "That's the beauty of Newmarket. You never can tell just what might happen here."

A warm sun beat down on the full stands that were arranged before the large tree-lined racing lane. Women held up fans or silk parasols. The edges fluttered in the summer breeze as clouds scudded across a bright blue sky. Men wore their periwigs and large plumed hats to shade their skin and eyes. The elite of London sat in their open coaches, opposite the stands. Buckhurst's midnight-blue coach was decorated with gold scrollwork, highlighted with the family crest on each of the two doors. Nell sat beside him on plush leather, wearing an exquisite dress of butter-yellow striped silk with a fitted bodice, a lace-edged collar, and a fashionable blue underskirt, which he had had made for her. It was still a foreign world, but one she had begun to enjoy.

While he was too tall and sturdy to be a serious rider, it was said that King Charles would be racing his own horse this afternoon. But then she already knew about Old Rowley. Nell sat straight on her seat, determined not to miss a moment. His brief kiss last night had been nothing more than flirtation from a devilish man whose wife and mistress were nowhere about. Men really were nothing more than errant little boys, she and Rose always laughed. The king was no exception. Yet still she smiled to herself, thinking how commanding he was. King Charles was not classically handsome, but he was so tall and elegant that when he faced her, he made her forget to breathe. Buckhurst did not do that to her, no matter how much she had hoped he would. Even after the events of last night, she still hoped to rescue him, and thus be rescued *by* him. She could, and would, forgive him his drunkenness, as he had forgiven the inelegance of her low birth. He was not the golden treasure Moll Davies had managed to find. But he was a lord, with lineage and money to share, and he would be quite magnificent enough for a girl like her.

Nell glanced out across the track as the riders were led on horseback to the starting positions. King Charles stood out for how high above the others he sat in his saddle. Yet even if he had not, she would have known him for the way he held himself, the long, dark curls of his periwig, beneath a tightly fitted tall crown hat, and the gold thread and rich silk of his quilted waistcoat. "There is the king," Buckhurst said offhandedly as he drew out a flask from his pocket and began to open it.

"Oh? Where?" asked Nell, feigning boredom herself, using the acting skills that had taken her to this unbelievable zenith.

"Just there. In azure and gold. He actually looks quite ridiculous on horseback, tall as he is. But he is such a vigorous sportsman; they say he cannot help himself, the competition of it all."

"One could do worse," she observed, feeling a sudden jolt of irritation.

"I, for one, cannot imagine all of that walking about for miles on end, the swimming, hunting, and, at night, the endless dancing. Then feeling the next morning as if you simply must be astride a horse, racing somewhere."

She felt a shiver of admiration. "'Is Majesty does all of that?"

"Daily, they say. And his poor collection of courtiers and servants are left to try to keep the pace. At the rate he goes along, I should think he will be dead before he's forty and without a proper heir to see to the succession."

"I thought 'Is Majesty 'ad nearly a dozen children."

"Bastards, all. And those are not much good for anything but a man's pride." He glanced over at her then, the flask hovering near his mouth. "Really, darling, how could you not have known the difference? Even a girl from . . ." His words trailed off.

"Even a girl from Coal Yard Alley?"

"You are what you are, Nell. We both are. Yet I love you quite desperately all the same." He took a long swallow from the flask, then kissed her cheek.

"You *love* me?"

He thought for a moment, considering the declaration. "Well, you are as close as I have ever come to caring about what someone thought of me. So, I expect I love you, yes."

A ringing romantic endorsement it was not. But the admission offered Nell the hope that, with patience and time, she might one day actually become Lady Buckhurst. If only she could continue to tolerate the drinking, the constant presence of his equally dissipated friends, and his falling asleep before he got anywhere close to a romantic show of affection, it might well be a sound and comfortable life. Nell settled back against the seat, ignoring the next large swallow of liquor he took, and the noxious odor of it as it permeated the warm air around them.

Charles sprang from his mount in a small gravel arena into which he had been led by his royal equerries at the race's end. He never knew whether they allowed him the win, but it was always more about the thrill of the contest than the hope of victory anyway.

A young towheaded page in royal livery offered him a goblet of cider as he was quickly surrounded by courtiers, servants, ambassadors, and a bevy of smiling women. It was then, at that precise moment, that he saw her again. On his other side, the Duke of Buckingham, that persistent fly begging to be swatted, was already chattering in his ear. But Charles did not listen. He felt like a boy, anxious, tentative. She was between Buckhurst and Sedley, and they paid her absolutely no attention, talking instead to each other in spite of how she seemed to glow in a dress of butter-yellow silk, her hair fanned out on her shoulders beneath a small, smart matching hat, trimmed with feathers, and shimmering against the light of the sun. Suddenly, he despised Buckhurst.

"Your Majesty."

"Your Majesty was brilliant just now," Sedley flattered.

They bowed and spoke in unison as Nell bobbed a curtsy.

"I merely won the race," he said with self-deprecation before he turned to Nell. "And Mrs. Gwynne. How did *you* find it?"

"I confess to knowin' precious little about 'orses, Your Majesty. But it was entertainin', it was."

His smile was sly. "I would have preferred to impress you."

"Oh, I was certainly *that*."

"Splendid to hear." He went on smiling. Seeing it, Sedley and Buckhurst exchanged a glance. *Good*, Charles thought. *They have noticed something other than themselves, at last.* "And shall I see the three of you tonight for the banquet?"

In a well-schooled fashion, Buckhurst bowed deeply to the sovereign. "It would be our great honor to join Your Majesty this evening," he said, as Nell's gaze met the king's.

Buckhurst had accorded Nell a stout maid, named Paulina, who was to lay out her clothes, help select her shoes and accessories, and arrange her hair. She had also been given the little girl she had seen that first afternoon, hiding beneath the staircase. Jeddy, who refused to speak, was there, Buckhurst explained, to amuse her. It was all the fashion, he said, to have a little black child to attend her when she went out.

"I really don't want 'er, Charles," Nell said that afternoon as Paulina dressed her hair, carefully stringing a rope of pearls through the upswept copper curls. Jeddy was a little girl without her mother. It was all Nell could think of every time she looked into her beautiful, sad eyes. Nell's life in Newmarket felt like an audition. She was being tried for the part of Lady Buckhurst with no guarantee of winning the role. "She makes me sad thinkin' of her servin' me."

As she stood before him, Buckhurst reached out and fingered the folds of her petticoat, a delicate thing of lace and ribbons. There was a little charged silence between them then, accentuating the creak of the floorboards as Paulina quietly led Jeddy from the room. As he lay with her, untying her petticoat laces, she closed her eyes, wishing it were the king instead. Buckhurst was drawing apart her legs then, hovering over her. She could feel his warm breath on her face, feel him pressing between her thighs. But his enthusiasm for her once again was a fleeting thing. She wrapped her arms around his neck and felt the perspiration there just as he lifted himself off her, and rolled onto his side.

"I'm sorry, Nell," he said once again. But that was all.

Nell stood before a full-length mirror, being clothed and ornamented by Paulina in a new sage-green dress looped back in front and held by gold ribbons, which Charles had bought for her. Jeddy lingered shyly near the door. A cool breeze blew in through the open window and scented the room with the fragrance of roses. At her throat was a fine lace collar that matched the fan from France waiting on her dressing table. Even after all these months, she still could not quite believe the reflection gazing back at her. Polished. Elegant. An almost believable lady stood before her. The years of searching for food and safety were masked well by fine fabric and neatly curled hair. Yet she was still Nell. Yes, she would always be that.

"It is the king," said Paulina, glancing out the open window at the commotion below. "Every time His Majesty passes, he draws a crowd."

Forgetting herself, Nell drew up her skirt and raced to the window, then balanced her hands on the ledge. She saw him across the street, tall and prominent, surrounded by courtiers, lingering for a moment to speak with one of them. As she stood watching him, something drew his gaze to her. It was too late to hide or even turn away. He had seen her. No, she must be bold. She was not certain what possessed her to do it, but in that moment, rather than be coy and demure, Nell smiled broadly at him and gave him a little wave with the tips of her fingers. Her heart began to race as he tipped back his head and laughed. The way his eyes brightened, then crinkled at the corners, made him seem even more handsome, she thought as their eyes held each other's until a courtier beside him tapped his shoulder, and he turned away. The moment was quickly extinguished, but not the impact it had made. He knew her. She made him smile. She was still, after all, not a real lady, no matter what she wore, but Nelly Gwynne, and something told her at that moment that it was that about her which he liked best.

Chapter 13

MY MERRY, MERRY ROUNDELAY
CONCLUDES WITH CUPID'S CURSE:
THEY THAT DO CHANGE OLD LOVE FOR NEW,
PRAY GODS, THEY CHANGE FOR WORSE!
—*George Peele*

THE vast tent, striped of blue-and-green silk and topped by a gold crown, swayed in the warm spring breeze on the vast lawns behind the king's palace. The royal musicians were playing a sprightly, "My Lovely Lady Mary," and glittering candles everywhere gave the tent a magical glow. In her new gown, Nell stood between Buckhurst and his companions. She looked lovely by the candlelight, and tonight she truly believed it.

"Where is the king?" Buckhurst murmured beneath his breath.

"I'd rather have a drink than give another bow," quipped Sedley. "Groveling can be so tiring."

"Now that you mention it," Buckhurst chuckled, raising a hand to his mouth, "I believe I saw champagne. You know our good king does love all things French."

Nell frowned at them. "We've only just arrived. Try to behave yourselves. Hmm?"

"Now, Nell," Sedley smiled sheepishly at her. "What fun would that be?"

A liveried servant, bearing a silver tray of glasses filled with champagne, passed them; Nell saw Buckhurst and Sedley exchange a glance.

"After you," Sedley said, and he and Buckhurst burst out laughing.

Buckhurst chucked Nell's chin, as if she were a child. "Do *you* behave *yourself*," he said, then pressed an absent kiss to her cheek. "Unless, of course, it involves the king!"

Before she could respond, Buckhurst, Ogle, and Sedley were gone, moving together toward the servant with the tray. He had never remarked about her gown, her hair, nor made any comment at all about wanting to dance with her, in spite of the lively music and the collection of guests already doing a branle near them.

"You are a vision this evening. Well recovered, I trust, from the events of our last meeting?"

The deep, well-schooled voice came from behind her. Nell turned, then curtsied to the Duke of Buckingham. She had softened toward him since his generous assistance with Buckhurst. Still, something about him made her want to be careful.

"May I call you Nell?"

She nodded, cautiously.

Buckingham smiled, "A dance later, perhaps?"

"Perhaps, is it? 'Ave you not made up your mind to ask me?"

"If His Majesty fancies your company as much as I believe he does, then I should be cautious asking anything of you. So we shall have to see as the evening progresses."

"Surely Your Grace knows that the king already 'as a mistress and a wife."

"He has several mistresses," Buckingham corrected her.

"And Your Grace? What do *you* 'ave?"

"More greed than sense, and more ambition than lust,

truthfully." She lifted a brow, openly scrutinizing him. He was smiling broadly. "I know we got off to a poor beginning. But, as it happens, I would like to be your friend, Nell."

"And why would a duke of the king's court want to befriend a lowly, retired actress?"

"Because I am a prudent man, and I happen to believe that you will have great power with the king one day. If the king does select you," he continued. "I would like to help you, once you have reached his bed, to learn how to keep yourself there."

"If he *selects* me? You make me sound like one of his 'orses."

"Knowing His Majesty, as I have had the privilege of doing lo these many years, I do not believe there is any doubt of his interest in you, Nell. But when he does proposition you, you should be wise enough to accept. I do not know yet if you are as wise as you are witty. I have had the misfortune, after all, of seeing you with Lord Buckhurst."

"Does any girl ever reject the king?"

"Only those who are not clever or wise," he said. "But I am going out on a limb and wagering that you are both, with a healthy dose of ambition thrown in."

"And I can see that Your Grace is a crafty man."

"So long as you are not afraid of the king, then we shall get on splendidly. He simply must have challenge in a woman, one who can meet him fully, or, to be blunt, she shall be gone after the first tumble."

King Charles stepped behind Buckingham then and put a firm hand on his shoulder, stopping their conversation instantly. "Open flirtation with a special guest of the king, is it, George?" he asked with a wry smile.

"Never, Your Majesty."

"Good to hear, old friend. Mrs. Gwynne," the king said deeply, gathering her hand in his and pressing it to his lips in the French manner. "I must say that tonight, you are a vision."

She smiled up at him, reminded how much taller he was, how much more commanding in stature alone from the other men around him, and thinking how magnificent he looked in claret-colored velvet, trimmed in gold braid. "And *you* are as smooth as a sow's ear. Every other woman 'ere makes me look a country cousin to 'er."

"I happen to like the country," the king said. Then he glanced at a group of guests in the middle of a lively branle danced to his favorite tune, "Come Kiss Me Now." "Shall we, then?"

"I'm afraid proper dancin' is not somethin' Lord Buckhurst's 'ad the time to teach me."

"You might wait a very long time if it is Buckhurst you intend as a teacher."

"Unless, perhaps," said Buckingham, "you held a drink to his nose and led him away from Charles Sedley."

The king laughed at that. Then he looked at Nell. "Forgive me. We were thoughtless. It is only knowing Buckhurst as we do, and his penchant for personal enjoyment above all other things, that sometimes makes ridicule simply too tempting."

The couples were assembling in a circle and joining hands. They would step forward, meeting with a slight pause, then step back. The music was light and happy. The dance, he told her, was a great court favorite, easy enough to learn. Nell was listening to the sound of the flute and the low rhythm of the drum, trying to make out the steps. Hart had taught her to do a wonderfully comic jig for the stage, but this was altogether different. She tried to hide her studied frown with a carefree smile. "I 'aven't a clue 'ow to begin!"

"Then I shall teach you."

Nell considered it. If the king of England wished to teach her to dance in Buckhurst's stead, who was she to object? This was a height to which a girl like her had no right to rise. Nell took the hand that the king had extended to her. His skin was warm and smooth; his grip, powerful. There was an energy between them as they touched. She smiled up at him then, doing her best to resemble the most carefree girl in the world. What the stage had not taught her, life had. She would be what he wished, the clever, carefree Nell from the King's Theater, the one men desired. She could not compete with noblewomen on their level, but she could use what she had.

As they advanced together, the other dancers fell into deep bows and curtsies, some of them whispering. If there was such a thing as magic, this certainly felt like it to Nell.

Amid candles and lamps that flickered like diamonds, and lively music that carried Nell along on the arm of a nearly mythic figure, she danced to two songs as his partner. Then a servant approached. Coming into the dancing area, he whispered something imperceptible to the king. Charles glanced at her in response.

"You must follow Chiffinch, my dear," he said. "It is to do with Lord Buckhurst."

Nell followed the tall stately man, and two guards, knowing that whatever she was being led to, it could not be good. Her gown trailing on the walkway, she walked silently behind the two guards, who smelled heavily of musk and sweat. They moved along a winding path through the garden in silence, the only sound the clicking of their shoe heels and the scratching of crickets in the shrubbery. They passed a tiny caretaker's cottage, heading for High Street, and a row of thatched houses beyond.

"It is just as they did in Covent Garden!" A man looking up

was saying in disbelief. "A year has passed, and people still speak of that!"

Charles and his friends Sedley and Ogle were standing on a second-story ironwork balcony. Buckhurst, who stood behind Sedley appearing to take him sexually from behind, although both were still dressed enough to make the jest clear, was laughing hysterically. Ogle had urinated into a bottle, and had just flung it into the gasping crowd. Horrified and nervous laughter flared as Buckhurst began to strip off his clothes, and the three began to climb down a vine-covered trellis against the house. Cold reality hit Nell. For this man, she had left a public who adored her. She had abandoned a sound life she had been building all on her own for *this*. Suddenly, she hated herself for it.

"His Majesty has authorized me to offer you a coach back to London, madam, should you decide to go," the servant called Chiffinch said evenly. He did not look at her as he spoke.

"The king knew about Lord Buckhurst?"

"His behavior has gained its own status, Mrs. Gwynne. His Majesty merely anticipated the possibility, and authorized me to act accordingly should the need arise."

Tears pressed at the back of her eyes. Fighting them, Nell felt her mouth tremble. She bit her bottom lip to stop it. "I'd no idea the extent—" The words fell away.

There was no point. It was done.

She had given up on her own wits and gambled on something, and someone, who was not real. Nell met Chiffinch's gaze. "Thank you, sir, for the offer. But I found my own way 'ere. It'll do me good to find my own way back."

She left Newmarket at dawn, before Buckhurst was awake—before he could object, if he meant to at all. She was riding through the undulating, mist-shrouded countryside, in a coach she had insisted on hiring for herself. As the Buckhurst manor grew ever smaller in the rear window, then disappeared beneath an emerald-green rise, Nell at last put her head in her hands, and for the first time in a very long time, safe in her solitude, let herself weep. Until she heard the rustling . . .

She heard the rustling before she saw the movement.

As the hired coach swayed and clattered over the winding dirt road leading back toward London, Nell gasped when she saw her. Her little ebony face shown smooth, and her teary eyes were wide as she pressed back the corner of a blanket to look up at Nell.

"How in blazes did you manage to hide yourself in here?"

Jeddy sat up huddled in the blanket, a bare foot poking out.

"Oh, never mind. You'll not answer me anyway, I suppose. The thing is, I 'aven't any proper place for you to stay."

Still the girl said nothing, only stared, eyes wide.

"I wonder if you *can* speak. But you must be hungry. I'll tell the coachman to stop at the next inn."

The little girl lunged, shaking her head in a pleading gesture that they not stop.

"I'm not sendin' you back. I'm only fetchin' us a proper meal!"

The child gripped Nell's forearm with surprising strength, still shaking her head. Nell reached out and put her hand on Jeddy's head. "It'll be all right," she said in a much softer voice. "I've no idea what the devil I will do with a little girl, but I'll not send you back to Newmarket. All right, then?" Nell moved her hand to touch the curve of the girl's chin in a gentle, motherly gesture. She thought how young the girl was, and how alone she must feel. Thinking of that made her heart squeeze. It was good, she thought, to feel something today besides regret.

Before she had left the King's Theater, Nell had paid for the room over the Cock & Pye for the two months' time she would be gone, so that her sister could have a roof over her head. It had been a great deal of money, but she had paid happily, not only because of her concern for Rose's health, but to honor the promise she had made to care for her always, no matter what.

Holding tight to Jeddy's tiny ebony hand, Nell opened the main door and, lowering her head, managed to make it up the steep staircase, just beyond the bar, without being stopped by Patrick Gound. That at least was one small blessing. She could not bear just yet to explain to anyone why she had returned from Newmarket early. But Jeddy resisted climbing, so that she had to drag her along. "It's all right," she murmured. "Come on. No one'll 'arm you. 'Twill not be the grand room you 'ad with Lord Buckhurst, though. What I'm to do with you I'll figure out later."

She opened the door to her old room, aching for a bed and the peace that only sleep brought. Her mind was still a jumble of so many things. Frustration, anger, and regret were tied up like a tightly knotted bow on one of the king's lace jabots; she felt an utter fool.

Rose looked up from a meal of fish pie set up on the rough-hewn little table beneath the soot-smudged window, a warming shawl around her shoulders. Her eyes were a bit brighter as she glanced up, the gray that rimmed them not nearly so dark now. Seeing Nell, she stood and absently wiped her hand on the front of her dress. "This cannot be good, that you're back so soon."

Nell sank onto the edge of the bed and kicked off her soft shoes. "I've left 'im."

"'E wasn't to marry ye then?"

"'E's a perfectly content drunk. Bad as Ma, only with fine clothes, and money."

"And what the devil are we to do with the likes of 'er?" asked Rose, with just the hint of her old cough as she glared at Jeddy, who was loitering at the door. Nell glanced at her sister, then over at the little girl of whom she had begun to feel fond. "Clearly, I've got to get a job to support 'er *and* you."

"Where's the sense in *that*? Keepin' a child, another mouth to feed?"

"You'll care for 'er when I'm out, 'tis that simple."

"I'm to take a little blackamoor down the Strand with me, like some sort of proper lady, when I actually feel well enough to get out of 'ere? Ballocks to that! I'd be the laughin'stock!"

Rose had been pretty once, full cheeked and smiling, her dark hair long and glossy. Nell understood only too well the sharp edges that their hard life had given her. She looked at her sister with patient sympathy. "With Jeddy, you'll 'ave a bit of company."

"Just because you've been on the stage, and been bedded by a lord, you'll not to go gettin' all 'igh and mighty on me now!"

"I don't suppose you're in a position to be lecturin' me about much of anythin', Rose Gwynne, straight from the gaol, are you!"

"That was cruel, comin' from you, Nelly."

Nell had not meant to say it. She had not meant to belittle her sister, whose release from Newgate prison seemed the greatest miracle of their lives. There was no one in the world to whom she was more devoted, nor cared for more. But Jeddy was an innocent child like she once had been, whose life was charted and determined by the accident of her birth, with no way of ever rising out of it. Especially not if she gave her away.

Groveling before Charles Hart was almost worse than going hungry. But there was no other choice. She knew she must return to work, and there was a limit to things she was qualified to do. If not for Rose and Jeddy, she would have gone back to selling oranges rather than bow down before Hart. But Rose was right—Nell did miss the stage, the adoring crowds, and the power and independence that that life brought.

Nell had no idea how she would ever make herself face Hart, or what she would say if she did manage to find the courage to appeal to him. In the meantime, Richard Bell had come to see her at the Cock & Pye two days after her return to London. "You have been missed!" he exclaimed as they embraced.

"You never did believe I would stay with 'im, did you?"

Richard held her out at arm's length in the noisy tavern as his smile faded. "No, I didn't. Do you want to tell me what happened?"

"There was nothin' of the fantasy I made it into," Nell said firmly. "Simple as that."

Richard took her hand again as they made their way to a small table in the back. "You don't need to be so tough, you know," he said as they sat opposite each other, and leaned in so they could speak in low tones. "Not with your friends."

"Oh, but I do. London's a rough place for a girl like me if your backside is anythin' softer than shoe leather. So who told you I was back in London?"

He took a long swallow of ale from a pewter tankard before he answered. "Moll Davies, actually. She came to poke about the theater and see if you intended going back on the stage. Word was that the king was at Newmarket when you were there, and that he left the same day you did. Things like that set people to talking."

"The king's whore believes *I* am some sort of competition?" A smile broke across Nell's face. It was the first spark of happiness she had felt for days.

"Should she?"

"I saw 'im. But 'e didn't offer to whisk me away, if that's what you mean."

"Did he tarry with you, at least?"

"I'd warrant the king would tarry with a rosebush if 'e thought it would bring 'im flowers!"

Richard laughed. "That *is* his reputation."

"I made a mistake with Lord Buckhurst. Now I'm back, and I'll never make the same mistake again, thinkin' a man'll provide for me, I can promise you that. Eleanor Gwynne pays her own way from now on, and mends 'er own mistakes."

"Like Mr. Hart?"

"Does 'e still despise me?" She bit her lip as her expression became worried.

"Quite openly."

"But do you suppose 'e would 'ave me back on the stage? I might've embarrassed 'im by leavin', but I'd gotten pretty good for business—"

"I don't suppose he would, Nell, no. Not the way he talks about you."

Nell felt the heavy blow in that.

"But fortunately for you"—his eyes glittered with amusement—"it really isn't up to him. Thomas Killigrew holds the royal warrant for the King's Theater. And he would very much like you back."

"Oh, you absolute angel of mercy! 'Tis the real reason you came 'ere in the first place just now, isn't it?"

"I did think you might have a few financial complications if you'd returned to London without Lord Buckhurst, so I thought I'd see to it for myself."

"You can't imagine the 'alf of it! Complications everywhere!"

"When I spoke to Mr. Hart on your behalf yesterday, it seems Mr. Killigrew overheard me."

"Overheard?"

He grinned impishly as he shrugged. "Well, I *might* have watched to see that Mr. Killigrew was nearby when I mentioned your return to Mr. Hart."

"Richard Bell!" Nell lunged across the table and threw her arms around his neck. "I do swear I could kiss you!"

"Wouldn't mind if you did." He heard himself and how it had sounded. He quickly added, "I only meant that you're extraordinary, and I'm fond of you, and—"

"I know what you meant, Richard." Nell was beaming at him, her copper hair loose and full, seemingly lit by the candles on the tables in the very dark room. "So 'ow am I to do it, then?"

"According to Mr. Killigrew, who is thrilled to have the return of his star, you are to be there tomorrow morning for rehearsal. We've only just begun a new play, called *The Indian Emperor*, and he wants you to play the emperor's daughter. It's the lead, of course."

"Tell me it's a comedy."

"It could well be with you in it, Nell! Seriously, though, I don't know. We haven't had a real success since you left us, and they've been scrambling a bit with the material. I'm not at all certain yet about this new play."

"I'm nervous."

"Don't be." He took her hand again. "You've got friends in the theater, and a very adoring audience who will cheer your return, no matter what material you perform."

"I certainly 'ope so," said Nell, shaking her head.

Nell stood back a step from the stage for a moment, cloaked in shadows, watching the others rehearse. Charles Hart was directing the actors in every nuance of what they said and did. If he could have told them how he wished them to breathe, she thought ruefully, he would likely have done that as well.

Just as Beck Marshall began a short monologue, facing Richard and Mary Knepp, Hart caught a glimpse of Nell from the corner of his eye. "Well, well. Do look, everyone, what the proverbial cat has dragged home," he said loudly enough to silence the scene. "Or have I mixed up my metaphors, and it is chickens that have come home to roost? Eleanor Gwynne, everyone—" He held out an arm and his voice went louder, a sharp unmistakable edge to it. "The actress too good for the King's Theater, but not good enough, it would seem, for Lord Buckhurst!"

A collection of embarrassed chuckles sounded from the actors, then quickly faded.

"Perhaps we should speak privately," Nell offered, stepping forward into the bright sunlight cast from the glass cupola above them.

"There is not a thing I should wish to say or do to you *privately*, Mrs. Gwynne. As you know, were it up to me, I would not have taken you back, no matter how you groveled. Apparently, Mr. Killigrew and I do not share the same standard."

"I groveled to no one!"

"Unfortunately," Hart continued, unaffected, "your return was not my decision to make."

"And you'd do well to remember that!" Nell seethed. She was angry now. It was bad enough coming back. She'd be damned to hell if he was going to humiliate her publicly, as well. "I'm 'ere to do my job, so you'd best let me get on with it, Mr. 'Art."

All eyes were on the lovers turned adversaries, as Charles Hart moved toward Nell in two long, commanding steps. He was close enough now for her to feel his warm breath on her face. His nostrils flared, like a bull ready to charge. "Things have changed in your absence, Mrs. Gwynne. I may be forced to take you back, and even to give you the leading role, but, as it happens it was I who was left to select and contract our current production, a wonderful *dramatic* story, *The Indian Emperor*, in which you play the tragic heroine. So, we shall see if you are more clever at adapting to drama than you were at adapting to a life of leisure in Newmarket."

"I think she takes your point, Mr. Hart," Richard Bell bravely interjected when no one else dared speak a syllable. Charles Hart pivoted back in response.

"*You* think? Since when does this theater pay an imbecile to think? You are here, Mr. Bell, to sweep up the rubbish in the pit and occasionally to fill in the background when there is absolutely no one else." Then he added, with a cruel flourish, "Rather like in your own life. Now, shall we all get back to work?"

Nell took a copy of the script from Mary Knepp and glanced at it. Reading for her was still almost impossible, but she rarely allowed anyone to know it. Fortunately, she was a quick study, able to memorize her own lines as well as the lines of the other actors as someone ran through them with her the first time. She glanced down at the jumble of words until one jumped out. The emperor's daughter was supposed to weep. There was no part of herself she was willing to touch to make that really happen, certainly not before a raucous London crowd bent on a good time. This play would be, she knew from the first word, a disaster. Exactly what Charles Hart wanted. Punishing her publicly would be well worth a very brief financial flop.

There would be no choice but to hold her head up and endure it.

Not if she meant to stay at the theater, and pay her own way.

Watching the rehearsal, they sat in the back of the theater, beneath the upper tier, in an overhang of seats in which the noble class viewed performances. Both Ogle and Buckhurst were dressed for an evening out, wearing long, curled periwigs, feather-trimmed hats, coats decorated with looped ribbon, and breeches to the knee. The actors were running through their lines before them on the stage as two men hung a large curtain in preparation for one of the scenes.

"I was such a fool!" Buckhurst murmured as Nell entered and spoke her first line.

"On that much we agree," said Ogle.

"I haven't a clue what I was thinking, treating her that way, as if she would be around forever." It was the same sentiment he had muttered all the way from Newmarket, and Thomas Ogle knew what he was expected to say next.

"You weren't thinking. You were drinking. A bit of fun cost you the most celebrated girl in London."

"I am an utter, daft fool!"

"You did rather make a mess of things."

"I must apologize. I want her back, and she has got to know it."

"She looks awfully content up there."

"What's that life compared to the one I can give her?"

"Dependable, I should say, to begin with. You don't mean to marry the girl after all, do you?"

"I don't know that I wouldn't," Buckhurst hedged, opening a small silver snuffbox and pressing a bit into his left nostril. "I haven't actually thought that far ahead."

"We don't, our kind, do we—"

Buckhurst glanced at him sharply.

"—think well ahead of the moment, or marry girls like that," Ogle amended.

"I don't know that I mightn't." Buckhurst was now looking dead ahead again, watching Nell's every move on the stage. "You said yourself she was different."

"Different certainly does not mean suitable as the wife of a Sackville."

"Probably not. But I want her all the same, and you know perfectly well I've had a lifetime of getting what I want. I am not prepared to lose now."

He flicked his friend's shoulder in a false show of bravado, but as he stood and prepared to move toward the stage, he felt a hand clamp tightly onto his shoulder to stop him. A tall, broad-shouldered man with a square jaw and intense dark eyes said, "There is someone outside who wishes a word with you, my lord."

"Not now, my good man," Buckhurst responded, trying to break free of the man's iron grip.

The bigger man would not let go. "The Duke of Buckingham, sir, is desirous of your company."

"I don't care if it's the ruddy king of England himself! I am engaged just now."

The man led Buckhurst then, quite against his will, and very forcefully, from the theater, and out into the street, where a large black coach with six horses on silver harnesses waited.

The coach door was pulled back by a stone-faced liveried footman, and Buckhurst was pressed with a single short thrust up the steps and inside the large and luxurious coach. Tucked inside, on the far end of the studded black-leather seat, the Duke of Buckingham sat, his hand on the ivory knob of a walking stick, and he stared straight ahead. Charles Sackville had always found George Villiers cold-blooded. Whatever this summons was about, he knew it could not be good. He sank onto the edge of the seat facing Buckingham, and waited, determined not to speak first for what it might cost him if he did.

"The king wishes to bestow a great honor upon you, Buckhurst," Buckingham announced without ceremony, and without changing the direction of his gaze. There was a slight pause before he added, "You are to leave for Paris as His Majesty's personal emissary."

"Paris? Good Lord, why me?"

"Because your sovereign wishes it. In light of that, you would be wise to see it as the honor it is, complying swiftly and quietly."

Buckhurst leaned forward, surprise still on his face. "I do appreciate the honor, but it is simply not the best time—"

The duke, resplendent in his gleaming blond periwig and jeweled hands, looked fully at Lord Buckhurst for the first time. His expression was cold. "I do believe, my lord, that you do not quite take my meaning. This is not a request."

"Am I being exiled, then? Punished for something?"

The duke rolled his eyes and let out an irritated sigh. "Leave it to a wastrel to see the king's largesse as punishment. The situation with the French is a delicate one after the Dutch wars, as I am sure you are aware. You shall be in France to express the king's regrets to King Louis over the illness of his son, the dauphin. Also, while there, you shall collect from His Majesty's sister a covert report on the state of relations, and see it brought back to England."

"But I am not a spy!" Buckhurst was on the edge of the seat now, hands curled around the edges of the plush black leather. "Or a diplomat, for that matter. I am, as you said, a wastrel!"

"Apparently, His Majesty sees something more in you. It is an opportunity to better yourself, boy, and your rapidly declining reputation. You would be wise to seize your bit of good fortune in this and be grateful."

Buckhurst glanced through the fogged coach window, back to the wide stone steps leading up to the King's Theater, and Nell. It was a crossroads, yet there was only one road open for him to take. "Very well, then. But I've someone back inside to speak with first."

"There isn't time for that. The king's barge is waiting to take you to Dover tonight."

"Tonight?"

"You leave at once."

He glanced at the stairs again. Nell would never forgive him. She would never understand how dear she had become to him, or how, in following her back to London, he had hoped to improve himself because of her. He considered that for a moment. Perhaps it was better this way? Perhaps in France he actually could make a real man of himself? He would lose Nell, of course. But she would not have him as he was now anyway.

He looked back at the duke. It felt like a contrivance, this honor, though for the life of him he could not imagine the benefit to anyone in being rid of him. As the coach pulled forward with a little jerk onto Drury Lane, and away from Nell Gwynne, Charles Sackville wondered for a moment if he would ever know the real reason why he was being so swiftly spirited out of London.

The king was playing tennis when Buckingham returned to Whitehall from Drury Lane. The duke stood to the side, arms crossed over his chest, watching the sovereign volley the ball across the court to his son, Monmouth. Charles's superior athletic skill still made Buckingham angry. He struggled at everything the king did with ease. Especially the getting of women. Not just the easy marks brought up the back stairs by Chiffinch, but with real, sensual, thinking women, as Castlemaine in the early days had been. Or his early love, Monmouth's mother, Lucy Walters, before her.

Castlemaine had only ever slept with him to make the king jealous. George knew that. It had not made the competition any less fierce. But what the king wished was always the priority. It was everyone's priority. And so now, too, this morning at the theater, Buckingham had acted on behalf of his sovereign. Even if he had not yet revealed the scope of his plans for Nell. After all, King Charles may be the superior athlete, but who could argue, he wondered, with his own vastly superior mind? Who else would ever think to replace the powerful Castlemaine with a hungry young actress who could so easily be molded by the person wise enough to install her?

"Ah, George!" the king called out with a friendly wave.

The match was suddenly over in mid volley. He took an embroidered towel from the tray held by a waiting page, daubed the sweat from his face, then tossed it at the servant as he approached his old friend. "So, then? Was he amenable?"

"Of course, Your Majesty. What good servant of the king would not humbly comply with so great an honor?"

"Oh, cease the flattery, George, it doesn't suit you. He had Nell to himself. That alone would be reason enough to hang on to the cliffs of Dover by his thumbnails."

"Not every man appreciates a diamond in the rough as Your Majesty does." Buckingham nodded decorously. "You saw for yourself how he behaved at Newmarket."

"So she's back at work at the theater?"

"As it happens, she's preparing to perform this very afternoon."

"And Hart. Tell me, George, does he wish her return to his bed?"

"My spies tell me the old fellow does not handle rejection at all well. Hart has told anyone who will listen that he hopes she dies a miserable death in this new play, and he hasn't said he meant a figurative demise, either."

Charles smiled and walked in long-legged strides away from the tennis court and back toward the stairway to his private apartments as Buckingham, and everyone else, struggled to keep the same sure pace. "Marvelous." The king smiled again.

"The road does seem paved, should Your Majesty desire to take it."

"For now, I suddenly wish to go to the theater. See it arranged, would you, Georgie?"

"Of course, sire. As I see to every wish on your behalf."

Yes, indeed, thought Buckingham. He may not be named chancellor yet. But thanks to their enduring friendship, he was still the second most powerful man in England, no matter his lack of title. It was he who really had full control of everyone's destiny, particularly the destiny of Nell Gwynne.

Chapter 14

... TO THE KING'S PLAYHOUSE AND THERE SAW *THE INDIAN EMPEROR;* WHERE I FIND NELL COME AGAIN, WHICH I AM GLAD OF, BUT WAS MOST INFINITELY DISPLEASED WITH HER BEING PUT TO ACT THE EMPEROR'S DAUGHTER, WHICH IS A GREAT AND SERIOUS PART, WHICH SHE DOTH MOST BASELY.
—*The Diary of Samuel Pepys*

NELL felt the old familiar butterflies fluttering against the wall of her stomach as she stood waiting behind the curtain for her cue, her hand steadied on the swagged strip of fringed velvet, the candle lamps bright and dancing before her.

The play was dreadful.

It was not a comedy, at which she had so shined, but an overly dramatic tragedy. In a scene suspiciously convenient for him, Hart was killed off in the early part of the first act. Nell was left to soldier on by herself, weeping and hand-wringing. Her costume was scarlet velvet; her hair was tamed back tightly and fitted into a mock crown of rubies. No pratfalls or ribald jokes were possible. The play was tailor-made for Charles Hart to have revenge, and it was the worst possible return to the stage for a comedic star. Nell glanced into the flickering golden glare of the stage lamps, feeling her throat seize up. A full house. She felt like a lamb being led to the slaughter. She drew in a very large breath to calm her racing heart. What was the first line? Then, at what could not have felt a worse moment, she glanced up at the royal box and saw the king. In the next instant, she heard her cue, and was ushered onto the stage.

The ovation and whistles of welcome were raucous and sustained, and Nell fought a smile. This was, she remembered, a serious moment in the play. "My father is dead," she declared, trying to force dramatic tears to her eyes.

Four dandies in the front of the pit began to laugh.

"Did he die of boredom with this play?" a man called out amid growing laughter, though in the bright lamplight she could not see him.

She delivered another line, her dread growing.

"Aw, give us a laugh, Nelly!" someone called out from the back of the pit.

She heard the splat of an orange onstage, and was relieved to be joined by Hart's mistress, Mary Knepp, who was to play her nurse. But it did not matter. It was nothing like the other times she had been onstage, cheered and adored. This, the papers would say, was a disaster.

Nell made it through the play by sheer will. As she moved to her place behind the curtain for the final time, her body was awash in perspiration. Half the pit had cleared out during the final scene, and they had not gone quietly. There was more tossed fruit. More jeers. And when she had looked up, the king, as well, was gone from his box. She sank onto her stool in the tiring-room, wanting to sink into the core of the earth, when Richard Bell gently touched her shoulder. "Come now," he said with a half smile. "It wasn't that bad."

"No, it was much worse."

He waited for a moment as she looked up at his reflection behind hers in the mirror. He would not lie to her further. Their friendship was too strong for that. "All right, it was not good. But there's always the next play. You must think ahead to that."

"After today, I'll be lucky if anyone in London will give me another chance."

She took her time walking back to the Cock & Pye, meandering from Drury Lane to Maypole Alley, where she bought a leg of mutton and some cheese for dinner. She wanted desperately to avoid the expectation she knew she would see on Rose's face when she returned.

Just as she turned to go into the tavern, a painted sign on iron swinging above, two men emerged toward her from the shadows cast by the jutting roof of the house next door. Nell turned with a start, feeling a jolt of panic, until she recognized one of them. The Duke of Buckingham.

He was dressed like a common butcher or tailor, someone who actually belonged, like her, in this low place. He wore no periwig or fine buckle shoes, but rather a brown linen hat pulled low, a buff-colored shirt and plain buttoned doublet, and buskins, as the other man did.

"There is someone who would like a word with you," Buckingham said as the king himself, equally disguised, emerged from the same shadows.

She felt herself smile at the absurdity of the entire scene. But the three men seemed to be taking enormous pleasure in their charade.

"Say you will have supper with me."

"Oh, I don't think dinin' with a king is a very good idea. Too much attention I don't need just now when I'm tryin' to get back to work."

"And if, by a rather clever disguise, I were not a king, and were to bring along a friend, would it be a good idea then?"

"No less than three friends would do."

"I am not usually required to bargain with the fairer sex. But I find that *you* are a force with which to be reckoned."

"I'll not be taken lightly by Your Majesty just because I 'aven't come from anythin', if you've got that in mind," she warned, trying to be serious, but still utterly charmed by him.

He gathered up both of her hands and pressed a lingering kiss gently onto them. "Who in their right mind would take you lightly?"

"It would be nice to be appreciated. But only just for supper." She was thinking of Moll Davies. And survival. Moll may have a king's house, and a royal child, but if he was not fully tired of her, he soon would be, and then she would be alone. That much was clear enough as he looked at Nell with his best rakish smile.

"Two, these two, and it's agreed." He pressed her hands against the length his chest with a humorously dramatic flourish.

The king of England, his brother, the Duke of York, and the Duke of Buckingham led Nell to Bridges Street, and into the back of the Rose Tavern. The savory aroma of roasting meat was very strong inside the warm place. They took a large plank table behind a red swagged curtain. The click of snuffboxes and the roar of raucous laughter and continuous conversation was loud, making the little party all but invisible.

Buckingham sat across from her, the king beside her, the Duke of York on her other side. She had only met the king's brother this evening, but she liked him. James was not so tall or handsome, and he was more round at the middle than Charles, but he had an honest face.

"Juniper ale all 'round," Buckingham called to the innkeeper. Turning to Nell, he added, "It's famous for curing whatever might ail you, from rheumatism to palsy, and even your digestion."

"But can it quench your thirst?"

Everyone laughed. She knew the king liked her clever tongue, and so she had decided to say whatever came into her mind.

As platter after platter of roast lamb, rich oysters, and the king's favorite, pigeon pie, arrived, Nell's cup was continuously filled, until everything seemed particularly humorous. Amid the laughter and rapid banter, Nell felt herself begin to relax. She enjoyed the elevated company; Charles had an easygoing manner, a wicked sense of humor, and a bold zest for life.

"So, Nell," James said. "How did you find our little town of Newmarket?"

"I found it quite by accident, Your Grace, and paid dearly for my lack of direction. Sadly, I suspect I'll go on payin', so long as Mr. 'Art 'as any control at 'Is Majesty's theater."

Glances darted nervously back and forth as the men tried to discern how serious she was.

"Ah, splendid!" Buckingham announced, pointing across the room. "A game of dice!"

At another table, around which both men and women were crowded, some of them were beginning to toss down coins for betting.

"Shall we?" he said to York, clearly wanting to give the king time alone with Nell. As they began to stand and brush crumbs from their waistcoats, the innkeeper returned, asking payment for the enormous and costly meal.

For Nell's sake, they had carried the ruse fully forward, wearing costumes with no pockets or satchels. In the shadow of a request for money, the king glanced at Buckingham. "Well, pay the man, George."

"I haven't a penny with me," he said in a flustered tone. "James?"

The Duke of York's face went ashen. "I don't carry money with me. I never have."

The men exchanged cautious, darting glances with one another as the king leaned back exploding with a burst of amused laughter. "Oddsfish!" the king said. "How do you men expect me to charm the girl when I cannot even buy her a plate of mutton?"

Nell bit back a smile as the innkeeper hovered over them, a frown creasing his sweaty brow. "This is surely the poorest company that I ever kept in a tavern!" she said, laughing the wonderful laugh that the theater patrons loved so well, deep and up from her soul. "It's all right, *Charles.* I believe I've enough of my wages to settle the debt. Although, after today, it could well be the last I have for a while."

"Oh, nonsense, Nelly. You're brilliant onstage," James earnestly proclaimed. "Everyone knows it was a miserable play, even if it was written by Dryden."

"George here will, of course, reimburse you before you lay your head on a pillow this evening," said the king. Then he leaned over to whisper, "And if I have my way, as king of England, that pillow shall be mine."

George and James left the table then.

Charles took up Nell's hand, turned it over, and ran the tip of his tongue along the inside of her wrist, as he had done at Newmarket. Then, without warning, he leaned across, pulled her to him, and kissed her deeply.

"You'll not be havin' your way with me as king of England," Nell said. "But for the man I saw here tonight, I could be very complyin' indeed."

"Then he is the man you shall have."

The innkeeper showed them up a creaking set of back stairs to a room overlooking the street, paid for by one of the king's coachmen, from whom the Duke of York had gone out to fetch coins. Charles closed the door, and pressed Nell against it. She could feel the warmth of his strong fingers through the thin fabric of her bodice. She looked into his eyes as he carefully peeled the fabric of her corset back from her breasts. He touched each with the tip of his tongue, as his arms encircled her again, exploring the contours of her back. It was the first time a man had touched her in that way, with lips, tongue, teeth. The sensation was pure pleasure, and Nell heard herself moan.

"Shall I stop, Nelly? If so, you've got to tell me now, as I'm one man who'll never force himself on you," the king declared on a ragged breath.

"Then I'll never tell you to stop."

He led her to the old creaking bed near the window, as the sounds of clinking glasses and laughter below filled the charged air around them.

The Indian Emperor played for four days at the King's Theater, until dwindling ticket sales called an end to Charles Hart's vendetta. Then a new play was chosen, another drama, called *The Surprisal*, and once again Nell Gwynne was given the dramatic lead.

"A pox on him!" Nell ranted in the tiring-room, her face white with rage. "He's doin' this to spite me!"

"At least you've got steady work," offered Richard, not convincingly.

"And for how long?" Nell shot him an angry stare. "At this rate, I'll be out on my ear with not even oranges to sell to pay for Rose and Jeddy's supper!"

Richard hesitated a moment, looked around, then said, "Ask the king to intercede."

"The king?" she said angrily. "What makes you believe I have influence with the king?"

"I saw you leaving here with His Majesty that day. *Everyone's* talking about it."

"Well . . . if it's gossip you're after, Mary Knepp told *me* the king is back in bed with Moll Davies, that they were seen yesterday out in His Majesty's carriage right on the Strand, pretty as you please, and she was so low as to even 'ave brought their bastard, and 'eld 'im up to the window!"

"And you believe Mrs. Knepp, of all people? You know she's never forgiven you for being in Charles Hart's bed before she was."

Nell put her face in her hands for a moment. When she looked up again, her expression had softened. So had her tone. "'E 'asn't called on me again, Richard, and I don't *want* to care! 'Twas a moment between us, and 'e took it. 'Twas I who let 'im do it. Foolish, I know, after Buckhurst, but I'll not be fooled a third time, not even for the king of England."

She went on playing the role of Samira the next afternoon.

Each performance was a punishment to endure, each line and the response to it was excruciating. But she would not be chased away. She could not. Eventually, the theater would need a success; they would need to return to comedy. The audience was steadily calling for it.

Before the sixth and final performance of *The Surprisal*, Nell sat before a mirror in the bustling tiring-room, having her hair curled into long ringlets by an old woman with heavily veined hands. Other actors dashed back and forth around her chattering, laughing, and in various states of undress, when very suddenly there came a new whirlwind of commotion. Nell glanced in the mirror and saw, behind her, a thin, very elegantly dressed woman with ash blond hair done up with ribbons. She was wearing rich green velvet with white lace ruffles at her collar and cuffs, and Beck Marshall was rising from a chair to greet her. Nell had seen the face once before, fleetingly, as the woman had made her way up to the king's box to sit beside him.

"'Tis an honor, my Lady Castlemaine, to have you here," said Beck, her voice dripping with a solicitous, honeyed tone.

Nell slowly turned away from the mirror to face the infamous royal mistress.

She was lovely enough, though a far sight more *mature* than any woman she could imagine retaining the attentions of King Charles for as many years as she had. She was certainly nothing like Moll Davies. Though it was Lady Castlemaine, not an actress, who bore a title and six acknowledged royal children, she reminded herself. Nell felt a sudden spark of envy as she looked into Barbara Palmer's smooth, delicately carved face, and her sharp, assessing sea-green eyes.

"It has been ages," Castlemaine said to Beck, who appeared to be a close friend. "We've come to invite you to dinner after the performance. You must be pleased this ghastly run is over."

Nell had heard the gossip that Lady Castlemaine enjoyed the company of actors, and often attended the theater without her royal lover.

Someone drew up a chair for Lady Castlemaine, who took it without acknowledging the gesture. Her chin was high, and the marble-sized pearl at her throat glittered in the candlelight from the long row of dressing-table mirrors.

"Since Mrs. Gwynne has returned, it seems we cannot find a success."

Suddenly, all eyes were on Nell. In the palpable silence that followed, Lady Castlemaine turned and looked directly at her. Nell was forced to stand and curtsy.

"Your Ladyship," she said.

"So you are the famous Nell Gwynne everyone chatters on about."

For a painful heartbeat, Nell thought Lady Castlemaine knew what had happened between herself and the king. She felt the blood drain from her face at the prospect. "I'm probably more infamous at this point than anything else, since things did change 'ere upon my return, and most will tell you, not for the better."

Castlemaine studied her for a moment with those assessing green eyes, and Nell saw her mouth twitch slightly. Then she pursed her lips, as if she had smelled something foul. "Self-deprecation can be a useful tool, Mrs. Gwynne. But only when used in careful moderation."

"I shall remember that, Your Ladyship. Thank you," she said, then bobbed a second curtsy.

She smiled at the show of deference, and Nell saw straight teeth, and then something more: One tooth at the center had a slight chip. A flaw. So the great lady was not so perfect after all. The strain Nell felt at the encounter began to abate as swiftly as a retreating tide, and she felt her sense of self return.

"I saw you in *The Mad Couple* last spring. I found you to be quite good."

"Thank you, my lady."

"Very funny."

Richard Bell chose this moment to speak. "The Duke Buckingham, and even His Majesty, have told her that, as well. She only needs another comedy here to—"

He had been anxious to help, but he had gone too far, mentioning the king in connection with an actress. Everyone in the tiring-room could sense it. Nell watched Lady Castlemaine realize, once again, just how pervasive the king's appetites could be.

Richard lowered his head at the awkward silence he had created.

"Ah, well," said Castlemaine tartly. "His Majesty is a great patron of the theater. But he is also taken up with his children of late, and no longer given to the peculiar plunges into folly he once was."

"Five minutes, everyone!" A young man called into the tiring-room, signaling the commencement of the play.

"Fascinating to have met you, Mrs. Gwynne," Castlemaine smiled tightly. "I wish you good fortune on the stage today. By the sound of things, you are going to need it."

In the two-minute encounter, Nell had met the infamous Lady Castlemaine, an aging beauty apparently clever, or ruthless, enough to have won back the king. If she were ever to come upon His Majesty again, Nell would consider herself warned.

Chapter 15

ALL THAT IS AND SHALL BE,
AND ALL THE PAST, IS HIS
—*Sophocles*

THERE was blood, dripping, oozing, washing across everything. It became tears, hot and salty. They fell into his eyes so that he could not see, but it was there, on his lips, the gritty taste of blood, the king's blood, sprayed outward from the neck, and Charles's ears were full of the weeping. It surrounded him until the sound became a roar, became unbearable. "No! *No!* Don't kill him! You cannot kill him!"

Charles bolted upright, his face awash in perspiration, and his heart slamming so hard he could not catch his breath. It was a moment before he could see his own bed, the collection of spaniels at his feet. It had only been a dream . . . the same dream as always. The girl beside him was, incredibly, still asleep, thank God, as he had no idea who she was. Nor did he wish to. Another procurement of William Chiffinch, a young body to help him forget that he loved no one and no one loved him. The vivid dream so close in his mind brought a rush of bile to his throat. It was all so pathetic at this hour of the night: the women, the idleness, and, with it, the pervasive sense of loneliness that never quite went away. Lines of the satirist, the Earl of Rochester, came to mind: *Nor are his high desires above his strength; his sceptre and his prick are of a length.* Cruel words, but true. It was why Rochester thrived at court. Charles rose and tossed on a dressing gown. Still, the naked girl on the bed did not stir. Chiffinch's rooms were beside the king's bedchamber. One slight rap on the door and Chiffinch would have his wife rouse the girl, see her dressed, and on her way.

In bare feet and an untied dressing gown, he paused to knock on Chiffinch's door, then he continued on down the paneled corridor to the queen's private apartments at the other end of the Long Gallery, with its view over the river and ceiling painted over a century before by Holbein. On nights like these, though few and far between, he wished Catherine's rooms were nearer. He must be near to something good and kind, even if he did not love her as he should.

Catherine's lady, Maria Mariano, a homely Portuguese matron, met him at the door in her white cap, nightdress, and hastily tied dressing gown, her inky hair long on her shoulders.

"The queen has long ago retired, Your—"

Charles raised a hand, stopping her. "I wish only to look in on her for a moment."

He brushed past her and crossed through two sitting rooms to the queen's bedchamber. Catherine slept like a corpse, her pale skin hidden by a high lace collar, her dark hair bound into a linen nightcap, and her hands joined upon her breast. He sank into Maria's chair beside the bed. His wife was not beautiful or enticing, but her kindness had always been the draw for him to try and feel something for her. After a moment, she opened her eyes. "You've had the dream again, haven't you?" she asked him in English, thickly accented with her own Portuguese.

He took her hand tenderly. She did not know the details of his recurring dream; she knew only that it was a disturbing one. She knew it was likely about the former king's murder because once, when they were newly married, he had thrown water from the ewer and basin on himself and rubbed himself nearly raw, asking her all the while if she could still see blood on his skin.

"I'm all right. I just needed to see you," he said quietly.

"I wish you could speak of it, Charles. If not with me, then with someone."

"Perhaps one day."

He could see how frail and tired she looked, suffering, he knew, every herb and tincture possible to try to become pregnant. He had been wrong to come here seeking the kind of comfort she was not capable of giving him. After another moment, he leaned over and pressed a kiss onto her forehead in the shadowy twilight.

"Would you like to stay?" she asked, almost as an afterthought.

"You rest. It will be morning soon," he soothed her, watching her face soften with relief. "Perhaps we can walk together later."

"Only if you do not walk so quickly, as is your custom with others. I am never quite as quick at anything as the others."

He knew what she meant. They both knew. "You've been a good wife, Catherine."

"I have not done my duty to you, the one for which we married."

Charles gently placed her hand back atop her other hand, which had remained on her chest. "You have been a comfort to me. That's a duty in itself, and in it I have been well pleased."

She smiled softly, and he could see her eyelids begin to close once again. Lingering a moment more, he pressed a kiss onto her cheek, then quietly left the queen's bedchamber. This was not the answer for him, nor was she. He would go on looking elsewhere until he found it. But Catherine was safe with him—she would always be—and Charles was glad of it.

John Dryden stood in the innermost sanctum, the royal bed-chamber at Hampton Court, early the next morning, facing the king, who was being ceremoniously dressed before a collection of ambassadors, courtiers, and servants in front of a trio of floor-to-ceiling Flemish tapestries. The room was vast and grand, with a great poster bed and high crimson-velvet tester dominant behind it. The chairs were cushioned in plush crimson, and the cabinets gleamed with royal silver. He had been summoned there by the Duke of Buckingham, and he had expected to be received in the presence chamber, honor enough for a well-known yet modest London playwright. Being permitted here, into this inner sanctum, to watch the king's rituals, was a suspiciously high honor to be now accorded.

"Has Your Majesty had an opportunity to read the play you requested be written?" he asked, once he was brought forward.

"I have read it."

"And does the outcome please you, sire?"

"The role of Jacinta is written perfectly. She will be brilliant at it."

"It was my hope Your Majesty would find it so."

"And I wish to see *An Evening's Love* performed here at court first, to be certain of the outcome. With Mrs. Gwynne in the lead role. After what happened with the dramas, I should not wish her to take any unnecessary chances."

Dryden bowed to the king. "It is understood, Your Majesty."

"Can you see it arranged with all the players, Killigrew, Hart, and the rest?"

Dryden tried to gauge the king's wish before he responded. "Of course, I shall command her to Hampton Court, along with the other players. And we would all expect Mrs. Gwynne to be honored by the invitation to perform for Your Majesty here."

There was a little silence. A cough, and the echo, in the cavernous, vaulted bedchamber.

"And yet you are the playwright," the king went on, sounding oddly tentative. "Perhaps you would implore her with something more than her duty to her king. I do not wish her to come here simply at my command, Dryden."

"An alternative is to be my own notion, then?"

"There must be an element of desire on her part, or it will be pointless to me."

There was irritation in his voice. Dryden bowed deeply. "But you are the great king of England, sire. Attending you would be any young lady's desire."

Charles swatted the air, bored with flattery. "It is a good thing you are a better playwright than you are a sycophant, or I might never see Mrs. Gwynne again," he said.

In one of the coaches sent to London by the king, Nell, Beck Marshall, Rose, and Jeddy clattered along down the long gravel pathway to the massive palace of Hampton Court. The summer day was warm and fragrant. The sky was full of birds, and the emerald-green route, with the vast palace before them, was more grand than anything Nell could have imagined. The royal summer home was a grand Tudor compound of red brick and stone, dating to the days of Henry VIII. A line of shiny lacquered coaches, bearing the other actors, scenery, props, and costumes, followed them. Nell sat quietly inside the coach as they moved beneath an arched porte cochere and the coachman pulled them to a swaying stop. She had not wanted to come, but in the end she had been given no choice in the matter. It was the King's Theater of which she was a part, Thomas Killigrew, the manager, had advised her, and it was at the king's pleasure they would all perform here. Her only requirement, in return, was that her sister and Jeddy accompany her as wardrobe mistress and companion.

She exchanged an encouraging little smile with Jeddy just after she was helped down by a royal footman in red-and-gold livery. Then she stood waiting for him to emerge amid the commotion of all the other coaches coming to a stop behind them. Two performances, and they would be on their way back to London. That was part of the arrangement. She could tolerate that, and shine, she had decided. With any luck, a new paramour would be beside him as the king watched her perform. She would take her bows and be on her way back to London with her pride and her heart fully intact.

The play itself was better, at least there was that, written once again particularly for her by Mr. Dryden. And the part fit her like a glove. This one at last, she had breathed a sigh of relief, was a comedy.

"I can hardly believe my eyes," Rose said in a low voice as they made their way through an inner courtyard, then past a small chapel where Henry VIII had married his notorious second queen, Anne Boleyn. The echo of shoe heels and whispers were the only sounds as each of the actors was shown to their own apartments; Nell's room was left for last. She held Jeddy's small hand protectively, as a palace guard opened the final carved, rounded door. It made a low squeal as it moved back on its hinges. Nell entered first, and Rose followed, gasping and gawking at the grandeur like a street vendor in Pudding Lane. The fragrance of roses and lilacs in large crystal vases overwhelmed them, as a warm summer breeze through an open oriel window ruffled the gold silk draperies on their heavy iron pole.

The room was dominated by a massive poster bed and two intricately carved chests on which the flowers had been placed. The walls were adorned with three Flemish tapestries, each depicting hunting scenes. There were lacquered cabinets and silver on all of the tabletops, and a trundle bed for a small servant. There was also an adjoining room with a smaller bed, dressing table, and French folding screen.

"The performance will be at three, and His Majesty wishes you to join him for dinner at one."

"You may tell the king I never eat before a performance."

"Nelly!" Rose gasped. "You're not serious! 'E is the king, after all!"

"And I am an independent woman. Never again will I make the mistake of forgettin' it."

The guard bit back a smile. "His Majesty anticipated your response, Mrs. Gwynne," he said. "I am to tell you if that is the case, His Majesty has left you something on the night table that he hopes will help you find inspiration in wearing it as you perform today." Dutifully, he made a bow and was gone.

"Well, you can't very well say no to that and keep your head, can you?" Rose pressed her sister excitedly.

Nell moved slowly toward the bed as Rose and Jeddy stood in stunned silence. There, on a small carved walnut table beside a candle lamp and a book of prayer, was a glittering pear-shaped diamond suspended from a thick gold chain.

"'Oly mother of . . . ," Rose sputtered as they all inched closer to it. Her fingers trembled as they splayed across her mouth. "Look at that, will you, Nelly!"

"'Ow could I look at anythin' else!"

"I fancy 'e *is* serious about you, after all."

Nell picked up the necklace and touched the diamond with one careful fingertip. "Now don't go readin' more into it than there is, Rose. 'E is a very rich man with power enough to get what 'e wants without thinkin' much of it."

"Well, 'e certainly 'as gone to a lot of trouble to get you out to 'Ampton Court if 'e's not serious!"

Nell frowned, looking at her sister. "The king of England could 'ave any woman in the world, Rose, ladies, countesses, and duchesses alike, and, if the stories are right, 'e 'as done just that, many times over."

"Maybe all that is not what gives 'im a shiver any longer. Maybe 'tis a low sort with the power to give 'im more simple pleasures 'e favors?"

"A girl like me doesn't flatter 'erself. 'Tis a tumble 'e wants with a popular, young actress, as 'e did with Moll Davies, nothin' more." She set the necklace back on the night table and looked at Rose and Jeddy, still standing there before her, both with stunned expressions. "Don't look at me like that, the two of you. I know what I am. What *we* are. I'm 'ere now, by 'is command, so I'll take what 'e offers. But don't 'ave me go lookin' for more than that!"

The vast chamber in which they performed, with its vaulted ceiling, was done up so well it looked like the theater back in London, Nell thought, as she lingered behind the curtain of the stage that had been erected there. It certainly had the feel of the King's Theater, with a broad wooden platform, heavy velvet draperies, and all of the same lushly painted scenery. Costumed as a boy, with huge bell sleeves and knee-length pants, Nell came onto the stage to uproarious applause from the king's courtiers and friends.

Each time she delivered a line, the crowd broke into fits of laughter. Nell was back on her game. There was a rhythm to the entire play. She was at ease, and, for the first time in a long time, she did not want it to end. And as the last lines were spoken, as Nell looked out over the glittering lamplight and the grand crystal chandeliers dripping their ivory-colored wax, the king's smile was brightest among the others. She bobbed a whimsical little curtsy in response, holding her wide knee pants out to the sides, and tilting her head comically as the king's diamond glittered prominently against her throat. Everyone laughed. Lord, but she loved that sound! She fed on it. It meant their approval. Audiences gave her a kind of acceptance she never had in any aspect of her life. Now, here, before nobles and royalty, she was a success.

Exhilarated by the heady triumph, and full of renewed pride, Nell skipped off the stage at the play's end, and dashed back behind the heavy curtain. As she knew he would be, the king was there a moment later, his strong, dark eyes shining, arms crossed over his chest. He was dressed elegantly, in a claret-colored coat, with gleaming gold buttons down the length of it. He wore a white-lace jabot, and a dark, curled periwig that matched his mustache. She did not want it to matter. She did not want to crave his touch. She did not want to feel the excitement flipping over and over inside of her as he looked at her. Yet she did.

"I don't believe anyone has ever refused me," he said with a twisted smile.

"I don't believe *I* would be said to have altered that fact."

His smile lengthened. "What would you call your reply, then?"

"I said only that I could not eat before the performance."

He took her hand in his own and raised it to his lips.

"Your Majesty could have done with makin' your intentions a trifle more clear, since it 'as been such a long time since I 'ave seen you."

"Very well." Charles tipped up her chin then and kissed her, his lips lingering on hers as his arms went around her. To be kissed by him was unlike anything she had ever felt. The connection was different. The moment. His touch. The way he looked at her, as if she were the most magnificent creature in the world. Her desire for him in return was powerful. How easy it would be, she thought, to submit more to this man, with not just her body but her heart.

Feeling her yield, he drew away and raised a brow. "And how did you find that?"

"Much more clear." She tried to smile.

He fingered the jewel at her throat. "You do look glorious in diamonds."

"If only it 'ad not taken you so long to realize it, sire."

"You do say just what comes to your mind, don't you?"

"Nearly always, I'm afraid."

"Ah, Nelly, how you make me laugh! And I do so need humor in my life."

"The weight of England must be a heavy burden for one man."

"You know not the half of it."

"Laughter then should be a potent tonic."

He ran the back of his finger along her cheek. "You do not eat before a performance, and I cannot think for want of you now after it."

"I warn Your Majesty, I'll not come to you cheaply, nor go quietly this time."

"Duly warned," he teased her in a husky voice, linking her hand with his own, and leading her through a small paneled side door that gave way to a concealed staircase with direct access to his private apartments.

"So, I've not put you off entirely?" she asked with a little laugh as they climbed the steep stone steps.

"I look forward to every fascinating moment. You inspire me, Nelly. You truly do."

His vaulted bedchamber, hung with three massive Gobelin tapestries, and draperies of heavy green silk, was littered with spaniels. A few lifted their sleepy heads from his bed, a chair, and the carpet near the fire, grunted, and then fell back to sleep. Others scuttled toward the door, tumbled over one another, and growled. The scent of their fur, and a hint of urine, mingled with old fabric and candle wax.

"Don't mind them," he said of his spaniels. "They really are everywhere."

"Why do you 'ave so many?"

"You know how it is: Two make four, then one day it's six. I can't bear to give any of them up. It's a bad habit I have with a great many things. They'll not bite you, however. That, you will be leaving up to me!"

They moved to his bed, a grand old canopied thing, curtained in heavy tapestry fabric of green, blue, and gold. He lifted her on top of the rich tapestried silk bedcover, and met her upon his knees. He kissed her again and again, and her heart began to hammer. The king took his time showing her the things they might do together, the ways of pleasuring each other he liked the best. It was a secret world nothing had prepared her for, but she did not blush nor shrink away. Nell felt her body respond to everything, and she was changed by it. The world she knew with Hart and Buckhurst was gone, ages old. Forgotten.

A king's desire had become her own.

As they lay sated and chuckling about everything and nothing, as lovers do, Charles said, "I want to know about you, how you survived all of life's obstacles, how exactly you managed to triumph as you have. I want to know everything."

"As with most things, the fantasy is far more entertainin' than the reality."

"You told me once that your mother was not an enthusiast for reality."

"Your Majesty remembers."

"You must call me Charles when we are alone, sweetheart," he said. "Difficult for us to be on an equal footing when we are like this together, without it."

"We're hardly equal." Nell smiled and wrapped her arms around her knees. "If we were, I'd be callin' you Charlie."

"Then do it."

"You can't mean it. You're the king!"

"I already believe you are the one person who would tell me the unvarnished truth if I asked. That is a rare thing. I trust you to call me what you like."

"You *trust* me?"

"You cannot imagine how much I would like to entirely trust you, yes."

"You do talk a sweet game."

"Truthfully, I've had a lifetime of practice at that. And in spite of how trivial this sounds, it is different with you. I'm not certain I can tell you why. Lord, I could scarcely function, knowing you were arriving here at Hampton Court today."

Nell smiled. "A finer compliment a girl could not 'ave from 'er king."

Charles pressed her back and arched over her again. "And from her man?"

"Are you my man, sire?"

"I don't suppose so, no. The king, *he* belongs to too many people already. His life is forever complicated. No, not the king. But Charles, the man, now there is a soul ripe for the taking."

She laughed then, a rich, earthy sound that was pure Nell. "Then take it I shall!"

"What the devil are you blathering on about?" Barbara Palmer ranted, hands on her hips as she stood poised outside the door to the king's private apartments in sunlight that came in like streamers through the long hallway windows. "I am welcome at Hampton Court any time I please!"

"Not this time," replied Buckingham flatly, barring her way. He met her thread for thread, dressed elegantly in gray silk, brocade shoes, and a plumed hat.

He had promised to keep the other women in the king's life at bay while he romanced Nell. And so, with William Chiffinch to alert him, the king's dearest friend would keep his word. It was all part of the duty, he had mused.

Barbara tried to push past him through the door. But Buckingham held firm to his stance.

"Allow me to pass, George!"

"I'm afraid not, milady."

"It's that Davies trollop again, isn't it?"

"I can safely say that he is quite finished with her."

"Oh, nonsense! You know perfectly well the tart bore his child, assuring he shall *never* be truly finished with her!"

Knowing of Castlemaine's growing paranoia and suspicion as her grip on the king loosened more each day made it all the more sporting for the vengeful duke. Buckingham was quite enjoying this. A bit of turnabout was not only fair play, it was absolutely delicious. Everything was working exactly according to plan.

"Tell me who she is, damn you!"

"No one my Lady Castlemaine knows or cares about, I assure you."

"I know them *all* sooner or later, and all I care about any of them is that they are gone!"

George leaned against the wall and crossed his arms over his chest. "That is not entirely true. You quite touted the merits of Frances Stuart, and to her face directly, if memory serves."

"Your memory is obviously the cesspool your mind is! You know perfectly well I only touted her, as you say, to secure my own place, as His Majesty was angry over my bedding *you*!"

The absurdity of that hit them at the same moment and they both began to laugh, one spurred on the more by the other, until both slid down together, onto the floor, in a voluminous pile of silk, lace, and stockinged legs.

"We are positively a pair!" Barbara giggled in a way that did not seem totally in touch with sanity.

"On that we at least can agree."

She grabbed his collar at both sides then suddenly, her expression changed as quickly as her mood. "Tell me who she is, George. He would not have ordered you to bar my way if she weren't a serious contender."

"She's certainly nothing like you."

"You know her well?"

"We've met," he hedged.

"Will he be showing her off then, making her official?"

"I should rather think you could depend upon it."

Barbara struggled to stand again, holding up the skirts of her dress. "You simply must tell me her name!"

"Oh, now. Surprises are so much more fun, don't you agree?"

"He'll not cast me over for her, if that's what you are counting on, with your twinkling eyes and clever grin. You who I rescued myself from the Tower. And now I am coming to rue that particular day!"

He stood then as well and pressed down the rumpled parts of her gown in a way a father might do to a child. "You know perfectly well that I have always counted on you." *Especially when you are your own worst enemy,* he thought. But he did not speak the words, for what that much honesty would cost him with her. He wished to be rid of her at court, of course. But he knew only too well that she was not gone yet.

There was to be a banquet once the king's players had returned to London. Nell was meant to remain at Hampton Court and attend it as the king's personal guest. Rose Gwynne sat on the edge of her sister's bed in astonishment as a league of royal dressers, a seamstress, and a Frenchman to style her hair began the intricate process of covering Nell in rich fabrics and elegant shoes, transforming her into a proper court lady.

The two leaded-glass windows with tinted crests near the bed were open, ushering in sweet, warm air. The sun began to set on the horizon, just beyond the formal rose gardens and pond dotted with white swans. The sound of the splashing fountains that had lulled them to sleep at night, along with the music of the crickets in the hedgerows, was now all but drowned out by the chattering and dashing about of the king's personal staff.

"If mother could see us now," Rose mused, while Jeddy sat at her heels rolling a small blue ball back and forth in her hands, as if she were any other little child of a royal household.

"She'd take every bit of this away, too. Just like always." Nell glanced over at Jeddy. This odd, silent little girl had been the best thing to come out of her disastrous summer liaison with Lord Buckhurst. In so brief a time, she had come to care for the child with the huge eyes so full of mystery and fear.

"You really *must* hold still, mistress!" the dresser exclaimed, a stout, middle-aged woman with gray, deep-set eyes and turned-up nose, as she wrestled with the corset stays at Nell's already tiny waist.

Nell regarded her reflection in the full-length mirror. She had never felt so pushed or poured into anything, yet never in her life had she looked so elegant. Her hair was swept back into a twist with long side ringlets; and beneath the diamond choker given her by the king, she had been pinched and pressed into a sapphire blue gown pulled back at the knee with silk ribbons to show a blue-and-yellow striped satin skirt underneath. The bodice was fitted tightly, the square neckline cut so low that her bosom was forced up and forward seductively. Behind her mirrored reflection, she was surprised to see Jeddy's upturned face and her open, approving smile.

"I don't look an absolute fool in this?" she asked Rose, who alone could be trusted to tell her the truth.

"You look like a princess, Nelly," Rose said as she gripped a fringed velvet pillow and drew it against her chest. "I'm envious down to my toes!"

Nell took a step back, then spun around. The beaded hem of her dress whispered along the floor, sounding like little bells. Jeddy let out a joyful little huff, almost a giggle, and Nell felt her own heart give way for her even further. "And what do *you* think, Jeddy? A jade dressed up like a proper lady, am I?"

The little girl smiled keenly, but still she did not answer. In her months with Nell, she had yet to utter a word, though Nell knew by her face and expression-filled eyes that she understood everything. It was likely she had been beaten in her past; certainly, she was still very frightened. To the world, Jeddy was supposed to be a charming little token, a pet. But to Nell, she was someone dear. Trust took time, Nell knew.

"All right, then. I suppose I'm ready as I'll ever be!"

She entered the glittering banqueting hall that evening half a pace behind the king. For most of their parade through the crowd of guests, both foreign dignitaries and courtiers, she could not quite catch her breath. Images played across her mind: of an earlier time, one in which it seemed she was another girl entirely, one who had begged for scraps, fought off foul-smelling men as her own mother lured them upstairs in a bawdy house. And later, as she sold oranges for a few shillings in a soiled linen dress, and never had quite enough herself to eat.

By midnight, she had lost track of how many notable people to whom she had been introduced, and all the while he kept her hand carefully pressed upon his arm, leading her, guiding her. The evening whirled by with Nell in a cocoon of joy, laughing, dancing, and sharing a world with the king of England that only a short time before, in Newmarket, she could not have begun to imagine.

After they had danced until Nell's feet ached, they took a stroll together through the grounds, past decades-old gardens with hedges and fountains, and vast lawns with dark woodlands beyond. They went then into a second wing of the palace and into an intimate little wood-paneled room beside the gallery where the music and laughter could still be heard. But here, the air was clear and more full of clever quips than raucous laughter. Around a table, seven or eight of the king's friends were playing an intense game of cards. Upon their entrance, they all stood and bowed to him until he nodded. Then, without ceremony, they returned to their game.

"And here we have the *real* festivities," said Charles. "And not just any card game, mind you. This is basset. Very competitive, indeed, with this wily group."

"Life's so much more of a thrill in that sort of company." Nell smiled.

"Well, now," exclaimed a barrel-chested man with pepper-gray hair and a thick Scottish accent. Having heard her, he looked up from the card-strewn table to assess her with a more critical eye. "Are ye no' just a wee breath of fresh air, lass."

The king's smile bore a hint of pride. "Nell Gwynne, may I present the Duke of Lauderdale, John Maitland, one of my Privy Council, and a rather notorious and rakish old jackanapes, I'm afraid. His wife is clever and bold, and certainly his better half, which is why I keep him around."

"I'll consider myself warned," Nell said, her friendly voice warming the air around them.

"Could an old friend invite Mrs. Gwynne to try her luck with us?"

"If she is not made to lose too dreadfully to an old schemer like you," quipped the king.

With his approval, and beneath a very watchful eye, Nell sat with the others and quickly picked up the rules of the game. Before long, she was even winning a bit. She sank more easily into the chair and took a long swallow of French brandy from Lauderdale's glass, then held up her cards as if she belonged there every bit as much as each of them. Lauderdale exchanged an approving glance with the king.

"So tell me, Mrs. Gwynne," the Duke of York offhandedly asked as he lay down a card. "Which do you find more rewarding these days, performing for all of London or simply for our king?"

The double entendre was clear, and Nell felt the king tense beside her. Her smile was unfazed. She put down her own card with a flourish and met him head-on. "There's no denyin' I do love an audience, Your Grace. But there's somethin' to be said for the benefits of one very big—and important—standin' ovation."

Everyone at the table erupted in approving laughter, even the king, and Nell felt the tension slide away as they all realized that she had won another hand.

"So what is it like to have been dreadfully poor and now to find such overwhelming favor?" the king's brother pressed indelicately, for the challenge of it.

"Very like taking the nasty cod liver oil your sort fancy, I should imagine. Not all that pleasin' to the taste, but you can do it if you set your mind right properly to it."

They looked down at her cards and were all amused that she had won yet again. "Do not tell us, Your Majesty, that she has never played this game."

"Ah, Nell is, among other things, an amazingly quick study."

"'Amazing' being the operative word," laughed the Duke of Lauderdale. "Your Mrs. Gwynne most certainly is that!"

"Thank you for teachin' me," she said when it was over, and she had not, as the king commanded, lost too badly.

"It was a rare pleasure," Lauderdale said, nodding to her in such a grand and courtly gesture that Nell felt delighted. Here with these people, on the arm of the king himself, she felt almost at ease.

As they strolled out into the moonlight of the little inner courtyard again, with its ordered French parterre, dotted with Greek stone statuary, Charles took her hand. Then he stopped her suddenly, and pressed a kiss onto each of her fingers, working the tip of his tongue over each gently rounded fingernail. "Spend the night with me, Nell. The whole night."

She bit her bottom lip to stop a smile. "You mean like a proper mistress?"

"I mean like Nell Gwynne, the woman who has captured my heart. My friends love you, London loves you, and I have been entirely won over."

"Your heart, you say?" she asked, with her usual wry smile.

"I did indeed," replied the king.

Chapter 16

NONE EVER HAD SO STRANGE AN ART HIS
PASSION TO CONVEY INTO A LIST'NING VIRGIN'S HEART
AND STEAL HER SOUL AWAY.
—*Sir Charles Sedley*

A T the end of October, Nell was back on the stage in London and the king, she was told, had just returned from Windsor with the queen. During the first ten days of their separation, he had sent her a small token each day. Among them was an ivory-handled hair comb, a silver patch box, a bracelet, and a strand of pearls.

But as the days became weeks, once again he did not send for her.

Three weeks passed, and Nell sat in the tiring-room, surrounded by other actresses, having rouge applied to her cheeks. Everyone at the theater had clambered for details of what had occurred at Hampton Court after they had returned to the city, and if she was meant to be a new, proper mistress to His Majesty now. The truth was that she knew even less about their future than she did about who his other companions might be. It seemed to her a very delicate dance. Say too much and appear boastful, as Moll Davies had. Say nothing at all, appear uninterested, and end like Beck Marshall's older sister, Anne, who had briefly, two years earlier, had her own royal affair.

"The king is here! He's here!" Richard cried out.

Her heart began to pound, almost as it had before her very first performance. It was sudden and unexpected. She had missed him so desperately, but she dare not admit that to him. Emotion was weakness, and she could not be weak with the king if she meant to win some substantial part in his life. There should be not a spark of jealousy in her behavior. "Is the queen with him?" she quietly asked.

"No—"

"Hello, Nell."

It was not the voice she expected just then cutting between Richard and herself. Still, she knew it before she turned around. The sense of dread at the haughty tone turned her skin to goose-flesh.

"Hello, Moll," she said in reply.

Richard stayed glued to the spot near the door as Nell stood, and the two actresses faced each other, just before the play was to begin. The sound of laughter and the commotion out in the theater filled the awkward silence.

"I thought I should come back and extend my regards since you're back on the stage. I'd 'eard you'd gone off with Lord Buckhurst."

"Ancient 'istory, I'm afraid."

"Well, *I* am 'ere, of course, makin' *new* 'istory with 'Is Majesty," she said boastfully. "I tell you, Nell, I so needed an afternoon out with our daughter. She's growin' so fast, you can't rightly imagine."

Reference to a child. It was a direct hit, and Nell felt it deep in the center of her chest, not far off from her heart. "Congratulations," she forced herself to say. She was a better actress than Moll Davies would ever be.

"Thank you then, Nell. 'Twas a long and difficult pregnancy, and not without its, shall we say, *complications*, for 'Is Majesty and I. But," she added, honing her gaze, "I'm pleased to report that now everythin' is back to normal."

One beat, then two. Nell felt fury rise up—not at the king's infidelity, that was to be expected. She understood it. She forced herself to accept it. But this woman's flaunting of it at her intentionally was too much. "Well, I *do* 'ope that you get everythin' you deserve and more," Nell said.

"Oh, believe me, I intend to." The angry sparks between them now were hot enough to ignite a fire, yet still they smiled as if they were the very best of friends.

After Moll left, Nell flung an oak-handled hairbrush at the door, barely missing Beck Marshall, who was just coming around the corner to tell Nell she was due onstage. Richard led Nell gently toward the door. "Lie down with dogs, you get fleas," he said.

"Moll Davies is *no* companion of mine!"

"Seems to me you lie down in the same places."

"'Tis not like that between us! Unlike that cow, Moll Davies, *I* actually love 'im!"

"*Love?* Is *that* what you've had to tell yourself in order to bed such a notorious lecher?"

Nell slapped him hard across the face, and the crack of flesh stilled things in the room for a moment. "I thought you were my friend, Richard."

"I have always been your friend. Certainly the only one bold enough to tell you the truth."

"You're only jealous!"

"Yes, Nell, I suppose I am at that."

So it was out between them. Nell had always known it somewhere deep down, but it was an entirely different thing to have it admitted to, as it was now. And then, in the next moment, the truth became a great barrier. They stood looking at each other as the activity slowly rose back to a crescendo around them." I'm sorry," Nell said awkwardly.

"It's my own fault. I always knew what would happen."

"I do love you dearly, Richard." She held out a hand to touch his face, but he stepped back.

"As a friend?"

"As a friend."

"Nell! It's time!" Beck Marshall called to her, holding on to the doorjamb as she stood in the doorway. Nell was still looking into the face of tender kindness and patience, wishing so dearly that she felt differently about him.

"Well," he said to her, and exhaled when she did not respond. "You'd better go. Another brilliant performance awaits."

"You're right, I should go," she replied. She was ashamed that she could not force herself to say more to her first real friend in the theater, a man who had rescued her not once, but twice.

She thought about Richard, not Charles, as she ran through the motions, and her lines, as she made her curtsies, and received the adoring crowd. The king had a grand bouquet of blue hyacinths delivered to her in a crystal vase when the play was over, but he did not come to her himself. She knew why, of course. So did Richard Bell. Moll Davies had cleverly recovered that place in his world. It really was a more intricate game than she had bargained for, suitable for only the very best players. And just now, Nell felt as if she would never quite know all of the rules.

❧❧

The king sat in the first row of chairs in his vaulted chapel facing the river at Whitehall. Beside him was the queen in a dress of gray wool and ivory lace. Beside her was the Duke of York, who sat stone-faced as a psalm was read, echoing across the ancient stones and the soaring, arched ceiling above them. Beside the king was the Duke of Buckingham, but his mind was miles from this place and this moment. Carefully, Buckingham watched the king's brother for open signs of his ever-growing Catholic loyalties, something he might use as a weapon when the moment came.

Like a skein of yarn, it could all unravel, and he must be prepared. With the potential for Monmouth to one day be legitimatized as true heir, the Duke of York could conceivably be displaced. Monmouth needed an adviser if that were to happen. York had Arlington, Buckingham's rival. Monmouth was desperate and, thus, more malleable. A grateful Monmouth—or, if not that, perhaps a fertile new queen—he could control. A zealous Duke of York, led by the fervor of his faith, he never would.

Control at court—power—was everything.

After the service, Buckingham stepped into stride with the king beneath a truncated stone archway that faced a little inner courtyard. It was always a contest among the privy councillors to see who would get there first. Their shoe heels clicked in time on the ancient tile walkway. Everyone else, including the queen, walked behind them much more slowly, chattering in low tones. "Did you see it?" George carefully asked the king. He saw the troubled expression, the heavy frown, in response.

"So my brother made the sign of the cross. What of it?"

"He's a Catholic heir in a Protestant country," the duke countered, his voice urgent, low.

"Zounds, man! I well know it! But what would you have me do about it?"

"The people have already been through too much! I tell you, if they knew—"

"I love Monmouth with every fiber of my being, but I'll not recognize a bastard child in my brother's stead!"

"But if he is your legitimate son—"

"You know very well that he is not."

"Come on, Charles, this is me! I was there with the two of you! I saw you with Lucy myself, calling yourselves husband and wife."

Their eyes met. The king's were hard, full of opposition. "Youthful zeal, not fact!"

"All it would take would be confirmation from you. No one else was there to say it didn't happen, and poor Lucy Walter is dead now. Your brother would be reduced from the succession, thus the Catholic threat to Protestant England would be vanquished. And you would have the heir you have always needed."

"Catherine is the only woman I have ever married."

They broke off from the others then and walked alone through a long stone gallery, which held the night's cold in spite of the warm autumn air beyond. "Then, if you won't name Monmouth, for the love of God, divorce Catherine, and get a wife who can give you proper heir! Your involvement in Lord Roos's petition for divorce has opened the way wide for yourself. You cannot tell me you didn't know it would when you interceded."

It was true the bill had just passed through the House of Lords, allowing the legally divorced Lord Roos the ability to remarry, and Charles had allowed himself to consider what it might be like, in spite of all his earlier promises.

"Why do you want this so desperately?"

"Since we were children," Buckingham began, "I have only *ever* had your best interest at heart. I love you enough to remind you of your duty to leave a proper legacy."

"And what of your own legacy, George? Where is that in all of this?"

"My future has always been wrapped up with your own, Charles. I am, you well know, a faithful servant." He nodded in a courtly gesture that was awkward between two old friends.

Charles put his hand on George's shoulder, trying to bridge the chasm his friend had created by constantly harping on this objectionable point. "I shall speak with him, all right?" he said gently. "But there must be some sort of tolerance in England for the Catholics. I am not without understanding as to their passion for God."

"You cannot mean to put *their* passion over the wishes of *your* Protestant country?"

Charles looked back at the group, which lingered now a few steps behind them, near a marble statue of Henry VII. The truth was, as king, he walked a fine line religiously and politically. The Dutch wars had been such a disaster that he felt the need for absolute caution in all circumstances that might risk the good of England.

"I am, above all things, desirous of security for England, and I am *not* certain I can maintain that if the Dutch and the French remain such staunch allies against me. That is a dangerous and very delicate position to be in. Can you imagine what would happen if my Catholic brother was removed from the line of succession? If I openly berate my brother for his faith, and King Louis hears of it, it could well backfire in the French allying ever more strongly with the Dutch against me."

"Trying to be all things to all people is difficult work."

"George, trust me, you will never know." An affable smile broke then across the king's face. "Come, old friend. Ride with me out to Enfield Chase. That will clear my head for the excursion to the theater later this afternoon."

"Joining Your Majesty in that shall be my pleasure," Buckingham smiled.

As the coach turned, nearing the grand stone Holbein Gate, Nell felt her mouth go very dry. Her heart was racing. The great iron gates were lit by huge flambeaux and the coach paused only briefly, the royal crest on its door being the route to access. It felt as if her whole life was at stake in this evening; the welfare of Rose, Jeddy, and herself depended on it. What the king liked about her was her humor and simplicity. She must remember that with every smile and every carefree laugh, even though she felt far more deeply for him, felt much more than the need to find security. She loved him. She knew that. But it was too soon for him to know it.

"I'm glad you agreed to come," he said with a note of hesitation as she stood in the little entry alcove to his private bedchamber after her performance that afternoon. Near the hearth, a pup roused from a dream, squealed, then dropped off to sleep once again.

Nell pressed her hands onto her hips. "Did you honestly think I'd refuse?"

"All I know for certain is that I have been distracted since last we met."

"'Ave you, now?"

"Well, I have been keenly aware that through circumstances of my own foolish making, I have not paid attention to you in nearly the way I wished."

"And you mean to change that, do you?"

"Oh, indeed I do." He kissed her, his mouth lingering.

He pulled her close, and she shivered at the way he so quickly possessed all of her. Nell drew him closer and wrapped her arms around his broad back as he pulled her down with him onto the bed. There was nothing like this in all the world, she thought now as she always did. Touching him, being touched, that was all.

Afterward, he moved away from her and reached toward his bedside table, where, among the stack of leather-bound books, there was a small silver chest studded with pearls. He handed it to her, still smiling. "Open it."

She pressed back the lid a little warily, and saw a single key lying on a bed of red velvet. "The key to your 'eart?" she quipped.

"Better than that, I hope, at least for now. The key unlocks the front door to a house in Lincoln's Inn Fields. It is your new home."

She could not quite believe what she had just heard. She knew that it was the largest square in London. Lord Buckhurst had once told her that the lords of Coventry lived there, as well as the Earl of Sandwich. Nell kissed each of his cheeks, his nose, and then his mouth. "'Ow will I ever be able to thank you, Charlie?"

"I do hope you'll think of a way. In fact"—he grinned—"I am counting on it."

"My own 'ouse?" she asked, still incredulous.

"With furniture and all the particulars. Most important, with only a single key—yours."

She could see by his smile how enormously pleased he was with himself.

A small side door, partially hidden, opened, and a tall man entered the bedchamber wearing starched black and a tall, white cravat. "Does Your Majesty wish me to escort the lady away now?"

An awkward silence followed. Nell's world felt wrapped up in this moment because what the man said had made her suddenly feel tawdry.

"No, thank you, Chiffinch," said the king. "Mrs. Gwynne will be staying the night, and as many, from now on, as she likes. In the morning, see that my coach is readied. We shall be going together to Lincoln's Inn Fields once we have broken our fast."

Chapter 17

NEXT TO COMING TO A GOOD UNDERSTANDING WITH
A NEW MISTRESS, I LOVE A QUARREL WITH AN OLD ONE.
—*George Etheridge*

THE king was still in his dressing gown, Nell in her chemise, and their feet were bare. Charles sat with her in a tall armchair covered in Spanish leather. They were in the elegantly paneled, high-ceilinged drawing room of the house in Lincoln's Inn Fields, not far beyond the Strand. Coaches clattered along the cobblestones beyond the velvet-draped windows as Nell sat on the king's lap, hands linked behind his neck. Her hair was only partially bound by the ivory clip he had given her; the rest of her unruly curls lay on her silk covered shoulders. Across from them, seated on two matching straight-backed chairs upholstered in needlepoint and a red-velvet-covered divan, sat the Duke of Buckingham, the Earl of Arlington, Thomas Clifford, and the Duke of Lauderdale.

"This is all rather unorthodox, if I may say, Your Majesty," Clifford said with obvious discomfort as Rose Gwynne trod carefully, laying a tray of marzipan and peeled oranges onto a small pearl-inlaid table between them. The air was made instantly sweet. Rose was healthier now, and it showed in the color that had risen back into her cheeks; her cough had at last disappeared. With a hint of pride, Nell glanced at her sister, smiled, and nodded a thanks. There were other servants, naturally, to perform such functions, but it gave Rose a purpose, now that she had recovered, to move about and do things for Nell and the king.

"Quite a change," Buckingham agreed with a cautious smile.

Charles kissed Nell's cheek. "Well, gentlemen, it seems a great many things are changing these days. At present, I do not wish to be parted from Nell here. So you take your king as you find him, and happily, I presume."

"Indeed, Your Majesty," Arlington flattered, with an overly solicitous smile.

Buckingham, his great rival, shot him a nasty stare.

Since they had first set foot together inside the impressive three-story house, with its great bow window, ivy-covered brick facade, and neatly trimmed hedge to the street, Charles had brought the court here. It was better, he said, than to be forced to leave the little world he was building with Nell. He did not wish to take her to his palace by the river. Too many interests competed with the old ghosts there, and he wanted to focus only on this new and wonderful world between them. As if life were all fresh and interesting to him again, Charles had personally helped Nell organize the household; he even advised her on hiring a proper maid to teach Rose how to comport herself. A spindly woman named Bridget Long was selected, even though Nell found her dour. He also helped her with a few court dance steps, and advised her on the proper tone with which to speak to her servants so that they would abide by her wishes. He seemed perfectly content to remain in this constant state of semiundress, in and out of bed with Nell. But now the business of being sovereign was at hand.

Louis XIV had gone to war against Spain. If England did not take a definitive stand, it would be seen as weak and indecisive, and they would be vulnerable abroad. Charles was ready to listen to his advisers on which way to proceed.

"We still cannot openly ally ourselves with France, of course, because of the religious question," Arlington began with his usual note of caution. "But your sister, the Princess Henrietta Anne, is well ensconced by her marriage to the king's brother at that court. Perhaps it is time to ask her to remind the French king that he is free to buy your neutrality."

"The good Lord knows England could use the capital," said Lauderdale.

"Support such as England's is clearly worth a strong price," Clifford pointed out.

"We certainly do not want to go up again against the united strength of the Dutch and French," Arlington chimed in. "Deals simply must be made. A stand taken."

Charles glanced at Buckingham as Nell toyed absently with the lace sleeve of her dressing gown. The king rubbed his chin between his thumb and forefinger, considering. "George, what have you to say of this?"

"I say, for our loyalty, we should ask of Louis a share of the Spanish conquests and commercial privileges once France wins. But do it through your sister, so it is not made known to our own people. Have the princess tell him covertly the price for our neutrality."

"Interesting," Charles contemplated.

"And if Your Majesty would not mind my saying," Arlington gently interjected, "if we ally with Holland, pressuring Spain into concessions toward France, that can only increase Louis's loyalty. Thus, we win on two fronts."

"Nell?" Charles suddenly turned to ask. His dark eyes were wide, and the expression in them absolutely serious as he stroked her hair. "What do *you* think of all this?"

In response, Nell tipped back her head and laughed. It was a deep, earthy sound that made the others around her smile. "What I think, sire, is that I'm well out of my league!"

"Never. Sharp as a tack, you are," Charles said with a bemused chuckle. Obligingly, his Privy Council laughed with him.

Nell was filled with pride that he thought enough of her to ask. She could have enormous power, Buckhurst once had told her, if she was ambitious and wise enough.

Before they adjourned, it was agreed by all but Buckingham that Lord Arlington, the most cautious and experienced diplomat among them, would be dispatched to Holland to solidify an alliance. Meanwhile, Princess Henrietta Anne, the favorite sister Charles called Minette, who was married to the French king's brother, would be called upon to privately make certain Louis understood it was an alliance entered into only to help France succeed with Spain.

When the others had begun to thank Nell for her hospitality, and to make their way back out onto the square, coaches and sedan chairs bustling past, Buckingham hung back from the rest. "Since you are having Minette privately reassure Louis as to your intentions, sire, might I advise something similar with the Dutch, just to keep England on firm footing all around?"

"What have you in mind?" Charles asked, his arm around Nell's waist, his mind already in her bed.

"Have Arlington, if he must be the one to go to them, indicate a secret clause in the arrangement, so they do not fear double-dealing against them. It would be my suggestion that

we make clear that we know that Louis has a power lust, and if
he has any intention of reneging on his promises to either
England or Holland, that we will turn on France. I believe it
would go a long way to mending old fences with our Dutch
enemy."

"Former enemy," Charles corrected.

"Of course, Your Majesty."

"Double-dealing with them both, is it then?"

"You must behave as a force to be respected and feared, one
who has the foresight to make powerful alliances. As your father
before you did."

"George, I would not presume to be as my father was."

Buckingham leaned closer to his childhood friend. "It is a
height to which you can aspire. And in that, Charles, he would be
proud of you."

Barbara Palmer waited impatiently in the dressing rooms of His
Majesty's privy apartments at Whitehall, commanded there by
the king, then left alone. With a bobbed curtsy, the maid told her
that the king was preparing to leave for Windsor but would be
with her presently. In the next room, just beyond the closed,
heavily carved doors, she could hear Buckingham, Clifford, and
the king whispering and then laughing. Her new shoes were too
tight, her feet hurt, and she was angry that Charles would dare
to keep her waiting like this. Two guards were posted on her side
of the door to see that she did not burst through them. There was
a time, not so long ago, when he could not bear to be separated
from her, nor would he bar her from any place in any of his
palaces. He sought her counsel, as well as her body. They were
partners in all things.

Now, apparently, she was to consider it great fortune to be summoned like a servant.

After more than half an hour, the heavy carved-oak doors were pulled open, the laughter beyond them faded, and the king strode through, hands linked behind his back. She was reminded in that instant, as the sun gleamed through the wall of windows, the bright light hitting his face, what a gloriously masculine man he still was. He radiated confidence, sensuality oozed from him. It seemed a very long time since they had lain together, and a lifetime ago that he had loved her.

She stood regally, every bit the noblewoman, in a dress of emerald brocade, as the doors were closed by two liveried guards, and Charles approached her, shoe heels echoing across parquet flooring. The dogs were not at his heels, which was a poor sign. She knew there was another girl—another pathetic actress, of all things—and that he had bought her a house, as he had Moll Davies.

Charles held both of her arms above the elbow in a play of sincerity, then kissed her cheek. "It is good to see you," he said, the strain between them now a palpable thing.

"Is it?"

"Of course, it is. But I shall come straight to the point."

"Please do."

"I'm leaving for Windsor within the hour—"

"So I've heard."

"While I am gone, I wish you to vacate your apartments here at Whitehall."

For the first time in many years, something of the real Barbara Palmer bled though, and her face and voice filled with panic. "Leave? This is my home! Our children's home!"

"Please do not make this any more difficult than it must be."

Her eyes narrowed. "Did you honestly believe that I would make this moment easy on you? That after all of these years together, I would simply pack up and walk away? Good Lord, Charles, tell me, please, this is not about that two-penny bottom-feeding *actress*—"

His eyes were angry now, his expression closed to her. "Stop it, Barbara."

"Stop what? Reminding you of our years together? Of our children?" She put her hands on his face to make him look at her, to see her as he once had. "Will you feel less guilt if you are not reminded of them here running about the gallery?"

"They will all be well cared for. You know that."

"And me? What of me, Charles? Now that you have a shiny new jade to chase and woo, am I to be tossed out like a used-up old tavern whore?"

"Your mouth is as foul and tiresome as the rest of you has become!"

"Now *there* is a great irony! The king with the open bedchamber door, and his own personal procurer, telling *me* what is foul!"

He slapped her hard across the face—harder, she saw by his expression, than he had meant to. Her hand went up to strike him in return, but he caught her by the wrist until she jerked her hand free. "How can you possibly look at me in surprise for where we've gotten to? All the time you were professing your love to me," Charles said in a seething tone, "you were bedding my best friend, and then my own son!"

"That was pure survival, Charles! The only way any woman can survive a lover with more ballocks than heart is to give him back as good as she's gotten!"

"You knew how I was, right from the start! I never lied to you about the others!"

"I knew! And I was fool enough then to think I could change you!"

His face was mottled red now, and a vein above his brow pulsed as he closed his fists and held them up to her. "I am king of England, by God, and I shall do as I please!"

"How well I know it! But does your precious Nell know it?" Barbara's expression was as full of anger as his. "Ah, well. If not now, she will soon enough. It's unavoidable, really."

A moment passed. There was a muscle still twitching in his jaw. "I've bought you a grand new house on Pall Mall," he flatly announced.

She studied him for a moment and then smiled, slyly. "For me to go quietly, to leave Whitehall without a fuss, I will go there a duchess."

"Impossible."

"Oh, now. We both know nothing is impossible. You've only just reminded me that you do precisely as you please. So let it please you, Charles." Her voice was cold and low. "Make me Duchess of Cleveland, just as we've spoken of for years, as you have taunted me with. I won't go quietly for less."

"I do despise you!"

"The feeling at this moment, I assure you, is more than mutual."

She spun away from him then, her emerald skirts swishing across the cold floor. "Duchess of Cleveland, *and* the house. That is my price."

Later that same afternoon, Nell sat beside the king in His Majesty's black coach, with six pure-white horses out in front, as they neared Windsor Castle. Gilded and emblazoned with the royal crest, and outfitted in red velvet within, it was a luxurious conveyance, and Nell sank against the seat, still not quite able to fathom her good fortune. She had asked to have her sister come along for support, and the king, who had yet to deny Nell anything, happily obliged, giving Rose and Jeddy a place in the coach directly behind his own.

Like Newmarket, Windsor was one of the king's favorite places to pass the warm months of summer, those too dangerous to remain in London for the constant risk of plague. His gaze out the coach window was distant as she took his arm and leaned against his shoulder.

"What troubles you?" she asked, pressing two fingertips onto his furrowed brow.

"I don't believe you'd want to know that."

"Then you'd be wrong. I've an interest in everythin' about you."

"Even if it concerns another of my mistresses?"

"So long as you've no idea of *me* lyin' with her, I'll gladly 'ear."

A smile played at the corners of his mouth as the coach jarred and swayed. "My Nelly. You do lighten my burden, you truly do."

"Then from now on, I'll consider it my official job. When I'm not troddin' the boards at Your Majesty's theater, that is."

"I've broken my ties with Lady Castlemaine. I asked her to leave Whitehall."

"Did you now?" She paused for a moment as the coach turned, and swayed, onto a more narrow, shadowy tree-lined lane. "Did you do that because of me?"

Charles looked over at her again, then took up both of her hands in his. "It was time. That is all. I do not love her."

"Did you once?"

"I believed I did."

"For years, they say."

"Aye, and other loves as well, even so. Several others." He lowered his eyes and was silent for a moment. "This is not an excuse, knowing what your own life has been, because there isn't one. But rather, it is an explanation. My youth was a miserable one, full of far too much sacrifice for anyone's liking." He closed his eyes then; images that pushed forward from the back of his mind were there now. But he would not let them forward. He could not. "The world of a king is responsibility and decisions."

"A fair bit of privilege, as well, I'd say."

"My goal since the day of my father's murder has been to sample every possible pleasure that I can, and, yes, with as many others as I can. It is the variety that wins me, and it is a fearsome, relentless draw. That is the cold truth of it." He looked at her then, his dark eyes distant and a little wary of her feelings. "Does knowing it make you care for me less?"

"I'm no one's innocent, Charlie. I know your 'eart and your prick are very different parts of you, indeed."

"If you really do understand, you would be the first."

"I rather fancy bein' the first at somethin'."

"Nell Gwynne, you are truly one in a million."

"And *you* are one in three, all of you named Charles!"

He ran a hand up beneath her skirt and along the length of her thigh. "Have you ever made love in a moving carriage?"

"Another new adventure with the king of England?"

"And another new one tomorrow, I hope. And to answer your question, I find I'm rather more pleased than ever to be your Charles the Third!"

Evenings at Windsor were a continuing cycle of banquets, dancing, card parties, cockfights, and debauched games. But the comparisons to any world Nell had ever known abruptly ended there. There were also daylong hunting trips from which the women at court were excluded. Nell began to spend much of the day in the company of the wives, mistresses, and ladies of the king's court. They were well-trained women who had a far better mastery of things, even down to how to wear their clothes. Nell was certain that the sheer weight of her petticoats, hidden beneath her new and complex fussy dresses and cagelike bodices, would be her undoing. It was so different from wearing a costume she thought, where movements were exaggerated intentionally. These women could glide in their petticoat armor, they smoothly dipped into curtsies, whereas she collapsed beneath the weight of the movement, the dress, and the underclothes contrivances.

Worst of all was that they softly chuckled when her laughter erupted quite beyond her control, highlighting the great difference between them.

Nell's general discomfort was made all the more intense by the round of unrelenting invitations from the wives who knew Queen Catherine and Lady Castlemaine. Nell knew they tolerated her, in her new, daringly low gown with her swelling bosom and awkward new hairstyle, only because she was in the highest favor with the king. But they made it clear, as they smiled at her while she forgot not to say "ain't," that she would only ever be an actress and a jade.

Still, they played cards in her company, and did needlework beside her in the privy gardens, with its clipped yew hedges and blossoming rosebushes. And they gossiped incessantly. Mary Fairfax, soon to marry the Duke of Buckingham, was the least abrasive. She sewed, smiled, and said little. Anna Maria, Lady Shrewsbury, with her thick, pursed lips, turned-up nose, and deep-set eyes, made up for it. Nell thought she, Buckingham's new mistress, was the worst.

"Poor dear *madame*, as they call our own Henrietta Anne in France," Shrewsbury scowled as she exchanged a glance with the Duchess of York. "I do not know how she can bear her days at the French court, with a husband who finds greater worth in the company of young men than in her."

Their heavy skirts rustled as they moved, and the air was too full of perfume.

"It is a scandal," Isabella, Lady Arlington, concurred, tittering obnoxiously behind an intricate lace fan. She had raised it suddenly, as if there was even a modicum of modesty about her. Her position as wife of the secretary of state had made her more bold than wise.

Margaret Ashley, wife of the chancellor of the exchequer, did not do needlework, she said, as her eyesight was poor; she could focus exclusively on stirring scandalous topics for a group of bored women to contemplate and laugh over.

"His Majesty's sister does her duty to the English Crown, first and foremost. But the Duke of Orléans much prefers to do his duty to the chevalier de Lorraine," said Lady Ashley, bringing a bawdy fit of laughter up from all of them.

Nell bit her lip and tried again to focus on the mass of thread and fabric on the hoop before her, making it resemble something near to a rose. She had no idea how so tedious an endeavor could be either entertaining or relaxing, or how they might have spent a lifetime practicing.

They sat collected on a wide flagstone path at the center of a lush flower garden, brimming with fat, fragrant pink roses and clematis, accented by huge statues of Greek goddesses. Beside them was a stone pond full of moss and water lilies. It had been the garden of

Queen Henrietta Maria, the king's mother, before the murder of her husband, before the dark days of Oliver Cromwell, and her exiled years in France, when all of the flowers were allowed to die, and the joys at court passed away behind sober form and prayer. Now the garden was back, and for the use of anyone at court, to gossip in, or while away the hours, since the new queen was away so often.

"Poor dear. Do you suppose she has the good sense to take her own lover yet?" Isabella asked.

"Hopefully, not a young coxcomb like Lord Buckhurst," Margaret Ashley cackled, tapping her knee. "That truly would be going from the kettle into the fire!"

They were like crows, Nell thought. Elegant, silk-clad crows. Nipping back and forth. Harsh. Crude. She was struggling not to spring up, toss down her needlework hoop, and run all the way back to London at the very moment she heard Buckhurst's name.

His image came flooding back at her. Their time together . . . the awkward parting. He was in France? At the court of Louis XIV? *That* was why he had never spoken to her after her return from Newmarket? "Why is Lord Buckhurst in France?" she heard herself ask.

"Sent by His Majesty personally, sweeting. Official business for the Crown," replied Lady Ashley nonchalantly.

"Business?"

"Trickery business only, I'll warrant you!" Shrewsbury laughed, and the sound was very like fingernails scratching brick. "'Tis what he gets for daring to tamper with someone who's already caught the king's wandering eye!"

Lady Arlington's gaze darted from Shrewsbury, who hushed suddenly. Nell's eyes shifted from one woman to the next. Slowly, all the court wives lowered their heads and went intently back to their needlework. But not before Nell saw a mocking smile, then two, as their chins hit their chests. It felt as if a huge stone in her throat was preventing her from speaking further.

It had been far simpler back in London, with her own house a protective barrier from this harshness. The king might care for her, but a future of trying her best to spar with these women, who had made a career of it, seemed at the moment a high price to pay.

"Forgive me, my dear," Isabella Arlington said insincerely. "We'd all forgotten that it was *your* favor from whom His Majesty sent the boy abroad."

Nell reddened. "Of course you 'ad."

Her corset cut into her rib cage. The shoes pinched her feet. She thought how the true Nell Gwynne had vanished. This strange concoction of a court girl remained. Even royal desire and a king's influence cannot make a lady from a common wench, that was becoming all too clear.

At the very moment when Nell felt certain she would either say something horrid or run foolishly back to her apartments, a small contingent of young men approached, wearing periwigs, smart summer cassock coats in brightly colored silk, and broad-brimmed, fashionable hats plumed with ostrich feathers. They looked like the fops and dandies back at the theater in London—wealthy, idle, and utterly condescending.

"Ah, there they are," said one, a thin young man with coal-black hair, his face and hands the color of a tallow candle. "Our own pack of she-wolves and a new lamb ready for slaughter."

"Well, if it isn't the merry band, come to taunt us," Shrewsbury countered dryly, then looked back at her needlepoint.

The other men laughed subtly as he drew nearer and extended a hand to Nell. "Do be cautious of this group, Mrs. Gwynne," he said in a low, cultured voice. "They will eat you alive, and smile all the while as they do it. Allow me to introduce myself, and my friends. I am John Wilmot, informally called Rochester by those who do not find me as entertaining as do my companions. And this is my closest friend, Henry Savile. Our squinting friend over there in the red cravat is Sir Carr Scrope, and our fourth is Laurence Hyde, son of the poor wretch who was once His Majesty's greatest friend. Now, thanks to Lady Shrewsbury's own *good friend*, the Duke of Buckingham, he is, alas, a father in exile."

Everyone at court knew of the torrid affair between Buckingham and Lady Shrewsbury, so the reference was lost on no one. Yet here she sat, unashamed, and right beside the naive girl Buckingham was poised to marry, Nell realized.

"Careful, Rochester," said John Maitland's wife, Elizabeth. "I've heard the king himself say he only finds your poems and your sense of humor moderately entertaining these days."

Nell was feeling as if she had been rescued. "You're a poet, Mr. Rochester?"

At that, the ladies around her laughed cruelly. "Mrs. Gwynne, this libertine before you, quite inexcusably, is no mister, but the second Earl of Rochester."

"Forgive me," she said.

"'Tis a tiresome old family title, useful only to give me passage into court, and out of less-fortunate entanglements."

"Since you are here now," said Lady Ashley, "do share a poem with us. It can be so tedious without the men around."

"Not that again, Margaret. I've never understood any of his obscene trifles." Lady Arlington rolled her eyes.

"That's only because you live such a remarkably dull life," Henry Savile joked.

Rochester smiled slyly and sank onto the ground, sprawling out, his head propped up by an elbow. A moment later, his companions joined him in various states of repose. Plucking a blade of grass and inserting it between his lips, Rochester thought for a moment, then began:

> *"Naked she lay, clasped in my longing arms,*
> *I, filled with love, and she all over charms;*
> *Both equally inspired with eager fire.*
> *Melting through kindness, flaming in desire.*
> *With arms, legs, lips close clinging to embrace,*
> *She clips me to her breast, and sucks me to her face.*
> *Her nimble tongue with——"*

"My Lord of Rochester!" Margaret Ashley gasped. "I believe we have heard quite enough!"

"What do you call that?" Nell asked. She was feeling suddenly among friends at last.

"The poem is called 'The Imperfect Enjoyment,' my dear. Do you like it so far?"

"Quite. Only what is imperfect about it?"

"As it goes on, I'm afraid the poor boy spends himself in her hand and, alas, cannot give her the great joy they both desire."

"A lamentable problem of the very young," Scrope remarked cleverly.

"Not always exclusively," Hyde put in, which brought laughter from the three other men, even the tawdry Lady Shrewsbury. But Margaret Ashley was stone-faced.

"Presenting filth as poetry is as vulgar as you are!"

"I follow only the dictates of our good king, Lady Ashley. He enjoys lewd humor, so I simply indulge him in what he desires. Rather, I suppose, as does Mrs. Gwynne here, or anyone else who expects to remain in his favor."

"He *does* have a point, milady," chuckled Henry Savile. "What *do* you give him, a girl like you, who has him so entirely besotted?"

"Clearly, there is great power in low charms," Scrope laughed.

When Rose and Jeddy returned from a walk around the grounds, the vast bedchamber was shot with the pink light from the sun setting bold and vivid through the windows. The room itself was littered with a spray of dresses. The bed was covered with a silken rainbow of topaz, emerald, violet, and crimson, the floor held a tidy pile of shoes, and Nell was in the center of the disarray. Before her stood William Chiffinch, doing his best to help. The king's page of the back stairs was a thin, square-shouldered man. His face was dominated by a high forehead and a neat little pointed beard, and his salt-and-pepper-colored hair gave him a fatherly impression.

"Those women are vultures! Bugger 'em all!"

"You must give as good as you get, Mrs. Gwynne," said Chiffinch, "and do it with a smile. It is the thing that fascinates His Majesty about you."

A woman came through the same door then and sank against the jamb, looking weary. Mary Chiffinch, a royal seamstress, had a kind, middle-aged face and a small, blunt nose. Her hair had gone gray, but her genuine smile recaptured a spark of her youth. "My husband is right, child. It has been years since either of us have seen His Majesty so truly contented."

Rose brought Nell a small cordial and led her gently to a chair.

"'Tis difficult to believe 'e's 'ad women for the choosin' since 'e was old enough to know what to do with 'em. I've been a dalliance to powerful men, and I'll not be that again!"

"There is a difference, my dear, when it is someone about whom he cares. It's just bedmates my husband finds for him; he hates to be alone at night, you see. His Majesty, poor man, has nightmares."

Chiffinch held up his hand. "That'll do, Mary. The girl has enough on her mind without hearing all of that. Fact is, I have been in His Majesty's service for a very long time, and I tell you, you have a great opportunity here. You can walk away, if you must. I have already seen to the coach you requested and it waits out in the courtyard. Or, you can meet His Majesty, as he wishes, for a sunset ride down on the river on his private barge."

"I don't know . . ."

"Take my advice, my dear. I know the king's habits well. When he is smitten, the world belongs to the object of his affections. He longs to care deeply for a woman. Truthfully, he longs to be in love, though if you tell him I said so, I shall deny it forcefully," Mary Chiffinch said.

"He told me so 'imself."

"Did he now?" Mary smiled.

"But Lady Castlemaine?"

"That was over with long ago," Mary interjected again. "It was only milady's cruel threats that carried it on for as long as it did."

"And Moll Davies?"

"Och." She chuckled, slapping her thigh. "She was a diversion, only an actress!"

"I am only an actress . . ."

"You are much more to His Majesty than that," William said calmly, commanding the moment. "He wishes to see you beside him in the morning. That, my dear, speaks volumes. Now, my wife here can teach you all you need to know. She may not be a lady herself, but she has known enough of them to help you."

"Where do we begin? I ain't got the first idea!"

"First, you must stand up straight. But a better corset will help with that. You will meet with the royal dresser tomorrow. Then curtsy not for the stage, but more modestly. I can show you that as well. And you must never, ever again say, 'ain't,' if you can possibly help it."

Nell paused for a moment, reflecting. "Why would the two of you do this for me?"

"Truthfully, because we have great experience with the alternatives," Mary Chiffinch replied. William smiled kindly. "Let us only say it is our little attempt to help His Majesty find a bit of peace. If you succeed in the bargain, so much the better."

"And you believe I can do that for 'im when the queen 'erself, and a long parade of other women, 'aven't?"

They looked at one another, then back at her. "But then none of them were quite you, were they now, Mrs. Gwynne?"

Buckingham was reviewing petitions on a painted desk when William Chiffinch rapped softly on the door to the duke's private paneled closet. The small room overlooked an inner courtyard at Windsor, and the splashing stone fountain there.

"Has it been done, then?" Buckingham asked. Sun shot golden light through the windowpanes across the side of his face. "Have you convinced Mrs. Gwynne to take on a bit of . . . refinement in order to withstand the impending challenge here?"

"I believe she convinced herself, Your Grace."

"Splendid," Buckingham replied without emotion.

With Nell Gwynne in the royal bed, there would be no true risk of serious competition for the king's influence. Castlemaine was gone. Lady Stuart as well. Even Moll Davies. Things had worked out brilliantly. Now came the real challenge. He had begun things with her at Newmarket, befriending her, gaining her trust. Now she must be educated in how to succeed for the long term. Above all else, he must make her believe she required him to help her succeed.

He had heard the report about the needlepoint gathering. Shrewsbury had been brilliantly insipid, breaking her down in order for him to build her back up in the manner he required. Lord, but she could seduce him with her cruelty as well as her body! She was so like Castlemaine, only decidedly better. "Has Mrs. Gwynne gone with His Majesty out onto the barge, then?"

"She has."

"Splendid news." He pushed a pouch full of silver crowns across the long desk without looking up. "And you will keep me abreast of all things between them?"

William Chiffinch took the coins and slipped them into an inside pocket of his waistcoat with ease. "I do believe she will be good for him, your Grace. This one, it seems, truly does care for the king, which, if I may say, is a welcome change."

Buckingham glanced up with a changed expression. "When I want your opinion, Chiffinch, I shall ask for it. In the meantime, keep your eyes open and your mouth shut, as always, and the continued extra money shall be yours."

William Chiffinch bowed deeply. "I am Your Grace's humble servant."

"Excellent," Buckingham said. "See that you remain so."

The king's barge silently slipped down the river at sunset, cutting through the motionless water like glass as crickets chirped in the reeds along the muddy incline of shore. Nell reclined on a banquette of crimson-colored velvet and a spray of cushions, while Charles sat beside her. He propped a shoe heel on a tufted stool and gazed at her intensely. "I want Lely to paint you."

"The painter who did that lovely portrait at Whitehall of Lady Castlemaine?" she asked, unable to seem too cavalier for the surprise in it.

"The very same."

"A right grand honor."

"I want an image of you beside my bed on any night we might be parted."

Nell smiled slyly. "I'll just bet you tell that to all the mistresses, wives, doxies, and jades."

"It would be an awfully crowded wall if I did." Charles moved across the banquette, took up her hand, and kissed her palm. Nell felt herself grow hot. His touch alone had that power over her now; she wanted only to give in to him. She would deny herself, and him, nothing any longer.

"You are so wonderful."

"And *you* are very drunk!" she purred as he arched over her, brushing a hair the breeze had blown across her cheek. She hoped he would say he loved her because she wanted to say it to him. She would feel so much more confident about remaining his mistress if he did. But she could see, by how carefully he chose his words at moments like these, that he was far from ready to love her. She was to be fun for him, a diversion. And she had risen higher than an orange girl should. So a diversion she would be.

"Will you allow him to paint you?" the king asked, as the barge swayed upon the water, moved ever so slightly by the sudden breeze.

"You *are* the king, after all. Now 'ow would I dare deny you anythin'?"

"I want him to paint you nude, so that I might remember all of you."

"So you are king *and* a right lecherous one, you are at that!" laughed Nell.

Rose lingered in the corner of the large dressing room, fingering the tassel on a blue damask curtain, and watching as Nell tried again. Dressed only in a high, crushingly tight corset laced in back, and tall heeled shoes, in which she wobbled slightly, Nell bobbed a graceful curtsy. The effect was much better this time, as her ability to mimic was great, and her desire to improve was strong. But it was a tenuous balancing act: she must improve enough so she would not embarrass herself at court and yet still remain the real Nell, for whom the king so dearly cared.

"Say it again, then," Mary Chiffinch directed from a stool at the dressing table. William stood beside her.

"Good evening, Your Ladyship. 'Ow did you enjoy the consort today?"

Mary nodded. "And?"

"And *is it not* a grand day?"

"Much improved." William beamed. "Not an 'ain't' lingering anywhere."

Behind her, Rose had bobbed the same curtsy, then moved her lips as she whispered the words her sister had spoken aloud. They still felt foreign and awkward in her mind. She had enviously yet proudly watched her younger sister's amazing transformation all of these months, and it should have been enough. She was at the king's court! To exist even in the shadow of such fortune at first had been enough. But now she wanted more. For the first time in her life, Rose wanted something for herself enough to believe that she, too, might, with a bit of effort, actually win it.

Again she moved her lips, listening critically to herself. It was not so far off from how Nell now sounded. Rose counted slowly to five as she bobbed a small curtsy of her own. With all of the attention on Nell, no one noticed. She glanced down at her dress, costly topaz satin with ivory lace, then touched the fabric with the tips of her fingers to reassure herself that it was real. She looked up at Nell again, who was biting her lower lip in concentration as she tried to recall the first few steps of the branle. Nell began to smile and, just as suddenly, looked over at her sister.

"Come dance with me, Rose Gwynne!" she said, and held out her hand. "You probably know this better than I do. You've always 'ad a way with dances!"

Rose felt her face flush. "I couldn't."

"Like when we were girls. Remember?" Nell was smiling. "Come on! I need you!"

Three days later, the king stood across the bedchamber in a white shirt, open at the chest, and black knee-length breeches, as he stared out the window down into the gardens below. Nell woke slowly and, as she did, she saw him there, tall, slim, and graceful. She smiled to herself, her body sore from the night of lovemaking, and her eyelids still heavy. But she had never felt so content.

For a fortnight, he had escorted her to his banquets, dinners, card parties, everywhere. She had new gowns with which he had surprised her, made especially for her gamine shape. A dresser was brought to her from Paris, who made certain her petticoats were crisp and new, the strings of her busk were properly tight, and her shoes were *à la mode française.* A French stylist came to arrange her hair into the latest fashion, and ornament it with tiny flowers and ribbons to match her gowns. Rose and Jeddy, who were with her everywhere as companions, had new clothes as well. The latter had a sweet little dress of shiny blue serge. "Forever" was becoming a fantasy she had nearly begun to allow herself to believe.

The king turned and saw her lying on her side, with three of his favorite spaniels lounging at the foot of the bed from where he had only just risen. Instead of coming back to her, he rested his hands behind him on the window sash and exhaled. She could see his intense expression, even across the room. "The queen is arriving today," he said bluntly.

Nell sat up, pulling a sheet across her bare breasts, feeling suddenly as if she had been dropped from a great height. It took a moment to catch her breath so that he would not notice the change. "Here at Windsor?"

"I only received word last night that she desired to speak with me about something particular, and then to remain here for a few days afterward, if I would consent."

He came to her then, across the parquet flooring that creaked with each step before he settled onto the edge of the bed beside her. "I want you to remain. We will only need to show a bit of care in . . ." His words fell away. "She's a good woman, Nell, a kind woman, and I have no wish to flaunt anything before her that might bring her more pain than she has already suffered."

"Of course." Nell swung her legs to the side of the bed and drew on the dressing gown of ivory-colored Spanish lace that she had left atop the bedcovers. Then she stood and shook out her long hair. The movements were disjointed and too purposeful, designed only to buy her a moment to press back her disappointment, and to give him what he wanted from her now, the freedom to see his wife. "I 'ad no chance to tell you, but Mr. Dryden 'as sent me another play. As it 'appens, right from the first that this one was read to me I could tell 'twill be uproariously funny."

Charles cupped a hand beneath her jaw and kissed her tenderly. "I do not wish you to return to the theater. I need you here with me."

She gave him her best carefree smile. "Oh, now," she said, taking his palm from her face, where it stilled for a moment, and pressing a kiss onto it in return. "Once an actress, always an actress. You know that. I miss it, I really do: the crowds, the applause."

"Will they do Dryden's play next?" he asked as two of the dogs suddenly bounded from the bed and scampered across the room.

"They'll do anythin' to have me back troddin' the boards. Mr. Killigrew as much as told me so. Whenever I was ready, 'e said. After all, I *am* Nell Gwynne. I fill the King's Theater! And it doesn't 'urt a bit that I've been mistress to that same sovereign!"

"You *are* mistress to that sovereign king for as long as you desire it." He kissed her more deeply then, and she could see the conflict on his face, his brow furrowing with guilt and regret.

"Then I desire it *and* you." She was smiling as determination alone pressed back the tears fighting to fall. "Besides, Lely's portrait of me is not yet finished, nor adornin' your wall. I'll 'ave to return to see to that!"

"I do not wish you to remain in London during the summer. There is too much risk there."

"Then if Mr. Dryden 'asn't another brilliant play for me to act in, you've but to send for me, after the run is over."

"I'm sorry about this, Nell. I truly am."

"No regrets, Charlie," she said, working hard to smile endearingly. "I've got none. Nor should you."

Out along the private corridor, Nell sank against the oak paneled wall, arms wrapped around her waist. Silent tears fell in long ribbons onto her cheeks. She had closed her eyes so she did not see Mary Chiffinch approach. Nor did she see William linger in the next doorway just beyond them. There was only the shadow of his long face, etched with concern, before he slipped back inside.

"Come, child. 'Twill do you no good. You've got to be stronger than the others, and smarter by half." Mary's voice was soothing, her arm across Nell's shoulder a gentle balm. Like a mother's love. A thing Nell had forgotten how to long for. "Come with me. We'll practice your curtsy again, and then I'll feed you a nice bowl of porridge with a bit of honey. Nothing like honey to set you to rights," she said, as if that alone could stop all of the uncertainty.

Chapter 18

A CROWN GOLDEN IN SHOW IS BUT A WREATH OF THORNS.
—*John Milton*

CHARLES sat alone in his small, private writing cabinet, beside his bedchamber, where the light filtered in across diamond-shaped red-and-blue windowpanes. He thought of it as Minette's room, because it was here, in a space arranged precisely the same in each of his homes, that he wrote to his dearest sister, who he had consigned to a loveless marriage in France. She had done it in order to keep the door open wide enough with Louis XIV. He had heard back from Arlington that the French king was not at all pleased by his proposition of money for loyalty against the Dutch. Buckhurst had written the same as well. Although that fool Buckhurst, he thought, could be trusted no further than he could be thrown. The echo of an ink dipped pen scratching paper filled the silence.

My dearest Minette . . .

Thoughts of Buckhurst brought his mind back to Nell. She had been gone from Windsor for four days, and he could do nothing but think of her, long for her. He closed his eyes for a moment, the pen poised over the paper. Ah, the things they had done together!

Her naked body stretched out before him, her raucous laughter, her quick, bawdy tongue . . . images moved across his mind as he tried to write to his sister.

I am at Windsor where memories of you and I hiding as children together in the maze, the sound of your laughter, always bring me such a spark of happiness when I allow myself thoughts of those care-free days. But life is no longer carefree for you and I, and the images of our childhood have begun to fade into all the layers of duty . . .

Buckingham was pressuring him again to consider divorcing Catherine, and she had come to Windsor to say she would not contest an annulment due to the shame of her barrenness. She knew what a laughingstock she was in the taverns and the fine salons of London—the only woman in the world, it seemed, upon whom the king could not get a child. They did not speak of that painful detail, but Charles knew it was there in the depth of those wide brown eyes, always just on the brink of tears, eyes he could not quite look into for the guilt he felt. Even as he had gone one more time to her bed, the night before last, and tried to get her with a child who would survive, and end all of the speculation about divorce, it all lay between them.

He wanted to be free of her, of all of it, but in the end, he still simply could not divorce her or annul their marriage. He had told her that she was his wife in the eyes of God Almighty, and there she would remain until death parted them.

Your husband, I hear, has been ill and that you have been as kind a nurse to him as he could ever hope for, and I wait for word of your own health. You must tell him to allow you a visit home so that you may tend to your own heart as you have done so well for him. There is such a great deal I want to tell you, so much has happened, that only a sister

who knew of the fields behind Greenwich, and who shares with me the
memory of our father's caress, and his loss, could ever understand . . .

He wrote the last with a determined flourish, knowing how true
it was, and how much he missed her counsel, not just their recol-
lections. Minette would chide him about his obsession with yet
another actress. But in the end, she would ask all about Nell, and
she would even wish to meet her if she made her brother happy.
There was no one else in the world he could trust with the truth of
an honest answer as Minette would give him in all things.

I think of you always, and pray for you daily.
Darling sister, you possess my love as no other.

> *Your devoted brother always,*
> CHARLES

After he had signed it, Charles pressed the chair back and
stood. A long, elaborate supper in the queen's honor awaited him,
as well as a puppet show afterward. Following that, there would
be an endless evening of cards with Rochester, Buckingham, and
Catherine, who loved nothing so much as a game of basset, and
the poetic wit of Rochester, who today would be tamed mightily
to recite for the queen. Then he would spend the night with his
wife, hoping against hope that it would make him long even a
little less for Nell.

He knocked on the cabinet wall, and a moment later the paneled door swung back on its hinges. William Chiffinch stood
straight spined and ready to take the letter and affix the royal seal.
"Did you send the string of pearls to Mrs. Gwynne?" Charles
asked as his closest servant moved toward the writing table.

"Indeed, sire. It was done immediately."

"And what of the play? Has she been a success in London?"

"Indeed, she has. A rousing success. The theater is packed, they say, every afternoon. Killigrew and Hart are planning to hold the production over for another week."

"Splendid, then," he said. But his voice lacked enthusiasm.

"Is Your Majesty all right?"

"Alas, boredom is not a malady, or by now I would likely be buried in Westminster Abbey," the king sighed.

"If you would permit the impertinent thought, sire," Chiffinch ventured calmly. "My wife has met the loveliest young girl, daughter of a tailor here in Windsor, most eager to meet Your Majesty, and—"

"I will accompany the queen this evening, William, and only the queen."

Chiffinch nodded deeply. "Of course, sire."

Charles turned, and the two men stood facing each other in the small room, although Chiffinch busied himself with ensuring the seal on the letter was dry.

"Yet I am reminded, sire, that the queen does so like to retire early with this country air."

"Does the girl's family approve of her visit here?"

"They consider the prospect to be the greatest honor, as would any family, Your Majesty."

Charles closed his eyes. This was not the answer, he knew that. But it was a diversion. Yes, at least it was that. "Arrange it, then," he said flatly. "But see to it she uses the privy stairwell. And I will want her out before dawn."

Chapter 19

FATE NOW FOR HER DID ITS WHOLE FORCE ENGAGE,
AND FROM THE PIT SHE MOUNTED THE STAGE. THERE
IN FULL LUSTRE DID HER GLORIES SHINE,
AND LONG ECLIPS'D SPREAD THEIR LIGHT DIVINE.
—*The Earl of Rochester*

"FIVE minutes, Nelly!"

It had been almost a month since she had heard the queen was pregnant. At last, the country chanted, there would be an heir. Nell stood and adjusted her skirts. The costume, a gown once belonging to the Duchess of Argyll, too big by half, was bound by a belt. The sleeves as well were too long, but Nell was accustomed to making do, and thriving.

"Are you ready?" asked Richard Bell. The revival of *The Sisters* was a smashing success; he was finally playing the second lead. He stood now in the doorway, arms crossed over his chest, wearing a gray wig and the costume of an old country squire. Nell turned and smiled at her old friend, happy to be with him again, old admissions and disappointments forgotten.

"Ready as I'll ever be."

"You were divine yesterday," he smiled. "Let's give it to 'em again today just like that!"

"Agreed. Only better!" she laughed, the first time in days.

The theater was a solace to Nell, the place where she was happy to be herself. Bold. Funny. Flirtatious. A place where everyone encouraged her, where they accepted her. She was so accustomed to the process of acting before hundreds of people now that she could speak her lines with total believability, yet look out among the audience, see theatergoers she knew, and enjoy bringing out their each and every response to her lines.

In the theater, like nowhere else in the world, Nell was in control.

As the performance came to an end, and flowers were tossed onto the stage, from the pit and from the boxes, and as Nell tossed kisses to the crowd, she saw Lord Rochester and his friend Henry Savile. They sat three rows back, on a bench in the pit that was thick with old orange rinds. Both of them were leading the ovation with hoots and whistles as Nell took her curtsies, which had become a performance itself, with her lifting the hem of her dress, demurely pressing her fingers to her chin, and bobbing comically. It was not at all like the one she had been taught to perform by Mary Chiffinch. It was good, Nell thought, looking at Rochester and Savile, not to be forgotten by those who knew the king. They were a small tie back to that other world she had left, but which she was not entirely ready to abandon.

After she had gone backstage, as the wardrobe mistress was removing her costume, and Nell was daubing the perspiration from her chest, a young stagehand came to her with a stiff white calling card. Beck Marshall, now in her petticoats, with a celery-green shawl tossed across her shoulders, glanced over at her from her own dressing table. "That didn't take long," she laughed.

"What didn't?"

"Why, replacing the king with a new string of suitors, of course."

"Don't be daft," Nell said, tossing the card onto her dressing table with the collection of jars, bottles, and boxes there. "These are friends who wish to come back and congratulate us."

"I would doubt they care a whit about me, Nell."

"Nonsense. Like every other man in London, they're taken by all pretty actresses."

As she stood, John Wilmot, who was Lord Rochester, and Henry Savile, his baby-faced, blond friend, arrived. "Mrs. Gwynne, you were absolutely brilliant just now!" Rochester flattered.

"I've never laughed so much in my life," Savile concurred, then he glanced at Beck.

"My Lord Rochester, Mr. Savile," said Nell properly, as she had learned to do at court. "May I present my friend, and fellow actress, Mrs. Marshall."

Henry Savile took her hands in his own. "I am beyond charmed, Mrs. Marshall."

Beck's smile, as she looked at him, was as silly as a child's, her wide eyes and long lashes fluttering at him. Nell bit back a smile. "And Mrs. Gwynne," said Rochester. "I shall forever be charmed by *you*. No one has ever set those women on their ears at court quite as you did. I do believe they are *still* as perplexed by your allure as we were the day we met."

"It's true. He's even written a poem about you!" Savile and Rochester exchanged a glance, and then both of them began to laugh. "Although, with John's sense of humor, and prurient verse, that's more a warning than a compliment."

They all laughed before Lord Rochester said, "Have supper with us, both of you. I know a wonderful tavern near here. The oysters and champagne are divine, and we are guaranteed the very best seat."

Nell demurred. "Come to my home instead," she suggested. "It will all be quite proper, I promise. We'll even invite our friend Mr. Bell over there, to keep it aboveboard."

"Now that would be a shame," Rochester quipped. "A dissolute evening is so much more entertaining."

"I 'ave a wonderful cook who came with the house, and I'll serve you my own oysters and French champagne, but *only* if you recite poems for us," Nell bartered.

"Ah, beware of a deal like that!" Savile laughed. "Lord Rochester's verses are hardly for polite company!"

"Even ones about me?" Nell asked with a devilish smile.

"Particularly ones involving beautiful women," Rochester chimed. "I'm quite incorrigible."

"Then we'll consider ourselves warned!" said Nell with a seductive laugh.

Nell and Beck passed through the front gate of her home, along with Richard, who had come along with them under protest. Lord Rochester and Henry Savile lingered a moment outside with the coach, giving their driver and groomsmen instruction as Nell and the others went inside.

As they passed across the threshold, and into the black marble foyer, a young man with tawny hair and gray-green eyes was just coming down the wide staircase, buttoning his vest. Rose lingered a few steps above him. Seeing Nell, his face blanched, and he paused. The tall clock in the hallway beyond struck the hour then with its tinny chime.

"Who might you be?" Nell asked in surprise.

There was a silence. The young man scanned all three of their shocked expressions before he bowed deeply and said, "Captain

John Cassells, guardsman to the Duke of Monmouth, madam, at your service." And then, without another word, he went past them and out into the warm afternoon sunlight. Near the wrought-iron gate, he tripped on a little shrub, and then was gone.

Richard, Beck, and Nell all exchanged a glance before they burst into laughter. "Yet another suitor, Nelly? How *do* you keep them all straight?" Beck asked on a chuckle.

"Oh, no! But with any luck, 'e was 'ere for my sister!"

They sat together in her most formal room to the left of the entrance foyer. A grand marble fireplace dominated; the room was decorated expensively with richly upholstered furniture and paintings on the walls framed in heavy gold. There were little objects placed on tables, none of them of her own choosing: a plaster bust of someone in military dress, a rosewood box inlaid with ivory in the shape of a heart, and a stack of classic books, which Nell herself knew she could never read.

"And *that* is your sister?" Henry Savile asked, crossing his legs as Rose went out of the room. "She's not nearly so ravishing as you."

"I'm younger. Life 'as 'ad decidedly more time to scar her," Nell said simply, looking at the empty doorway through which Rose had only just passed.

"Poor, dear Nelly," said Rochester in a mocking tone meant to lighten the pall suddenly cast over the room. "Such a gloriously complex creature you are, of which His Majesty shall only ever appreciate one facet."

"Is that what your poem says?"

"Among other things."

"And certainly not so properly," Savile added.

"Life at court has nothing to do with being proper! And it is certainly not for the faint of heart. But it is delicious gossip we live by." Rochester laughed. "I write about that. For example, did you realize that unappealing cow you met at Windsor, Anne, daughter of the once-great chancellor of England, is the Duchess of York, married to His Majesty's own brother?"

"How about the Countess of Shrewsbury. Now *there* is good fodder for gossip!" chimed Savile. "The she-devil herself, who was so caustic with you, behaves that way to absolutely everyone, even her lover, the great Duke of Buckingham, and right there beneath the very pert nose of the woman he intends to marry in a week's time!"

"Great in his own mind, if not in his bed, or at least that's what they say!" They laughed together, enormously pleased with themselves when they saw by her expression that Nell had absolutely no idea as to either revelation.

"But poor Mary Fairfax was so fair and naive. She sat right there beside the countess, smiling all the while," said Nell.

"Oh, my dear." Rochester shook his head. "Whoever told you that desire had anything at all to do with an important marriage?"

They were stopped then by a commanding click of the large brass front-door knocker. For an instant, until Jeddy turned the handle and opened the door, a very hopeful image of the king darted across Nell's mind. "I am looking for Lord Rochester," declared a cultured voice. Nell drew in a breath, determined to slow her heart as Rochester and Savile stood.

"Why, speak of the devil," Savile said beneath his breath.

"We really must be careful about that in future," Rochester concurred with a smile.

"Your Grace," they said, bowing reverently to the Duke of Buckingham, who stood now in Nell's drawing room, dressed formally in dark-blue long velvet coat and breeches, lace spilling from his sleeves. His hat, with a waving purple ostrich plume, topped a long golden wig.

"I saw your coach outside as I passed," Buckingham declared with a surprisingly easy smile. "And thought perhaps I might once again find a damsel in distress."

"Mrs. Gwynne can certainly take care of herself, as she so cleverly cares for the king," said Rochester as he and Buckingham smiled at each other, carefree as childhood chums. "But since you are here, do join us for champagne and great topics of the world, yet untapped."

"Oh, and give us the poem you promised," said Beck, swallowing a large mouthful of champagne and batting her eyes at Henry Savile.

"Very well, then, shall I?"

"You must," Nell declared.

Biting back a smile, Rochester began:

> *"She knew so well to wield the royal tool,*
> *That none had such a knack to please the fool.*
> *When he was dumpish, she would still be jocund*
> *And chuck the royal chin of Charles the Second."*

"Of course, it's all in the way you say it: *second*. It really is a poem to be appreciated verbally, not read.

> *"This you'd believe if I had time to tell ye*
> *The pains it costs to poor, laborious Nelly,*
> *Whilst she employs hands, fingers, mouth and thighs,*
> *Ere she can raise the member she enjoys."*

"Well," said Beck, into an awkward silence. "You did warn us."

Nell's eyes darted in turn to each of her guests. Finally, they settled on Rochester. "And do you know me well enough to write a poem like that?"

"Oh, I write them about all of the king's mistresses. He says it is one of his greatest delights."

"'Is Majesty's 'eard this, then?" Nell's tone was incredulous.

"Just two days past at Newmarket," revealed the duke.

"And you've still not been sent to the Tower for it?" asked Richard Bell. It was the first words he had spoken since coming into the room.

"It is what the king fancies about you, Nell, how deliciously undiluted by life you are, how wonderfully earthy your charms. It holds greater power with him than you know," said Buckingham. "I was with him when Rochester recited the entire verse. I can tell you that His Majesty was most thoroughly entertained."

"I would imagine the queen was not with 'im, then," she said, pressing back a smile.

"Not then, no. Her Majesty has gone to Bath, hoping the waters there will ensure a healthy pregnancy this time. But he wishes to see you."

"And 'ow do you know that?"

"I am his oldest and dearest friend, my dear. There are times when I know the king better than he knows himself. And I know that he thinks of you most fondly."

She settled back, wrapping her hands around the carved arms on her chair. "'E 'asn't sent for me."

"Life is complex for one who rules an entire country, and he is very busy indeed. But he will, Nell. Trust that he will."

They stayed on into the evening, drinking and playing cards as the lamps and candles were lit throughout the echoing rooms and hallways. Then they stumbled out onto the flagstone, in a fit of laughter, to Lord Rochester's waiting coach. Through the hours, they had spoken of the French, the Dutch, the economy, and sex, and heard more of Lord Rochester's poems.

"We would indeed like to return, if you would have us," Rochester slurred as he was helped up the coach steps.

"We could make it a regular event," Nell called out from her front porch, torch lamps flickering on either side of her. "And I shall call you my merry band."

"A truly splendid idea," Buckingham concurred. "Perhaps, if he is fortunate indeed, one day we shall even invite the king!"

After glancing into the mirror but still grimacing at the reflection, Rose sank onto the edge of the bed. She drew her knees against her chest and only then felt herself smile. He cared for her as she was. It still amazed her. What had begun as a flirtation in the corridors at court was becoming something real. She could actually feel it. Possibility. Promise. Then she caught sight of her hands.

No amount of cleaning, lotion, or oil could hide the scars there. No one would ever know the cruelties of life in the gaol, or the indignities of her childhood. But having a man like John say he cared for her went a long way toward healing a heart she had thought would be wounded forever. She would never be like Nell, she would always live in the shadow of her famous sister. But just now, as the scent of him still lingered in this room, Rose Gwynne knew that today marked the beginning of her own little miracle.

That night, Nell sat slumped against the dust-blue padded chair at her dressing table, wearing her cotton and lace petticoats, letting Rose brush out her curls. Jeddy, on the other side, silently rubbed scented balm of Gilead into the palms of her hands and then her fingertips.

"Did you actually enjoy the company of men like that?" Rose finally asked.

"'Twas what I was supposed to do. They are 'Is Majesty's friends, after all."

"But are they *your* friends? Enough to call them your band?"

"'Tis all a very different world. I'm only tryin' to learn to fit in. I need allies to survive, and they were 'elpful to me in it. Beyond that, just now I can't say. Speakin' of that, is John Cassells *your* friend? Or is 'e already, perhaps, more?"

Rose stood and set the brush down onto the dressing table. Color crept into her neck and into her face. "We were speakin' about the king's world, not mine."

"I don't 'ave a right to ask my sister about somethin' that goes on in my own 'ouse?"

"The man in *your* bed is the only one you should be worryin' yourself about."

Nell ignored her slight. "Captain Cassells is 'andsome enough. And we know 'e's got an income to keep you." She bit back a smile, cleverly changing the subject back, but Rose grew suddenly serious.

"I'm not known for my judgment with men any more than Ma, Nelly. And I can't say I think the world of yours."

"I'm a girl from the back alleys of London who, by some strange miracle, 'as found 'er way to the king of England's bed! 'Ow can you ever find fault with that?"

"The king 'as a wife, Nell, and 'e'll always 'ave a wife."

"So long as 'e loves me, what I've got is more than I've a right to," Nell declared. "And, for me, 'tis enough. Now tell me all about John!"

Two days later, as Nell and Rose were arguing over a selection of fabrics sent to them for new dresses, a footman in royal livery stood at her front door with a message. His presence silenced them and drew them both forward as Bridget Long, Nell's maid, held open the door. Sir Peter Lely wished to finish his painting of her, and by order of the king her presence was requested at the royal palace of Richmond. This was the king's way of beginning things with her again. It was a portrait he had said he very much wanted. But with the queen pregnant, and herself now the subject of lewd poetry and court gossip, the notion of returning to that tumultuous world was not appealing.

Nell glanced over at her sister as the expressionless footman stood waiting.

"What'll you do?" Rose asked cautiously. "The king'll be there."

"'Tis my fortune, and yours, that 'Is Majesty finds diversion in actresses."

"But those old crows will likely be there, and if memory serves, you couldn't wait to get out of Windsor."

"They're a part of 'is world I'm not likely to avoid, if I want to continue on. I've got to learn to live with 'em."

"I just don't want to see you 'urt, Nelly. You 'eard that awful poem yourself. 'Tis the way things are at court. You're a diversion, and a bit of lowbrow comedy to make 'em all laugh for a while. Like Moll Davies was. But it didn't last for 'er, and you'd best prepare that it won't last for you."

"I've got to do this."

"Because you love him?"

"Because I love him." A moment later, Nell touched her sister's arm, and her voice went lower. "And I love you. I don't know what I'd do without you, Rose."

Rose smiled. "Good. Then you'll never 'ave to find out."

"Only *I* can make myself irreplaceable to a king. For all that was beyond us growin' up, this much the Fates have left up to me. I'm determined to figure my way round them this time. Watch and see if I don't."

Chapter 20

I GIVE YOU FREELY ALL DELIGHTS
WITH PLEASANT DAYS AND EASY NIGHTS.
—*From* Venus and Adonis

Two days after she had been summoned by the king's painter, Nell lay nude on a wide daybed, covered in rich azure velvet, fringed in shimmering gold. In the vast salon, two tall windows filtered the afternoon sunlight. It shimmered on her smooth, ivory skin, as Peter Lely attacked the canvas before him with a palette of bold colors. The odor of paint and linseed oil was pungent in the closed room. There was something oddly sensual in posing, Nell thought, as she lay silently watching Lely's expression, and his movements. First an intense glance at her body, studying each turn and rise, then focus back on the canvas. It had been going on that way for hours.

It had been a fortnight since news had spread across London that once again Queen Catherine had miscarried her child. Three months had passed since Nell and Charles had seen each other.

She could not imagine the sadness, or conflict, either of them felt. She even pitied the queen. It was odd how many lives intersected because of one man, she thought. Thoughts of him turned to sensation. Her skin turned to gooseflesh. But Lely had been very firm. She could not, must not, move if they were to make important progress today.

"Is that not sufficient for one sitting?" A voice suddenly filled the great chasm of high beams and wood floors. She heard firm footsteps follow the question as the king added, "We want to immortalize the lady, not paralyze her."

"As Your Majesty wishes," Lely said in English, thickly accented by his Dutch roots. "I have reached an appropriate point to stop for today, in any case."

Charles moved into Nell's view, and she watched him scan the canvas. He was in a magnificent coat of sapphire blue, with wide silver cuffs trimmed with loops of silver ribbon. The onyx curls of his wig lay on broad sapphire shoulders. His expression was so intense as he looked at the work that it quickly became a frown. Finally, he looked away from the canvas and directly at her. His gaze rested appreciatively on her nude body for only a moment before Lely handed her an ivory-colored dressing gown, edged in Belgian lace. Nell took her time putting her arms into each of the sleeves, and even longer closing it over her bare breasts, in what she hoped would seem a slightly erotic dance.

"Nell," the king finally said with a glint in his dark eyes. "I don't believe I have ever seen you look lovelier."

"And *I* don't believe I've ever seen Your Majesty look at me longer," she said on an infectious chuckle that quickly broke the frown, and had him smiling.

Lely bit back his own smile at that. Nell stood and was embraced by the king. "I've missed you, sweetheart," Charles said in a low tone, meant for only her to hear, as his arms surrounded her and he pulled her small body against himself.

"I can tell."

His mouth went down on hers then in a deep, languorous kiss. "Will you not tell me you've missed me as well?"

"And be like all the others who mean to flatter you instead of love you? Not a chance!" she laughed, and ran a finger down his chest to the row of shimmering silver buttons, each emblazoned with his coat of arms. "But you still and always will be my own Charles the Third!"

After Lely had gone, Charles gently pressed Nell back onto the daybed upon which she had posed. Arching over her, he kissed her neck, and then the lobe of her ear. "I'll have you right here and now if you'll not object," he murmured into her unbound hair.

"Your Majesty can 'ave me anywhere you fancy, and in any particular way you please," Nell replied with a carefree laugh that excited him all the more, as the shoe heels of the Yeomen of the Guard clicked out a rhythm in the corridor beyond them.

She touched the fitted, boned bodice of the luxurious gown into which she was pulled, pressed, and tied. It was an elegant creation that, at the king's pleasure, had been styled in France particularly for Nell. It was the country and culture that he enjoyed most, he told her. And his much-loved sister lived there. The dress, sewn of champagne-colored silk, had a full skirt over layers of petticoats. It was sprinkled with tiny white silk roses. How far she had come. She could still see the king's reflection in her mirror, as she had stood before him earlier, her hair dressed with a sheen of pearls, her neck and shoulders smelling of essence of pear. He had placed one very discreet and fashionable black patch beside her left eye, just above where they crinkled when she smiled, just before he clothed her neck in a glittering pearl-and-diamond choker.

Now, her arm in his, the king had placed his other hand atop hers. She knew the small movement was to steady her. He must feel her trembling. Even her best acting could not entirely mask that. There were just so many people, bows, nods, and curtsies, and she had not yet had nearly enough practice. There would be no ribald jokes or comedy tonight. She must make the king proud; she must behave as if she had always been meant to be here.

That was what the Duke of Buckingham had advised her.

"Would you like a glass of champagne?" the king asked as they took command of the room, continuing to nod and chat as they strolled. The gold braid on his shoulders glinted in the candlelight and caught her eye as she turned to him. "I'd prefer three, to tell you the truth."

Amused, he said beneath his breath, "At the moment, I suspect I could arrange for two without causing a commotion."

"Then that'll have to do," she replied as they moved gracefully toward the dancing area.

Nell looked up into the king's eyes and followed his lead. "You're doing marvelously!" he whispered to her as they passed during the final measure. He bowed and she curtsied, and Nell realized only then that the entire court had stopped to watch them.

"She walks like one of the king's dogs," she then heard a woman snidely say.

"She does have rather a loping stride," remarked another.

The king plucked another glass of champagne from a silver tray held by a page. "Here you are. The third glass. Never let it be said your king does not give you all that you hope for."

"I'm hoping for quite a bit more of somethin' else later," she seductively murmured, just as a gentleman and lady she did not know approached His Majesty, along with their youthful daughter. By the color that rose on the girl's cheeks as they neared, and the expression of near terror in her eyes, Nell assumed the girl was new at court. While he was not flirtatious with her, Nell felt a small spark of unease at the way he took the girl's hand at the introduction, and held it just an instant too long.

While the king was distracted by the trio, Buckingham quietly advanced. "I told you he would send for you," the duke said with studied calm. He was smiling kindly at her, wearing a coat of scarlet satin and a long blond periwig, yet standing formally, hands clasped behind his back. He seemed so different from the relaxed gentleman who sat affably drinking champagne and gossiping in her drawing room not a week ago.

"I shall 'ave to remember in the future to listen to you."

"You look delicious enough to eat this evening, my dear. Always remember I told you *that* as well."

Her smile was twisted. "Does everyone 'ere 'ave your way with words?"

"Not nearly enough to make it a challenge, I'm afraid. Which is what makes you such a delight."

"Well, just now I'm nervous as a kitten caught in a chimney pipe."

"His Majesty would never know it. And, if I may, a word of advice? Lock your fear away. The old crones, and the young jackals, for that matter, smell fear most distinctly. Once they've gotten the scent, they shan't rest until you've been entirely done away with."

"'Tis just what Lord Rochester said."

"He's not always tactful, but he *is* right."

"Thank you, Your Grace. I fancy all the 'elp you'll give me, if I'm to survive 'ere."

"I've seen for myself how resourceful you are, and been charmed by it more than once. You would survive here on your own. But I expect you to thrive! You've only begun to get your footing. Consider me a steady hand to shore you up."

She wanted to say that considering the sort of company he was known to keep, she did not seem at all like one a duke would fancy helping. But she bit back the words. She needed allies at court. She needed the great Duke of Buckingham.

He was spirited away a moment later by Lady Shrewsbury, her arm wound proprietarily through his. Then they began to dance an allemande right before the nose of the humiliated Duchess of Buckingham, who stood near the doors surrounded in a tight cluster by her supporters. Suddenly alone, Nell watched the king escort the young girl to whom he had just been introduced. They made their way, with great ceremony, out to dance. Court was a difficult place to exist when one could not stand in the light. She saw that boldly in the face of poor Mary Fairfax, now the unhappily married Duchess of Buckingham. And Nell felt it in the pit of her own stomach. But she pressed it away. *Determination*, she reminded herself. *No one from a place like Coal Yard Alley should even be here. You have already come so very far . . .*

The king reclaimed Nell after the dance, pressing an affectionate kiss onto her cheek, and winding her arm back through his, the other girl seemingly forgotten in a new round of introductions and laughter. A snide comment about the girl's extreme youth nearly clawed its way over her tongue, but instead Nell accepted a fourth glass of champagne from one of the many royal pages who circled the crowded room. And then another.

There was a small entourage of courtiers around them, vying for the king's favor, all listening intently so that they could laugh heartily at a joke he might tell. There was Arlington; his compliant wife, Isabella; John Maitland, the rough-tongued, burly Scotsman; and his dowdy wife, Elizabeth. The Earl of Rochester, whose poetry had stunned Nell, was at their head, and a pale, irritating Thomas Clifford did his best to laugh at everything.

No matter what he said, the group surrounding him, so as not to offend His Royal Majesty, nodded in total agreement. Nell was finishing her fifth glass of champagne when she heard the king ask, "Pray, tell me, is this room as warm as it feels, or am I the only one to notice?"

Everyone agreed that it was quite warm indeed within the confines so large a crowd.

"Well, then," he said. "A moonlight stroll should invigorate us all!"

As she strolled outside into the night along with the others, Nell began to feel the full effects of the champagne. The air seemed to her suddenly unbearably still. She bit back an erupting giggle at Elizabeth Maitland's irritatingly high, nasal drone. The aroma of Isabella's heady ambergris perfume was cloying, and she had never noticed how much Lady Maitland's footfalls reminded her of a waddling duck. Her head was spinning, and the conversations behind her took on a comic, unreal tone. The cagelike corset she was wearing seemed to be cutting the life out of her. She moved away from the group, down the steep incline behind the palace toward the stand of full, leafy trees, and the flowing river beyond, all of it lit in a silvery glow of moonlight. She heard the king call out to her. The champagne made her long to cast off the gown, the petticoats and jewels, the pretensions and conventions into which she struggled every moment of every day here to fit.

"Oddsfish!" She heard the king's deep voice. "Where the devil is she going?" But her own laughter was louder, mingling with the throb of her heart as she ran steadily nearer the water. "Nell, really!" Again the king's voice, deeper now, censorious. "Do cease this!"

"Mrs. Gwynne! I daresay, what on earth *is* she doing?" The irritatingly high voice of Elizabeth Maitland broke through her heart's deep pounding.

"Careful, sweetheart! You're very likely to—"

And that was the last thing she remembered before she slid on a slick patch of moss, tumbling headlong into a wave of cold water. Entirely submerged for a moment, and fully clothed, she felt the weight of the gown and the jewels as an anchor. Then, as she bobbed to the surface, Nell's senses reemerged. Along with them came the sobering realization of what she had just done . . . and right before Charles's most valued courtiers and their wives! For a moment, she did not want to come out of the water. Censure waited along the shore, along with disapproval, two things she almost could not bear, for how hard she had struggled against them. As she moved, drenched and dripping, nearer the collected, horrified guests, from the corner of her eye she could see two other figures approach, both adjusting their clothing and hair. It was the Duke of Buckingham and the Countess of Shrewsbury. Both figures were lit well by the light of the full moon above them.

"How absolutely marvelous!" Buckingham called out loudly on the tone of a carefree laugh. "An evening swim in this dreadful heat! Nell you are a positive innovator of frivolity!"

There was grumbling from the others as he and his mistress drew steadily nearer, both properly reassembled now.

"It wouldn't at all do to undress with our ladies, but we can certainly enjoy a swim in our clothes!" he laughed. Then, without missing a beat, Buckingham cast off his shoes, dashed down to the water's edge, and plunged headlong beside her.

Nell stood, still ankle deep in water, dumbstruck.

"Come, everyone! The water's grand, and we have Nell to thank for the notion!"

The countess was the first to follow, only removing her shoes before she plunged headlong into the river. Next, to Nell's great surprise, Isabella, Arlington's wife, began to giggle and remove her shoes. "Mrs. Gwynne," she called out. "You *do* certainly know how to brighten a banquet!"

Once she had been joined by enough of the others to dare, Nell glanced back up at the king, whose frown, to her relief, had now softened. His expression, in the moonlight and shadows, was something more of cautious surprise. It was better, she thought, to have him believe that she was a grand innovator rather than to reveal the truth to him. There was nothing at all innovative in her burst of insecurity, driven by too much heat and champagne. She certainly owed the duke a debt, and it was one she would not forget to repay. Nell began to splash about and to laugh genuinely, her own special infectious laugh, that in the beginning so endeared her to the king. It was that part of herself she had neglected these past few days, trying to be so like the rest of them. "Come, Your Majesty!" she dared to call out to him, as if it had been her plan all along. "Join us!"

To her absolute shock, a moment later, he did.

Suddenly, the king of England was chuckling, head back joyously, and wiping a hand across his face. "Ah, Nell! You do make me laugh!"

"Your Majesty is a fortunate man," Buckingham called out as they all splashed beneath the brightly shining silvery moon, to the sound of music and bristling trees.

He lay beside her before dawn, twisting and turning beneath the crimson-and-gold damask coverlet, his face awash in sweat and rousing the collection of spaniels asleep at their feet. Nell rolled onto her side in a spray of pillows, and saw his face twisted into an expression of agony.

"No! No, I won't! Stop, YOU MUST STOP!"

A moment later, Charles shot upright, calling out. Nell wrapped her arms around him. "You've 'ad a dream! 'Tis all," she crooned as she held him. "'Twas only a dream."

"God's blood, but it seemed so real . . . ," he muttered, rousing slowly from his dream-soaked sleep.

"I was right 'ere with you the entire time. I promise." She could see that her reassuring smile was a balm on the raw past that tormented him, and finally he drew in a deep breath, exhaled, and fell back against the pillows with her.

"Will you tell me about the dream?"

She saw him consider whether he could reveal things from his past that so defined who he was.

"It is always the same one. I see myself there among the spectators, watching. But my hands are tied."

"Your father's death?"

"His barbaric execution. I call out to him, I plead with the guards, with the executioner. But it always ends the same as it did. And his blood is always covering me, until I am drenched, and I cannot see. Then I wake up."

Nell reached over to the side table and poured him a glass of wine from the crystal pitcher there. "Where were you that day?" she asked as he drank it in one long swallow.

"I was already forced into exile in France by my father's own men. They were men who had betrayed the Crown and him to support Cromwell. For my own good, they said. It was the last place I wanted to be. I wanted to help my father. I was the eldest.

I should have been able to help him . . . We tried so hard to avoid the inevitable . . . God, the helplessness of that. I was powerless to change things."

He touched her, and the bed moved with the shifting of his weight. Nell melted against him. He held her face in his hands and pressed an urgent kiss onto her mouth. "Stay with me. I want you to be with me everywhere. I need you to be by my side," he declared.

"'Twould surely make 'em talk."

"I do not give a whit about gossip, Nell. You bring me too much joy and too much peace."

She swung her legs over the edge of the bed and ran her fingers through her unruly hair, trying to tame it. It was a nervous gesture to avoid the absolute power he had over her, especially like this, when he was vulnerable. "I'll not give up the theater again, even for you. I can't do it."

"But I want to care for you. I will see that you and your sister never want for money."

"'Twas a hard-won lesson, Charlie, but I'll not 'ave that arrangement with a man again."

"I'm not any man."

"Nor shall I ever be just any woman."

"All of my life I have been heir to a throne, a king's son, then a king. People have always told me what they thought I wanted to hear. You have never done that."

"I fancy the truth," she said. "It's easier to recall what I've said that way."

"Then I shall be with you when you trod the boards so brilliantly, so long as you are with me here in return. I should have said this long ago, and I'm a fool for not saying it . . ."

"Shh." She pressed a finger against his lips. "Say not what you're not ready to say."

"But I want to say it. With all my heart, I want to tell you that I love you, Nell. I love you, in fact, quite madly."

"In that case, Your Majesty"—she smiled up at him—"speak on!"

"I need a loan, George."

The king's declaration hung between them for a moment, heavy and awkward as they strolled together through the royal aviary in St. James's Park. It was full of exotic birds from all over the world in tall, impressive cages, all squawking and chirping.

"So the mighty comes to the meek?" asked the Duke of Buckingham with a particularly unattractive smirk. He could see very quickly that the king was not amused by his response.

It had been a difficult year, wherein Charles had been forced to go before Parliament and plead his case for money in order to try to begin rebuilding the decimated naval fleet so that he might once again strike out at the Dutch to reclaim his country's deeply wounded honor. But his own Parliament had been less than enthusiastic about granting his request in any meaningful way. They informed him instead that they had little faith he would not spend the money for his own increasingly grand and ostentatious lifestyle.

"You know perfectly well the royal coffers are drained. I've used every avenue I could think of to move funds around, but I need to find some creative way to see to a stipend for Nell."

"Perhaps if you hadn't bought that unspeakably garish house for Lady Castlemaine—"

"Don't be impertinent, you wretched friend! I need a loan, and that is all! Lord knows, I've seen to it that the Crown pays you plenty! Besides, I can either ask, or simply take it, if I must, when you are housed again in the Tower!"

After three previous forays into the prison for arguments that had gone too far, George knew the threat was anything but empty. "How much do you need?"

"Well, I've given her what I can, but she needs a full and proper staff, gowns, shoes, a woman to dress her hair. I've sent to Paris for her own wardrobe mistress. Then she will need more dancing lessons, reading and writing lessons, and comportment—"

"And yet, one might be moved to ask, is Your Majesty not trying to change the very things that attracted you to her in the first place?"

"Nonsense! I have no wish to change Nell!" he declared as they paused before a massive cage. "You know how difficult it is to exist in our world. I simply desire to make the transition easier."

"Until your next great distraction comes along?"

Charles's face hardened.

"You are very close to the line, George. I would watch myself if I were you."

"If Your Majesty were me, a gem like Nell would never have given you so much as a second look. Fortunately, you are far more clever, and certainly more handsome than I."

The flattery worked, as always, and a moment later Charles softened. "I care for her, George, and I mean to give her the life she's never had. That is *all* I mean to do."

"Of course, you can have the money, whatever you need. I'm only suggesting you take care. We both know there will be others one day."

"I'm not so certain."

"And was that the lovely daughter of Lord Kildare I saw coming out of your bedchamber yesterday afternoon, finally conquered?"

"That is lust, George, a very different thing from what I have with Nell."

"Be careful of your heart, Charles. Nell Gwynne may not always be so understanding of that, or willing to tolerate it."

"I have told her the truth about me, and she loves me, George, truly loves me, and she takes me as I am. Not even Frances offered me that. My own, in return, is a commodity I have not considered surrendering to anyone since Minette."

"A sister and a mistress are as different things as lust and love."

"But if I could, one day, actually find them both in one woman—"

"Like a needle in a proverbial stack of hay, Your Majesty."

Chapter 21

I N late November, the court returned to Whitehall so that Charles could resume the negotiations with France. The situation with the Dutch was increasingly tense. In addition, the king was forced to wrestle with an angry Parliament over his increasing alliance with Catholic France, and his just issued Declaration of Indulgence, meant to protect his Catholic friends and family from persecution. Parliament was withholding money from him because of it.

Meanwhile, Nell had agreed to work again with Charles Hart in her friend Charles Sedley's first play, *The Mulberry Garden*. The king was in his box every afternoon to watch her delight the masses, but his own existence gave him very little about which to laugh. When he was not watching Nell, he was consumed by the complexities of making himself a significant player on the world stage. If England meant to become a force with which to be reckoned, he knew that he must maintain a delicate political balance. After the devastating losses to the Dutch, England's national honor was at stake in it. *I will make you proud.* Every day he made that promise to the small painting of his father he kept in his private closet, making it a prayer. *I will see to it, Father, that what you wanted for England will happen, that your death will not be in vain.* But he knew he must also cultivate France. Catholic France.

It all played across his mind, distracting him, in the royal box, chin propped by his hand, as he watched Nell easily seduce an entire theater. She pranced across the stage and smiled to the crowd. She winked and skipped and delivered her lines so charmingly that men called out during the acts declaring their love for her, even while knowing her powerful lover loomed above them.

When it was over, he did not wait for her in the theater, but rather inside his coach, preferring to give her the moment with an adoring public, which she had earned. Buckingham, Lady Shrewsbury, and Thomas Clifford, who had also attended the play that day, had gone ahead back to Whitehall to await the king to play pall-mall. The game was all the rage now, and Charles could not get enough of hitting the wooden ball with a long mallet farther and more directly than anyone else.

A quarter of an hour later, the door of the great gilded royal coach was opened by a footman. Nell was helped up the steps, then inside, heady with triumph. Her smile was broad and infectious as she pressed a happy kiss onto his cheek. Jeddy, who went everywhere with her, pushed the train of her dress inside, then hopped up onto the seat across from her as the door was closed.

"Thanks for waitin', love," Nell said with a soft giggle.

"I have already waited a lifetime for you; what's another quarter of an hour? You were brilliant today."

"I dropped a line in the third act."

"Not so anyone would notice. Everyone was far too busy

cheering you on," he said, taking her hand as the coach lurched forward merging onto bustling Drury Lane.

Charles reached across to pat Jeddy's head, then smiled over at Nell. He liked the little girl because he loved all children, but mainly because the girl was dear to Nell. "If you're not too tired, I told George and a couple of others we would join them for a round of pall-mall."

"I'm never too tired for anythin' with you."

"And that *is* one of your attributes I most admire."

The coach rattled and rocked over the cobbles on Drury Lane, then down the busy, paved Strand, and through Charing Cross, heading toward Pall Mall, where it was the custom for a great parade of coaches to ride slowly in order to be seen. The king drew a small blue-velvet pouch from his surcoat, and Nell giggled delightedly. No matter how many tokens he gave her, it was still a surprise when another arrived; it was a confirmation that he still cared for her. Inside the pouch were two perfect emerald earrings. Each the size of a fingernail, they were exquisitely teardrop shaped.

"To make you sparkle," Charles said, taking one of the earrings from her hand to insert it into the tiny hole in her earlobe.

There was a round mirror sewn into the tufted fabric of the carriage wall behind Jeddy. Nell lurched across to regard herself with the earrings, even as they swayed. Jeddy smiled, seeing her pleasure. "You're too good to me, Charlie," she said, settling back beside him and wrapping her arms around his neck.

"I treat you only as you have always deserved to be treated, sweetheart. And you, my girl . . ." He glanced across at Jeddy, who was always careful never to look directly at the king unless, as now, she was addressed. "You deserve something as well for making your mistress so content as you do, and watching out for her when I cannot be there."

He handed Jeddy a shiny silver crown. It was the first the child had ever held. "Won't someone believe she's stolen it?" Nell asked as soon as it occurred to her.

"If they do ask, she shall tip up her head and say proudly that it was a gift from her king." He looked at Jeddy again, whose black eyes were as big as saucers. "Keep it. Money is power, and power is freedom. This can be the beginning of both of those for you."

Suddenly, a coach slowed beside them and Nell looked across, just as the king did. His smile fell as they both looked over and through the window saw the queen.

Nell felt hot color creep up her neck and onto her face at the awkward moment. The woman with slick ebony hair and expressive dark eyes sat surrounded by her ladies and was unwilling to break her proud gaze from Nell's. For a moment, the two women were connected. The queen's huge, dark-brown eyes shimmered. Pride mixed with great heartbreak was what Nell saw.

Nell's gaze slid away from the window, back to the king. His face had tensed.

The king's coach moved ahead of the queen's then and the moment was over, but it had an impact on Nell. As they emerged from the coach minutes later, with a swish of Nell's skirts and a flash of the king's jeweled fingers, Charles was engulfed by a crowd of his courtiers. The incident was replaced in Nell's mind by the overbearing solicitations of the Duke of Buckingham as he led her toward Pall Mall. Nell stood beside him, smiling wisely, yet saying nothing. Always attentive. Always learning, paying careful heed to how people spoke, and the sort of things they said. She knew now that the best tutor she could ever have was her own desire to improve.

She was joined by Lady Shrewsbury, the Duchess of Lauderdale, and Lady Arlington, all of whom had shown a drastic softening toward Nell since that first horrid afternoon in the Hampton Court gardens. Such was the power of her growing importance to the king.

Smiling and conversing, they followed the men, and their collection of pages and aides, as well as several of the king's guard. It became a great crowd of perfumed, finely dressed courtiers, all bows, beads, wigs, hats, and plumes. It was a warm afternoon, and the wind was dry and soothing beneath the protective canopy of trees in a sentinel row down the length of the park. Charles had only just taken up his mallet, the others collecting in a ring beside him, when a diminutive man of middle age, with a wildly angry expression, approached with two of his own servants. One of them Nell recognized as John Cassells, Rose's lover, who was in service to the king's eldest son. The men did not stop beside the king. Rather, they drew up directly before the Duke of Buckingham, to the shock and whispers of the crowd.

"Who is that?" Nell leaned over to Lady Shrewsbury to ask in a whisper.

"That, Mrs. Gwynne, is my husband."

"I didn't know he had it in him," the Duchess of Lauderdale said dryly.

"Sadly, nor did I," Lady Shrewsbury countered.

"Sir," the Earl of Shrewsbury said to the Duke of Buckingham in a stilted tone, "this theft of my honor must come to an end here and now. It would be one thing for you simply to go on bedding my wife. But I can no longer tolerate your open mocking of me with her to the entire court."

George bit back an amused smile at the formality. "Do stop before you say something we all know you will regret."

Shrewsbury was rigid as a corpse, fingering the dagger sheathed at his hip. "The only thing I regret, sir, is allowing this to go on for as long as it has. That, and marrying her."

The ladies let out a collective gasp at the slight, delighted in the drama of it all.

"Oh, Shrewsbury, do have a heart and leave us before this gets out of hand."

"I no longer have a heart. And all that is left to me are the shreds of my honor!"

"Good Lord, but you're drunk!" said his wife.

"I may be drunk, but I believe this is the wisest thing I have ever done!"

There was another collective gasp of disbelief as Buckingham turned very slowly and asked, "You are not seriously challenging me to a duel, are you? And without a formal written declaration? Good Lord, no wonder your wife finds you so great a coward!"

"If you decline, sir, to meet my challenge, tomorrow at dawn in the close near Barne Elmes, it is *you* who shall be thought a coward!"

"I'll not decline, and you'll not survive," George said coldly.

"You're going to let them fight?" Nell asked the king, clinging to his arm as they walked back to the royal coach, the easy afternoon for which he had hoped now at an end.

"There is little I can do about it."

"You're the king of England! Can you not make a law or somethin'?"

In fact, there were many rules and customs that governed such a challenge. There were weapons to be decided—pistols or swords; the location—most often an open field; and seconds to be decided upon for each opponent. But, as to stopping the process, he calmly told her, it was an agreement between gentlemen that not even royalty could upend.

"But what if someone should get 'urt?"

"That is more than likely."

"But these are your friends, your subjects!"

"And, more precisely, George has been a friend to *you*."

"'E 'as been, indeed!"

"If he has helped you understand anything about life at court, then you must know he would not want this stopped."

"Even if it means his own death?"

He turned to her then, but his face was expressionless. "Even if."

Lending a modicum of propriety to what was already a scandalous affair, Lady Shrewsbury left England to visit France the next morning.

Or so the court was told, though there was no one who had actually seen her depart.

As the sun rose, Nell sat in her dressing gown in the little alcove beside her bed. Charles had left at dawn to return to Whitehall to have breakfast with his eldest son, Monmouth, and so Nell waited alone for Rose to return. She had been out with John Cassells, who, presumably, had told her everything that had occurred. Perhaps her sister understood things more clearly and could explain them to her. Yet Rose had not seen the expression of anger on Shrewsbury's face, or the look of confident resignation the Duke of Buckingham presented. Worst of all was the evil glee with which Lady Shrewsbury observed it all unfolding. It did not seem to Nell, based on her response, that the lady cared who won or who lost the duel, so long as they fought over her.

Nell gazed out her large bedroom window facing the square. The glass panes were covered with an early morning autumnal frost. Jeddy was still asleep in the little low bed beside her own, warmed by the fire. Her face was softened by the full belly, and sugary marchpane, with which she had gone to sleep. She smiled to herself thinking how content she would feel, if not for the battle that was likely to cost someone his life.

When Rose came in finally, Nell heard the front-door latch click. She descended the wide staircase alone, her dressing gown sweeping over the polished oak steps, and stood facing her in the still-shadowy entrance hall. Then, without a word, they embraced, each knowing what the other knew. A moment later, Rose followed Nell into the grand drawing room, where the servants had already lit a fire.

"John is to be present at the duel today," Rose quietly announced, warming her back at the hearth. "And I've told 'im I must be with 'im somehow."

"'E's not in danger, is 'e?"

"'E's not one of the seconds, so not directly in danger. Yet still, I've got to be there. If somethin' were accidentally to 'appen, I'd never forgive myself."

"You're a woman, and 'Is Majesty wouldn't want you to be there. You know that," said Nell.

"'E wouldn't want *you* to be there. But I suspect you're comin' with me anyway, aren't you?"

"'Ow ever could we do it?"

"As it 'appens, John 'as offered to dress us up like page boys." She smiled as the foolish image circled in both their minds. "We can 'ide in the shrubbery there, surroundin' everything, yet be close enough to see."

"An ingenious fellow, your Captain Cassells," said Nell. Then she laughed. "Lord above, Rose, I would never even attempt such a thing without you beside me!" Nell's expression changed again, mirroring the worry she felt. "'Is Grace 'as been so good to me, Rose. I 'ate that 'e's gotten 'imself into this."

"You can't afford to think like that now. John's reminded me, as you once did, that court is a very different world, and we've got to learn to fit in with them, not the other way round."

A voice interrupted them. "She's right, you know, Nell."

It was a man's easy tenor that came from behind them, beneath the archway into the drawing room. Both Rose and Nell pivoted around to see the last person they ever expected. Charles Sackville, Lord Buckhurst, was standing there, handsome and carefree as ever, in a suit of sea-green silk, with a matching cloak and shoes with shining silver buckles. His hat was plumed with an ostrich feather, and his mouth, as always, wore the same slightly twisted smile that once had won her for a time when she was still one of Mary Meggs's orange girls.

"But you're in France!" Nell cried out in surprise.

"I was indeed. But apparently I was drinking the ambassador dry, and testing his hospitality in it. He sent me back without incident."

"Clever way to get home." Rose smiled at him.

"Your girl let me in," he said. "I hope you don't mind. I'd no idea you'd kept her."

"She's not my girl, and her name is Jeddy," Nell replied.

After an awkward silence, considering what was proper, and what was her deeper wish, Nell dashed across the room and embraced him. She knew that she should be angry with him for how he had let it end, yet she wasn't. "Oh, 'tis good to see you!" she said, laughing as they embraced.

"And it is a feast for the eyes to see you." He held her out at arm's length. "My, but the royal purse has made you into a remarkably elegant lady in my absence."

"My sister worked right 'ard to become proper, all on her own," Rose defended, as the two continued to embrace.

"I wouldn't doubt that for a moment." He kissed each of her cheeks as Rose left the room by a small arched doorway beside the fireplace. "Yet I can see that wonderful, refreshing Nell is still there just beneath the surface, for anyone who truly cares to look."

"A great deal's 'appened while you've been gone."

"To begin with, I hear you've quite captivated the king. That is certainly a change from the girl I chased through a certain meadow in Newmarket not so awfully long ago."

She sank onto a small settee covered in blue Florentine silk, fanning out her dressing gown. A moment later, he sat beside her, and took up her hand. The feel of it was so different from the king's. There was no great command in the way he gripped her fingers, yet there still was a potent history there.

"I'm sorry I left like that, Charles."

A smile played at the corners of his mouth in response. "You really did break my heart, you know."

"Your 'eart is meant for revelry, not love. When I discovered that, 'twas time to leave."

"And His Majesty's is different?"

"'E says 'e loves me."

"Well, now. That does put a crimp in the notion of a reconciliation between us." He lifted her hand to his lips and gently kissed it, in spite of his cavalier tone. "So, then. There's no chance at all, I don't suppose, of us having, at the least, an assignation on the side when His Majesty is otherwise engaged?"

"None at all, I'm afraid."

"Seems a waste of such a lovely home, so suspiciously far from court. Have you ever asked yourself why he put you so far from the

center of everything—and everyone else—with whom he lives, if
it is genuine love between the two of you?"

Nell stood then and smoothed out her dressing gown, feeling a
hint of defensiveness overtake her genuine regard for him. "I told
him once, in passing, that this particular square had always
seemed the most elegant in the world."

"Convenient wish to grant to keep you and Lady Castlemaine
from one another's throats."

"You have been gone a while, Charles. Lady Castlemaine was
asked to leave court last summer."

"Is that a fact?"

"It is."

"Do yourself a favor, in any case, and do not go making the
inference that it means you have him exclusively, no matter what
he tells you in order to keep a place in your bed. Their romance
had been winding down for years, and he had been on the march
to replace her. Needless to say, you are not the first woman for
whom His Majesty bought a house. Nor are you likely to be the
last."

"You've no idea what you're talkin' about! 'Is Majesty adores
me!"

"He adores all pretty things, Nell, and in abundance."

"At least for now 'e's chosen me over a bottle of gin!"

"Dearest Nell." He sighed, feeling the sting. "Now I've
angered you, and my greatest wish was only to come here and
apologize for my behavior in Newmarket. You really did break
my heart when you left me. You know, that is absolutely the
truth."

She softened again, but her expression was still hostile. "Oh,
did I?"

"More than anyone else ever has."

"Then tell me this, would you ever have married me if I had stayed with you?"

For a moment, he studied her. "Based on your expression just now, I am forced to ask, if I reply to that honestly, will you have me thrown out of your house?"

"After most of the people I've met at court, if you're honest, I believe you'll 'ave a friend in me for life."

He moved a step nearer, closing the chasm between them. He embraced her very gently then, and, with great sincerity, pressed a kiss onto her forehead. "Nell," he said very gently. "You are the most exciting, funny, desirable woman it has been my great honor to know. And you were the first person I wanted to see the moment I set foot back in London. But I don't suppose I shall ever be a marrying sort of man."

She smiled up at him. "You are every bit the libertine they say you are."

"Hopelessly, I'm afraid."

"Pray, tell me you'll not disappoint me as a friend."

"I shall be your friend, dear Nell, above all other things."

Nell chuckled. "The love of revelry could do much to change that promise."

"But it is nothing compared to the power of our friendship."

"Well, I could certainly use a friend these days. And, as my friend, will you go to the duel this mornin' between Lord Shrewsbury and the Duke of Buckingham?"

"That's not exactly an occasion to which one is issued in happy attendance. And I can proudly say I've managed to reach this ripe old age without having been invited to one directly, either!"

"Rose and I are goin'." She smiled. "We're dressin' up as boys."

"Now why does that not surprise me, coming from a woman who conquered the stage as a dozen different people?"

"Seriously, Charles. 'Is Grace's been a friend while you've been gone, and I couldn't bear to think that 'e might—"

"The only person George Villiers is a friend to is himself, Nell. And perhaps, on occasion, the king, *if* he thinks it might get him somewhere."

"You'd best be careful, Charles Sackville. I may be an actress, but your own mask's begun to slip," she declared. "In spite of everythin', though, the truth is, I'm awfully glad you're back!"

Nell and Rose arrived at the grand estate, Barne Elmes, early enough to steal together across the soggy grass and into a loose bush large enough to conceal them. The beige coats and hats provided by John Cassells hid them well in places the low-lying fog did not conceal. As the first grand coach pulled down the gravel drive of the estate, Nell's heart raced. She could not believe that she was actually going to watch this.

Suddenly, all the men were present on the great open close with its thick grass waving. They saw John, who carried messages to the duke and his two seconds. Words were exchanged that they were too distant to hear. One of the horses whinnied, then pawed at the gravel, pulling against its harness. Nell's eyes shifted from one man to the next. Their rivalry was a palpable thing.

"I wish I knew how to stop this!" she whispered, her voice rising in panic.

"Hush!" her sister bade her. "You know 'Is Majesty would be furious if you were caught 'ere!"

"That Shrewsbury trollop could never be worth this!"

"There's two men across that field of grass who believe otherwise."

It happened quickly after that. A series of blades glinting in the morning sunlight as it poked through the clouds and fog. Sharp movements back and forth. A deep cry. A small puncture on Buckingham's upper arm was the first wound. A stream of blood darkened the sleeve of his white shirt, and Nell felt her mouth go dry.

"Please, no!" she gasped before Rose covered her mouth with her own hand.

The six men were now moving, lunging and darting. There was little grace in it, the way the king had once described. Rather, it seemed a reckless tangle of showmanship and vengeance. Suddenly, more blood. This time it was Will Jenkins, Buckingham's tall, stately second who took the blade. A wound like a crimson sash darkened across the front of his shirt. He recoiled in response, then sank like a stone onto the wild grass. Before anyone dared go to him, Buckingham seized the distraction and plunged his sword into Shrewsbury's unprotected side to the sound of a deep-throated gasp.

"He's killed Lord Shrewsbury!"

That was the whispered refrain around them as Nell clutched the king's arm. They stood together that evening on the balcony to watch a glorious nighttime display of candlelit boats and barges, their banners flapping in the cool breeze as they paraded along the river. The lantern light hit the snaking water, turning it to silver before them. Around Nell and the king stood his friend John Maitland, Duke of Lauderdale, Thomas Clifford, the Earl of Arlington, and their wives, watching the magnificent spectacle in the king's honor. But everyone's mind was on the gossip of the day.

"Is 'e dead then?" Nell quietly asked Charles.

"Not yet. But the wound is very bad."

He was still unaware that Nell had been present at the duel, and she had no intention of telling him. She thought of it now, hours later, as the most horrendous thing she had ever seen, including all of the seamy elements of the darker world that her mother had exposed her to.

"'Tis dreadful," Nell said, pretending to watch the magnificent display of boats and barges before them, as the warm breeze up off the water ruffled her sleeves and the curled ends of her hair.

"Fool should never have challenged Buckingham. He's a talented swordsman."

"Perhaps 'e thought 'e must. For 'is wife's 'onor, I mean."

"Lady Shrewsbury has no honor," Charles scoffed. "None worth trying to save, anyway. She's a court whore, here to gain what she can at any expense. Everyone here knows women like that for what they are. And losing sight of that now will likely cost him his life."

The offhand comment wounded Nell in a way she had not expected. It reminded her pointedly that she was not so different from Lady Shrewsbury. She, too, was a mistress, a court whore. Expendable. As much as she loved Charles, and he cared for her, she must never lose sight of that, and she must work every day to keep her place, unlike a wife—or a real lady.

It was late when the festivities finally ended, so, instead of returning to her Lincoln's Inn Fields house, Nell remained at Whitehall. But she slept little. As she lay alone in the king's grand bed, with long swags of tapestry fabric wrapped around heavy turned posts, her stomach was sour and roiling. Nell could deny it to herself no longer. She felt certain she was pregnant. The signs had been there for weeks, in spite of how she tried to reason them away. The reality filled her with both a sense of joy and a deep dread. Another royal bastard. The butt of more jests. More cruel poems written for a laugh by Rochester. Nell thought how a child between them would likely hasten their end. As it had with Moll Davies. How would a bulbous tottering mass go on enticing a king? William Chiffinch was standing over her holding a large cup of steaming chocolate when she woke.

"I thought perhaps you could use this," he said kindly, as she fought a new surge of nausea and moved to the edge of the bed, which was still covered by a spray of the king's spaniels.

"Where is 'e?" she asked, afraid of the answer.

"Gone for one of his walks, ma'am."

"Alone?"

"His Grace, the Duke of Buckingham, and the Earl of Rochester are with him."

Chiffinch covered her with one of the king's own dressing gowns. "My wife is in the next room. She will see to something suitable for you to wear today should you wish to wait for His Majesty's return."

Nell looked up at him, tall and stoic, his face giving nothing away; his voice, however, held an uncommon tenderness. "'Tis all so complicated." She sank back onto the bed, wrapped in silk and tassels. "There seems so much still to learn. So many traps around nearly every corner."

"I can easily arrange a coach if—"

"But what's the right thing to do, Mr. Chiffinch? I wouldn't want to be a nuisance. But I shouldn't like to end up like Moll Davies."

"Pardon me for saying, Mrs. Nelly, but you are not at all like Mrs. Davies."

She smiled at that, grateful. "Thank you, sir."

"I would be honored if you would call me William."

Nell studied him for a moment. "Why are you so nice to me?"

He leaned in very close, pausing before he replied. "I shouldn't say, Mrs. Nelly. But Mrs. Chiffinch and I had a daughter once. You are very like her. Same fire and spirit. My wife noticed it straightaway."

"And tell me, William, what would you both have thought of your very spirited daughter in bed with the king like this?"

"She was once. She died in childbirth because of it."

Nell covered her mouth with a hand. "Pray, forgive me. I'd no idea."

"It was a long time ago."

"And the baby? Your grandchild?"

"Gone to memory as well, I'm afraid. Now we've got only our duty to him. It keeps us both tied to this life, connecting us back to her in a way." He turned away from her then. "If you will excuse me, I shall call Mrs. Chiffinch to find you something extraordinary to wear." He was moving toward the door when she called to him:

"William, thank you."

"Your servant," he said with a courtly nod as he left the chamber.

Nell went to the window. She leaned against the casement and looked down onto the formal gardens in the courtyard before the river. In the distance, she saw Charles, the Duke of Buckingham, and the Earl of Rochester, just where William had said they would be. But, between them, walked a woman, cloaked in blue velvet and ermine. At first, for the ermine-covered hat she wore, Nell could not make out who it was. Then, as the woman tipped her head back and laughed at something the king said, Nell could see who Chiffinch had forgotten to mention. It was Lady Castlemaine, the woman supposedly well out of the king's life.

Nell watched her link her arm with the king's, then lay her head on his shoulder as they strolled a pace ahead of Buckingham and Rochester.

Nell felt as if something pierced through her, going straight to her heart. She felt the press of tears at the back of her eyes. It was the suddenness of it. But she was determined not to cry, or to feel the disappointment that was almost overwhelming her. Instead, with utter determination, she forced a smile. She would not be pitied, like the queen, nor avoided like any of the others, when his eye wandered. If Nell was to outlast them all—and by God, she now meant to—she must learn to happily coexist with anyone King Charles put in her path, no matter how her heart was secretly pained because of it.

Two months later, in March of 1669, Lord Shrewsbury died of wounds suffered in the duel with the Duke of Buckingham. As a consequence, Lady Shrewsbury was invited to live openly with His Grace. When the duchess protested so startling an arrangement, the duke asked his own wife to find other accommodations. The court was rocked by the scandal.

Nell continued on in a revival of *Catiline His Conspiracy*, at the King's Theater. Her own scandal was bitterly brewing. It was one that would not only eclipse the Shrewsbury affair, but would engulf the entire gossip-hungry court. She was pregnant with the king's child, and when she was forced to refuse a new role written for her once again by John Dryden, scandalmongers spread the news like wildfire, saying that for the duration of her pregnancy, her influence would be diminished. The question endlessly debated in coffeehouses and taverns along the busy Strand was who was likely to challenge Nell Gwynne's place with the king.

Chapter 22

RELATIONS between England and France had become sound enough by the following spring that Louis XIV's brother granted his wife a visit home. It was to be a great state occasion: Charles, James, and Minette, the three surviving children of the murdered Charles I, would see one another for the first time in over nine years. But the true reason for the visit was that after years of hard and complex negotiations, with their sister as the envoy, the two sides had finally agreed to a secret alliance. In exchange for substantial monetary aid, Charles had privately agreed to announce, at the time of his choosing, his conversion to Catholicism.

Minette had been dispatched to see the highly secret document signed on behalf of France. Only Arlington and Clifford of the English king's Privy Council (privately both Catholic) had read and signed the actual treaty. Charles was so afraid of their attempts to dissuade him that the bulk of his privy councillors—including the Duke of Buckingham—knew nothing about the real elements that had been agreed to. Instead, the others were presented a second manufactured treaty to keep them unaware.

And none of them were invited to join the king and the Duke of York for the reunion in Dover. Charles was playing a high-stakes game, intent on gaining money and power. Charles I would be proud of what he had been clever enough to achieve. And that was reason enough to attempt it.

There was one great caveat to his complete satisfaction at the impending reunion.

Minette's husband insisted that the visit be not only brief, but also extend no further than Dover; Charles could not bring his sister home to London. So he could not introduce her to Nell, who had begun her lying-in at the house in Lincoln's Inn Fields. He had not seen her for several weeks, at her insistence. "Wait till I can be gorgeous for you again, and I'll warrant you, I will be!" she had insisted. He had done his best to understand. But he had wanted Nell there. Her honest, easygoing style would have won Minette's fondness immediately. Even though his sister loved Catherine, he knew she loved her brother more.

He stood on the dock with his brother, James, and watched the ship sail slowly nearer, bobbing on the whitecapped waves as a huge French flag fluttered in the wind. Salt spray and a spring mist peppered their faces. His heart raced like a child's from the anticipation. Minette was the one person in the world he loved completely. When she stepped down the gangway, wrapped in forest-green velvet, Charles wiped the tears from his cheek. They were the first he had dared shed since the day of their father's murder. He and James encircled her, standing like that for a very long time, silently shocked at how drastically poor Minette had changed. She had always been petite, but now the girl they embraced was hauntingly thin, and there were feather-gray shadows embedded deeply beneath her pale, hazel eyes. Nevertheless, she smiled up at her brothers, Charles most particularly, and then embraced them each again with all of her strength. "We are all that's left of Father now," she whispered to them as they stood huddled together against the buffeting winds.

"I believe we have all three made him proud," Charles said in reply, and his smile reflected everything—their history, their losses, and their abiding love for one another. As he glanced up, his gaze caught on the collection of ladies who were following Minette from the ship. All of them wore French fashions, lacy and more intricate than the English designs. And at the head of the little delegation, intentionally setting herself a few steps apart, strode a girl with smooth, corn-yellow hair, her back regally straight, her nose tipped up as she came toward them. Charles was instantly captivated by her face. It was smooth and oddly full, with wide, impossibly blue eyes, and a little rosebud mouth. The silk fabric at her bell sleeves and ankles ruffled in the breeze, and he watched her proudly attempt to keep everything in its proper place. Her look was so childlike, her manner so full of pride, that she reminded him of a very small girl playing dress-up. Only when Minette and James began to chuckle at him did he even realize they had been speaking.

"I can see you have not changed," Minette said, taking his arm.

"Truthfully, our brother has only added more trophies to his cabinet in your absence."

Realizing the implications suddenly, Minette's smile fell. "Well, you are not to add Louise de Kéroualle to your conquests. I promised her parents myself I would protect her, and return her to them the chaste girl she is now, and I mean to do just that."

Charles embraced his sister again, and held her tightly as they all began to shiver from the cold breeze. "I'm here to see *you*. That is all I wish to do these next preciously few days that James and I have you," he said sincerely. But his mind skipped onto other things. *Louise*, he thought as they strolled arm in arm together back toward shore, the little group of his sister's ladies close at their heels. *What a simply exquisite name for so luscious a child-woman* . . . Everything else at that moment, especially his life back in London, seemed very far away.

Chapter 23

BUT THESE THINGS ARE PAST AND GONE.

—*Catullus*

Rose waited down in the walled back garden of Nell's house, amid a neat little orangery planted by the king. John had said that he would come as soon as she sent word, and she believed him. But it was a cold early morning, and she had slept little these past two nights. Finally, he came through the wooden side gate that the groundskeeper used. He was flushed and out of breath from having run, he said, half the way, because he could find a hackney coach to take him only so far from Whitehall as Covent Garden.

"Has she had the child, then?" he asked.

"She was safely delivered of a boy late last night."

"Another son for the king's growing collection."

"As long as my sister is made secure by it, I'll rejoice in their 'avin' a dozen more."

A floor above them, as they spoke, Nell lay curled beneath a mound of heavy bedding, the sleeping infant tucked into the crook of her arm. At first, it had frightened her to look at him. A royal child. The king's son. Better just by his birth than she could ever be. But it had been nine hours now. The servants had gone back downstairs. Rose had gone, as well. The weighted draperies had been pulled back, and the excruciating pain of his birth was like a nightmare gone into the light of day, diminished now by pure joy. She glanced down at him again. Foolishly, she had thought he would look like the king. He had a little crown of dark hair, but other than that, he looked to her like a tiny old man, wrinkled and foreign. Would he be ashamed of her one day? She could wear the most expensive fashions, learn all of the proper things to say, yet, in the end, she would always be Nelly Gwynne, daughter of a whore, from the rough slums of London.

For a moment, she dared to miss Charles. She had not allowed herself this weakness during the entire ordeal. His sister would always be first in his heart. He had gone to her at Dover, and Nell was glad of it. Almost glad. The little face beneath her puckered, then let out a tiny gasp. To her surprise, Nell felt her heart squeeze in response, and she pulled the infant just a little bit closer to her breast so that he could feel her heart beating.

He would be secure, she thought. Charles did his duty to all of his offspring. And, no matter how casual the affair with the women that created them, he cared financially for their mothers for the rest of their lives. A knock sounded at the door then, bringing her from her thoughts. Perhaps the king had come to—

"We simply could not wait a moment longer!" Buckhurst happily exclaimed, his arm laden with boxes, as he strode through the door into the bedchamber. He was followed by Sedley, Rochester, and the Duke of Buckingham, each of them bearing an equally weighty haul of gifts wrapped up in silk ribbons. Nell felt a smile turn up the corners of her mouth as they clumsily approached her.

"I'm no lady," said Nell. "But this cannot be proper, all of you tumbling into anyone's bedchamber."

"It is decidedly not." Rochester affably grinned. "But your little man there simply could not be made to wait to meet his three most-earnest uncles!"

"Uncles, are you?"

"That is what we shall call ourselves to him. If, of course, you'll let us," Sedley announced with a smile of his own.

"We all adore his mother enough to be her brothers."

"Since being her lover is long out of the question!" Buckhurst quipped. "Unless, of course, you've taken to your senses and changed your mind!"

In response, Nell tossed one of the packages at him playfully, and they all laughed. She was surprised, with the king so far away, how much she needed their company just now, and the reassurance of their interest in her.

Sedley plumped the spray of beaded-silk bed pillows for her, and Buckhurst helped her sit up, while Rochester unlatched the window and let in a welcoming burst of fresh air.

"You all really should not 'ave come," she said as Buckhurst sat at the foot of her bed. Sedley and Rochester leaned on the wall near the window, and Buckingham, regal in black velvet with white slashing, brought a carved oak chair nearest the bedside for himself. "But I find I'm quite glad that you 'ave, my dear, merry band."

"Have you heard from him yet?" Rochester asked, sending an awkward shard of tension into the happy moment. Everyone knew he had meant the king. And whatever was said in response, he was likely to make a poem out of it.

"'Is sister has only just arrived at Dover. I would expect no message for a few days at least."

"Of course, that's right," they stoically concurred with nodding and grumbles of agreement. But they all knew the reality. This was simply another of the king's illegitimate offspring lying before them in an ivory silk gown and bonnet. Nell could not expect more than he felt inclined to offer.

"A game of basset, perhaps?" Buckhurst cautiously offered.

"I'm a bit tired, actually," she said. "But thank all of you, truly. And next week, you'd best bring a loaded purse, or I'll take the shirts right off your back!"

After they had each pressed a kiss onto Nell's forehead, and were headed toward the door, Buckhurst lingered, taking the baby from her and placing him in the cradle beside her. After the others had gone downstairs, he returned to her, sank onto the edge of her bed, and they embraced.

"Thanks for knowin'," she whispered, weeping softly into his collar as he held her.

"Careful of that, or you'll have even me believing I've a redeeming quality or two."

Nell laughed in spite of herself, and wiped the tears from her cheeks. "You'll not be tellin' anyone about this, will you?"

"About what?" he asked with a deliberate smile. Then he grew serious and put his hand gently on top of hers. "Some moments are just between friends, Nell. And I'm awfully glad to have been admitted back into your good graces. Now, tell your old friend, Buckhurst, what troubles you."

"'Tis only I 'aven't any idea the way I'm to keep 'is fancy now, with a child."

"You're not pretty, witty Nell any longer? Is that it?"

"'Ave a good look at me, Charles," She pointed to her middle, then rolled her eyes. "I may still be Nell Gwynne, but I'm surely not the girl I was."

"Then you'll work hard to bring her back better than ever. He won't be in Dover all that long, after all. And he'll expect to see you upon his return."

"His little tart with a crying babe at her breast? That doesn't work so well for kings and actresses."

"Is it Moll you're thinking of?"

"He told me 'imself 'twas never the same between them after the child came."

"Ah, but then *she* wanted security. *You* want his heart."

"And who am I to think I could ever keep it?"

"Because you challenge a man, Nell. And the whole sorry lot of us adore that. You must admit, I speak from experience in that respect."

Nell shook her head, then reached over to press a finger along the cheek of her son, asleep in his cradle. "They're all out for blood, you know. All of 'em waitin' for me to trip up."

"Ah, but they don't know about your secret weapon."

She looked at him, her tears dry now. "What on earth could that be?"

"Why, the great and clever Lord Buckhurst, of course!" he slyly smiled.

Nell realized that evening that she had not seen Jeddy since her labor had begun, and it was unlike her not to be lurking around a corner watching. After dark fell, Nell became concerned, sending Rose, as well as her maid, Bridget Long, and her steward, Jimmy Burnett, to hunt for the little girl.

"She doesn't want to come in," Rose finally announced, a hint of exasperation tingeing her voice, an hour later when they had located the child. "She believes you're dead."

Nell sat up. "Well, let 'er come and see for 'erself that I'm not!"

"She's afraid."

"Gracious, of what? I'm perfectly fine! I've just 'ad a baby, is all."

"'Tis somethin', I think, to do with where she came from. Somethin' to do with 'er own ma, perhaps."

"Oh, pox take it!" she exclaimed with a sigh. Nell's thoughts wound back over the past weeks, to little moments with the girl that should have been clues, but she had been so taken up with her own fears, and with impending childbirth, that she had not seen them. "Well, if she'll not come in 'ere, you tell 'er I'll just 'ave to come out there."

"Nelly, you can't! You're not to get up yet!"

"Well, I'll not 'ave my girl thinkin' I'm dead or dyin'."

And she did think of her in that way, as her girl. Jeddy had been the first child to bring out maternal feeling in her. The first to make her believe she might make an acceptable mother. The first to make her believe that history did not always bear repeating.

When Jeddy was brought into the room a few minutes later, it was reluctantly. She clung to the doorjamb, wide eyes full of fear and hesitation, even as Nell smiled over at her. "I'm sorry I worried you with all the wailin' and such. But I wanted you to see that I really am perfectly fine." Jeddy's eyes began to glisten with tears. Nell's encouraging smile fell. "Now you listen; I've always been plain with you, and I've been good to you, too. 'Twill not change now. 'Twas painful bearin' my son, and you might've 'eard sounds to that effect. But I didn't die, and I'm not goin' to anytime soon! Now close that door and come closer to me."

Nell waited for the little girl to comply. Timid though she was, in all the past months Nell had never seen her like this. Once Jeddy was beside the bed, in her little blue silk dress and bare feet, Nell took her hand. "'Twas your own ma, wasn't it?"

Jeddy nodded her head; the unshed tears that glistened so brightly in her eyes fell slowly now onto her cheeks. Then, in a soft, almost imperceptible voice, she said, "On da boat. She sick.

No water. No food. Dey toss her into da water, and I don't cry. I don't say nothin' 'cause we jes' keeps goin'.'"

"God's death . . . ," Nell murmured. She had never believed the horror of anyone's childhood could exceed her own. She had no idea at all what to say, how to help heal a wound in a little girl's heart that had been bleeding for as long as she probably could remember.

"I'm sorrier, Jeddy, than I can say. I know I can't change the past, not what they did to your family. But what I can do is be your family now, and you can be a part of mine."

"I's a blackamoor, ma'am," she said, her child's voice made brittle as an old woman's by the life she already had lived.

"I know perfectly well what you are. And *I* was raised in a bawdy house. But it doesn't change who we are now with each other."

When the child could not answer that, Nell instructed her to fetch the small silver jewelry casket she kept on her dressing table and to bring it to her directly. Jeddy complied, and stood at the side of the bed watching as Nell withdrew a short, slim rope of pearls that Lord Buckhurst had given her in Newmarket. She placed them behind the little girl's neck, clasped the hook, then smiled. It seemed important to do this.

"The king gave you money, and now I've given you something as well. These are very fine pearls, Jeddy, as fine as you are. Your life'll never be what it was with your ma. But I want you to 'ave them, and wear them, to 'elp remind you that you've a good life now with us."

Jeddy nodded to her in response but did not speak. Nell watched her tentatively finger the fine strand of pearls at her neck with just the smallest hint of a smile playing at the corners of her mouth. And that would have to do, for now. It had taken her a lifetime to heal the raw wound of her own childhood, and, while she was not there yet, Nell knew this was a beginning.

Two weeks later, Nell lay awake in her bed late in the afternoon. Physically, she felt invigorated now, her body healing, but her mind was a torrent of fears and worries when Rose came personally to tell her that she had guests. They were collected in the drawing room beside the entrance hall. She sat up and raked her loose hair back from her face.

"I knew you'd not be asleep."

"Sleep seems impossible just now."

"I suspect they knew that."

"Lord Buckhurst again?"

"Along with his new shadows, Buckingham, Hyde, Rochester, and Savile, come to help you, they say."

Nell came into the room in a dressing gown of Burgundian lace, silk ties at her wrists and neck where the collar folded out beneath her chin like a flower. Her hair was long down her back, and pulled from her face with a little silver comb. She looked angelic, but she felt quite terrified. It had been one thing in the beginning to seduce the king and hold him in the bedchamber with her bawdy humor and slim girl's body. But between the Chiffinches' lessons and now a child, it all was becoming quite another thing.

"If we're goin' to work together, I can't think of you all as lords and dukes, or I'll not learn a thing. From now on, in my merry band," she pronounced, looking first at Rochester, "you shall be Roddy. Buckhurst, you must be Sackville from now on, as there can only be one Charles. Hyde, I shall call 'Lory,' since Lawrence is so conventional . . . but you, great duke, to me shall always be Lord Buck."

It was a secret society, away from the contrivances of court, and they all were seemingly pleased with the new monikers. Buckhurst rocked back on his heels then nodded to each the others. "Are you ready to go to work?" Buckhurst asked.

"Ready as I'll ever be," Nell replied.

All afternoon, they sat together conducting her education in the things that were quite beyond the Chiffinches' ability to teach. These four alone could help her in perfecting the art of courtly conversation. While Buckingham and Savile spoke to her of politics and familiarized her with events of the day so that she would make no great gaffe, the fine art of clever banter was left to Rochester and Buckhurst. Since she was such an incredibly fast study, they would help refine her comedic retorts from what she could freely use in the theater to what even the queen might find amusing. Although the afternoon was long and the lessons tedious, in the end Nell was able to mimic each of them for inflection, as well as create short, clever replies that would keep her from danger in conversation.

"You are indeed a marvelous student," Rochester said at last.

"I would not have believed it if I had not seen it myself," Savile concurred.

"I am duly impressed," said Buckingham.

"But will His Majesty be impressed?" she asked them all, a hint of vulnerability bleeding through the affable tone.

"It is not the king about whom you must worry. He adores you as you are," Buckhurst replied. "As do the four of us. But now you have a bit of knowledge, which is a weapon against the worst of them at court."

As Buckhurst, Savile, Hyde, and Rochester, one by one, kissed her on the cheek, and said their good-byes at the open front door, this time it was the Duke of Buckingham who lingered. Nell never quite knew what to expect from any of these men. The sun was setting beyond the brick wall and iron gate, a fiery crimson slashed across the sky. Nell waved to them and watched the coaches pull away. When she turned around, Buckingham placed a hand on her shoulder.

"Is there somethin' you want?" Startled by his nearness, she regretted the question the moment it left her lips.

"Indeed there is, and I have reason to believe it's what you wish, as well, since at last we find ourselves alone." He pulled at a tendril of her hair, fingering it sensually. Nell tensed as he released her hair and ran his fingers down along the slim column of her neck. "Dear girl, the king and I have shared our bad fortunes and good, alike, and since he is not anywhere near here—"

Before he could finish his sentence, Nell slapped him so hard across the face that his head made a little snap back, and his hat tumbled to the floor. "By God, you'll not share me! I owe Your Grace a great many things, but I'll never owe you that! I've only just 'ad your best friend's child!"

"That was weeks ago, Nell, a lifetime in this king's world. You don't honestly believe he is spending his nights alone in Dover." He rubbed his cheek for a moment, and then stooped to pick up his fallen hat.

"No matter where 'e is, I know not why I would eat mutton when spring lamb awaits!"

"Depending on what the king finds in Dover, you may well be waiting a long time."

"I'll take my chances." She opened the front door wider to him, and held on to it to stop herself from trembling. "'Is Majesty is the only one who'll 'ave any part of me, and if you *ever* try to touch me again, I swear to tell 'im everythin'."

The Duke of Buckingham swept through the doorway and tapped the hat back onto his head.

"Love really *is* blind, if that is indeed what you call it. " He did not wait for her reply.

Chapter 24

SECRET GUILT BY SILENCE IS BETRAYED.
—*John Dryden*

THE king held Nell to him, feeling an unexpected surge of something very like guilt. In the beginning, he had not expected to love her so much, nor to miss her desperately when they were parted. Beyond the ivy-covered brick wall surrounding the small garden at the house on Lincoln's Inn Fields, coaches and carts clacked over the cobblestones. Horses whinnied as they passed. The sunset was golden and ruby red above the little collection of orange trees he had planted there for her as a reminder of how it had begun between them.

"He's a beautiful boy, sweetheart," Charles murmured as he held her. Having her in his arms again felt like falling very fast into something dark and warmly welcoming. The urge to commit to her alone, and for the rest of his life, was strong—but he could not do that to her. He could not betray her with a lie like that.

"Rose thinks 'e looks like you."

"Oddsfish, but he is a poor dear child, as I'm an ugly specimen, indeed."

"*I* think you're the 'andsomest man in the world, Charlie." Her tone was not solicitous; she was simply speaking a fact. "Though you're not to let that go to your 'ead any more than you absolutely must."

He stroked the back of her long hair as they moved to a wrought-iron bench and sat together. "I expect you shall keep me in line."

"As if any woman in the world could actually do that. Would it be too absolutely absurd to name 'im Charles when you've other sons by that name already?"

"None are your sons."

"Because there really is no other name that fits, and I—"

"You honor me, Nell Gwynne. More surely than I deserve." As she nestled against him, the fragrance of musk, champagne, and orange blossoms was very strong around them. In this reunion, the pain of missing Minette eased, and he felt himself begin to breathe again in a way he had not since leaving Nell in London. "You truly do make me want to be a better man, Nell," he confessed, and pressed a gentle kiss onto her forehead. "Even if I never achieve it, you are the only one who has ever made me want to attempt it."

"'Tis a start, then," she quipped.

She was refusing, he saw, to let him make promises rooted in the sentiment of the new life sleeping upstairs. Charles smiled at her and moved to draw a velvet pouch from his waistcoat. "I've brought you a gift to celebrate the magnificent son you have given me."

Nell untied the ribbon, drew back the top of the box, and gazed down at a teardrop-shaped ruby pendant set in gleaming gold.

It had come from his mother's collection—she had worn it when he was a child, and had been wearing it in the last portrait ever painted of their family. He knew the moment Nell became pregnant with his child that it was meant for her. The tears sparkling in her eyes pleased him. He had never seen much beyond avarice in the eyes of the other women upon whom he had lavished wealth and jewels. "Do you truly like it?"

She touched the jewel with the tips of her fingers. Then she looked up again, searching his face. "'Tis too grand for me, Charlie."

"You're the only one in the world I would ever give it to, so on that we disagree."

She wrapped her arms around his neck then, and the depth of her kiss stunned him. He had left a vixen who he cared for, and loved to seduce, and he had returned to a complicated, lovely woman who he adored more than life. A smile spread slowly across his face. *If only . . .* , he thought. But he could not finish the thought.

Later that night, when the rest of London had bolted their doors, and everything was silent but for the linkboys who roamed the streets, lighting the way with their torches for hire, the king was wide awake. He slouched unnoticed, without his periwig or finery, on a wooden bench at the back of the Rose Tavern. Around him, Buckingham, Rochester, Savile, and Ogle drank tankard after tankard of foaming ale, amid a scattering of playing cards and shillings. They sat talking and laughing with the rest of the miscreant society that found their way here behind the large painted door and into the airless room, full of private nooks and alcoves, designed to harbor any dark activity that might be desired, and paid for.

The king loved to steal out like this, smell the ale, hear the clank of plates and tankards, and itch the underbelly of his own dangerously diverse society. All of his friends complied happily whenever the mood took him. But tonight Charles wanted to feel very little; the numbness of too much alcohol was a preference to thoughts of that beautiful French girl already back in Paris with his sister. He forced his thoughts from her, and from this place, and back to images of Nell. A shard of the guilt startled him. For a moment, and only that, he wished he could change. For Nell. But then the moment was gone. She would be asleep by now anyway. Thank God. That kept the guilt from advancing into something he must address. He pressed a tankard of ale to his lips, his fifth, then tipped back his head, and drank. As he finished the swallow, he saw a woman across the room. Her hair was down in long copper coils, darker than Nell's and more coarse, but there was something invitingly similar about her. Her eyes were a deep green, and there was that same sensual rawness. Huge breasts bulged over the top of the white bodice of a dress stained with food and perspiration. She was on the lap of Samuel Pepys, who came here often once his wife was asleep. Sam would not give him away, as the loss was too great for either of them. Buckingham saw the king's face and knew the expression well.

"Do you want me to arrange it, Charles?" his old friend slurred, drunk himself.

The king's eyes were glazed, and it took a moment for the words to register. What he should do was go back to Whitehall and find Catherine's bed. It was his duty, and the fate of England still teetered precariously on the entire question of what would happen if together they could not produce a live heir. Would it be their Protestant child that would continue on for England, or would his brother's Catholic progeny shift the balance entirely? And there was still the Monmouth question. Yes, always that . . . *You know you married my mother in secret all those years ago! In your heart, you know that I am your rightful heir!* He closed his eyes for a moment, dizzy and distracted from the noise and heat. If not Catherine, he should at least go to Nell, in spite of how late the hour. He knew how she could soothe him just by being herself, even if it was too soon for her to give him the full pleasure he would always desire of her.

"Pepys won't mind," Buckingham murmured, his hand of cards held up to obscure his words. "The ol' jackdaw owes me a favor for providing him an alibi last week for his wife."

The king rubbed his eyes. When he opened them, he saw the woman whispering seductively in Pepys's ear. Her legs were crossed, the skin of her fleshy calves glistening with sweat in the stifling room. As he watched her, the last days, the last hours, peeled away like old paint. Something about her reminded him of Nell as she was in the beginning. That first lust. The newness of what they had shared. He drank the rest of his ale, feeling more and more aroused. *Sins of the flesh*, he could hear his mother say. She was dead, and yet she still sought to remind him how different he would ever be from his father. *Why keep trying for a goal I can never attain? I will never be him . . . Never.*

The devil take me," he murmured, looking back at the woman, who was blurred in his vision now but still seductive to him. He took Rochester's glass of sack and drank it too. "Talk to Pepys," he said flatly.

Chapter 25

WHAT'S PAST AND WHAT'S TO COME IS STREW'D WITH HUSKS
AND FORMLESS RUIN OF OBLIVION . . .
—*Shakespeare*, Troilus and Cressida, *Act IV, Scene V*

Two weeks after Henrietta Anne returned to France, she fell critically ill. By the time word was sent to Charles of his sister's condition, Minette was already dead. Theaters were closed, taverns were silenced, and so was Whitehall Palace, where black crepe was hung.

When a knock sounded at Nell's door a few days following the official announcement, she was hopeful her visitor would be Charles. She had been able to think of little else, knowing better than most of the deep bond he had with his young sister. When Rose brought Richard Bell into the sitting room instead, Nell dashed across to him and they embraced. But the moment was broken when she looked up over his shoulder to see Charles Hart standing behind them.

Richard lifted a hand to stop her. "Don't be too cross, Nelly. He promised he'd stay only a moment if I agreed to bring him."

"And what did 'e promise *you?*"

She could hear the servants whispering beyond the closed door. This visit would be the new tale they would gossip about tonight after she, the baby, and Rose had gone off to bed. In truth, she thought of Richard like a dear older brother. She was not capable of anger toward him, but she would not tell him that just now.

"Before you slay me, it was Mr. Dryden who sent me," Charles Hart said. "Can you quite imagine it? Absurd as it sounds, he thought I particularly might have some pull convincing you to take the part he wrote for you in his new play."

"Imagine it, indeed," she said sarcastically, unwilling to give an inch to a man who had treated her so poorly.

He moved a step nearer, and Nell felt herself take a reflexive step back. She crossed her arms over her chest and set her face. "And you, of course, 'ave no interest whatsoever in my response. You came 'ere out of . . . out of what, the goodness of your small and shriveling 'eart?"

"I suspect I deserved that."

"That, and more."

"Come on, Nelly." He smiled, trying to recapture something from her that he believed she once had felt, his tone going humbly low. "I think you know I wouldn't be here if there was any other way. The fact is, I'm not too proud to say it. I need you."

"Mr. Dryden won't do the play without you," Richard cautiously offered. "I heard him say so myself."

"Without myself *and* 'art together, is what you mean."

"It is entirely true," said Hart, without his characteristic bravado.

In that oddly triumphant moment, Nell felt the overwhelming urge to order Hart onto his knees while she considered. Yet it would not alter her response. Her life now was with her son, and with the king. "I'm sorry, Charles, but I don't think—"

"Nell, listen to reason." Hart's hands were out now in a pleading gesture, his expression reduced to something resembling sincerity. "The play is called *The Conquest of Granada*, and we are to play the lead roles. If it must, let it be your great swan song, one last bow to your audience, to those who have clambered at the stage door every day since you departed it! They deserve that for their support of you! Now, I know I was injurious to you in a dozen different ways these last years, and if you refuse me, I will not be able to honestly blame you; but in your heart of hearts, can you truly say there is not a part of you that does not long for that applause for which you worked and earned and so richly deserve?"

His words resonated in the silent room. They had sounded like the last poignant lines from one of their plays.

"I'll consider it. For now, 'twill 'ave to be good enough."

She knew she would have to speak about it first with the king. But he had not sent for her, nor visited her, in the month since his sister's death. Whether she could continue working, now that she was mother to a royal child, had been left an open question.

She jostled about alone inside the hired coach, listening to the harness jingle and the horses' hooves clop a rhythm on cobbles, bringing her even nearer to Whitehall Palace. She had considered the move for hours. It was a risk to seek him out, but they had a child he had acknowledged. Surely, he would accept an impromptu visit. Had he not told her he loved her quite madly? Nearing the Holbein Gate, Nell glanced heavenward, saying a silent prayer to give her courage. Even so, her heart was racing so that she almost could not draw breath. This visit was brash, impulsive. He liked that about her. He would respect her for it now. He must.

As she emerged from the coach, bound by a tightly cinched corset and petticoats, all traces of her pregnancy were gone. Her normally small breasts, now full of milk, swelled more voluptuously than she had expected over the lacy décolleté. Although she must see him, Nell fought with every ounce of determination she had not to turn and run once she saw William Chiffinch emerge from the shadows surrounding a stone staircase to the royal apartments.

"My dear." He extended his hand to her, and a genuine, though controlled, smile softened the angles of his gaunt face.

"I see news travels fast around 'ere."

"I am paid to know everything that concerns His Majesty, and to handle it on his behalf."

She met his gaze. "Then I shall tell the king that you deserve an increase immediately since you could not possibly 'ave known I intended a visit."

"My apartments overlook this courtyard, madam, that is all."

"Better accommodations then, *and* a raise in your pay."

"Mrs. Gwynne." She watched him draw a short breath, preparing to say more, yet choosing his words delicately. "Madam. You cannot see him now."

"'E's not 'ere?"

She saw a small muscle in his jaw tighten in response. His lips closed into a straight line. "He is a complicated man."

Nell felt a tiny twitch of indignance. "Do you not mean 'e is a restless man, William?"

"That, as well, madam. And if I may say, it is the chase that keeps him, not being chased."

"But I've got to know 'ow 'e is. It 'as been weeks since 'is sister died, and there is so much to discuss about—"

"Since the princess passed from this earth, it has not been easy for His Majesty, and he has required a period of private mourning in order to reflect. I do realize you are very young, madam, but playing in this world is a skill you simply must master if you mean to stand the test."

"The test, Mr. Chiffinch?"

"The test of time, madam. Pray, love him if you must, but do not pursue him. He must be made to chase you—and, given time, he will. That is my advice to you."

Nell glanced around, the weight of foolishness descending upon her fully then, and having no earthly idea how she might leave with any small bit of her pride intact. Gazing around at the windows, she wondered how many courtiers had just witnessed her arrival. William Chiffinch took hold of her arm, above the elbow, and drew her back to him. "It is not much," he said to her gently. "But my wife and I were about to share a lamb pasty and some wine beside the fire. We would be grateful for the company if you would consent to join us."

She looked at the waiting coach, then glanced back at him. It was likely she was being viewed from the honeycomb of windows above and around them. If she departed now, people would know she had been turned away. William Chiffinch was offering a way through her miscalculation, and she must not be too prideful to reject it.

"I wouldn't wish to trouble you."

"My wife fancies that you are a breath of fresh air around this place, child, and I find I agree with her. We would like it very much if you would join us."

Nell smiled tentatively as he extended his arm. The apartment to which he led her from the prying eyes of Whitehall was well appointed and charming, not the modest servant quarters she had expected. The dark wood furniture was oversized and stately.

There were two gold-framed landscapes on the wall, and an impressive tapestry on an iron rod to further warm the room. Mary Chiffinch came quickly to the door with a welcoming smile and a motherly embrace. "How lovely, indeed. It can get rather dreary, just the two of us," she said. "Do come and sit beside me, child. I have so longed for a visit like this with you. Pray, tell us, how is your new son?"

"'E looks like 'is father."

Nell saw her exchange a glance with William. There was a slight pause before she smiled more broadly and said, "Then he is destined to become a most magnificent man, indeed."

Nell felt free to speak about many things after that, as they served her Rhenish wine around a little inlaid table that had been moved into a cozy nook beside the fire.

"And you, my dear. How are you?" Mary asked.

"Bearin' a child changes your life," said Nell.

"And bearing a king's child will change it forever."

"You understand?"

"One sees a lot living within these old walls, Mrs. Gwynne. It can be hard to watch at times. One only hopes to be of service."

"After all you've done for me, you really must call me Nell."

The two women smiled at each other as William looked on, the friendship among the trio deepening. Then, as the afternoon sky darkened, a light rain began to fall, sounding like tiny pebbles as it hit the window glass. Nell loved the rain. It cooled everything. It cleaned everything that had been wretched on Lewkenor Lane. Mary Chiffinch stood upon hearing the sound of coach wheels churning gravel in the courtyard below them. Nell was smiling at her, until William's eyes followed his wife's, with an expression that had suddenly grown serious. He glanced up at the tall clock, then looked at Nell in an awkward little silence.

Her eyes shifting from one of them to the other, Nell stood then and went to the window, the hem of her dress sweeping across the floor tiles. She touched the windowsill just as the king emerged with a great smile, shoulders back, chest out, even in the steadily worsening rain. He was elegant in claret-colored satin and gold lace, and his onyx periwig, beneath a plumed hat, as he turned and held out his hand. Then an arm emerged from the coach. A woman's hand, lace spilling back from a tiny wrist. The breath caught in Nell's throat. It began to burn. The arm became a swirl of blue, became an impossibly beautiful, smiling girl. Blond hair pulled away from full flushed cheeks. The face resembled a child's. The body was voluptuous. The smile was coy, the gaze purposeful. Nell gripped the windowsill. Ah, yes . . . the other women. She accepted it as a portion of the price for a royal lover, but to see this played out before her eyes when her own body had yet to fully recover from the child she had borne him . . .

Nell closed her eyes, exhaled a breath, then opened them again, catching a last glimpse of them running together and laughing, hands linked, through the rain toward the entrance to his privy apartments. When she turned around, William's expression was stoic. His hands were linked behind his rigid back. "Her name is Louise de Kéroualle, although some at court, who do not fancy her, have taken to calling her Carwell. She was sent from France as a gift from Louis XIV to revive His Majesty. They initially met at Dover."

"'Ow very thoughtful to give 'im such a *sensual* reminder of 'is sister."

"His sister understood, and accepted, what pleases him, Nell, as do you."

"I understand no woman will ever settle 'im."

"Then, indeed, you do understand him well."

"I've meant only to love the part of 'im I 'ave, and be pleased with it."

"Then keep to that, child, keep to that."

She searched their faces. "Why are you tellin' me all of this?"

"Because you matter, Nell. To him and to us."

"I should go."

"Perhaps for now," William agreed. "But when he calls upon you, which he shall, I trust you will not show him the disappointment you feel, but only your pretty, very witty self, to remind him how much he needs you in his life."

"'Ow can you be so certain 'e'll call upon me with a new and even prettier girl to chase?"

"Because, Nell," said Mary. "Quite simply, Mademoiselle de Kéroualle is not surrendering herself to the king, and His Majesty will entertain virtue for only so long."

"Well, then," Nell replied, pressing back the hurt as she turned around, and began to make her way across the room toward the door. "Perhaps I'm still in the game, after all."

Although, in the end, she had not gotten the chance to speak to him about it directly, Nell's decision to return to the theater was actually made for her by the king. She decided she would retain her dignity, and her lover, by remaining occupied. For all he had given her, stepping aside to share his favor seemed a relatively simple thing to do. She had not really lost him, after all. No one had ever really possessed him that way. And, she reminded herself, she had responsibilities.

She stood with Richard Bell at the back of the theater, the day after she had gone to Whitehall. They were behind the stage in the little corridor outside Hart's private tiring-room, the door still closed. As they waited, Nell chatted with several other actors who were excited at the prospect of her return. Her presence in a play assured them all work, and ovations over jeers. Beck Marshall came to her then as well, and the two women embraced fondly. Beck's expression was full of such joy that Nell did not see the door open and Hart emerge with Lady Castlemaine, who was still adjusting her gown.

"Well, well. What have we here?" Castlemaine asked haughtily. "Groveling, Mrs. Gwynne?"

Nell met Castlemaine's gaze directly. "If so, then 'tis Grovelin' who's right pleased to meet Arrogant, Lady Castlemaine," she daringly returned. "'Tis a right fancy word I learned from Mr. Dryden." She glanced at Hart, his face drained of its color. "Hello, Charles," she said with an easy smile. "Surprisin' company you keep these days."

"Well, we do all have to be somewhere when we're not sharing His Majesty's bed," Barbara retorted, her small nose tipped up as she bit back a contemptuous smile. "And variety, they say, is the spice of life."

"But does not one usually rise *from* an actor *to* a king and not the other way around?"

"Clever tongue for a tart."

"I don't flatter myself, my lady. I'm just a 'umble girl, like a dozen others, from Coal Yard Alley."

"Trust me, Mrs. Gwynne. Humility really is an overrated commodity."

"On par with loyalty?"

Beck coughed into her hand. Richard bit his lip. Glances were exchanged as everyone went absolutely silent. Then Nell's gaze met Lady Castlemaine's again, like two opposing cats, backs hunched. Castlemaine's blue eyes were hard and cold.

"The game, not the motivation, is the thing, *Nell*. Has His Majesty taught you so little?"

"I've learned well what 'e wishes me to know. Which is why both of us are 'ere and not with 'im at this moment, I expect."

Castlemaine's smile became a foxlike grin. "So you've met the new French whore."

"I've seen 'er."

"There's quite a buzz about her, you know. The girl looks ten, but can play Frances Stuart's game better than any expert doxy, myself included. He's quite on the string over her already."

Nell had heard from Buckhurst just how long Lady Stuart had held the king with little more than a tempting smile. But the king's lust was a powerful thing, and that was precisely where she could do battle against anyone. She lifted her chin and smiled confidently. "I'm not worried. Besides, at the moment, I've a job to do." She looked back at Charles Hart. "I've come to tell you I've decided to do the play."

"Oh, bless you, Nell!" He lunged at her, embracing her tightly. "You'll not be sorry! We shall be brilliant together!" He touched her cheek. "As we always have been."

Nell stepped back. Her smile fell. "I'm 'ere to work, Charles. Only that. For anythin' else, I leave you to Lady Castlemaine's very capable 'ands."

"Oh, now. Don't be a spoilsport, Nell," Castlemaine purred. "You took the king from me, and I took Mr. Hart. Can we not share and share alike without this reproach?"

"No reproach, Lady Castlemaine, just the truth. I've no interest now in any man but my son's father."

"Would that he were capable of returning your fidelity, my dear."

"The part of 'im I've got is enough. And, after all, while 'e's occupied, so am I."

Charles Hart moved a step away from Castlemaine. "I cannot thank you enough. I know I don't deserve this, after everything."

Nell tossed her head and the coppery curls, done into fashionable ringlets, bounced on her shoulders. "Oh, "I'm not doin' it for you, Mr. 'Art. Surely you knew that. There are people dependin' on me. Every day that I'm near you, 'twill only ever be for them."

With her words still hanging in the air, she turned and walked away, basking in the heady glow of a powerful moment that had taken her two years to earn, and which she knew she would savor forever.

Chapter 26

"WHAT STRONGER BREASTPLATE THAN A HEART UNTAINTED!"
—*Shakespeare*, Henry VI, Part Two, *Act III, Scene II*

Louise de Kéroualle's manner was as haughty as any courtier or princess. The noble, yet impoverished, *famille de Kéroualle* had raised their beautiful daughter well, and then laid all of their aspirations on what she might do to reclaim their financial standing. Upon the treaty with France, in which Charles had promised, in secret, his conversion to Catholicism, the girl he had seen at Dover was sent as a reward. Some at court whispered she was a well-placed French spy.

To ensure her success, there must be a guide, the French court resolved. The French ambassador, Charles Colbert, marquis de Croissy, was perfect for the challenge. A tiny, bald man with opaque blue eyes like a bird's and an unassuming manner, he was nevertheless a ruthless patriot. Gaining elevation for his seductively beautiful charge was his sole occupation from the moment he met her ship at the windswept Dover shore. De Croissy stood behind her now in a suit of robin's-egg-blue silk, his small feet made smaller by large silver buckles on his pointed black shoes. The king had invited Louise to join him for a stroll through St. James's Park, just newly, and very grandly, opened to the public.

His presence there, beneath the lanes shaded by sweet-smelling lime trees, was an event that would be attended by many of the most influential people. De Croissy hoped it would also endear Louise, finally, to a few of the king's court.

De Croissy watched her as she stood now in her petticoats, corset, and open dressing gown before a full-length mirror. Succumbing to a childish pout, she crossed her arms over her chest, lace sleeves spilling onto her gown, and stuck out her lower lip as Mary Chiffinch, the chief seamstress at court, and an assistant, held up a dress for her approval.

"I'll not wear zat 'orrible ting! Eet looks like a sack! Take eet away!"

The women exchanged a glance before the garment was swept off by a third assistant. Louise remained standing, her arms crossed, her pale face reddened with anger.

"Engleesh fashions are so vulgar!"

"However, here," de Croissy said calmly, "you honor the king by wearing them."

"Believe me," she said, suddenly switching to her native French so that only the ambassador would understand. "He has no interest in anything honorable regarding me!"

"And yet still, *chérie,*" he returned in their native tongue. "The competition is fierce, and this is a game we must play by their rules in order to win."

"What makes you so certain I want to win him?"

"Your family's diminished accounts make it reasonably assured."

"I have been here for almost two months' time with no word at all of the king's divorce, which Buckingham promised me."

"That is not an easy thing to achieve, *ma précieuse.* You must wait with the greatest patience for him."

Again, her lower lip turned out in a pout, and she stamped her satin-toed foot with childish petulance. "*Eh bien*. Then he must wait for *me*."

The ambassador lowered his voice and turned her from the two wardrobe women, who lingered near a window. "Take great care with that approach. There are a bevy of others who would gladly take that place he desires for you in his bed, and often do!"

"Pif! *Le roi* attends me now like one of those spaniels, following me, pleading with me . . ."

The ladies moved forward now and held out a second dress for her consideration, neither of them speaking during the flurry of French flying past them. Louise studied the dress for a moment, then turned back to Ambassador de Croissy, giving them no response.

"You may be beautiful and ambitious, Louise, but here at this court you must also be wise, or you shall never take dominance in his life."

"Take it from who?"

"Nell Gwynne, *bien sûr*."

She laughed at that. "The actress? You believe a slut can rival a noble Kéroualle?"

"In the bedchamber, I have little doubt."

"He also shares his bed with his dogs, for all the power in his life they possess!"

"Take great care, Louise. She has already seen the ouster of Madam Davies, Lady Castlemaine, too, and then borne him a son. *Oui*, if you are not careful, I believe she can indeed be a great rival, and our goal to assist France will be for naught."

"*My* goal, monsieur, is to become queen of England!"

"Ambition, *ma petite*, is essential in measured doses. And *that* must be tempered with wisdom, or it will be as caustic to this court as lye, and none of us shall have what we desire."

"Well, I'll not be a fool like all of the others and give him my maidenhead for nothing. At least I shall be given Lady Castle-maine's apartments while you engage his advisers in a serious discussion of the divorce that I was promised by the Duke of Buckingham. Only then will I seriously entertain the case of his royal ardor."

"You play a dangerous game, mademoiselle. He cares deeply for Mrs. Gwynne; they have a formidable history. You have had a unique opportunity during her lying-in to challenge that. But that time is swiftly passing. Let not your opportunity, and France's, go with it." Having said what he desired her to hear, de Croissy inclined his head, then turned to leave. When he reached the door, amid an echo of clicking shoe heels across parquet, he turned back. As if an afterthought, he said, "And do wear the first dress, *chérie*. To obtain what you desire in England, you must first please an English king."

The prince had accepted his uncle's invitation to this state visit, which would take place at Windor Castle, with the greatest cau-tion. Charles's appetite for Dutch wealth was well enough known.

Charles's goal was to see this nephew installed one day as sov-ereign prince of all Holland: his own powerful Dutch ally would be family, easily manipulated into generosity. Yet first he must proceed with the French in a war against them. It was Minette's legacy, Charles believed, the cause toward which she had worked faithfully in Paris, and which she had not been able to see to fruition. "Your crossing was mild, I trust?"

"Mild enough, Your Majesty," the young prince replied, and the plume in his wide hat danced with the slight nod that followed.

They stood opposing each other in the vast gallery, hands linked behind their backs. Its mammoth wall tapestries and an intricately painted ceiling were a grand backdrop for the collection of courtiers, ambassadors, and eligible Englishwomen who whispered behind raised fans at this great state visit.

Buckingham stood beside William Chiffinch, a hand raised casually before his mouth. "Well, tonight the French chit shall finally get her way, being present at a true and official state ball without Mrs. Gwynne, which should at last quiet her."

"On the contrary, Your Grace," said Chiffinch. "Both mistresses are to be present this evening, along with the queen."

"The comedy actress at a state occasion?"

"It seems our king, for the moment, prefers the easy companionship of a sure thing to the frustrations of the hunt."

"I've always liked Mrs. Gwynne," Buckingham said, laughing.

"But was Your Grace not the very one to bring the Kéroualle girl from France to replace her?"

"That was my king's wish. You know perfectly well that Nell is far more to everyone's liking here at court. Yet attending something so formal? About that, the mind does reel."

"The French girl and the actress here at Windsor, and the queen somewhere in between?"

"Now, William." Buckingham smiled, touching his shoulder affably. "What would His Majesty's life be without a bit of spirited competition in it?"

"Or in your own life, Your Grace?" William Chiffinch said.

He had missed her more than he thought he possibly could.

As Charles waited alone before the banquet to reunite with her in his bedchamber, he felt the anticipation of a much younger man.

It was not only sexual need that had moved him to request Nell's companionship at Windsor over that of Louise. Nor was it his wounded pride over Louise's continual refusal of her favors. But Nell made things easy for him. With her, Charles could forget. The French . . . the Dutch . . . the Catholic question. Conversions . . . *Minette* . . . grief. The nightmares that took hold of him every time he allowed it. Charles indulged himself entirely in the open knowledge that Nell Gwynne adored him. It was a comfort like no other, almost like the innocence of childhood. And he did love her in return.

He had told her so once, and he had meant it. But a part of him loved Catherine as well. And Barbara, although to a far lesser degree now. But they were each chapters to him in a long and complicated book. Before that had been Hortense Mancini, in France, who had rejected his youthful proposal of marriage. Lucy Walter, Monmouth's mother, in the beginning. But it was Nelly he wanted. Her goodness and humor made it impossible not to. And now, this afternoon, she was late. It made him feel childlike and slightly peevish that she was not yet here with him. He had been so much the fool. He must give up this reckless chase of the Kéroualle girl. And he would. *Ah, Nell . . .* He gazed up at the tall ebony clock again, trying not to be angry. She would be here. He trusted her. And there were precious few whom Charles II trusted.

Clutching the folds of her blue velvet skirts, Nell was swept quietly up a narrow back staircase at Windsor by William Chiffinch, followed by two palace guards. There was evening mist still on her cheeks and pure panic in her heart. On the landing outside the king's privy apartments, she paused and touched William's arm. A tasteful pearl necklace glinted at her bare breastbone. "I don't know if I can do this," she murmured. "Lie with 'im, aye, but attend so fancy a state ball afterward? I tell you, I'm bound to do the wrong thing as I did once before when the Duke of Buckingham was forced to—"

Chiffinch knew about the impromptu swim in the lake. He turned to meet her gaze in the lamplight that danced on the old pale-yellow stone walls. He smiled tenderly at her. "Only be yourself, Nelly. Remember, that is what he finds most endearing."

Her head spun wildly with a barrage of questions. What about the French chit? Where was the queen? Would presenting her publicly not offend half of the staid court, who already resented her rise? "But why is 'e doin' somethin' like this now? Perhaps if I know why now 'e wishes to take me out of the shadows . . ."

"I believe it is His Majesty's way of displaying the prominent place you hold in his life."

The well-shared place, she thought. But she did not say it.

"And the Carwell woman?" she cautiously asked instead, as they reached the landing.

William reached for the large brass handle, then turned back to her. "Make of this opportunity all that you are meant to, and think nothing of her. That is my best advice to you tonight."

Nell wondered then if it were true about her prominence of place, why she still must be brought up the back stairs like all of the other girls who were brought almost nightly to the king of England's bed?

"I have missed you."

Nell lay cushioned by the dark tufts of hair covering his chest, one leg slung over his thigh, on top of a spray of silk-covered pillows sewn with the royal crest. She smiled mischievously at him. "And, apparently, I arrived not a moment too soon."

He chuckled and caressed her bare shoulder. "There's no one like you, Nelly. Nor shall there ever be."

She rolled onto her side, then propped her head on her hand. Her hair fell in a cascade onto the thick, inky coils of his chest hair. "And 'tis a good thing, is it?"

"It is a very, good thing."

"Will ye be as 'appy with me when I go back to work?"

"I was told about that." He sighed then, and his expression became grave. "You know I shall take care of you and our son. I've told you before, you need not return to the stage at all."

"And I love you for it. But 'tis more than you and I to consider." Charles Hart's contrition alone was worth returning to the stage. And there was Rose and Jeddy. Life had taught her that independence must be the lesson most well learned. "Mr. Dryden 'ad already written the play, so I told them I'd do it one more time. Then I would need to consider little Charles and 'is future."

"What of *our* future, Nell?"

"You know I'll be yours for as long as you want me."

"Well, I want you. I want you very much indeed." He kissed her then and very gently caressed her cheek with the back of his large hand. "Why on earth do you love a devilish rake like me, king or not?"

She kissed his cheek in return. She could be the bawd for him. That was a playing field she need not share with the French virgin. Nell sat back playfully on her knees, bare to him, and smiled broadly with her best stage smile. She poised her hands on her hips and tipped her head. "Because you are, and always will be, my very own Charles the Third—my Charlie—and make no mistake, 'tis a place to be reckoned with!"

"Blasted Buckhurst and Hart," he said, glancing away, then back at her. "You watch that actor, then, if you mean to go on with this, Nell. I would just as soon see his head on a pike at Tower Bridge if he ever touches you again."

"Oh, I've it on good authority that 'e's got entertainment enough these days without lookin' to 'is past for it." An image of Lady Castlemaine, her hair tossed, dress askew, emerging from Charles Hart's tiring-room bloomed then in her mind. She wondered what the king would think if he knew Barbara also had a taste for the lower classes. That day at the theater, Richard Bell had told her of a certain circus performer with whom the once-powerful favorite now divided her time.

"Pray, tell me, does your house here at Windsor please you well?" Charles asked her, surprisingly earnest.

She thought of the little place on the cobbled street wedged between a tavern and a cobbler shop, with its tall, narrow rooms, diamond-shaped windows, and little sea-coal fire blazing in the drawing room. "'Tis right snug, it is, Charlie."

"It is the most prominent on Church Street, with a secret tunnel to the palace any time we like. And it's yours now, Nelly. I bought it for you and Charles last month, so you shall always have your very own home to do with as you please whenever we are here. And I mean to bring you here quite often."

She hugged him then, and let their kisses become passionate, expertly teasing him in the way she knew would most swiftly arouse him, because she did not want to think about the future. Or the truth: Lady Castlemaine had long possessed elegant and vast apartments, both at Whitehall and at Windsor. They were the very rooms, it was whispered, in which Louise de Kéroualle now lived. He could not be ashamed of her, she reasoned, because he had personally commanded her presence among the guests tonight at the official reception in his nephew's honor. Yet there was still the slight sting of disappointment: a house, but not quite a place in the palace. Still, he had given her a miracle. He had given her the world. She would always give him what he desired, and keep her thoughts to herself.

Music from the banquet hall at Windsor Castle filtered from the open doors and down the hill as Nell came back into the bedchamber in the little house on Church Street. She had been dressed for the evening by two court ladies sent over by the king to assist her. Her hair was fashioned into tight curls, and her face was covered with a thin layer of powder. A single small black patch was applied near her eye as she stood completely unnerved, yet waiting for approval. Before her, Rose sat on the edge of the bed, holding baby Charles. Jeddy was beside her, dressed as a grand little lady in her blue silk dress. Mary Chiffinch stood near the door.

The gown Nell wore was grass-green watered silk, with a gathered skirt, and a tight bodice that laced in front. As Nell stood before them now, it was clear that she had added a small personal touch of her own to the fashionable gown. By untying the top two laces just enough, her plain country corset, a thing of coarse linen, was visible. It caught the eye most particularly because she had declined to wear the royal jewelry the king had sent with the court ladies to complete her ensemble.

"You cannot possibly," Mary Chiffinch shook her head. "It makes you look—"

"It makes her look like what she is," Rose declared in defense. "She'll never fully get away from that."

Rose knew how intimidated her sister was by the courtiers and the nobility around which she was forced to survive and thrive. The two sisters had spoken of it endlessly as they lay together in the dark at night, talking and gossiping about the day's events.

Even the lessons from the Chiffinches and her merry band had not bolstered Nell's confidence entirely. And tonight was an actual state occasion.

"I really just think that you should—" Mary Chiffinch began, but Rose swiftly and firmly cut her off. "You go on as you are, Nelly. Be as you are, and proudly, too!"

Nell looked at her sister, feeling an enormous burst of love and gratitude for the only person in the world who could truly know what all of this was like for her. Rose alone, with a single look, could give her the confidence she needed to go forward tonight.

And she had.

Nell was escorted by the Duke of Buckingham into the long, narrow banquet hall. It was paneled in dark oak, and lit to a golden glow by candles in sconces and blazing lamps set along the walls. She saw Lady Shrewsbury talking with the Duchess of Lauderdale, and even caught a glimpse of Lady Castlemaine and her husband. And nearest the door stood the French ambassador, a little bald man in deep conversation with Louise de Kéroualle, who, from a distance, she now knew well. What a snug little evening, thought Nell with well-masked disdain.

"Chin up," Buckingham whispered to her, their complex friendship deepening. "If I can see what you are thinking, they can as well."

A seeming eternity later, the guests all turned in response to the opening of a pair of inlaid doors, pulled back by two stone-faced liveried servants, and the flourish of trumpets. Everyone fell into deep bows and curtsies as the music changed to a stoic, formal pavane, and King Charles and Queen Catherine slowly came into view, progressing together, hand in hand, and made their formal entrance. Behind them strode the king's nephew, William of Orange, the guest of honor.

Nell stood among the crowd that ringed the grand room and watched them dance a more lively branle. She smiled and nodded, leaning in toward Buckingham, then smiling, as though he had just spoken to her, in case anyone was watching.

The evening droned on from there, through a series of lofty welcome speeches to the king's esteemed guest. An interminably long meal followed. Then a servant touched Nell's shoulder. He whispered that the queen wished to meet her. She glanced in panic across the room at the dais, draped in folds of burgundy-colored silk, and piled with gold goblets and plates of fruit and marzipan. The king sat beside his wife. Nell caught the exchange between them that was clearly about her. She saw Charles grow increasingly tense. Lady Castlemaine, seated near the queen, was looking at Nell, with an unmistakable smirk, as the servant led her toward them.

A moment later, the chasm that had always separated them fell away as Nell curtsied low before the queen, who was resplendent, seated in a throne of silver-and-blue velvet, her chin tipped up, her neck and wrists covered in jewels. Up close, she was prettier than Nell had expected. She was petite, as Nell was, and her nose was overly long, but her dark, watery eyes held a kindness that was apparent even behind the reserve.

"You are smaller than I had envisioned," said the queen in a surprisingly soft tone, as the king sat silently watching.

"They say I've a rather irritatingly large voice to make up for it."

Someone behind Nell stifled a cough.

"Do they?"

"They do, Your Majesty."

"I remember you in *The Indian Emperor.*"

"Thank you, ma'am."

"I did not like you in it."

Nell nodded.

"You were much better in *The Maiden Queen.*"

"I was, at that."

"Ironic a role as that was for one such as yourself."

Their eyes met. Catherine's expression was stoic, until Nell smiled. "I never did master drama on the stage. I was actually quite dreadful at it."

"Some roles are simply not suited, no matter how much one wishes to play them," the queen said pointedly. "See that you take care with the unique role you are carving out for yourself in this world, my dear, as true favor is fleeting."

"I shall remember that, Your Majesty."

"The world can be a dark place for those who no longer possess it. Do learn to tread carefully. And tie up your laces, if you are going to attend this court in future."

Nell understood her, and her meaning. She was ushered back to Buckingham's side then, knowing precisely where she stood with the tolerant queen of England. Which was more than she could say for most of the rest of England's court. Amid a rising crescendo of whispers, and with all eyes upon her, the musicians began a sprightly country tune. Nell was uncertain who said it, but as she neared the safety of Buckhurst's side she heard a woman's voice, and then another.

"Charming girl," said one.

"She certainly has set this court on its ear."

"And, if I may say, breathed a bit of new life into staid, old vulgarities."

"Well, I think it is positively shameful, trotting her out like this as he does, and she from the very bowels of London! At least if he must, he should escort one of his *proper* whores. What must the poor queen think?"

"I would imagine Her Majesty is well used to it by now," the second woman remarked, just as Buckhurst took Nell's hand and smiled, full of sympathy.

Chapter 27

WITH HOW MUCH EASE BELIEVE WE WHAT WE WISH!
—*John Dryden*

NELL stood center stage, in a crested helmet, belted tunic, and buskins, costumed as Queen Almahide. Her hands were on her hips, and a bow and quiver hung from her left shoulder. She had taken the stage in the empty King's Theater, summer sun streaming in through the glass roof above them. It was late in the morning, and the players were doing a last run-through of *The Conquest of Granada*. Hart was her exotic lover, Beck Marshall was the seductress, and Richard Bell was to play Nell's jealous husband.

The theater manager, Thomas Killigrew, sat with Dryden watching from the pit, and Nell saw them there, studying her. It was good to be back, caught up in the easy camaraderie of the other players, the jesting, and the laughter. Here, being herself took no thought, and for it she paid no price. Yet, even so, she still felt tension. It came with a name: *Carwell*. Nell could not bring herself to say it properly. Gossip about Carwell had grown like wildfire at the theater. Louise continued, they said, to entice the king by refusing him. It was said that the tactic had led to a predictable result. The king was now so obsessed with winning her that she was with him at Hampton Court at this very moment, joining him for his nephew's remaining few days in England. Forcefully, Nell pressed back her jealousy. She was accustomed now to rejecting it. She knew the king would send for her again. And when he did, unlike Carwell, she would not play with his heart.

"Shall we go over that last scene again?"

"Oh, come on, Nell. We've all got it down! I'm hungry," Hart moaned.

"We *have* been at it for hours, Nelly," Beck carefully agreed.

Everyone at the King's Theater understood that work was the best distraction for Nell. Glances were exchanged amid the silence. "Come on, all of you," Richard finally said, then turned to wink at Nell, in a show of solidarity. "Let's give the scene one last go-round, shall we? A bit of hard work won't kill any of us."

Afterward, Nell and Richard walked together out onto Drury Lane. Several mud-splashed hacks sat lined against the curb, their horses pawing at the cobbled stones as they waited for the actors, who were all just now emerging with somewhere to go.

"God, but it is good to have you back," Richard said, taking up her hand, then pressing a kiss onto her cheek. The freckles slashed across his nose seemed brighter in the sun, and so did his affectionate smile. "It really hasn't been the same without you."

"So I hear."

"You know Hart is bedding Lady Castlemaine?"

"So apparently is half of London. Everyone, that is, but the king." She chuckled. "I've 'eard tales of a tightrope walker, as well."

"I think they are both trying to get back at you."

"And I've 'eard that you are seeing Beck."

Richard's easy smile fell. He raked his limp hair back from his forehead as Nell felt his hand tense in hers. "How'd you know?"

"You don't think I keep those old connections for nothin', do you?" She touched his face then, more serious. "But I'm glad for you."

"You know it's always been you, Nelly."

"Beck's lovely."

"I know she'll break my heart one day, just as you did. I'm certainly no lord fit to keep her. But for now, I'm happy."

The king's coach at her disposal, drawn by six horses, their silver harnesses jangling, pulled up before them then, just as a light breeze caught the hem of her dress. Nell descended the last step away from the theater, then turned back to Richard. "See you tomorrow, then?"

"You couldn't keep me away. This is the biggest part I've ever had, and I'm planning to get a laugh if it kills me!" Richard smiled. "That is, after you do, of course!"

The house on the square, when she returned to it after the rehearsal, was hot for midday. Only the kitchen window at the back was open, so the rest of the house had the feeling of a tomb when the square-shouldered Bridget Long closed the door behind her. As she removed her gloves, Nell saw that Rose and John Cassells were together on the divan in her drawing room. Cassells was not wearing his uniform, but rather a plain nut-colored surcoat with dull brass buttons down the length. Their hands were linked, and they were whispering.

"Where are the children?" Nell asked as Cassells came to his feet, nervously pressing out his surcoat with his palms. Rose stood beside him a moment later.

"The baby's asleep, and I sent Jeddy to the little room beyond the kitchen, as she felt feverish and wouldn't eat."

"A fever in summer?" Nell came forward. "'ave you called for a doctor?"

"For Jeddy? Well, no, I only thought—"

Nell turned back to the door. "Bridget, go fetch one promptly!"

"I'll go," John said, nodding politely to her. Before Nell could object, he was gone, the heavy front door closing with a thud behind him.

"What were you thinkin', Rose?"

"John's asked me to marry 'im! And other things've 'appened today, as well. I wasn't thinkin'—"

Nell turned away, not allowing the full explanation, and began to weave through the house toward the snug little room behind the kitchen where Jeddy often slept if the king was present and she was not allowed in Nell's bedchamber. Rose followed her.

"Nelly, I really think you should let me explain—"

Nell rounded on the small door near the larder, her dress sailing out behind her, but as she burst into the room, she stopped stone still. The last person in the world she had expected to see was sitting before her. On a stool beside a sleeping Jeddy, holding a cloth to her forehead, was Helena Gwynne, the mother Nell had not seen in well over a year.

The doctor John Cassells managed to find did not believe it was the plague, for which Nell felt as much relief as if she had given birth to the little girl herself. She ran the back of her hand across her forehead, sank down at the scarred wooden table, piled with vegetables beneath a rack of copper pots and kettles, in the center of the room, and heaved a heavy sigh. Helena and Rose were seated across from her.

"What the devil are you doin' in my 'ouse?" Nell asked at last.

Helena and Rose exchanged a glance. "I've no place to go, Nelly," her mother said. "And I've changed my ways, I promise you that."

"Ballocks! You've been dreadful your whole life, and *now* you've changed your ways, just when there's a bit of royal favor to be 'ad?"

"Nell!" Rose gasped. "'Twas the drink! And she's given that up!"

Nell studied her mother, the round face mottled red, the fat, chapped hands, and the layers of rosy flesh. "And you believed 'er!"

"She's our ma, and she's come to ask for 'elp, for lord's sake!"

"Rose, you cannot be serious. 'Ave you forgotten?"

"I've forgotten nothin', Nelly. But it seems that your tolerance extends no further than the king's bedchamber!"

Nell glanced bitterly at her mother, sitting beside Rose. "I can't talk about this any longer," she declared, charging out of the door as fast as her legs could carry her.

Nell waited in the wings for her cue. Beck had told her it was a full house, and for the first time in a long time she felt a nervous anticipation over making her entrance. She drew back the heavy curtain and peered out into the pit. There was the Duke of Buckingham, now her good friend, with his infamous mistress, clearly pregnant; there was Samuel Pepys, certain as always to spread news of her performance to everyone he knew. There was the Duchess of Argyll and Lord Rochester, and a woman in a long black cape, her face covered by a vizard, gesturing like an actor. And, in front of them near the stage, stood an orange girl in a gray linen dress and apron, basket over her arm. In that girl, she saw herself not so very long ago.

The image forced Nell to see how far she had come, and she was grateful for the reminder.

The cue came, and she stepped onto the stage to the deafening roar of applause. She grinned, then curtsied low for the crowd. As she rose, her gaze settled on the royal box above her, half in shadows from all of the lamplight. But the images and the faces were clear to her. The king had come to see her return to the stage. And he had brought Louise de Kéroualle.

As she began to speak her lines, to curtsy and wink at the audience, the nervousness slipped away. Nell was entirely believable, endearing as an innocent, and the more they laughed, the more Nell felt the wound of the king's action fade, replaced by the open adoration of the crowd.

After the performance, Beck came to her as she was being helped from her costume, to tell her the king wished to pay her his compliments.

"Is the girl with 'im?"

"It was a servant who addressed me. I'm sorry, Nell, I didn't see."

Nell forced herself to smile. "He's the king of England and can do precisely as he wishes. Especially with me." She stood, glanced at her own reflection, forced an even more carefree smile, then prepared to receive him. Perhaps he believed she did not know about Carwell's presence. That was how she intended to proceed. *You are an actress; now act!*

The tiring-room door opened.

"Your Majesty, it is an 'onor," Nell said, curtsying low along with Beck and the other actresses around her, then rising with her usual smile.

"You were right to take the role. I do believe it was your best performance yet."

"My greatest desire is to please you."

"And your second-greatest desire?"

"*That*, Charlie, I can only tell you privately."

Everyone watched the exchange, knowing who lingered just beyond the door, all of them anxious to see if it might erupt into anything about which they could gossip.

He took her hand and gently, seductively, kissed it. "Then I shall call on you privately again very soon."

"And *I* shall look forward to that with the greatest anticipation."

In the next moment, he was gone in a flash of silver and a swirl of his blue velvet.

The others crowded around her so excitedly that she did not see John Cassells coming toward her, his handsome face drawn with a grave expression. "Rose has sent me to fetch you," he said. "Your girl has taken a turn for the worse."

There was silence between her and John as the musty-smelling hired hack jostled up Drury Lane to Maypole Alley and toward Lincoln's Inn Fields. The moment the coach pulled to a stop, Nell sprang from inside, leaving John to settle the fare. She was through the kitchen a moment later, to find her mother on a small stool beside Jeddy's bed, pressing a cloth onto her forehead.

"Where's Rose?"

"Upstairs with your son. I figured you'd rather 'ave it that way than me with 'im."

That was accurate enough, but Nell chose not to say anything. As her mother glanced up at her, Nell realized that she was not drunk and swaying, cursing, or begging for money. It startled her into silence, until she could think again of the little girl who had no family now but Nell's.

"I know what the doctor said, but I've seen it myself, and it really might be the pox after all, so you really shouldn't be in 'ere yourself, Nelly. You're a right proper lady now."

"Jeddy is my responsibility."

"As are a lot of people."

"Including you, Ma?"

"You mustn't jeopardize your own 'ealth for the sake of a black-amoor, little girl or not. 'Tis all I'm sayin'."

"Because, on occasion, the king wishes to bed me? Not so long ago, Ma, 'er lot in life was better than my own. She 'ad little silk dresses, and she slept in a clean bed, while I was fightin' off your lovers!" Nell hadn't realized she was yelling until Jeddy opened her eyes and looked at her. "I die?" she asked Nell in a weak voice that pulled at Nell's heart.

"You most certainly will not! You just need to rest, and I'm goin' to see to that," Nell said soothingly. "Did the physician do nothin' for 'er, then?"

"The girl was bled, but 'twas all 'e felt he should do when there's yet no sign of the sores."

"Bugger that! Worthless sorts, doctors!" Nell looked at John Cassells, who was now leaning awkwardly against the doorjamb. "Pray, tell me you know an apothecary, Captain?"

"Aye. One over on Butcher's Row."

"Take me?"

"But I've only just sent the hack away."

"Then we'll walk!"

"I'll stay with the girl," said Helena Gwynne.

"You do that, Ma. But don't believe I've forgiven you."

"I wouldn't think anythin' of the sort, Nelly."

Once again, Louise had refused him, retiring with a headache suspiciously akin to the ones the queen often professed when she did not desire his company. Now that Her Majesty had suffered yet another miscarriage, that seemed a newly consistent state between them.

For solace, the king had gone off with a group of his best companions. On horseback, they thundered through Hounslow Heath, the breeze cooling them as it tossed their hair, cooled their skin, and pulled back the rich fabric of their capes. They darted through a thick stand of trees, shading them from the blazing sun. It occurred to him then, as he led the way, upright in his saddle, that Louise could be punishing him for escorting her to Nell's performance. Perhaps, in light of that, he deserved her refusal. But on the other hand, Nell had become a priority in his life, pure and simple, and Louise must come to accept that, if she meant to remain at his court. For now, he wished her to remain, if only to see where it all might lead. It was not only Louise's elegant beauty that drew him, nor the excitement of the challenge she posed. Her heritage made her at ease in his world, in a way Nell never would be. Lord, how he hated to admit that, even to himself, for how he adored her. He was not above contemplating the criticisms of his sweet Nell, who had been elevated to the status of *favorite* after the birth of their son. Nell . . . dear uncomplicated Nell. Accompanying him, loving him, sharing his life as she did with such an open and tender heart. Yet she was still so achingly out of place at the rituals of royal life, rituals from which he could never entirely be free. His own earliest memories were of the great dignity his father brought to his role as monarch, and Charles felt the weight of his obligation to England in it.

He pulled the reins hard then and came to a halt in a grassy clearing through which ran a pebble-strewn stream.

All of them dismounted to rest the horses. Buckingham had not accompanied them, and Charles was glad, since he knew the bond of friendship George had formed with Nell. Lady Shrewsbury was, at this moment, giving birth to Buckingham's first child, and he was with her. So now Charles strolled across the clearing with Thomas Osborne, Earl of Danby, a rising star in Parliament, an outspoken supporter of Louise and her elevation in court. Everyone, it seemed, but Buckingham knew that Danby was intent on replacing Nell. For that reason, Danby would be honest, and just now the king needed honesty.

"So tell me, Thomas. What is my court saying of Mrs. Gwynne these days?"

Osborne, a tall, pale man with thin blond hair, looked warily at the king, cautioned by the words and not the tone of nonchalance. "They say she is the finest actress in all of London, sire."

"Of course that. But tell me, did you speak with her at my banquet for the Prince of Orange?"

"No, sire."

"And why was that?"

"Well . . ." He paused. "In part, because she was taken up much of the time by the attentions of Lord Buckhurst and Lord Rochester."

"And the other part?"

"My wife would not allow it, Your Majesty."

"I see."

They paused while the horses grazed on the long blades of grass at their feet.

They took a few steps more together before Charles stopped again. He said, "I am very fond of her, you know."

"Aye, sire. That is clear."

"And how do you see her growing role in my court over these next years?"

Thomas grimaced. "Oh, sire. Please do not ask me that."

The king knew the others, who had drawn near and then loitered beneath the trees, were listening, but he did not care. "I command your opinion, Thomas. What good are you to me at all if you will not give me that?"

"Very well. I believe the quiet insults will escalate. And come to match the slights from not only the ladies of your court who envy her, but from the men who secretly desire her. And you cannot surrender everyone's head to the block in her defense."

Charles shrugged. "Harsh, but honest."

"You did ask me to be, sire."

"So I did." He held the bridle of his horse, pausing a moment as an odd sensation overtook him. He knew that he loved Nell. He missed her. That must be it. Acknowledging that, he swung back up into the tooled black saddle studded with Spanish silver. All of the courtiers followed the king's lead, and once again the group began to gallop farther into the forest, churning earth and the carpet of coppery needles beneath them. A moment later, Charles called out to one of his aides, who was keeping pace with the others behind him. "Return to Whitehall. Have Chiffinch send for Mrs. Gwynne. See that she is waiting in my bedchamber when I return."

Chapter 28

BUT WHEN I CONSIDER THE TRUTH OF HER HEART, SUCH
AN INNOCENT PASSION, SO KIND WITHOUT ART; I FEAR
I HAVE WRONGED HER, AND HOPE SHE MAY BE SO FULL OF
TRUE LOVE TO BE JEALOUS OF ME AND THEN TIS I THINK
THAT NO JOYS ARE ABOVE THE PLEASURES OF LOVE.
—Choice Ayres, *Charles II*

B Y midnight, the fever had broken, with the addition of
julep and glysters from an apothecary, but Jeddy remained
delirious. Nell spent the night, along with Helena Gwynne,
in the dark and stifling little room behind the kitchen. Mother
and daughter did not speak, yet an uneasy camaraderie seemed to
develop through the night as they tended the girl. Bathed in perspiration, and lit in hues of umber and gold from the candlelight,
lumbering back and forth to fetch cool water and cloths, Helena
spoke no words of complaint, and Nell did not offer any relief.
She was happy for the help. It was the least her mother could do
for her, she thought, when she had done little for anyone before
but cause damage. She was also relieved to have Rose tend to her
baby son safely upstairs.

Near dawn, as Jeddy fell into what seemed a less fitful sleep, Helena softly said, "I reckon there ain't many who'd 'ave done what you 'ave for a servant, Nelly. I'm proud of you."

Nell was on her knees beside the small bed. She sat on her heels, then ran the back of her hand across her brow. For the first time since she had come home, she actually looked at Helena. "I'd like to say I've been proud of you at some point in my life, Ma, but I really can't think of a single moment."

"I suppose I deserved that."

"You did 'orrid things to Rose 'n me."

"I was alone. We 'ad to survive. 'Tis the unvarnished truth of it."

"And is it the truth about my father you've always told?"

"You know I don't talk about that."

"Rose and I never believed 'e was a captain in the king's army, killed in the war to save our own king's father."

"Whatever the truth, Nelly, 'e's gone just the same." She paused for a moment, looking at her daughter, before she said, "And once 'e was gone, I was left to survive with the two of you, the best I could. 'Tis not an excuse, because there ain't one."

"I want the truth about 'im. I deserve that much."

"And I want those years back! Look, my girl, in the low life we lived, things 'appen. I made choices, bad ones. But I kept you girls with me. At least I did that much."

"And with my whole 'eart, Ma, I wish you'd left us behind. Bein' alone could not 'ave been worse than the life you gave us!"

The eyes of mother and daughter met. There was pain reflected back at each of them. When she finally spoke again, Helena's voice was low and fragile in a way Nell had never heard before. "And will you put me out now as you wish I'd done to you, Nelly? Is that what you want to do?"

She meant to say she had no idea what she would do, when she

heard Mrs. Long, her housekeeper, come to the small door leading in from the kitchen. "The king, Mrs. Gwynne, has come, and
he's brought his own physician with him."

Nell stood and smoothed down her skirt. The bodice of her
dress was soiled, her hair was falling free of its tight arrangement,
and her eyes burned with fatigue. He would not find the blithe,
gamine actress who provided him with carefree pleasure. But
tonight there was something she cared about more. In the midst
of that thought, Charles was at the door. Only the elderly court
physician, gray-haired and stooped-shouldered, was with him. As
he moved forward, his face was spiked with concern. "How is the
girl?" the king asked.

"She is resting, at least."

Charles nodded to his physician to personally examine Jeddy,
then led Nell from the small, unbearably warm room and out
into the kitchen. There, he embraced her. Exhausted, she melted
against him, grateful for the reassuring strength of his tall, strong
body.

"I came the moment I heard."

"You needn't 'ave."

Charles pressed a kiss gently onto her lips, then looked at her.
"Oh, but I did. You should have called on me from the first."

So many responses moved through her mind, light and clever
retorts, about the teetering focus of his attentions. But so near
dawn, she had not the energy or inclination to speak any of
them. She was happy he had come out in the middle of the night,
happy that she was still a priority in his glittering, powerful
world.

He sat her down gently at the kitchen table with its two long,
rough-hewn benches, and poured her a glass of wine from a jug
beside a wooden bowl full of potatoes. Then he smoothed the hair

back from her forehead as she took a swallow. "Now, I'll check on the girl if you will stay here and catch your breath."

As he turned away, Nell called out, "It may be the pox, Charlie. You shouldn't go in there."

But the king only paused to turn and give her a gentle smile. "Drink that. It will do you good," he said, before going back into the little room with Helena and the physician.

A few moments later, Rose came down the back stairs with the baby, who was fussing in her arms. "*Now* can we hire a wet nurse?" Rose asked, as she tiredly handed the baby to Nell.

Perhaps if she were more like Lady Castlemaine or Louise, or even Moll Davies, she could.

But he was the dearest thing in the world to her, and Nell simply could not force herself to give him over like that, in such an intimate way. Nell put her son to her breast and then for a moment wearily closed her eyes. She was determined to be a better mother than her own had been. This child already was helping to heal the wounds of her past, especially when she pressed him so close to her wounded heart. She felt the king's hand on her shoulder, and realized that for a moment she had actually nodded off. He was smiling down at her as his physician packed up his instruments and bottles of potions on the table before her, then tapped his hat back onto his head.

"It's not the pox or the plague, thankfully," Charles announced. "Whatever it is, she's already better."

"Pray God!"

"She's resting now," the old physician announced. "But it's a good, sound sleep, and there is no longer any sign of the fever."

Nell felt herself go limp as she handed the drowsy baby back to Rose. "So it's off to bed with you," the king declared, helping her to her feet as a fiery orange sunrise began to peek through the window.

"I'll bet you say that to all the girls," she wearily quipped, and he bit back a smile in response. Then she let him lead her upstairs.

In her bedchamber, the bedcovers were pulled back and the draperies were drawn across the windows, barring the swiftly coming daylight. She let Charles help her onto the feathery mattress and then cover her over with only a light summer wrap. Her eyelids were heavy and sleep beckoned her as he settled her on the pillows. He sank into the wing chair beside her bed. "Will you not lay with me?" she asked him with stifled yawn.

"I shall be here when you wake, but despite my rather notorious reputation, I am not quite so low as to take advantage of a lady who cannot meet me fully."

"I've always been able to do that," she smiled, her eyes heavy and closing.

"Indeed you have. And better than anyone else." He chuckled, then, for a moment, there was silence between them. "She's going to be all right, you know."

"I believe that now. I'm glad you came."

"It was simple enough. I love you, Nell," he said, but she did not hear it. She was already asleep.

Nell went back to the theater the next afternoon, the play proving a great success. In spite of it having been meant as a serious production, audiences adored Nell, and pealed with laughter at her being cast as a virtuous queen wrongly accused of adultery. Once again, Nell chose to win them over with her comedic skills. She had decided humor was the only way so notorious an actress as herself could ever hope to deliver the impassioned plea for purity, which was a part of her character's lines.

Afterward, she went to Hart's private tiring-room and closed the door behind herself. "When the run is over, it will 'ave been my final performance," she announced as he sat at his dressing table. His hand paused in midair as he looked up at her reflection behind him. "I've already spoken to Mr. Dryden, before 'e comes up with another role for me."

"You're not serious?"

"I am entirely."

"But the play is a rousing success, and *you* are the toast of London again!"

"Better to go out on my own accord than be chased from my pedestal by tossed rotten fruit, or a prettier actress," she said, twisting one of her coppery curls.

"That could never happen."

"We're all replaceable, Charles. Just ask Lady Castlemaine next time you see 'er."

He turned around and stood. "Don't do this, Nell. The theater needs you."

"The king needs me more."

Richard Bell was at the door then with Beck Marshall and Thomas Killigrew. "I, for one, think it's brilliant," Richard said with a smile. "Why trod around with the lot of us when you can sip sweet French champagne on the royal barge?"

"I second that," said Beck, smiling. Nell looked back at Charles Hart, who stood there, entirely bereft. She was surprised that she felt no joy now, as she once would have, in seeing him like this. "Look Charles, 'tis really quite simple. 'Is Majesty will grow tired of me one day, and doubtless I'll be back 'ere when 'e is. But for now, I need to nurture the king's investment in me."

"I hope that means fighting the French chit for your place, tooth and nail," said Richard.

"Tooth, nail, or seduction. Whatever works," Nell quipped.

Beck chuckled. Hart rolled his eyes. Louise de Kéroualle's reputation in London had grown notorious. Everyone, it seemed, had an opinion, not only of her, but of why she was in England, and what she really desired from the king. The predominant rumor still flying rampant was that she was a spy for France.

That evening, Nell felt pleased enough with herself, and confident enough, to host a small, informal birthday party for the king and those at court who had aligned themselves publicly with her, the Duke of York, Buckingham, Rochester, Lord Buckhurst, and Charles Sedley among them. Now that Arlington and his wife had chosen Louise de Kéroualle, Nell knew that alliances were more important than ever. And she was glad to have cultivated her own camp.

Fortunately, the king now spent most of his evenings with her, and their intimate circle.

"It is a lovely evening you've planned, sweetheart. But I would have hoped you would have seen your way to inviting the Countess of Shrewsbury tonight," the king said. "If not for me, at least as a favor to your friend, Buckingham, who is so fond of her company."

Nell sank onto his lap, then kissed him seductively as the others gathered in her increasingly elegant drawing room. "Ah, one whore at a time is quite enough for you, sire," Nell said wryly. The king laughed, and then so did everyone else, even the increasingly endangered Duke of Buckingham.

"I, for one, think Nell is a wise woman," Buckingham said with a smile. "We men are always better off focusing on one luscious beauty at a time."

"You mortal men, perhaps," the king returned with a pompous chuckle.

Glances were exchanged, and in the awkward silence that followed, Nell looked at Charles. They had not been speaking of herself and Louise de Kéroualle directly, but the comparison was impossible not to make. Everyone knew of His Majesty's growing obsession with her. But Nell meant to make light of it. She had fought too hard, and come too far, to play this particular scene in her life any other way. "Then two at the utmost, Your Majesty, for even royalty has its limits," she declared with a raucous, carefree laugh, until the others began to laugh along with her.

Later, as Charles sat trading indecent poems with Rochester, Nell joined Buckingham outside in her garden. He had gone there alone with a glass of champagne and stood among her rose-bushes, all full of fat pink and white blossoms. He turned when he heard her footsteps. She was smiling, and they embraced.

"Thanks for bein' 'ere, Lord Buck."

"Would I have missed the king's birthday?"

"Perhaps for Lady Shrewsbury's sake you might 'ave."

"We understand each other, you and I, and we have learned from each other. One must always consider *all* of one's alliances, not only the amorous ones. And, adore her though I do, my darling can be a bit, shall we say, *abrasive*. As for you, it is imperative that you save your strength for the most critical battles ahead of you."

Nell smiled charmingly. "Carwell does appear to be a worthy opponent. Although I've only the king's divided attentions, and a couple of distant glimpses, to tell me that. We've not met."

"Yet."

"And shall we?"

"My dear girl, knowing the king, I believe you can safely count upon it."

She wound her arm through his, and they strolled a little way along the brick pathway lined with orange trees, and their deeply sweet scent.

"Did I ever tell you how I forgot Mademoiselle de Kéroualle in Dieppe on my way to escort her here from France?"

Nell giggled, put a finger to her lips, and looked over at him. "You didn't!"

"I did indeed. Or so His Majesty shall always believe. It seems that I was greatly taken up with business in Paris, you see, and so, after instructing the lady to wait for me there to make the crossing, I entirely forgot her, and made my way back to England by Calais."

"So *that* was how Lord Arlington came to her rescue?"

"And, alas, why she was not able to make the grand entrance into London she had planned. But I hope that shall remain our little secret."

Nell tipped her head back then and sounded that rich, deep laugh of hers that everyone at court had come to know well. "George Villiers, I do believe I love you!"

"So long as the king doesn't know, I say I am well pleased to hear it!"

Nell did not see Charles again for the rest of the summer, as he had left London for his progress to Windsor, and then moved on to Hampton Court, while she finished out the run of the play. When autumn came, and His Majesty returned to the palace at Whitehall, two major changes had occurred.

Louise de Kéroualle was officially His Majesty's other ac-knowledged mistress.

And Nell Gwynne knew for certain what she had suspected for weeks: She was once again pregnant with the king's child.

Chapter 29

VARIETY IS THE SOUL OF PLEASURE.

—*Aphra Behn*

O N Christmas day in the year 1670, Nell gave birth to a
second son. She chose to name him James, after the Duke
of York, who, slowly and at first reluctantly, had become one of her greatest admirers. The brothers went together
to visit her as a light snow fell; London appeared coated with a
dusting of sweet powdered sugar.

"He looks like our father," James said as he descended the
stairs behind the king.

The house was alive with activity, and everything was heavily
decorated for the holiday with holly and ivy and big green velvet
sashes. Servants were bustling about, and laughing children were
dashing through the corridors.

"Praise God, he is healthy, as Nell is. I am truly a blessed man."

"I like her, Charles. I know I gave you a difficult time over her
in the beginning. I didn't think I could truly care about her, considering everything. But I do. Everyone does."

"As opposed to anyone in particular?"

James shrugged. "I bid you only to take care with her competition, my brother."

"As you have with your own mistresses?"

"I am not a king."

"Yet."

"She is not thought of the way Nell is, Charles. The people despise your Louise."

"They are very different women."

"Look. There is only you and I left now from all father and mother created, from all their hopes and dreams, and I have tried only to be the counsel to you that father would have been. That Minette was to us both."

Charles softened. "Mademoiselle de Kéroualle is a pleasant and lovely diversion, James, and she dresses up nicely for formal occasions. You needn't trouble yourself about her beyond that."

"They say she is a spy for France, Charles, sent here by Louis personally to seduce you, and then from her post to keep him informed of your alliances and loyalty."

"Ah, *those* rumors."

"You make light of something serious."

"All of my life that has been my mode of survival, and you well know it. You cannot have forgotten, can you, what life was for us when we were sent from England, not so very long ago? I am the people's king, and their ruler every waking hour, but I'll be damned to hell if you, or anyone else, will tell me what to do when I wish to be merely a man."

"Concentrate on Nell, Charles, and take great caution with her rival. I bid you that only with the greatest brotherly affection."

Charles embraced his brother then, and, for a moment, they were silent. "And I am sorry about Anne."

"Whatever our problems, she was my wife. I should have been a better husband before she died."

"Perhaps to your *next* wife."

"God willing. I did not actually believe there would ever be one."

"I do not suppose there is any point in my asking you to consider the offer of Marie de Guise? It would go a long way to strengthening our alliance with France."

"I thought that was precisely what you were doing with Mademoiselle de Kéroualle."

"Bastard!" Charles laughed.

As they walked together back into the long hallway lined with ancient portraits in heavy gold, the ceiling paneled and gilded overhead, Charles slapped his brother's back. "So there is no chance at all of a Guise alliance?" he asked again with a half-bitten smile.

"About as much chance as my asking *you* not to continue on with my lady Carwell."

After several months in the same house, Nell and Helena Gwynne had begun to forge a tentative, if strained, coexistence. Helena had been there for the birth of her daughter's second child, holding Nell's hand throughout, refusing to leave the task to midwives. She helped with Charles and Jeddy, complaining little, and she seemed to have given up the urge for gin entirely. Helena was revealing a maternal side to herself, one Nell had never experienced, and it began to heal some of the deepest wounds that had long divided them.

On New Year's Day, Rose and John Cassells were married at St. Stephen's, a small ivy-covered stone church on the corner of Drury Lane, near the Cock & Pye. The King of England attended the small ceremony, as did the Duke of York, the Duke of Buckingham, and the rest of what Charles now affectionately called

Nell's merry band, rounding out the unlikely collection. Patrick Gound from the tavern was also among the guests.

The house, when they all returned to it, was decorated with white ribbons and garlands of ivy and roses, and everything smelled of flowers and lemon oil.

"'Is name was Rowland," Helena said in a soft voice, her face made vulnerable, unshed tears in her eyes. Nell glanced up, moved swiftly from the joy of the wedding, and not immediately understanding. Until her mother continued. They were alone together upstairs where Nell had gone to check on the children. "And 'e was indeed, once upon a time, every girl's fairy tale, a captain in 'Is Majesty's army. God, but we were 'appy then."

Stunned, Nell sank onto a hassock. "What 'appened to my father, Ma?"

"The end of 'is life was not so brilliant as the first. 'E died in debtor's prison in Oxford, where 'e'd been assigned, Nelly. A lost soul. A disgrace. There was the two of you by then, and only me, 'eartbroken, and left to figure things out."

"You didn't do a very good job of figurin'."

"True enough. And in the end, I made a livin' the only way I could."

"You should've told us, Ma. At least there was a tiny bit of 'is life Rose 'n me could 'ave 'ad to 'old on to if you'd told us."

"I 'adn't it to give to you. 'Twas all taken up with what came after 'e died."

"The drinkin' and the men."

"Aye, that. The point is, I'm sorry, Nelly."

Tears had come to her eyes, but Nell brushed them away with the back of her hand. She stood and looked out the windows onto the busy square. The music and laughter from the wedding party downstairs rose up around them, filling the odd silence. When

she turned back, Helena was standing, too, half in shadows, and half in the slanting light coming in through the long window-panes. But neither of them knew what more to say.

Louise rounded a corner, stalking through one corridor of White-hall and then another, her yellow silk taffeta skirts billowing out behind her like a lemony sail. Around her, a cortege of court ladies, her wardrobe mistress, the French ambassador, and other pretty young attendants scrambled to keep up with her charging pace.

"What business have you?" asked one of the two guards posted at the king's privy door as the collection of spaniels barked from the other side.

"I see ze king now!" she ordered in her fractured English soprano.

"His Majesty is not here, madam," he said dryly.

"Zen 'e is *where?*"

"Not here is all I know, madam."

Insolent fool, she thought. But she did not know the words in English, even if she had been unwise enough to speak them aloud. Her hand went to her hips, and she looked back at de Croissy. *"Eh bien,* he promised me the evening! I have bathed and prepared myself for him! Now he leaves me to wait in my bedchamber like one of his trollops!" she raged on in her native tongue.

"He is, after all, the king, Mademoiselle de Kéroualle," de Croissy cautiously observed.

"Et moi?"

"You are here to serve him, as are we all."

Feeling the dark press of humiliation, Louise lifted her chin, turned from the French ambassador, and began back down the corridor, the others following dutifully. For a moment, the sound of their shoes heels echoing over the grand length of parquet floors, and the swish of her taffeta skirts, were the only sounds.

"I don't understand any of this!" she muttered in a fast flurry of French. "He desires me, he chases me endlessly, and now that I have given in to him, I am worth not so much as an explanation when I am abandoned? He simply does as he pleases! *Dieu*, this will not stand! I shall see about this! I shall see about it all!"

De Croissy's hand pressed into her shoulder then, pulling her to an abrupt halt beneath a ceiling mural full of clouds and angels. Once again, Louise turned; this time her face was crimson with rage. "How *dare* you touch me!"

From behind gritted teeth, he coldly replied, "I had hoped to spare you the explanation, but you leave me no choice. We have too much at stake now, and I will not have you risk the place King Louis believes you have attained with these childish tirades of yours! Is that entirely clear? *Bon*. Then you should know he has gone off to that actress of his. An unpleasant truth, yet there it is. And from what I have observed, you are not so entirely indispensable to His Majesty as to go demanding his return. You would do well, as Mrs. Gwynne herself does, to tolerate his dalliances and be there, clean, pretty, and smiling, when he *does* again desire you, which may not be anytime soon if he sees you raging and stomping about like this!"

Louise's blue eyes narrowed. "How *dare* you! I will be queen of England one day, and I could have you drawn and quartered for speaking to me in this manner!"

He gripped her arm then and pulled her close so they would not be overheard. "Fantasies are delightful, *chérie*, until they interfere with business. You will never be queen; you are already a whore. Now, you have a job to do if you wish your family in

France to continue living in their newfound luxury. And I suggest you do it admirably, or you will be out on your ear and back to France, a disgraced harlot who could not keep an old lecher like King Charles from running off to a mere actress."

Tears pooled in her eyes, and she turned her lower lip out in a dramatic pout as it began to quiver. "This was not how it was supposed to be when I agreed to come to England."

"Life is difficult everywhere," he seethed and pinched her arm even more tightly. "I suggest now that you're here, you get creative, and make the best of it, *chérie.*"

Charles rode to Lincoln's Inn Fields with a heavy heart. He had told his advisers that he would tell Nell himself, that it would be easier for Nell, coming from him. But he knew there were no words that would suffice. In their endless hours of conversation, he had learned what Richard Bell had come to mean to her. Her first friend in the theater, Nell always proudly proclaimed. She had lobbied tirelessly for better parts for him, as he, in the beginning, had lobbied for her. Without Richard, Nell always said, she would still be selling oranges, and she most certainly would never have met the great love of her life.

Not bothering with the formality of a knock, a royal guardsman opened the front door for the king. Charles then stepped inside before Buckingham and the Duke of York, both of whom had insisted on accompanying him. The royal physician also followed. Nell was sitting beyond the archway, in the drawing room, playing basset with Rose. Helena Gwynne was sitting out in the entrance hall on the steps holding the new baby, James, surrounded by Jeddy and Charles, who were tossing balls down the stairs and giggling together. It was such an idyllic scene that the king's heart squeezed in his chest. She'd had too much trauma in her life already for this. He felt a thickness at the back of his throat, a burning at the prospect of what he would say, how this next moment was about to change everything. He nodded to Helena, then moved toward the archway. Nell glanced up, saw him, and sprang to her feet, smiling broadly. His appearance was not a surprise; he often came to her unannounced when he could steal a moment here or there.

The king steeled himself and took a step forward. *This is mine to do*, he thought. *She deserves as gentle a heartbreak as I can make it for her.* "It's Richard, Nell," he said.

She froze, stunned, before him.

"There has been a fire at the theater."

Suddenly, she was looking up, eyes wide, tears pooling there, and he was holding her arms, watching helplessly as the first tears slid down her cheeks. "God . . . Oh, God, no . . ."

"It is a terrible tragedy, sweetheart. The theater is completely destroyed. He was trapped in one of the tiring-rooms."

He stood there, still bracing her, watching helplessly as she collapsed. Her mind would be hurling images at her with cruel precision, he knew. Richard's laugh . . . his crooked smile . . . the utter kindness to her that she had always described to him. Her body jerked uncontrollably as she wept. "I just saw 'im yesterday . . . only just embraced 'im for the last time . . . 'e 'ad found the courage at last to ask Beck Marshall to marry 'im. Ballocks! Oh, ballocks!"

"Leave us, all of you," the king commanded then, and there was no other sound but Nell's sobbing as everyone moved across the wide Turkish carpet, through the drawing room, and back into the kitchen.

The house, so full of life only a moment before, was still now, with the quiet accentuating every sound. The tall clock in the entrance hall that ticked away. The floorboards beyond the drawing room straining as one of Nell's servants moved with the others. The king knew he could have his doctor administer something to make her sleep. But that would not take away the pain, only prolong it. How well he knew that himself. Instead, he knelt with her, and held her in his arms, knowing there was nothing in the world even a king could do to help. "I am so truly sorry, Nell," he whispered into her hair.

"Stay with me," she bid him in return.

She asked him for so little, Charles thought. He wanted to give her the world. Right now, he knew that all she wanted was the one thing even a king could not give her: the life of Richard Bell.

Chapter 30

HE WHO REINS WITHIN HIMSELF AND RULES PASSIONS,
DESIRES, AND FEARS, IS MORE THAN A KING.
—*John Milton*

L ATER that same afternoon, feeling nostalgia, and the heavy pull of his conscience, Charles summoned Lady Castlemaine. After their many and complicated years together, and for the sake of their children, whom he adored, he meant to set things right. And he would tell her in person, whatever consequences that might bring.

"Duchess of Cleveland?" she asked, a slight catch in her voice, as they stood facing each other in a small sitting room, a part of his private apartments. The pale pink light of late afternoon was showing in through the windows, casting shadows around them.

"You will be Countess of Southampton, as well."

"I don't understand. I bid you for years to give me this, and now, when I haven't seen you for months—"

"We had good years together, Barbara," he said evenly, as his ever-present collection of spaniel puppies tumbled and barked at his feet. "You gave me some of your very best. I know that now. You were there for me even in France, before the Crown was restored. You helped me borrow clothes suitable enough to ride back into London . . ."

In spite of herself, she bit back a smile. "I remember it well."

"So do I. You will also become Baroness Nonsuch, for helping me cover *that* particular indignity."

"And do I claim Henry VIII's palace that goes with that name?" she asked ungratefully.

"Of course." He knew how desperate she was for money. He had bailed her out more times than he could count, taking money from every source he could find to pay off her enormous gambling debts alone.

"So, my dear Charles, what has you feeling so magnanimous today?"

"Age and regrets, I suppose," he answered her honestly. "Perhaps I am trying at last to be a better man."

"A noble, if impossible, task. But the attempt, it is for Nell really, is it not?"

"And if it were?"

She looked at him for a long time before she replied. "I would much prefer to hate her, Charles. I think everyone would. But the truth is, your Nell is damnably likable."

"She is," said the king. "Isn't she?"

Three days later, on a crisp and cloudy Saturday afternoon, Charles strolled through St. James's Park with Louise. They were followed by the French ambassador, de Croissy, and several French attendants. The thought came to the king again, stubborn, like a child whining to be heard; he pressed it back, but it only came again more strongly: *She really was not quite what you had hoped she would be. And so now, what will you do?*

So there it was. Out. Acknowledged. Accepted. He faced the prospect not only of breaking her heart, but also of returning her to France, her reputation in tatters, and ill-suited for any sort of proper marriage. God help him, rogue that he was, still he wanted her gone. After their first time three months ago, Louise had gotten onto her knees beside the bed and begun to pray, exactly as his wife had done on their wedding night. It had done little to maintain his raging fantasy of bedding the chubby-faced French girl he had convinced himself he loved. A month later, and three days after the death of Richard Bell now, Charles tried not to remember that disappointing encounter. As they strolled together through the lushly landscaped park, Louise's arm linked through his felt like a noose around his neck.

What Louise de Kéroualle lacked in desirability she had, these last months, made up for in availability. Since she was housed now in Barbara's former suite of apartments at Whitehall, convenience certainly gave her the edge on his attentions, if not his heart. No, his blood did not burn any longer when he was with her. Nell had always been his fantasy. Ah, Nell! The passion between them was unmatched. He felt his heart quicken, remembering. With everyone else there were the motives, bribes, unrelenting power games, which, truthfully, at times had their own allure. But with Nell, it was only the lust and the love. Simple and powerful, as was she. Louise held her hand out to a small, timid deer that had approached them. She jumped back with a little squeal of delight when its wet nose touched her fingertips. Then she turned to smile at Charles. Nell . . . He should be there with her right now. Today was the funeral for Richard Bell. He should be there with Nell to comfort her, but she had asked him not to come. He had been hurt, and yet he understood. Too much would be made of their appearance together, and the memory of a dear friend would be lost to gossip.

Louise tightened her grip on his arm as he pointed his silver-tipped walking stick, and they began again beneath a shady canopy of plane trees, both of them warmed by ermine and velvet. She was so at home beside him, he thought, nodding and smiling to the passersby. Yet he must break it off with her. She must return to France. He would speak with de Croissy, who would negotiate with Louis a suitable settlement for the Kéroualle family. He would take care of her, just as he had cared for Castlemaine and Lucy Walter before her. He might well be a rogue, but at least he could be a decent one. He did not speak to her as they rode back to Whitehall. It was difficult to look at her, knowing what he must do if he were to set things right with Nell, and his wife. He felt his body growing more rigid with every heartbeat. He was not good at disappointing people.

"My dearest," he said cautiously as they rounded the corner onto King Street. He took her hand, though it felt false to him, and awkward. "I regret to say there is something we must discuss."

The coach slowed in traffic, and Charles could see people gawking and pointing to the young, elegantly dressed beauty beside him, and asking one another whether it was Mrs. Gwynne, who they adored, or that Carwell woman. He felt himself cringe. Then, before he could say another word, Louise buried her face in her hands and began to sob, the plume in her velvet hat bobbing up and down. "Now there. What is this?" he asked her, somewhere between concern and irritation. He had never been able to bear a woman's tears without weakening.

"I am to 'ave Your Majesty's child!" she announced on a wail so shrill that he grimaced.

For a moment, he almost laughed at how pitiful she sounded. Then he remembered what he had meant to say before her announcement. This changed everything. Irrevocably. He patted the back of her gloved hand, then reached to her chin so that he might draw her gaze up to meet his. Her nose was red, and her cheeks were swollen, making her appear pathetically childlike as the coach pulled past the Holbein Gate. "You are a dear, sweet Fubbs," he said as endearingly as he could manage. "And I know you will give us an exquisite child."

"Fubbs?" she sniffed as her nose began to run, catching on her top lip. "I know not zis word."

It was what he and James had called their childhood nanny, a cross between chubby and fat. That was the first thing he had thought when he looked at her crying. Instead of admitting this, he said, "It is a made-up word, *chérie.* One that reminds me of you, all gloriously soft and round, and so impossibly sweet."

"I am Your Majesty's own dear Fubbs, zen?" she asked as the sobbing slowly ceased.

He drew in a sharp breath. "Eternally."

The coach jerked to a halt in the courtyard before the privy stairwell. He heard a groom lower the steps beyond the door. "But Your Majesty wished to tell me somezing as well, *non?*"

Charles smiled, though for what earthly reason he was not sure. "It is unimportant now."

You are certain zen, *cher amour?*"

The king left his coach first, muttering beneath his breath as his shoes crunched the gravel. "I suppose from now on I shall have to be very certain," he said, but only to himself.

Chapter 31

HER ADVENTURES WERE THE TALK OF THE TOWN AND AMUSED
RATHER THAN SHOCKED THE GOOD FOLKS OF LONDON.
—*De Croissy about Nell, to the French foreign minister, Pomponne*

IT was spring before Nell felt able to leave the safety of her house, and the reassurance of her children. After Richard was buried, she still kept her draperies closed and strung with black crepe in his honor. Her friend had deserved at least that much. But she also remained away from court because she knew, as everyone did, that Louise de Kéroualle was pregnant. For the first time in three years, carefree acceptance seemed beyond her, and she would not risk Charles's knowing it. It hurt desperately.

Then, in April, just as Louise had done to her, Nell seized on the circumstances plainly available: She used Louise's increasing absence from public events to reestablish her own dominant place.

In those lovely, cool months of spring, Charles rewarded her with his almost exclusive attendance upon her, and she was by his side both day and night. As sun steadily warmed the Thames, and saw the greening of the trees in St. James's Park, Nell and Charles strolled in the park and played pall-mall, to huge crowds of onlookers who were there to cheer on Mrs. Nelly, as they called her now. In the afternoons, they often sat together in the royal box at the Duke's Theater. When they rode in His Majesty's coach, it was to huge applause. There was no pretense about her, the people said in the taverns and alehouses throughout London. No threat of France, or of the dreaded Catholics from her. Nell, quite simply, was one of them.

To mark her renewed place in his life, at the end of May, while Louise de Kéroualle began her lying-in, Charles surprised Nell with a new home at the most fashionable address in London, 79 Pall Mall. The grand estate on the edge of St. James's Park was so near to Whitehall Palace that His Majesty could stroll through his own grounds and come easily to her back garden whenever he pleased. She needed a prominent home, he told her. She deserved the very best, and he was giving it to her. But truly, Charles wanted Nell as near to him as he could make her without actually installing her at Whitehall, where Louise de Kéroualle now possessed forty of the most splendid rooms in the palace. The queen spent most of her time at Hampton Court in order to avoid the growing spectacle of the ménage à trois taking firm hold in her husband's life. The halls and stairwells of Whitehall rang day and night with the echo of Louise's shrill demands for more, for bigger, and always for better than that for which she had already strained the royal coffers. And as long as she carried a royal child, the king refused to listen to the litany of pleas, not only from Queen Catherine, but from his brother, James, and the Duke of Buckingham as well, to count his losses and be rid of her.

Nell, wisely, refused comment on the matter.

He was with Nell nearly every night, he was exceedingly generous to her and to their sons, and she had the security and love even a proper husband could never have given her. Her two royal sons were healthy, and, after four years, Charles still desired her as he did no other.

Tonight was Nell's twenty-second birthday. She had everything she ever could have wanted. All she had dreamed of. Gone was the desperate girl, one of Orange Moll's collection. Now her hair was done up elegantly, braided, then strung through with pearls and tiny diamonds. Her face was powdered and patched with one square of black beside her mouth. It was there precisely to high-light her best feature, her smile. Her dress had been chosen by Charles himself. They made their way together toward the ban-quet hall, drawn by the music. They danced together as the court watched, and then, after a sumptuous meal, the king called every-one to gather into an alcove that overlooked the river. Candles in grand gold sconces bathed the area in a creamy golden glow. They were lit in a semicircle around a large piece of black silk draped over an easel. The king took Nell's hand and brought her forward through the crowd with him.

"My friends," he proclaimed loudly. "Mrs. Gwynne posed for the great Sir Peter Lely, at my command; this glorious rendering of an exquisite woman is the result."

Charles himself drew away the drapery then to reveal a breath-taking depiction of Nell. She was recumbent on a bed as Venus, and, beside her, depicted as Cupid, Lely had painted their eldest son, Charles. It had been so long ago, Nell had entirely forgotten. And she had never known that her son had met the painter, much less found a way to secretly pose for him. And now here was the king of England presenting the large, voluptuously painted por-trait to the court as if she were the most important thing in the world to him. Speechless, she glanced at Charles.

"Happy birthday, my sweetheart," he said softly. "And, while it is a gift for you, I say that, with your permission, it shall hang in my bedchamber always so that you will never be allowed to leave my heart, or my mind."

The flurry of applause was interrupted by the shrill sound of a woman's heavily accented voice calling from across the room.

"In zee bedchamber which *I* visit?"

The guests parted as Louise de Kéroualle moved forward, heavily pregnant, lumbering in a dress of ivory silk that billowed and rippled as she walked, protruding at her abdomen from her neck down. Her cheeks were flushed, and her wide blue eyes were full of tears. She looked to Nell like a little girl come down in her nightdress from a bad dream, all forlorn. A rising flurry of whispers was broken by the king's advance toward Louise. Nell could feel the tension, a physical thing, rising up in the air. She held her breath. This next moment could clearly go two ways.

"I was told you would be resting this evening, *chérie*," he said softly, although everyone around him heard.

"So eet seems we each 'ave a surprise tonight."

The silence grew more strained as Nell stood beside the portrait, watching the scene play out. James, next to her, put a hand gently on her shoulder. She could feel his support, and was grateful for it. Louise de Kéroualle was now so awkwardly large and plump that it was difficult for Nell to imagine her as a true rival to anyone, heritage or not. She was young, yes, but so childlike, and her English was so fractured that she made a cockney actress from Coal Yard Alley feel positively confident. Nell watched as the king tried to lead Louise, with a minimum of commotion, back toward the doors. "I don't believe you bring 'er 'ere!" she sobbed aloud. Nell saw that her blue eyes were fending off tears so rapidly that she appeared to be squinting.

"Whitehall is my home," Charles said a degree more forcefully, taking Louise by the arm.

"My 'ome now, as well!"

"I am king! I do as I please!"

"*I* carry your child!"

"Get in line. 'Tis a long one," Nell quipped beneath her breath, not realizing that Lord Buck, standing on her other side, had heard her.

"Touché, my dear," he whispered.

They exchanged a glance, each of them biting back smiles. James, from the other side, nudged her with his elbow, an action meant to command restraint. But when Nell looked over at him, the king's brother himself was trying to contain his own smile at the awkwardness of the entire scene. A moment later, amid a crescendo of chatter and murmurs, designed by the courtiers to appear as if no one had actually witnessed the absurd scene, Louise de Kéroualle approached her. Nell met her gaze head-on. *The meeting, at last,* she thought, still smiling.

"Meesus Gwynne."

"Meesus Carwell," Nell said jeeringly, with a little nod.

Muffled snickers filled the strained silence as Louise's expression became stony. *Humor,* Nell thought, *is my prerogative, especially on my birthday.*

"Meesus Gwynne, you make a mockery of my very place 'ere."

"It seems to me, Meesus Carwell, you do that quite well indeed, all on your own."

More laughter erupted as Louise spun on her heel and waddled from the room, followed quickly by Lord and Lady Arlington. The last image that Nell and the rest of the court had of Louise de Kéroualle was of her head lowered into her hands, the last sound the plaintive note of her cry. So that was how she did it, Nell realized. Tears and guilt skillfully aimed at a soft-hearted king.

Charles looked at Nell, with just the slightest expression of censure, and then he, too, was smiling. "Forgive me, sweetheart. I won't be long. Dance awhile with my brother. Then wait for me in my bedchamber. I've left your birthday present there."

"'Tis the gift I mean to give *you* that I 'ope you'll be returnin' for," she cleverly replied.

The king paused to touch her cheek, then left the room. As he neared the door, Nell's eyes caught with Lady Castlemaine's, who had taken in the entire exchange. To Nell's surprise, the king's former mistress nodded to her with deference. It was a victory Nell would never forget.

"Dance with me?" she asked the king's brother. "Now that old Squintabella 'as retired for the evenin', I feel rather inclined to enjoy the rest of my birthday."

"I don't expect *Squintabella,* as you call our dear Carwell, is going any farther than her steadily enriched apartments, sadly, so I would advise you, my friend, to take care. At least until her royal child is born."

"Well, I'm not goin' anywhere either, Jamie. So the young mademoiselle might be well advised to take great care with the likes of *me,* since I seem to 'ave quite found my stride."

The king found Louise huddled dramatically on the top of her bed, arms over her knees, sobbing into her hands. Lord and Lady Arlington were doing their best to comfort her as a ring of ladies looked on. "There, there, now. Is it all really that bad?" he asked.

"Eet is 'orrible!"

He sank onto the edge of the bed with her and with a nod sent everyone away. Silently, they withdrew. As she sobbed, Charles produced a handkerchief and handed it to her. He despised the incessant weeping. It reminded him too much of the sounds of his early years. Of death. Of places in his heart he did not wish to revisit.

"What is so horrible, then?"

"I came 'ere believing I would be your queen, Charles, fooleesh as zat may seem to you! And now look at me!" She went on sobbing, then blew her nose loudly into the handkerchief. "I am from a good family, you know eet!"

"One of the finest," he softly flattered her.

"And yet 'ere I am, a whore! A grand joke for your court to laugh at!"

Charles wrapped his arm around her shoulder as she wept into the handkerchief now. "No one laughs at you."

"Meesus Gwynne?"

"Oh, Nelly mocks everyone. That's just the way she is. She has had a very different life than yours, and she has been forced by circumstance to manage it with humor rather than tears."

"I want ze life I was promised by Bucking'am! I am a noble girl. I must 'ave a noble title!"

"An English title? I'm sorry, *chérie*, but you are French."

"Zen make me Engleesh!"

He chuckled at something so preposterous, and wiped the tears from her cheeks. When she looked at him again, earnestly, openheartedly, her blue eyes were still liquid with tears.

"What do you suppose King Louis would say to that?"

Weary of English, she replied in French. "I believe he would say that if his good brother is happy, then your two countries are stronger together. Only tell me, Charles, would it please you if your lover were a duchess instead of a lowly girl with no title?"

The truth was, it pleased him greatly to have a lowly lover with no title.

Nell knew who she was, and never tried to be anything else. But his own life was not that simple. Louise was pregnant with a royal child; if she were to complain, if Louis XIV were angered, he might well put an abrupt end to his fiscal generosity. As a result of his secret promise to one day declare himself a Catholic, Charles had so far received the vast French reward of two million *livres tournois.* That could not be taken lightly.

Chapter 32

MADEMOISELLE DE KÉROUALLE HAS NOT BEEN DISAPPOINTED
IN ANYTHING SHE PROPOSED. . . . SHE AMASSES TREASURE, AND
MAKES HERSELF FEARED AND RESPECTED BY AS MANY AS SHE
CAN. BUT SHE DID NOT FORESEE THAT SHE SHOULD FIND A
YOUNG ACTRESS IN HER WAY, WHOM THE KING DOTES ON; AND
SHE HAS IT NOT IN HER POWER TO WITHDRAW HIM FROM HER.
—*Marquise de Sévigné*

CHARLES could not have it both ways.

As he readied the country to strike at the Dutch again with the full support of France, England's own Parliament became hostile to the country's king. The rumor of Charles's Catholic sympathies had reached a crescendo. In response, Parliament delivered him an ultimatum. There would be no additional funds granted for the war effort unless His Majesty personally rescinded his Declaration of Indulgence, which he had sought in order to protect his Catholic family and friends. Furthermore, if the king meant to find victory over the Dutch, he would be forced to approve the Test Act, a bill barring anyone but avowed Anglicans from holding public office. This would affect not only Arlington and Clifford, excluding them from his Privy Council, but it would change the life of his own brother James; the Duke of York would be forced to resign his post as

Lord High Admiral if he would not, along with the rest of prominent England, renounce the Catholic faith.

Charles, who, for what felt like one shining moment, had
believed he had regained something of his father's own grand ability to rule, was trapped between his ambitions for England, and his
loyalty to those he loved. As the battle with Holland began on the
high seas, one by one, like leaves from an autumn tree, members of
his most trusted circle peeled away from his court rather than
renounce their faith. Arlington was first. Then Clifford. And, in
the end, the Duke of York gave up his post and prepared to retire
to the countryside.

"I do not wish you to leave."

"You have the power to put things right, you know," James said
as the brothers stood together for the last time, against the limestone balustrade facing down into the king's vast privy gardens
along the banks of the Thames. "Minette's dying wish, and that
which she fought for in France, was that England would return
to her Catholic roots."

"I took the throne a Protestant ruler, and there I shall remain
to steer the course."

"Then you do so without a brother, at least formally, by your
side."

"The loss shall devastate me. But I fear you shall get your
Catholic country soon enough."

"If the queen remains barren?"

"Aye, that." Charles looked at James; so much of their father
staring back at him, in the lines and curves of his brother's face.
"You are my rightful heir, Jamie. Whatever that comes to mean
for this country."

"And Monmouth? You know there is growing sentiment that
he should succeed you."

"My son knows he will die a duke, not a king, and I pray God he accepts that."

"But will your subjects accept it?"

Charles gazed across the gardens to a small lake where a collection of white swans slid across the smooth surface of the water. Laughter filtered up from a collection of courtly ladies, elegantly dressed, their hair smoothed with scented pomade that caught in the air as they strolled past. "My son will not challenge me," he finally declared. "Monmouth loves me, and he is loyal. I would stake my life on that."

"And so how goes things in your own house, then?" James asked with just a hint of sarcasm, to chase away the dark nature of what they had been discussing. "What glorious scenes have I missed these past weeks while I was off in my final service to the Crown?"

"Louise still despises Nell, of course."

"Of course. And our dear Nell?"

"She has taken to calling Louise Weeping Willow."

"Not to her face!"

"You know Nell."

James stifled a laugh. "What happened to Squintabella?"

"That as well. But, between you and me, Louise does so invite every last bit of it."

"Sounds like tolerably good fun."

"Not to Louise," he sighed. "Oh, James. Truthfully, what am I to do?"

"You poor old grass widow. Two gorgeous women doing battle over you, and that doesn't even include your still-besotted wife!"

"You really think this is humorous, don't you?"

"Sensationally so. I *did* warn you, after all."

"If I were to dispose of Louise, and I do say *if*, so great an insult would very well make receiving my payments from the French next to impossible, and you know how in need of money I am to keep the country."

"The country, or your women?"

Charles rolled his eyes. "Wait until *you* are king."

"I'm only your brother."

"You are my heir. Monmouth knows I shall never acknowledge him as legitimate."

"And yet there might well be forces at work, Charles, stronger even than you in the matter," said the king's brother.

"I shall protect your right to succeed me, James, if there is no legitimate issue."

"You rarely see the queen, much less make arrangements to try to alter that."

"My bed these days is quite busy enough. And on poor Catherine, I'm afraid I've given up hope," he sighed. "She has barred me from taking those affections with her, as I once tried very diligently to do."

James paused a moment before he took the subject back to where he wished it. "So you have thought about it then, forgoing your Louise?"

"On almost a daily basis, I am afraid. I should have remembered how fleeting the lure of beauty can be when it is juxtaposed against weeping and pleading."

"Assuredly, you shall forget again the next time a beautiful young woman catches your eye. And Mademoiselle de Kéroualle has used the tactic to a *T.* She certainly has achieved more here than I ever would have given her credit for."

"I can safely say I have learned my lesson in that particular regard."

"Tell me that again the next time," James laughed. "I only wonder who she shall be."

⊱✦⊰

Everything at court was changing. At last, even Nell Gwynne.

In those first tentative years, with her poverty so newly abandoned, she had been grateful for any attention the king would show her. But now Nell understood that Charles needed her as much as she needed him. Her place in his life was secure, and accepting every slight dealt her without comment was no longer necessary.

Nell truly could be herself now without risking loss of favor.

If she was going to have to coexist in this odd triangle with the Carwell woman, as everyone still secretly called her, she was going to do it on her own terms. Over the months that followed the birth of Louise's child, a son that she, too, not surprisingly, had named Charles, and into the autumn of 1672, they were regularly forced to endure each other's company: at the theater, at court events, at the races in Newmarket. Nell tolerated each meeting with humor, Louise with tears. Both hoped to unseat the other. But only Nell realized it was unlikely. The king would give neither of them up, and he wished the two women in his life to forge some sort of alliance.

"Why d'you tolerate it?" Helena Gwynne asked one afternoon at her house at Windsor.

Nell sat at her dressing table cluttered with jars of cream, a silver patch box, and flagons of perfume, and slipped a pearl earring into the hole in her ear. She was preparing for dinner at Windsor Castle. She and Louise de Kéroualle were to be Charles's only guests; the three of them were to dine together beneath a packed gallery of onlookers who were important enough to witness the daily royal meal.

"You 'ave security now with the children, and two amazing 'ouses, 'ere in Windsor and in London, that makes me wonder why you would let that ol' Frenchy 'ave 'alf of your man?"

"Because I love him. Pure and simple, Ma. And, of course, I want to be the only one, but in this life, I'll settle 'appily indeed for bein' the last one."

"'Tain't proper, that's all."

Nell glanced at her. "You're a fine one to go on about what's proper!"

When Helena looked away, chastised, Nell turned from the mirror and caught her mother's fleshy arm. It was doughy and warm beneath her fingers, and these past months it had become slightly reassuring. "I know you mean well, Ma, I do. But Charlie is my life. 'E's given me more than I ever could 'ave dreamed, and 'e's provided for our children *and* even the rest of my family. From me, at least, 'e'll 'ave whatever 'e pleases. 'Tis just the way things are."

But there was more than a mother's concern in Helena's declaration.

While Nell now had a palatial home on Pall Mall with a staff of ten servants, her own French coach, and six horses to lead it, a recent announcement from the palace lay between them. Louise de Kéroualle, by the grace of His Majesty, Charles II, and her own unrelenting manipulation, was now Duchess of Portsmouth. The Weeping Willow had won her battle to receive an English title. And Nell was still simply Mrs. Gwynne, the actress. Louise had won this round, all of London knew it, Helena knew it. But Nell had no intention of allowing her to win the war.

Nell wore her best new dress, sewn of scarlet silk, with bolstered confidence. At her throat was a string of rubies. The jewels were from her birthday, a gift from His Majesty. Beside her eye was a single black patch. The lace hem of her skirts met the heels of her new silver shoes and brushed along the polished parquet floor. Nowadays, she entered Windsor Castle lavishly, straight-backed, with guards before her, and servants behind. She headed toward the Great Banqueting Hall.

Her heart was racing, knowing what lay ahead. Knowing that Louise de Kéroualle lived here and that she did not. *They can smell your fear* . . . Those were Lord Buck's words of long ago, and her own sentiment now. Her rival would *never* know her fear. God help her, she would smile and laugh and give them all her very best jests before that ever happened.

As she moved into the banquet hall Lady Shrewsbury, Lady Ashley, and the Duchess of Lauderdale lowered their heads respectfully to her as she passed. Flowers well past first bloom bent now on tired, overpainted stalks, Nell thought.

Across the room, she saw the new French Ambassador, de Ruvigny. Nell's eyes met his. Sharp features, steel-gray eyes, silver hair, and a tiny bud of a mouth. He acknowledged her with a stiff nod, then averted his gaze. They would, all of them, wait in the gallery and be allowed to watch from a distance while she dined privately with the king and Carwell. Nell began to smile as she crossed the floor of the vast and empty banquet room, the lit candles casting everything in a creamy golden glow. It was very like the moments just before the curtain went up, she decided. The same fear. The same uncertainty. But she had won them over there, and she would win now. The curtain went up. She felt the same old moment of fear. Then the confidence returned, full force.

Charles and Louise already sat at the end of the table when Nell entered the room. Their hands were clasped, heads pressed together as if in some deeply private moment. As she drew near,

Nell could see that Charles was coaxing Louise, bidding her to remain calm—to remain at all. She felt empowered. When she was close enough, she curtsied deeply before Louise, more deeply than was necessary. The gesture held a hint of mocking. "Your Grace," Nell said to Louise, her voice tinged with sarcasm.

Louise looked up at her. "Why, Nelly, I do believe tonight in zat dress you look fine enough to be a queen," she pressed, knowing how superior to the cockney girl the king had made her.

Cut me, will you? I think not. "Aye Carwell, and you look just whore enough to be a duchess."

Louise shot the king a brutal stare as Charles erupted with laughter, followed by the rest of the court, who had been watching from the gallery above. Nell nodded up to them, as if taking an understated curtain call.

"How *dare* you!" Louise grumbled as Nell, with great dramatic flourish and fluffing of her skirts, sat in the chair allotted to her. The ruby necklace glittered at her throat. Servants began to lay great silver platters before them.

"It was but a jest, *chérie*. If you would come to know Nell, surely you would see that."

"I would rather do battle with a porcupine," Louise answered in French. More laughter rose up from the onlookers, which only made matters worse. "Zat woman gets away wis *everything*!"

Charles responded in French. "I would like you to try. The reason for this meal together is to make a display of the unity in my household."

"Impossible."

Nell took a swallow of wine, then let her wide-eyed gaze wander the gallery. "A blessing, indeed, that Her Majesty finds herself at Hampton Court presently," she could not stop herself from saying. "Or this table would be crowded indeed."

Charles looked over at Nell and gave a snort of laughter again, which caused Louise to bolt from her chair in a huff, then cross her hands over her chest. "I weel not 'ave zees!"

"Zees?" Nell mimicked, eyes wide, her lashes fluttering. "And they say *I* have trouble speaking the king's English."

Louise stomped her foot, Charles fell into a new fit of laughter, and Louise stormed out of the banquet room to an uproar from those in the gallery. "Not all performances are best offered up on a public stage, Charlie."

Charles glanced up, along with Nell, and nodded to the courtiers collected above them as though it had all been a great humorous jest. He was still laughing. "I really *did* hope the two of you could learn to get along," he said.

"Should you go after her?"

"I suspect I should. But I'm not going to." The king took up her hand and kissed it adoringly. "You absolutely enchant me, you know. You always have."

"Are you enchanted enough to grant me one little wish then?"

"So long as it's not the same wish my Lady Portsmouth doubtless has about now, for me to cast you off one for the other."

"The truth is that as much as I enjoyed this little performance of ours, I do find myself 'earin' the call of the real stage, Charlie. After Richard died, it was the furthest thing from my mind, but now—"

His smile fell. He leaned forward so only she could hear. "It's out of the question, Nell. I need you near me all the time. Who the devil would there be to cheer me? Especially now, with the country at war, and all this confounded animosity about Catholics rising to a fever pitch. And if that were not enough, the constant money problems Parliament taunts me with, having me plead for every guinea!"

She leaned back in her chair more comfortably. "Well, I've got an answer for that as well, you know."

"I'm almost afraid to hear it."

"It's simple enough. Send the French back to France, set me on the stage again, and lock up your codpiece!"

Charles pealed with a new burst of laughter, not just at the words, but at the clever way she managed to say something that would have angered him coming from anyone else. "I'm afraid I cannot give you back the stage, my sweetheart. You are far too important to me here. But what I will give you is enough of Sherwood Forest, the land and all the deeds, to add to your worth, as you can ride around before breakfast. How will that do?"

Nell smiled demurely. "Your Majesty's generosity is boundless," she replied. A title would certainly have been better, she thought, if only so she might fully match wits with Carwell. But Nell wisely chose not to say that. After all, she had been out of her league before, and, clever or not, in that regard, nothing had changed. She was still and always would be an orange girl dressed up like a lady.

The February cold crawled across London with deadly fingers. Outside the air was frigid, and icicles hung from the eaves. There was ice on the rooftops, and the Thames had frozen over when the court returned from Windsor. Everything was bare and gray. But in the center of her apartments at Whitehall, Louise stood warm and resplendent in folds of warm ermine and forest-green silk, surveying placement of two new French chairs near the fireplace hearth in her private reception hall. The walls had been changed from the brick and mortar of Henry VIII to smooth plaster.

Around her, the massive room was a hive of construction and activity. Workmen were mounting rich damask on the walls and removing the ancient tapestries on their heavy iron poles. Everything was to be changed, altered, or discarded. She waved a fan before her face and sighed. She was still waiting for the king. He was late again. Always late.

The child she had borne, who had changed her body and caused more hair to come out in her brush than she cared to see, did little to cement her relationship with His Majesty. He was still preoccupied with that tenpenny actress with her laugh like a hen and her distasteful mass of hair the color of a Bristol bonfire. Louise rolled her eyes at the thought. It would serve the king right if she were to take a lover, as Lady Castlemaine had so publicly done. He had told her once, back in the beginning, how angry that affair had made him. How betrayed she had made him feel. Good.

"This is all to change as well, *chérie?*" he asked suddenly, coming up behind her then.

"*Tout à fait, oui.* All of eet."

"But I only just approved funds for that watered silk wallpaper you pleaded for and which they are now scraping away before my very eyes."

Enormously pleased with herself, Louise turned around, smiled, and kissed his cheek. "Zat was last year, Charles. Zis ees all ze latest from Paris."

He touched his mustache. "But you live in London now."

Louise shrugged. "Some sings about each of us are not so easily changed. I've 'ad to learn zat well enough." She watched the king survey the work. It really was very amusing, since she had learned all of the little tricks that worked so splendidly well on him.

"You can certainly change your penchant for decorating, my dear. At least slow it down to a reasonable pace."

"And Your Majesty can change *your* penchant for Meesus Gwynne, *non?*"

Charles stood facing her. His mouth became a hard line. The mention of Nell had quickly infuriated him. She had pressed too hard, and done it too swiftly. It would do her no good in this. Only Nell seemed to have that unique ability to press without angering him. Louise switched to French. "For my sake, *chéri*. It really is the most humiliating thing to be faced with her."

"I will not discuss this."

"But to have a woman like *her* as my rival!" Louise declared in her native tongue, pressing a hand to his chest. "Will you not say she is beneath us both, what we are together?"

"Do not speak to me of Nell."

She clung now to the lapels of his waistcoat. "For pity's sake, Charles! I have given you a child!"

"And some are saying I have given you more than you deserve!"

Now was the moment. She felt the tears begin. They were certainly not full of sincerity, but any would do. Her full lips parted, the lower one slightly quivering. Big fat tears pooled in Louise's wide blue eyes, then splashed onto her cheeks with perfect timing as soon as their eyes met. "I 'ave tried so to be perfect for Your Majesty! God knows eet!" She sobbed out the declaration, one she wagered sounded all the more pathetic to him in her fractured English.

Servants and workmen milled around them. She could see his discomfort at that rising. His voice went lower. He leaned near. "And you have done an admirable job of it."

"Not so admirable as Meesus Gwynne!" She burst into fresh tears, weeping loudly and dramatically. *A worthy performance*, she thought, *compared to the transparent theatrics Nell Gwynne so clumsily employed.* "Do you not see how she humiliates me?" Louise wailed. "Calling me names! Imitating my Engleesh! I cannot possibly do battle wis zat!"

"You should not allow her to get to you so," he replied, speaking in a more gentle tone, glancing around uncomfortably, on the very verge of ordering everyone from the room.

But she did not want that. She knew an audience always made a scene so much more effective. That much she had learned, and would use, from the great Nell Gwynne. "At least say you weel not 'ave her any more here at Whitehall, if it must continue on." Louise's voice quivered, then she sniffled. She added in French, "My heart cannot endure much more, Charles."

To her surprise, the king brought her to his chest very gently then and pressed a kiss onto her forehead. When he spoke, it was with surprising calm. "Let us have no more unpleasant talk of this, hmm? It seems we've enough to discuss with all of your decorating before us."

"Shall you come to my bedchamber zen, tonight at least?" She asked, sniffling away the last of her tears.

"Alas, I cannot, *chérie*. I must work on the speech to Parliament, and I can only imagine what ungodly hour they will set me free of it all."

"I weel wait up for you."

"I will not hear of it. You know how you adore your rest. Now, no more tears, hmm. You know I cannot bear it when you're sad." He pulled her closer then and held her for a moment, then he walked briskly out into the hallway and down the long, vaulted corridor, followed by a collection of pages and guards. But his thoughts were no longer of Louise, or even Parliament, and the grand plea for more money to support himself. Nor was it of the war being waged before him.

Nell's face alone rose strong and bright in his mind.

Happy, smiling. He wanted to see her, to be surrounded by the reassurance of her body, her scent, to sink himself into her happy, clever world, and forget all else. He was a king who could have anything, and usually did. But she still offered him something only she could give.

"Ready my coach," he declared, walking with long-legged strides.

"Yes, sire."

"Inform the Privy Council that they are to gather at the house on Pall Mall within the hour. We shall conduct our business there. Then tell Chiffinch personally that if he has need of me, he will be able to find me until tomorrow morning with Mrs. Gwynne."

Chapter 33

THE SETTING SUN, AND MUSIC AT THE CLOSE, AS THE LAST
TASTE OF SWEETS, IS SWEETEST LAST . . .
—*Shakespeare*, King Richard II, *Act II, Scene I*

B Y the summer of 1675, the war with the Dutch was over. In the end, the costly conflict gained Charles nothing but more debt, and a growing resentment from his people toward the French for their role in facilitating hostilities. By association, Catholics who lived among them were now more out of favor than before. Louise de Kéroualle, who was both, was so increasingly unpopular that it was not safe for her to walk in St. James's Park, or ride in a coach without the window shades drawn.

The Duke of York only fanned the flames of hostility when he took an admitted Catholic, Mary Beatrice d'Este of Modena, as his second wife. As a result, calls spread across London for the Protestant Duke of Monmouth to be named his father's heir instead. Charles's life, as he turned forty-five, was full of more secret dealings with France, endless wrangling with Parliament, and heated meetings with his privy councillors, who pleaded with him to consider the viability of his son as heir.

The only part of the king's life that lacked complication, as the months changed, was the one he shared with Nell and their friends. Everyone now referred to them by Nell's nickname, the merry band: Buckingham, Rochester, Hyde, Buckhurst, Sedley, and Scrope. The house on Pall Mall had become a second, more intimate court, where the king and Nell entertained and dined frequently, where he could escape the other mistress from whom he found himself estranged. Charles had stopped sharing Louise's bed more than a year before. Since making her a duchess, she had badgered him to give their son a title. Under the relentless pressure, and desire for calm, in August of that year, he did; the king saw his youngest son titled Duke of Richmond.

It was this that turned the tide for Nell.

She would tolerate any slight to herself, and had. But she knew her son was every bit the royal child as was the son of a Kéroualle. As another autumn approached, there was unspoken tension between the king and Nell. Charles did not address it, nor did she. But every time Nell looked at Charles, she was reminded that their son was a bastard child with no future, while her rival's son was now a duke, living in Whitehall Palace.

"Perhaps you should confront 'im, Nelly," Rose offered one morning as they were plucking the sweet, ripe oranges from the trees in her little back garden.

"And say what? Give our son a title or else?"

"Somethin' like that. She just shouldn't be allowed to get away with it."

"'Er lover is the king of England, Rose! She only gets as much as 'e'll give 'er!" Nell drew her cloak more tightly around herself.

Rose shook her head. "I still think you should speak with 'im about it."

"I've never once asked 'im for anythin'."

"'Tis 'igh time you start! That child 'e's just ennobled is the ruddy son of a French spy, and all of England knows it!"

Late that afternoon, as she lay in bed beside Charles, and a soft breeze passing through the open window rustled the velvet draperies on heavy iron poles, Nell looked over at him. Her eyes searched his face. He was relaxed, replete. She had loved him for so long, and with her whole heart. She had always given him everything that she had to give. But now there was this one thing. This grand injury. It was different from anything else because it involved her child. Their child.

Nell ran a finger through the tufts of black hair. She felt his chest rise and fall beneath her touch, knowing all of the rhythms of his body. His eyes opened. They were black and shining. He smiled and reached over to press the copper hair back from her face.

"I want what she has, Charlie. Only that."

He turned onto his side facing her, and propped his head with his hand. The floorboards outside her bedchamber creaked as servants passed in the corridor beyond. "You've always had more of me than she does. I adore you. I love you."

"But what does our son have?"

He looked at her a moment more, then sat up abruptly. "He is my son, Nell, and he shall never want for anything. You know that."

"Anything but a proper title?" She put her hand on his shoulder. "I only want for our son what Louise's son 'as, or Monmouth, or Lady Castlemaine's children. A rightful place in this world."

He swung his legs over the side of the bed and stood up. She did not try to stop him or even plead for a response. She said nothing else. He slipped on his clothes and shoes, and took up his periwig, resting on the back of her dressing table chair. He put it on his head and topped it with his plumed hat without checking his reflection in the gold-framed mirror there. He had never left without kissing her good-bye or without seeing his two sons. Today, she could see that he meant to make an exception, and her heart broke just a little bit more because of it.

At Whitehall, Charles stood at an open window, lost in thoughts of what had happened with Nell. He could still feel her disappointed gaze upon him as he had dressed. He could never make her understand. It was not that he had not considered it. He had planned to make Nell Countess of Plymouth, or even Greenwich. He had raised the question with his Privy Council for the second time only last month. But the notion had been swiftly quashed.

Thomas Osborne, Earl of Danby, who had replaced Thomas Clifford as Lord High Treasurer after the Test Act, had been particularly incensed. In the beginning, he had been sponsored in it by the Duke of Buckingham. Now, like a swift-growing cancer that takes root and begins wildly to spread, Danby had methodically carved out such an important place for himself with the king that he was eclipsing all others, particularly the Duke of Buckingham. The grand duke, who had manipulated so many, was being outwitted, and grandly so.

"She was an orange girl!" Danby pompously reminded the king. "An actress from the streets! Surely Your Majesty need not be reminded of that!" It was bad enough, Danby said, that a Frenchwoman was now an English duchess. But with the mood of the country what it was, such a move was dangerous.

Words he might have said, assurances he could have given, now played across Charles's mind. Explanations he could have given Nell about how difficult times were now, about how he had pushed so far with granting Louise's plea that there was no room left. A bee hovered, buzzing outside the open window. It caught his eye. He had been greedy with Nell, always taking what she so readily offered. Believing it would always be there. The bee droned on a moment more, then disappeared. *If I should lose you . . .*, he thought. *Ah, but then of course that is impossible . . .* Nell would forgive him this eventually, as she forgave everything else. And he would return to her tomorrow, and tomorrow . . . and tomorrow.

Danby, the Lord High Treasurer, sat up, the bedcovers falling away from his hairless chest. He was a cautious little man with a pallor pale as death. He had a weak chin, and dark, deep-set eyes that made the contrast all the more ghostly. He came to Louise's private apartments only when he had seen for himself that the king had gone to Mrs. Gwynne's house and therefore would make no inferences as to his motives for privately visiting a royal mistress. They were inferences that would have been well justified, considering what he and Louise had been doing with each other this past month. He found Louise to be a sulking, pouting, little pudge of a woman. But her breasts were as large as her appetite for sex, and he was only too willing to oblige her, since the king himself was no longer partaking. They were well matched in most things, particularly in manipulation.

First to go would be Buckingham, next the famous Nell Gwynne.

Buckingham had too much power, and he was too allied with Nell. They agreed something had to be done. Through cold calculation, and ruthlessness, Danby was close to actually vanquishing the powerful duke, supplanting him permanently as councillor closest to the king.

"Will she receive it zen?" Louise now asked without ceremony.

He knew what she meant. "I have counseled him as harshly as I dare against it, madam. His Majesty has now dropped the notion of making Mrs. Gwynne Countess of Plymouth, or Greenwich, as he had planned."

Louise smiled triumphantly. "*Excellente.* Can you just imagine eet?"

"Well, you needn't imagine it. Now you alone of the ladies who currently share His Majesty's life shall have a title, and your son will do so, as well. As of tomorrow morning, the warrant will be signed, and your little boy shall forever be Baron Settrington, Earl of March, Duke of Lennox, *and* Duke of Richmond."

"Before Castlemaine's sons?"

"Well, I don't know about that," he stammered, uncertain of the answer, and stunned by the ingratitude.

"My son *must* 'ave precedence over 'ers everywhere zay are presented togezzer! So eet must be signed *first!*"

"It is my understanding that the warrant for all the boys is to be signed together tomorrow. Therefore, technically, none of them would take precedence over the other."

With the new détente between Barbara and the king, the former royal favorite had managed to garner from Charles the promise of the title Duke of Southampton for their ten-year-old son, Charles Fitzroy. Their younger son, Henry, would be created Duke of Grafton. Through pleading and relentless tears, Louise de Kéroualle had managed to attain the same place for her child, far earlier, by his third birthday. "Zat weel not 'appen!" she ruthlessly declared.

There was a knock on the door. Louise closed her ivory silk dressing gown over her breasts. "My son shall be first in *all* sings!"

It did not seem to matter that her lawyer found her as she was, undressed, in the company of a man, smelling of sex, with the king nowhere to be found. The lawyer was French, after all, and well paid by King Louis.

"Deed you bring zem?" she asked, before he had come fully through the bedchamber door.

"The warrant is here, milady." The lawyer opened a large leather valise as he was conducted into the room and walked toward a carved French writing table.

Danby had been a worthy opponent to Buckingham, but with Louise de Kéroualle, he felt literally out of his league. It was both seductive and frightening.

"*Bon,*" she said coldly. "Sign them. Danby weel be witness."

Sometimes, when she lay awake, alone, unable to sleep in her grand poster bed with all of its splendor, great carved wooden boys holding candelabra on either side of her headboard, and beside a dressing table covered in brocade, Nell could still see her. She was almost an apparition now, the girl standing before the king with her two rotting oranges, her matted copper locks, and her wide eyes. She was like a ghost, though achingly vivid. Memories of that girl in her soiled dress brought with it the wild, helpless sounds of Coal Yard Alley. The rancid, cloying odors of the narrow streets. The feel of desperation. But she was not that girl any longer. Not tentative, Nor unsure. Privilege had buried that part of herself deep beneath the well of obligation that her life was now. For herself, Nell cared little. There had been only a moment's pain, like the prick of a needle, learning Louise de Kéroualle was to become titled. Then, when it happened, an acceptance with a smile. She could only imagine the pressure that had been brought to bear on Charles. But for her sons, her sweet boys, they were where she drew the line.

She watched them together now: little Charles, almost four, and little James, not even two, playing with Louise's son, the Duke of Richmond, on the vast, sloping lawns behind Greenwich Palace. They were led in it all by Jeddy, who was treated by Nell and Charles as one of her own children. Life was carefree for all of them. None of them knew the weight of obligation or disappointment. Certainly not of hunger or even shame. Nell sat beneath a fluttering white canopy at the crest of the great rolling lawn surrounded by Louise de Kéroualle; Monmouth's pregnant wife, Anne; Castlemaine's eldest daughter, Lady Anne Palmer, who was nearly fourteen; and Rose. Behind them were the French ambassador, the dukes of York and Lauderdale, Rochester, and Sedley.

The king was beside Danby, speaking in hushed tones.

Nell looked away, shaking her head. She despised the Lord High Treasurer. He took Louise's side in all things, and nearly rid the court of the Duke of Buckingham. Her dear Lord Buck was all but invisible at court these days, and she was quite certain Danby meant for her to be next. He remarked openly and often about Nell's humble beginnings, and she knew it was he who fought ruthlessly against any elevation for her or her children. Watching him whisper to the king, Nell grew angrier by the moment. Charles was laughing; Danby was leaning in toward him, whispering. She shot to her feet; the children were laughing, running. The summer breeze blew. Her eldest son was near enough, though. He would hear her. So would everyone else.

"Charles! Come 'ere, ye little bastard!"

A stunned silence fell hard through the collected courtiers. In spite of Nell's flair for the theatrical, it had been such an ungracious thing to say, and she had meant it that way exactly. Full impact, and she felt the king's eyes upon her immediately. Her heart was in her throat as her eldest son came toward her so dutifully that she felt certain her heart would break. But with a singleness of purpose, she blocked out everything else. "That's it, you little bastard, come on to your ma!"

The king was beside her then, his hand tight on her arm. "Why the devil do you call our son something so vile? And in front of all these people?"

"Well, sire, I've no other title for 'im," she calmly replied.

Nell watched him glance around uncomfortably. The children stood in a group, ringing his legs. No one beneath the canopy behind them spoke. She waited for the anger, steeled herself against it. But it did not come. Their young sons were both near now, looking up, watching silently with Jeddy between them. The king bent down to his boys, smiled, tousled their hair, then glanced back at Nell. There was not a courtier present who did not hang heavily on what either of them might say next.

"You and everyone else will call them my sons, Nell, for they both are that, and have been acknowledged as such."

"Aimless bastard sons without title or direction. A fear for 'er offspring a certain Weeping Willow shall not need suffer."

He lowered his voice. "Nell, I bid you—"

"They're my life, Charlie," she said now in the same low voice as he. "Blood is thicker than water. Don't make me choose between blood and love, for I cannot know any longer where that choice would take me!"

Two months to the day afterward, Charles II's eldest son by Nell Gwynne was created Baron Headington, Earl of Burford. Their second son, James, with his father's eyes and his mother's copper curls, became Lord Beauclerk. After seven years, Nell had learned to fight and win.

The victory had gained her more than she ever could have dreamed for two sons of a commoner from the harsh London slums. Yet, like every good thing in Nell's life, this hard-won victory had come at a price. Just when Nell's star at the court of Charles II seemed at its brightest, another star began to ascend beside her.

On Christmas Day 1675, another ship from Paris landed on the English shore. Emerging in a swirl of ermine and black velvet was the celebrated writer and adventuress Hortense Mancini, Duchess of Mazarin. All of London was set on its ear at the news. Particularly the king. The court, and all of London, was rife with gossip, since Hortense had been an adolescent infatuation while he was in exile, and the first woman the king had ever wanted to marry.

Chapter 34

WHY DOST THOU ABUSE THE AGE SO? METHINKS IT'S AS
PRETTY AN HONEST, DRINKING, WHORING AGE AS A MAN
WOULD WISH TO LIVE IN.
—*The Earl of Rochester*

1676 TO 1677

BUCKINGHAM, having been relegated the year before to his country estates by Lord Danby's manipulation, was suddenly summoned back to court by the king. The two old friends spent time hunting and walking in the park with the king's ever-growing pack of spaniels. Charles walked more slowly than once he had, and Buckingham, slightly gray now, and far less dynamic, followed. Between them was still the fact that Buckingham had spoken out of turn with Parliament. It was the incident that Danby had used most fully against him. Now the king was obliged to find an apology.

Speaking of everything but that, they found themselves together in the king's privy hall, where a throne was positioned against the wall beside the fire, and a leather chair sat opposite for conversation. Both of them sank back gratefully and gulped mulled wine, laughing at old jokes, private moments only the two of them could recall. Then the king interrupted the banter to receive one of his spies. The man presented his report, bowed deeply, and backed out of the room. Charles glanced through the contents, then tossed the leather folio onto the tile floor. "A pox on her! She is bedding with him!" It was one thing to have suspected. It was another thing entirely to know. A new addition to King Charles's court, one no one had counted on, was a tall French nobleman who had arrived from Paris. Philippe de Vendôme was as handsome as he was depraved, and he had taken an immediate interest in Louise de Kéroualle.

Buckingham's twisted grin was hidden as he turned and casually fingered a glass globe that sat on a long sideboard. Like everyone else, he had long known about Louise's dalliance with Danby; everyone had, it seemed, but the king. This new liaison, however, was delicious beyond measure, and Buckingham hoped it would pave the way for his return to power over the ruthless Lord High Treasurer. He had one final chance at glory now that was back. "I could say I warned you about Carwell."

"You could," Charles grumbled. "But displeasing your king is well known to be dangerous."

"You know the wildly angry sentiment here for the French since the end of the war. Carwell is chief among their targets. Does your dear Danby not tell you the truth about that?"

"Danby is not you."

A small victory, and Buckingham reveled in it. "Aye, he tells you what you wish to hear, something I always refused to do."

"For a time, I actually believed I preferred that to your incessant manipulations."

"You knew about those?"

"And your infernal gloating."

"The grass so often does look greener."

"Very well, then. If you were back here with me daily, what would *you* have me do with things as they are now?"

"Send Carwell back to Paris and be done with her. You've enough on your plate now with Mazarin and Nelly, do you not?"

The king stiffened. "I shall decide when I have had enough."

"Have Danby and Vendôme not decided that for you?"

"George, if you were anyone else!"

"But I am not, am I? What I am, first and foremost, is your oldest friend. And, admit it, you have missed me around here."

There was silence for a moment. "Very well then, perhaps they have decided things for me. I have made rather a pathetic mess of it, haven't I? Bestowing title after title on Louise, hoping to make her love me. And leaving Nelly to love me as she has for so long, with no acknowledgment of that. Time and time again, I let Danby talk me out of naming her Countess of Greenwich. I let everyone tell me she was not worthy. Worst of all, I let myself believe it."

"I warned you about Danby, as well."

"Gloating really is your greatest character flaw, George."

"You can still change that. You can still change a great many things."

Charles looked at the man who had been like a brother to him. "Danby was right about one thing, George. You must make your apologies for what you so publicly said. It is the reason I summoned you back. To settle this once and for all."

"For how I spoke against Parliament? I cannot, Charles. Parliament has held you, bound and gagged, since you took the throne. I loaned you money, by my troth, because of how they manipulated you. Their entire function is to thwart your will, and I said so! Unlike women, the acts of that body are *not* the worse for growing old!"

"My father supported his Parliament, and I shall rule as my father meant to."

"Then you are a live fool instead of a dead one, but a fool nonetheless!"

Mention of the king's father crossed a line. "Perhaps Danby was right. It was a mistake to bring you back here."

"Not everyone has the ability to see the truth when it is staring them in the face, but I would have thought better of not only my king but my friend!"

"Guard!"

"You cannot do it to me again, Charles! You won't send me to the Tower for telling you what you know to be true!"

"*Guard!*"

"I love Your Majesty with every part of my being! I always have!"

"Before you insult me, my father, or Parliament, tell that to the devil, George Villiers, for I sure in Hades do not care!"

Later that afternoon, as sun streamed in the wall of paned windows that faced the Thames, Louise strolled through the grand gallery. She moved toward an open chamber where Nell, Rochester, Buckhurst, Sedley, and Hyde were playing cards. Louise was wearing the same mourning gown of black silk and lace she had worn the previous day. Her expression, as she passed, was properly sober, her chin was lifted with courtly dignity. A group of her lady attendants followed.

"Don't look now," said Rochester beneath his breath, as he fanned out his cards and lay them on the table. "But here comes the one actress to actually better you with her theatrics."

"She would have you believe she actually knew the deceased," chuckled Lawrence Hyde.

"Great God, who died?" Buckhurst asked.

"The esteemed chevalier de Rohan," said Charles Sedley in a gossipy tone.

"The *what* of *what?*" Rochester muffled a snicker, exchanging a glance with Nell.

"One of her countrymen," Buckhurst explained in a low voice. "The chevalier, it seems, lost his head for treason; the duchess tells me that their families had ancient and indelible ties."

"Oh, where is Lord Buck when a great retort wants saying by clever lips?" asked Hyde.

Buckhurst tossed his cards onto the table and leaned back in his chair. "Considering the error of his ways at this very moment, I suspect."

"Lord Buck is back at court?" Nell asked him in surprise.

"He has been these past two days. But, as Danby and Carwell have so thoroughly muddied the king's mind over him, I hear our old friend is settling in to his former apartments in a certain nearby tower."

Nell's face went pale. "You cannot be serious!"

"Would I ever joke about something so inconvenient as a prison cell?" Rochester asked.

"Poor old Buck, the great manipulator was outmanipulated," Sedley replied with a deep sigh.

"Well, we've got to do somethin' for him."

They all looked at Nell, their glances sliding from one another to her. "Sorry, love. None of us would consider attempting something so dangerous as *that*," said Rochester. "No, Nelly, I'm afraid you are the only one to go toe-to-toe with the king, and keep your head off a pike in the end."

At the king's request, Nell came to court for dinner the next afternoon. Sweeping into the grand dining hall with a particular flourish, she was followed by Rochester, Buckhurst, Hyde, and Sedley, a whirl of clicking shoe heels and curled periwigs. Her entourage gave her courage, she had told them with a giggle as they made their way together up the stairs. And Nell was glad they were with her. She came through the doors a quarter of an hour late, draped from head to toe in layers of deep-black silk. To her eyes, she held a black lace handkerchief, and she was wiping away tears, weeping softly as she moved, her black-lace hem trailing along the inlaid parquet.

The king, Louise, who was still in her own mourning black, and the ever-present Earl of Danby sat together. Around them, the French ambassador and a collection of Louise's patched and perfumed ladies paused and glanced up at her—precisely the effect Nell desired.

"Mrs. Gwynne," asked Danby with disdain, "for whom are you mourning?"

"'Ave you not 'eard of my loss?" Nell replied in a tone worthy of her best stage heroine. "The Cham of Tartary?"

Delighted by her utterly brazen mockery, Rochester, Buckhurst, and Lawrence Hyde all muffled laughter. Surveying each of them in turn, and realizing that their muted laughter was at her expense, Louise's face darkened to crimson. In her defense, the ambassador spoke again. "And what relation, pray, was the Cham of Tartary to you?"

"Oh," Nell smiled innocently, her timing absolutely perfect. "Exactly the same relation that the chevalier de Rohan was to Carwell."

Louise bolted to her feet with an audible huff and said something indecipherable to the king. Then she spun on her heel, a whirl of black mourning silk, and left the room. Once Louise was gone, the king himself began to laugh, leaning back in his chair and slapping the table. Amid the crescendo of laughter and applause, Nell stood and took a deep and triumphant curtsy. A moment later, she went to the king, sank onto his lap, and linked her arms behind his neck. As chatter and music rose up around them, she said what she meant to say. "I want to go to him, Charlie. Please let me try to mend things for you."

It was a moment before the king realized that she meant Buckingham. "Out of the question."

"But 'e's my friend."

"And he is my enemy!"

"Oh, dear, dear Charlie." She ran a teasing finger along the line of his jaw as she smiled and spoke to him in a low, coaxing tone. "Now, you know perfectly well 'tis no truth in that."

"His insolence, and blatant refusal to do as I command, is dangerous here, and that makes him my enemy. I should never have allowed him to come sniveling and scraping back—"

"Sounds like Danby's words, not yours."

"Whoever spoke them, they are accurate."

This was her chance to repay Buckingham for his help with the incident in the pond, and for having become her friend, and Nell meant to have her way. "In all the years, I've never asked you for much, 'ave I, Charlie? I mean, really, 'ave I?"

"Actually, you are the only one who hasn't."

She leaned in closer and twirled a curl of his long periwig onto her finger. "Well, I'm askin' you now. Let me go to Lord Buck. Let me speak with 'im."

"You believe you can help that cunning old dog see the error of his ways, do you?"

"If anyone can, 'tis likely me."

"True enough," he laughed, pressing a kiss onto her cheek.

Chapter 35

METHINKS, I SEE THE WANTON HOURS FLEE, AND, AS THEY
PASS, TURN BACK AND LAUGH AT ME.
—*The Duke of Buckingham*

CLOAKED in folds of black velvet, her hair covered with a wide black hat, Nell moved past the guard and into the apartments set aside for the great Duke of Buckingham in the Tower of London. What she found was a man she would not have known. In the time since she had seen him at court, the proud man so full of confidence had disappeared. In his place was a fragile, slightly stooped man, his blue eyes faded, with deep shadows ringing beneath them. He was old. Wrinkled. The skin once smooth and shiny, now was lined like parchment, and his armpits were wet with stains. The days of duels and clever mistresses were well behind him. His days out of favor had not been kind to the duke.

"My Lord Buck," she curtsied deeply, theatrically. The little private joke between them made him smile, remembering how far their friendship had come.

"So the mountain has come to Muhammad in the form of a beautiful red-haired angel."

She moved toward him. He stood, and they embraced.

"'Ow exactly *do* you find yourself in the Tower so often?"

"A tongue too clever for my own good, apparently."

"That only works well when you've masses of red 'air and a neatly turned ankle."

"So I have seen."

She kissed his cheek, then helped him sit.

"So, then, has His Majesty sent you?"

"In a manner of speakin'. But you must read the letter I 'ave brought you."

"You asked if you could come?"

"But 'e did not deny me. 'E misses you."

"I miss how we once were. How we *all* were."

"The Tower makes men sentimental, does it?"

"Only old men, I'm afraid. Ones who now see mortality more clearly than their ambitions."

She patted his knee and smiled. "You're not old, Lord Buck. Just more realistic."

He looked away for a moment, then back at her before he was seized by a fit of coughing. Nell poured him a glass of ruby wine from a pitcher on a table near the window and brought it to him. Then they sat together as he drank it.

"Do you remember our first encounter?" he asked, his voice tired and full of nostalgia.

"'Ow could I forget? You called me a jade."

"And *you* called *me* a coxcomb. I didn't even believe you knew what that was."

"I was right to do it. And *you* were right. I didn't."

"You changed his life, you know."

"'E changed mine."

"But to alter the path of a king, my dear. No other woman ever has endured what you have from Charlie, nor remained so entirely by his side."

"No other woman ever loved 'im as I do, nor ever will."

"I suspect you're right about that." He suddenly sighed. "I've nowhere to go, even if I do get out of here. Alas, Anna Maria has thrown me out of my own house."

"Snakebites, they say, are lethal," Nell smiled.

"I suppose I deserve what I get after the fate I sealed for my own poor wife."

"You really were full of the devil back then."

"Certainly full of my own sense of power and glory. Such a fleeting thing; I had no idea there could ever be anyone more powerful or clever with the king than I."

Nell reached over to cover his hand with her own. "You know you can stay with me for as long as you like. So long as you buy yourself a new periwig and some shoes so you don't stink up the place as you're doing now."

George laughed. It was a thin, hollow sound. "Are you planning to arrange my release?"

"Are you planning to behave?"

"It's not at all likely."

"Then we should tell them to keep your cell at the ready!"

She had woven herself so cleverly into all of their lives that there were very few at court who did not depend upon her in some way, George thought. Only her enemies would keep themselves excluded, and Nell had precious few of those. He had heard that it amazed everyone how the queen now occasionally went to Nell for advice about the king, and it amazed them even more to learn that Nell freely gave it. Few had been told, but he also knew about the royal hospital in Chelsea that Nell had urged the king to build for old or injured soldiers, like her father. She had a heart, it seemed, as deep and full as her laugh.

"Once I was foolish enough to think I could control you, bend you to my will," he said on a tired chuckle. "Now I do believe you control us all."

"I'm a king's mistress, Lord Buck. Only ever that."

"To my mind, the perfect royal mistress," the Duke of Buckingham amended.

Empty gin bottles collecting beneath her bed had given Helena's sealed bedchamber the reeking stench of alcohol. Nell had not seen it coming, and she cursed herself for her blindness. She had not wanted to see it, but, of course, that was no excuse. It was too late, no matter what. Nell stood in the center of the room looking at the pile of glass. Her housemaid, Bridget Long, stood behind her in the doorway, holding onto the jamb." I'm sorry, Mrs. Nelly, if I should not have told you. I just didn't know what to do with all of them."

"'Tis not your fault. You 'adn't any choice," Nell replied, feeling the scrape of her words coming up over her throat as if they were hot coals.

"Did you know?" she asked Rose the next day. Their mother had not returned home the night before. They sat in the kitchen as the cook, standing behind them, peeled apples silently and put them into a kettle on the fire.

Rose looked away. "I didn't want you to turn 'er out."

"But if I'd known—"

"You would've turned 'er out."

"And I might've 'elped 'er!"

"I think she'd gone beyond that, Nelly. 'Twas all so twisted up among the three of us."

"She still shouldn't 'ave chosen the gin!" Nell shook her head, her anger bold and vicious. All of the old hurt resurfaced; Helena Gwynne had abandoned her daughters yet again.

"Some people fail in spite of tryin'. I don't believe she meant to 'urt us."

"She's been 'urtin' us our whole lives Rose!"

"Don't you think she knew that, Nelly?"

The king sent out his own Yeomen of the Guard to search for Helena Gwynne. Days passed; three, then four. The old hurt battered Nell. They waited. Rose and Nell paced the silent corridors of the Pall Mall house. They wrung their hands, embraced each other, sat in Helena's room, and said prayers for their mother's safe return. She had made them both love her again, damn her foul soul. "I never should 'ave believed 'er," Nell wept one night against Charles's shoulder, as they lay together in her grand bed, and he pulled her tightly against him.

"You have a good heart that cannot help but care, in spite of how you have been tested."

"A 'eart only the better to be fooled by."

"No one fools you, Nelly. You're the smartest woman I know."

"I'm not sure 'tis sayin' much, 'avin' seen my competition, in that regard."

He kissed her then and the love inside her flared, still such a brilliant flame. Even after all this time, it was still like that between them.

It was another three days before two of the king's guard came to her front door and were shown into the large room to the left of the entrance hall. Charles held her shoulders very tightly as he stood behind her. At first, looking at them, and knowing, she was not certain she felt anything. Something so unlikely, so new and fragile, had formed between mother and daughter in the past several years. Like the first leaf on a tree after a long winter, it had sat vulnerable, growing slowly. Now, in an instant, it was swept away in a swirling cloud of fire, and the dust of *if only*. Nell felt her knees buckle.

They had found Helena Gwynne in the river.

She had fallen in drunk, they said, and was drowned.

After the funeral, Charles took Nell to Greenwich to give her a change of scenery, and a break from all of the sadness that lingered for her in London. The early evening air was cooled by a soft breeze, and the scent of honeysuckle was everywhere. Lit by torches, Charles, Catherine, Nell, Louise, and a dozen courtiers strolled amid tall trees, and hip-height ferns that softened their path. The king's musicians followed, and stationed themselves upon the wide green lawn where the forest began. They played beneath the bright, silvery light of the full summer moon and sent away the sweet sound of the brook nearby.

Taking her hand as they boarded his royal barge, the little laces on her dress ruffling in the breeze as the rest of the court followed, Charles asked, "So tell me, darling Nell, how would you feel about being called Your Ladyship?"

"I'd feel someone confused me with Carwell or Castlemaine."

"You are to become Countess of Greenwich. Countess of all that surrounds you here."

After all these years, she thought. She knew how hard Danby had fought him on this. He despised her, she knew, because she was not Louise de Kéroualle. "I've no idea what to say."

He took his hand from one of the oars and put it atop hers. "Say you'll grow accustomed to it, and I shall tell you that there are other plans, as well."

She looked at him, his once-smooth face now etched with lines, the large black eyes more sunken. There was only a hint of his youthful beauty now, and yet still he was possessed of that same charm she had seen that first day outside the King's Theater. "Plans?"

"I have made arrangement for Jamie to go to Paris to further his education."

She thought of their younger son, blond, wide-eyed, so connected still to his mother in a way that helped her to mend so many old wounds. "Paris alone? But 'e's just a little boy, Charlie!"

"He's the son of a king first, Nell. Charles, as the oldest, and already Earl of Burford, shall find his way in life clearly marked for him. Jamie needs the same chance. I want that for him. I want both of our boys to have brilliant lives. Besides, he'll have a staff to attend him."

"But 'e won't 'ave *me*!"

He tightened his hand upon hers, then lifted it and very gently kissed the inside of her wrist. "I need you here, Nell. But Jamie has his entire life ahead of him, and I mean to see to it that he has every advantage this world, and his father, can offer him that. I'm sorry all this has taken me so long." His voice broke. Then he looked off into the distance at the blaze of orange sun setting over the trees on the horizon. "I've been a fool about so many things. No matter what, I always, *always* knew you loved me, Nelly. In that regard, there was no one else even close."

She touched the ruby necklace at her throat, another priceless gift from him. "You know, I'd 'ave to say I agree with that," she said with a broad, happy smile.

❧

The new production was called *The Duke's Wife*, starring London's new sensation, Rebecca Marshall. Beck at last was a star. As a crowd gathered on the steps outside of the King's Theater, the great royal coach drew forward and slowed. Glancing out the window, Nell saw them and smiled. This scene in front of the theater never ceased to bring with it a burst of nostalgia. Then she glanced across the seat, beside Rose, at her two sons. No matter what thoughts this theater brought, her two boys would always be her greatest achievement.

"Shall we go in?" Charles asked his sons, Nell's sister, and her husband.

"I wish we had seen mother on the stage," said James.

Charles took Nell's hand, and squeezed it. "Oh, that was a sight. There really was no one like her."

"Tell it again, Father?" his namesake asked.

Charles smiled indulgently. "Well. The theater was full. There were shouts from the audience and applause so that I could scarcely hear. When she came onto the stage, your mother made a humorous little bow like a man, in keeping with her character, then glanced up at me from the stage, and my heart was lost to her instantly and forevermore."

The boys exchanged a look and then began to chuckle, but the sound held a note of pride that their parents were here with them, together, and still happy.

They strode through the crowd then, the king greeting his subjects in a formal manner as Nell and their sons walked a pace behind.

"Mrs. Nelly! Back where she belongs, she is!" someone called through the crowd. Nell smiled and nodded her acknowledgement. A part of her would always belong here.

As they passed inside the theater and turned, preparing to ascend to the king's private staircase, a young girl drew forward from the passing crowd near the pit. In the crook of her arm was a garlanded basket brimming with oranges. The girl's expression became stricken, and she made an uncertain curtsy before Nell. But Nell reached out and drew the girl up. "What lovely oranges," she said, smiling. "I do believe I shall take one. And two more for my sons." She reached into her small velvet bag and handed the girl a shining silver coin. The girl's gasp at the amount was audible, even in the packed theater, and many had turned to stare at the exchange. "Best of luck to you," Nell said sincerely, as James took the three pieces of fruit for his famous mother. As the group made their way then up the stairs, Nell turned back to see that the young girl had not moved from the place where she stood. For a moment, their eyes met again, and Nell smiled warmly at her once more. Then she followed her sons, with Charles, Rose, and John, up to the king's private box to watch the performance.

Epilogue

LONDON, FEBRUARY 1685

SHE did not hear him at first as she sat beside the fire. But when he drew near enough, she turned, and the sadness in her son's face told her everything. After all she had been through these past years, the drowning of her mother, then his only brother's sudden and unexplained death in Paris, he would rather do anything than tell her the truth about this now. But she was his mother, and she owed her everything.

"I have just come from Whitehall. His Majesty is dying, Mother. I'm so sorry."

When she said nothing, Charles Beauclerk, tall for fifteen, sank onto his knees before the silk folds of blue French silk draping Nell's legs. He knew he was the very image of his father. She had told him that so many times. What must she think now, looking at him? Was she seeing the other Charles, king of England? For eighteen years, he had been the great love of her life.

Nell shot to her feet, her spine stiffening. "I must go to 'im."

"The queen will not want you there, Mother."

"Since when 'ave I given a fig what the queen wished, or any of 'is women, for that matter?" She began to walk briskly, her skirts swishing, the blue hem rippling out behind her. Charles tried to keep up as she passed through the foyer. "Where are my gloves? And I'll need a 'at!" she called out to no one in particular. Her son followed, then gripped her shoulders and turned her back around. "The queen has *specifically* asked you not to come to court now."

Bridget Long dashed down the staircase at that moment, curtsied, and held out her leather gloves and a small felt hat. Nell paused to put them on. "Carwell won't listen to an order like that! I don't see why I should 'ave to listen, either!"

"Mademoiselle de Kéroualle is a whore."

"So am I, Charles. Only a better one."

Bridget placed the hat onto her head, and Nell tipped it to the proper angle herself before she walked outside, while Bridget went to call for her coach.

"Mother," Charles said uneasily as he followed her. "I was hoping not to tell you this, but Her Majesty has said she will not allow you to see him. Nor will she allow it of the others."

Nell saw tears in her son's eyes. But she was not the sort of mother to weep. Life was to be mastered with humor, she had always blithely told him. It helped one to survive

"But I was never like the others to Charlie," she said softly, her voice breaking now. "What we 'ad, what we've 'ad for all these years, was always different. And it is what I do. I follow 'im wherever 'e needs me. I can't give up on 'im! I've never done that, and 'tis certainly no time to start!"

"I am told by Master Chiffinch personally that Her Majesty sees this as her opportunity, after so long and difficult a marriage, to at last have the king to herself, no matter how briefly."

"Folly! She shall never *'ave* 'im! Not 'is 'eart!"

A coach drew forward, and a liveried groomsman approached.

"Shall I come with you, then, if you absolutely mean to do this?"

"You'd face the 'ordes at court who will now feel free to be unkind to me?"

"I would do anything for you. As my father would have."

"It means the world knowing that you would. But I'll face today alone, whatever lies ahead for me. You're not to be tainted by this." She took the groom's gloved hand and stepped smoothly up into the coach. After the door was closed, she leaned forward and touched the window glass. Her son raised his hand to match hers on the other side. "I love you," she mouthed.

"And I love you," he whispered in reply.

The heavy clouds merged then, and the coach began to pull away. He had known all along that she would do this, no matter what he said. He knew that she at least would try. For her Charlie. She may not have been the queen, nor even his only mistress—far from that—but she knew with every fiber of her being, and so did their son, that she had been his only love.

Author's Note

I N spite of retaining three main mistresses—Nell Gwynne, Louise de Kéroualle, and the Duchess of Mazarin—it was only Nell, upon his deathbed, about whom Charles showed concern. It was recorded that his brother James was to personally see to her future, which he dutifully did. Nell Gwynne was relieved of all debts, and an income was settled upon her for the rest of her life. However, having lost her love was too great a burden. Nell Gwynne lived only two years beyond Charles II, dying herself after an illness. She never did receive the title the king had promised, although his intention to do so is well documented. She was buried at what today is the site of the National Portrait Gallery.

A Reader's Group Guide

THE PERFECT ROYAL MISTRESS

Diane Haeger

ABOUT THIS BOOK

A legendary actress. A mistress to a monarch. A woman who would rise from the ashes of London to take her place in history.

Nell Gwynne, born into poverty and raised in a brothel, starts her working life selling oranges in the pit at London's newly reopened King's Theater, just after the plague and the subsequent Great Fire have devastated the city. Her quick sense of humor and natural charm get her noticed by those who have the means to make her life easier, though Nell is street-smart enough to know that a woman doesn't get ahead by selling her body. Through talent, charm, intelligence, and sheer determination—as well as a realistic understanding of how the world works—Nell makes her way out of the pit and onto the stage to become the leading comedic actress of the day. Her skill and beauty quickly win the attention of all of London—eventually even catching the eye of the king himself. Before she knows it, the scrappy orange girl with the pretty face and the quick wit finds herself plunged into the confusing and dangerous world of the court, and she must learn quickly who to trust—and who to never turn her back on.

From the grit of the streets and the backstage glamour of London's theaters to the glittering court of Charles II, *The Perfect Royal Mistress* is a love story for the ages, the rags-to-riches tale of a truly remarkable heroine.

The questions in this guide are intended as a framework for your group's discussion of *The Perfect Royal Mistress*.

1. Very early on, Nell comments that to survive despite hardship, "one simply had to put one's head down and keep going along" (page 2). How does this attitude help her throughout her life? Are there others in the novel who either live by this rule or don't? How do they fare? Do you think Nell's approach changes as she grows older and more experienced, or not?

2. What is the turning point in young Nell's life? At what point does she become one who makes things happen, rather than one who things happen to? Can you pinpoint a moment where she discovers the power she has?

3. What is it about Nell that first catches the king's eye? Does what he sees in her change over time or remain constant? Why is this infatuation so lasting when so many of the other mistresses are fleeting?

4. Consider those who Nell encounters at the court of Charles II. What drives these men and women? In what ways are they similar to each other, and who stands out, positively or negatively, as different from the pack? Did anyone surprise you? How?

5. Why does Richard commit himself so fully to helping Nell? Why is he so loyal to her throughout his life, asking very little in return? What does he get out of their relationship?

6. Consider the impact of parental relationships on the main characters in *The Perfect Royal Mistress*. How are each of these people affected by the actions of their parents, and how does this legacy manifest itself? If you were to look one generation into the future, how would you see the cycle continuing? What effect do you imagine these characters' lives and choices having on their own children?

7. When Nell attends the state ball with Charles (with Louise on his other arm), why, despite her fear of making a fool of herself, does she go against Mary Chiffinch's advice and insist on wearing her dress with the laces unfastened, though she knows that it is not proper? What is it that Rose seems to understand about this choice?

8. Discuss the relationship between George Villiers, Duke of Buckingham, and Nell. From such a rocky beginning, were you surprised at the genuine friendship that develops between them? How does each win the other over? Did you question Nell's willingness to trust Buckingham at all? At what point did he show himself to be her true friend?

9. It is clear that Nell loves Charles dearly and honestly, but nevertheless, she still continues to manipulate him into doing

what she wants. Consider these manipulations and the reasons behind them. Why does she do this, and how does she accomplish her goals? What did you think of this? Does the fact that Nell has to use such tactics with the king to get a title for her son, for example, negate the gesture once it is made? What do these exchanges say about their relationship? Do you think Charles knows when he's being played?

10. At what point does Charles lose interest in Louise de Kéroualle, and why does he not dispatch with her immediately as he does his other discarded mistresses? Why is she allowed to stay by his side for the rest of his life? Did you think this fact lessens Nell's place at his side? Why or why not?

11. Do you believe that Charles is happy at the end of his life? Why or why not? What would happiness have entailed for the monarch? What does he want to accomplish, and what do you think would bring him peace? What is Charles's driving need and how does he go about filling it?

12. Throughout the novel, Nell is treated poorly by many of the people she encounters but holds very few grudges. In what cases does she hold past wrongs against the person who has committed them, and in what cases does she forgive and forget? Why do you think this is? What accounts for the difference? Did you agree with her choices in this respect?

13. What did you make of the character of Queen Catherine? Despite her estrangement from her husband, Catherine still wields an extraordinary amount of power over Charles. Is this entirely a result of her position as queen, or also due to something inherent in their relationship? What do you imagine the queen's life to be like?

14. Why does Nell refuse to give up acting for so long, even when the king wants her to? Is the reason financial independence, as she maintains to him, or is there something more in it for her? What is it about the theater that keeps her coming back?

15. Prior to reading *The Perfect Royal Mistress*, what, if anything, did you know about Nell's story? What did you think about this portrayal? What expectations did you have going in, and how did the novel fulfill them or surprise you?

About the Author

DIANE Haeger is also the author of *The Ruby Ring*, *Courtesan,* and *The Secret Wife of George IV*. She lives in California with her husband and family.

Also by *Diane Haeger*

An unforgettable story of love, loss, and immortal genius . . .

In *The Ruby Ring*, Diane Haeger brings the Italian Renaissance to life as she reveals the love affair between a humble baker's daughter named Margherita Luti and the painter Raphael.

The Ruby Ring
$12.95 paper (Canada: $17.95)
978-1-4000-5173-1

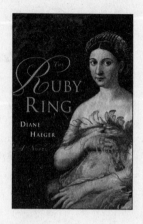

A love that knew no boundaries...
A *scandal that stunned France*

Set in sixteenth-century France, *Courtesan* tells with passion and extraordinary detail the story of King Henri II and his doomed, tempestuous affair with the beautiful widow Diane de Poitiers.

Courtesan
$13.00 paper (Canada: $17.00)
978-1-4000-5174-8

Available from Three Rivers Press wherever books are sold.